SEVEN

DEADLY

SHADOWS

COURTNEY ALAMEDA
AND VALYNNE E. MAETANI

SEVEN

DEADLY

SHADOWS

HARPER TEEN

An Imprint of HarperCollinsPublishers

HarperTeen is an imprint of HarperCollins Publishers.

Seven Deadly Shadows

Library of Congress Control Number: 2019946112
ISBN 978-0-06-257081-9

Typography by Erin Fitzsimmons
19 20 21 22 23   PC/LSCH   10 9 8 7 6 5 4 3 2 1

First Edition

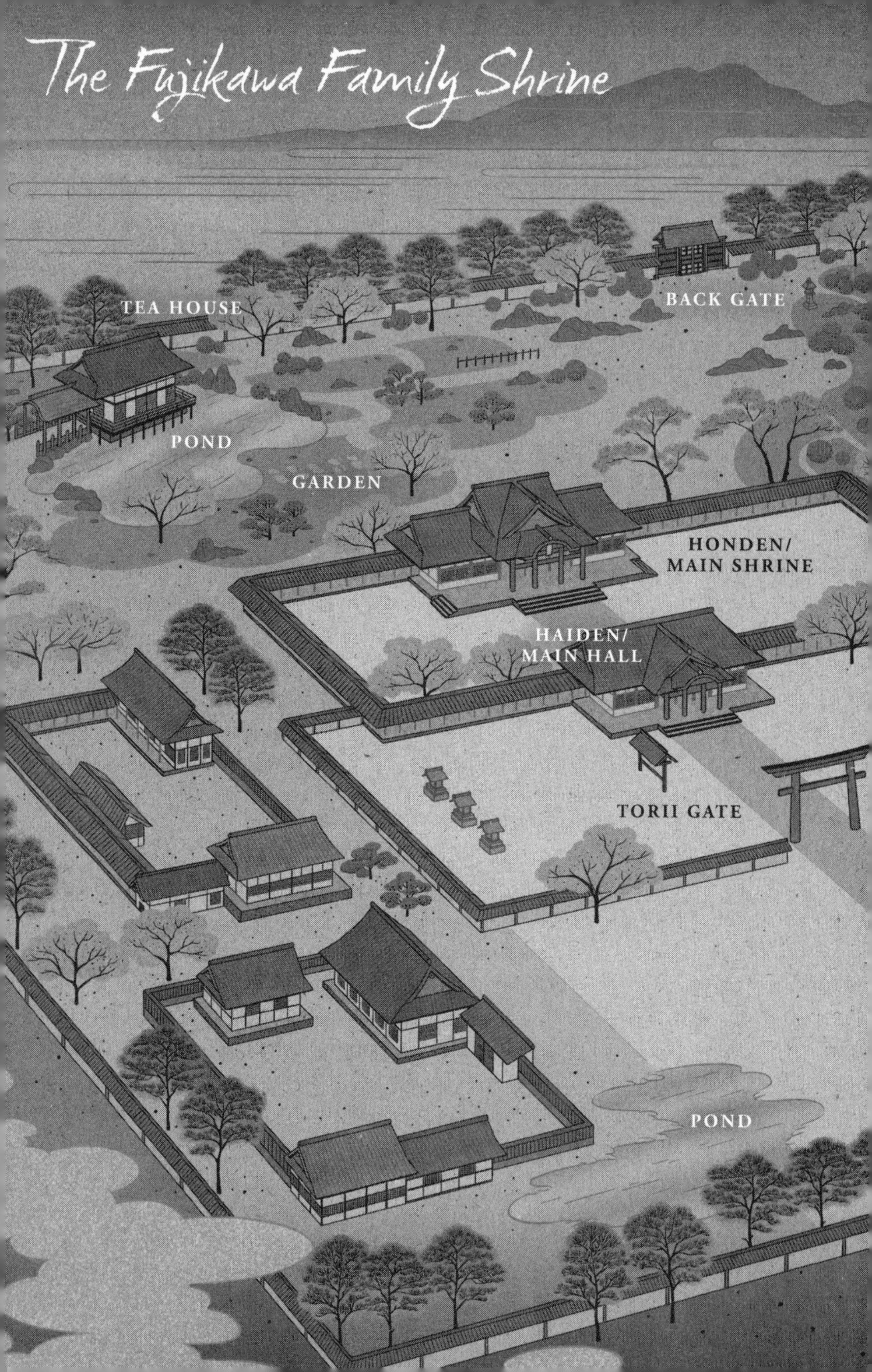

The Fujikawa Family Shrine

TEA HOUSE

BACK GATE

POND

GARDEN

HONDEN/
MAIN SHRINE

HAIDEN/
MAIN HALL

TORII GATE

POND

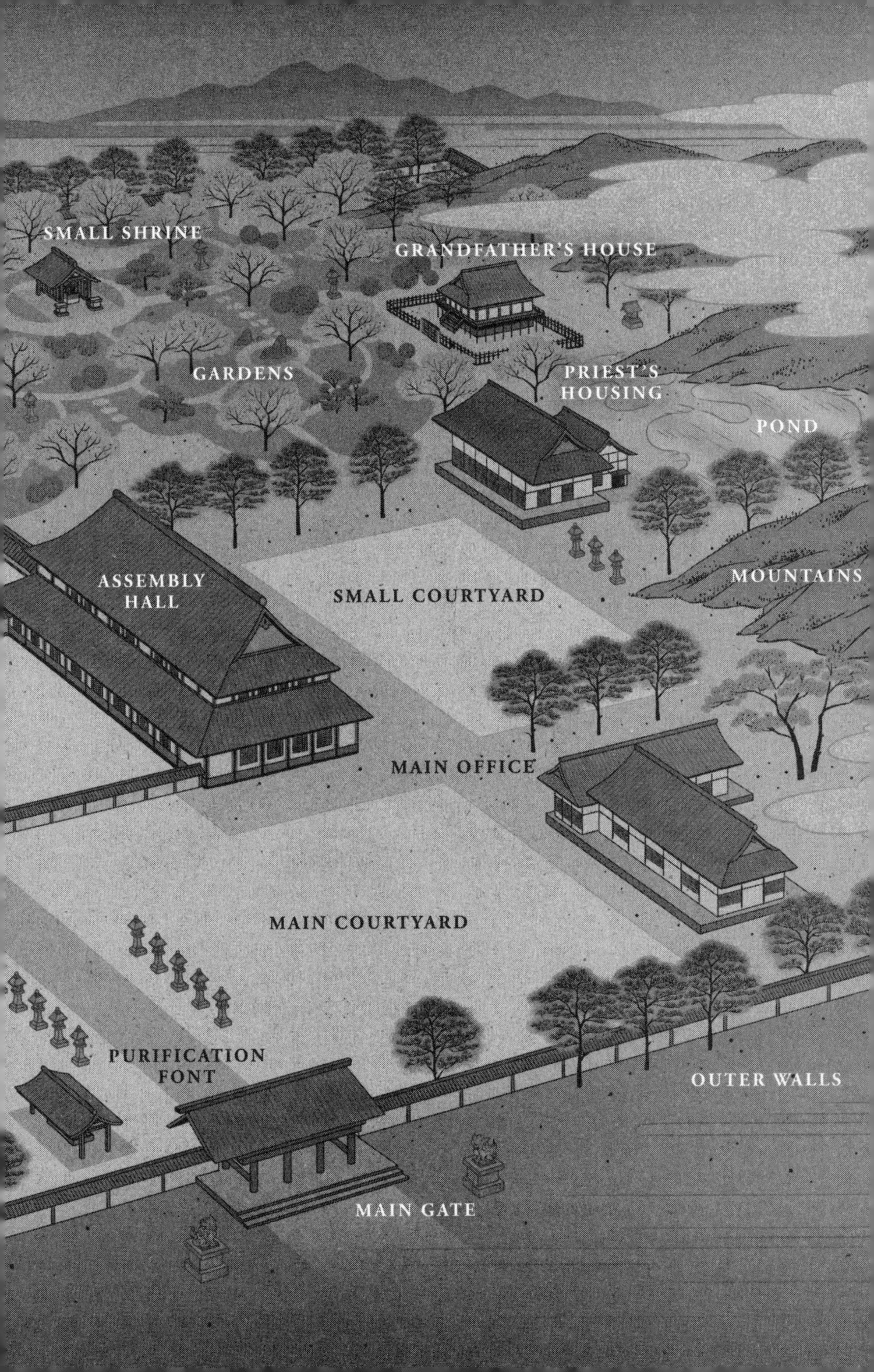

SMALL SHRINE

GRANDFATHER'S HOUSE

GARDENS

PRIEST'S
HOUSING

POND

ASSEMBLY
HALL

SMALL COURTYARD

MOUNTAINS

MAIN OFFICE

MAIN COURTYARD

PURIFICATION
FONT

OUTER WALLS

MAIN GATE

ONE

Kōgakkan High School

Kyoto, Japan

I am a girl surrounded by monsters and ghosts from an ancient world. Most days, they scare me less than people do.

"Baka!" Ayako-senpai snaps, shoving me to the ground in the school's courtyard. The contents of my messenger bag scatter across the asphalt. Some of my books fall open, their pages tearing and flapping in the wind: Chemistry. History. English. Colorful pens, pencils, and erasers flee from the girls who have trapped me.

Do you really think I'm the idiot here, senpai? The baka? I'm supposed to respect the upperclassmen at my school, but Ayako-senpai treats me like trash. She no more deserves the honorific of *-senpai* than I do the insult of *baka*. While her parents have the money to buy her a spot here at Kyoto's prestigious Kōgakkan

High School, I had to earn my way. Of course, being a newer student at Kōgakkan makes me an outsider, a girl on the fringe.

A *target*.

When I try to rise, Ayako puts a foot on my back. The girls circle tighter. Their shadows fall over me, surprisingly heavy in the hot sun. My cheeks burn. No matter how much shame I feel, no matter how violent their bullying may get, I will not cry.

I. Will. Not. Cry.

I clench my teeth and repeat these words like a mantra. From the ground, all I can see are the graceful stems of the girls' legs and the whiteness of their socks, styled fashionably loose and scrunched over their shoes. Their pleated skirts make jagged lines above their knees.

"You understand this is for your own good, don't you, Kira-chan?" Ayako says, removing her foot from my back and crouching down. She keeps her legs pressed together and clasps her hands in her lap. Her patella bones look like birds' skulls, white and fragile.

Of course you believe that, I think, wishing I could say the words aloud. But I know better than to talk back to an upperclassman—not only will Ayako make my life more hellish, but anyone I might complain to would tell me I was a fool for picking an argument with her.

"We're your big sisters, your senpai," Ayako continues. "We want you to fit in . . . but that might be difficult for a girl who's hardly more than a *scholarship* student. I'm surprised your parents can afford the tuition here."

The other girls snicker. Ayako slides a finger under my chin and turns my face toward hers. Movement draws my gaze left, where a ghostly tentacle curls over her shoulder and slides its tip into her ear. My heartbeat picks up. The bracelet I wear around my left wrist grows warmer, the protective metal charms reacting to the demon's presence. It's an old heirloom my grandfather gave me, one that has been passed down through the Fujikawa family for generations.

As a Shinto shrine maiden—a miko—cleansing evil is supposed to be part of my job. Few people can sense the yokai: the demons benevolent, malevolent, and everything in between. Yokai thrive on the energy created by extreme human emotions, which means it's best to try to avoid or ignore them. Most days, similar tactics work with human bullies: Keep your head down. Don't antagonize them. Ignore their insults. They feed on your embarrassment and your shame.

But evil is harder to deal with when it shows up wearing kneesocks and ombré extensions. I don't know what sort of yokai infests Ayako, but it must be why her bullying has escalated to a physical attack. Ayako and her friends have been shunning me since the first day I stepped foot on Kōgakkon's grounds. I've grown used to it, even if it makes me miserable.

Physical abuse, however, is more than unusual—it's almost unheard of, at least among female students.

Another tentacle slithers out of Ayako's mouth. I can't be certain that she means anything she says or if the yokai speaks for her: "Kōgakkan prides itself on its excellent student body, and we don't want anyone putting a mark on our sterling reputation. Especially not some priestess who works in a beat-up old shrine. Did the priests have to take you in because no proper after-school program wanted you?"

"I chose to work at my family's shrine, Ayako," I say, intentionally omitting the honorific.

The girls around me suck air through their teeth. "That's *Ayako-senpai* to you," one of Ayako's girls snaps, spitting on the ground. "Apologize!"

I let the command hang in the air, unanswered. The wind whistles through the school's courtyard, making the girls' skirts swing like bells. Ayako doesn't move.

Neither do I.

"Well?" another girl says. "Go on!"

"No," I say coldly. There are many ways to say no in Japanese without offense, but I'm done calling Ayako *senpai*. "My family has tended the Fujikawa Shrine for almost a thousand years, and I am proud to be a miko there. All your family's money couldn't buy a legacy like mine."

There's a beat, a moment of pure silence, before Ayako rises and kicks me, driving her shoe into my sternum. Pain clatters through my ribs. Choking, I collapse to the ground. The asphalt's heat bakes my cheek and reeks of burned rubber. Pebbles bite into my flesh. I curl my knees into my chest to protect my stomach.

I can't think. My lungs feel like they've deflated, making it difficult to breathe. I can't focus enough to push myself up from the ground.

"Ayako!" someone gasps. "You said you weren't going to hurt her!"

"Shut up," Ayako says, grabbing me by my hair.

My breath hisses through my gritted teeth. "Let me go—"

A shout rises from the other side of the yard. Ayako straightens, and her pack of girls turns toward the sound. Their legs tense.

Someone's coming our way.

"Go," Ayako snaps at the other girls. They stampede around me, fleeing and hiding their faces. Relief and embarrassment wash through me in equal amounts. I push up to a sitting position, wincing and rubbing my chest. My heart sinks when I see my younger sister, Ami, and one of the school's office secretaries hurrying toward me.

I've already lost enough dignity today. My little sister's pity is the last thing I want or need.

"Kira!" Ami's voice bounces across the courtyard, bright and high as a ball.

I don't want my sister to see me this way—my skirt is hiked up, exposing the tops of my thighs. Blood bubbles from the scrapes on my knees. My books and things are scattered around the empty courtyard, papers and assignments rolling in the breeze. Ayako's shoe left a large, dirty skid mark on the front of my white dress shirt.

Ami's pigtails bob as she runs toward me. I rise, squeezing a pebble out from under my skin and dropping it to the ground. It patters on the asphalt.

"Kira! Are you okay? Did she kick you?" my sister asks, almost crashing into me. She balls her fists in my blazer to keep her balance. She looks like she's about to cry.

I put my hand on Ami's head, refusing to make eye contact with her. "I'm fine, it was . . . a *misunderstanding*." My voice strangles on the last few syllables. I take a steadying breath. If I didn't cry in front of Ayako, I'm certainly not crying in front of my six-year-old sister.

"What happened, Fujikawa-san?" Miss Oba asks, calling me by my surname. "Are you all right?"

No, I'm not "all right." I wish people would stop asking that question—if someone needs to ask it, the answer is almost always no. I'm bruised down to the quiet, dark places of my soul. I tug my skirt into place and beat the dust off the pleats, succeeding only in smearing blood across the fabric. I curse mentally, knowing it will stain.

But I'd rather have blood on my skirt than evil slithering across my skin.

"Who were those girls?" Miss Oba asks. "They don't attend Kōgakkan, do they? Surely our students have more decorum than *that*."

You saw their uniforms. "I didn't see their faces. They knocked me down and wouldn't let me up."

Miss Oba purses her lips. I've never been a good liar, but neither is Miss Oba. She knows those girls were Kōgakkan students. I know who they were. It's easier for us both not to admit it and avoid the messy details. Neither of us wants Ayako making the consequences worse for us on Monday morning.

Besides, I can't tell Miss Oba about the yokai. Adults don't handle the inexplicable very well. Even my own parents refuse to believe that Grandfather and I can see and interact with yokai. Despite my mother's upbringing at the Fujikawa Shrine, the yokai exist only in the realms of pop culture and manga to her. And while Shinto is the cultural backbone of Japanese life, many people don't identify as religious. Not in the strictest sense, at least.

Miss Oba helps me gather my things off the ground. "Would you like to make a report?" she asks.

I shake my head, trying to shove my books into a bag too ripped to carry them. "I'm already late for work. I'll get some bandages at my family's shrine, it's not far."

"But Fujikawa-san—"

"I'm fine, thank you. Have a good day, Oba-san," I say with a short bow. With that, I usher my sister away from the courtyard before Miss Oba decides to ask any more questions.

Ami and I are fifteen paces away when Miss Oba calls out, "Fujikawa-san, wait!"

I pick the last rock out of my palm and pretend not to hear her.

TWO

Fujikawa Shrine

Kyoto, Japan

On our way to the shrine, my sister asks me enough of her own questions, tugging on my skirt to get my attention. I keep my head up and walk fast, clutching my tattered book bag to my chest, ignoring strangers' curious gazes. Despite the late November chill, sweat dampens my clothes, making them stick to the small of my back.

"Don't you need some bandages?" Ami asks. "You're hurt!"

Bandages can't fix me, I wish to say but don't. I'm too distracted by the number of yokai monsters on the street today, and I need to focus to keep us safe. Not all yokai are evil, but many love mischief for mischief's sake. They've adapted to living in modern Japan by concealing their true natures in human-looking glamours, concealing their hides, horns, and claws under expensive business suits, construction workers' clothing, or even grandmotherly flowered prints.

Ami waves to one of our "neighbors," Mrs. Nakamura, not realizing she's waving to a hone-onna, or "bone woman." Ami can't see the yokai's skeleton face, and always insists on greeting the neighbors on our route as we head home.

Some people, like Grandfather and me, are born with the ability to see through yokai glamours. Others can be trained. Once upon a time, Grandfather tried to teach my mother to spot the yokai. Mother was his heir, his eldest daughter, the pride of his life. I don't know what happened, only that their story didn't end happily. Now Mother visits the shrine only on major holidays. She and Grandfather hardly speak.

I'm Grandfather's backup heir, preparing to carry the legacy that my parents and elder brother, Ichigo, try so hard to ignore. In their minds, there's no fortune to be made in working at a shrine. My mother might have been raised in one, but neither she nor my father is religious. At least not anymore. And my brother, Ichigo, has no interest in becoming a priest.

"Kira?" Ami asks, tugging on my skirt again.

We pass a café's big windows. Inside, a young woman looks up from a magazine, sees my blood-spattered clothing and wrecked knees, and smiles. Ghostly whiskers ripple across her cheeks.

"Kira."

My bracelet burns almost as hot as summer sunlight.

Everywhere I look, I see yokai. *What's going on?* I wonder. *I never see this many of them on the street—*

"Kira!" my sister shrieks, startling our neighbors on the street. Their eyes narrow, blaming me, the elder sister, rather than the squawking child five paces back. Their thoughts are plain from their faces: *Kira should be able to control that child, she* is *the elder sibling.* Somehow, I've managed to disappoint even the neighbors and bystanders today.

I whirl around to face Ami, digging my fingernails into my palms. "What?"

"We passed the shrine, dummy." She pulls her lower eyelid down with one finger, sticks out her tongue, then turns on her heel to run down the sidewalk. I look up, realizing the Fujikawa Shrine's vermilion torii gate lies half a block behind us. I'd been so lost in my thoughts, I hadn't even noticed passing it by.

Ami sprints past the main gate, nearly colliding with a shrine visitor. She always forgets to walk under the left side of the torii gate, which is proper, and has barreled into our patrons more than once. With a sigh, I hurry after her.

"Don't take too long on your homework," I call out. "I don't want to be late getting home again!"

Ami waves me off and continues up the shrine's steps.

One of the shrine's priests stands at the bottom of the stone staircase, saying goodbye to a couple of elderly patrons. I hurry by with a short bow, not wanting to embarrass myself in front of our regulars. There are tourists on the steps, too, taking selfies with the stone lion guardians. They laugh too loudly, twisting their faces up in ugly grimaces, mocking the statues. Foreigners don't always respect our shrines the way they should, ignorant of what these spaces mean.

Step by step, the shrine comes into view. The Fujikawa Shrine is nearly a thousand years old, set like a gem into one of Kyoto's lush mountainsides. The main hall stands at the heart of the shrine. The resident kami spirits are enshrined inside the honden, or main shrine, behind the hall. While there are hundreds of thousands of kami—the spirits that animate the landscape around us, or the ancestors who graced this earth before us—chief among them all is Amaterasu, the Sun Goddess, and the most venerated kami in all Shinto.

The shrine's offering and assembly halls stand to the left and right of the main hall, respectively; the three buildings form a large public courtyard area, one that hides the more private places in the shrine from view.

The moment I slip past the shrine's gate, I breathe easier. The air cools my face, smelling verdant. Green. *Alive.* I pause at the purification font to cleanse my hands and mouth, then hurry past a large courtyard pond and racks of wooden ema plaques. The plaques bear our patrons' good wishes to the kami. At the shrine office counter, Usagi uses both hands to present a protective charm to a patron. If she's out front, it means the private office area might be empty. Good.

Priests pass me by, occupied with their own tasks or with

preparations for the upcoming autumn festivals. Everyone's busy, everyone's in a hurry. Nobody notices me. Which is great, because I'm not in the mood to explain the state of my school uniform.

To my relief, I find myself alone in the office. Stowing my books and busted backpack in a cubby, I grab my miko's uniform from a set of drawers, careful not to smear my blood on my white kimono. I go into the bathroom, close the door, and bang my forehead on it thrice.

Baka.

Fool.

Apologize, Kira.

I tell myself that they're wrong, that they're liars. I'm no fool. Still, their words stick to the insides of my ribs, like I've swallowed something rancid. Those girls can pretend they're defending Kōgakkon's "reputation," but in reality, they're cowards looking for an easy target. I just hate that their target is *me*.

Hanging my school jacket on a hook, I locate the first-aid kit under the sink. My hands shake with frustration as I pop the box's clasps. No, with *fury*, because there's nothing I can do to stop Ayako and her friends. Her father owns one of the largest J-pop record labels in the country, and were I to embarrass his daughter, I'd bring contempt down upon my family and the shrine.

I fight to open an antiseptic wipe, cursing when the paper tears but the plastic stretches. I *shouldn't* feel like such a failure: I get excellent grades, am polite to my teachers and classmates, and try not to stand out too much. My father runs a successful precision electronics company in Kyoto, and while his work may not be glamorous, it's profitable. Plus, it's an honor to work with my grandfather at the Fujikawa Shrine.

But 99 percent of my classmates are from a different economic sphere, one with different social rules and expectations. I'm often accused of "kuuki yomenai," or "not being able to read the air," because I sometimes miss the subtleties in social interactions.

In spite of my efforts, I stand out. A *lot*. It's hard to start over when you stick out so much. At least I belong here at the shrine, among the ancient rituals, talismans, and old cobblestones; I love every inch of this place—it's my sanctuary from the world.

I bandage my wounds. When I dress, my shrine maiden's uniform smells of cedar: crimson hakama pants, a pure white robe, and red hair ribbons. The feeling of crisp, clean fabric against my skin wicks the rest of my anger away. With a sigh, I consider doing some purification rituals before I begin work—I've spent too much of the day angry.

My inner peace lasts less than a second. As I exit the restroom, I look up and find I'm not alone anymore.

One of the shrine's kitsune guardians, Shiro, sits at the office desk. He's about my age, maybe a year or two older, with pop-idol good looks and a nose for mischief. Shiro looks human enough, except for the fox-shaped ears that poke out of his thick, reddish hair. Like most yokai, he keeps these ears glamoured while in public. Not all kitsune are benevolent, but shrine guardians like Shiro protect the sites dedicated to the worship of the kami and

Amaterasu. Shiro serves at the Fujikawa Shrine with his icy yet talented elder brother, Ryōsuke, who prefers to be called *Ronin*. When we were introduced, I thought his nickname was strange, but it seems to fit him.

Shiro looks like he's been waiting for me.

"Hey," he says, leaning forward in his chair to rest his forearms on his thighs. He wears a priest's teal hakama, rather than my red ones. "Rough day?"

I pause, clinging to the bathroom door handle. My kimono sleeves are long enough to hide the white bandages on my hands, but not the humiliation seared into my skin. I don't know Shiro well enough to burden him with my problems.

"I tripped and fell at school," I say, tugging on my sleeve. "I'm a little embarrassed, but I'll be fine."

He cocks one of his fox ears down, as if unconvinced. "You can't lie to me, Kira. I was raised by the best liar in all of Yomi, and can spot a lie before it's off your lips." He rises from the chair and starts across the room toward me. "Who hurt you?"

"I'm not lying." I step back as he approaches, but find myself bumping into the bathroom door. "I tripped."

Shiro's tawny eyes flash with mirth. He reaches down and takes my hand, lifting it gently, peeling back my sleeve to expose my injured hand. "I know a thing or two about not fitting in," he says, covering my hand with his own. "If you ever need to talk about things, I'll listen."

He'd be cute if he weren't so annoying, but he'd be *really* annoying if he weren't so cute. I don't like how easily he sees through my defenses, and his directness makes me uncomfortable. I won't tell him as much, though. "Thank you," I say, gently taking my hand from his. "But I should really get to work."

"Take a deep breath," he says. "Fujikawa isn't missing you yet—"

"You should call my grandfather *Fujikawa-san*, as is proper," I say.

"Typical Kira, using the rules to avoid having a real conversation." Shiro pretends to roll his eyes, voice lilting as he teases me.

His smile's so inviting, I'm almost tempted to tell him everything. But my scars and bruises, inside and out, are not the parts of me I want him or anyone else to see. When people know your weaknesses, they can exploit them. Or at the very least, they'll think less of you for them.

"I should go." I slip past him, heading for the door.

"At least let me walk you home tonight," Shiro says. "There were a lot of yokai in the streets earlier. I can help keep you and your sister safe."

I pause. Turn. Shiro leans against the bathroom door, arms crossed over his chest. When in his priest's garb, he always manages to look majestic and roguish. There is a quiver to him, almost, even when he's standing still. Perhaps it's the way he lifts his head an inch, nostrils flaring, as someone passes the office window. Or his sense of perpetual alertness, as if he expects an attack to come at any time, from any angle. That's the life of most anyone who deals with yokai daily.

"Do you know why they're here?" I ask.

He shakes his head. "No, but until their numbers thin out, nobody should leave the shrine alone. Something's not right."

"I'll meet you out front at sunset, then." At least this arrangement will make Ami happy; she *adores* Shiro. She'll probably pester him for a piggyback ride, and Shiro will oblige her all the way home.

He follows me out of the office. I step into the afternoon sunlight, pausing to let it thaw the rest of the fear from my soul. While it's my turn to sweep the shrine's courtyards, I'm almost looking forward to the work. At least I'll get to be alone for a little while.

"I suppose I should check the wards around the shrine, just in case," Shiro says with a sigh, placing his hands on his hips. "I'll see you in a few hours, okay?"

With a nod, I turn to the afternoon's work: sweeping. *Endless* sweeping. The Fujikawa Shrine is one of the larger shrines in Kyoto: it boasts two courtyards, an assembly hall, a teahouse, gardens, and dormitories for the priests, and that's to say nothing of the magnificent main shrine itself. And while Grandfather employs groundskeeping staff to keep the shrine immaculate, he still expects me to sweep the leaves. I guess he thinks it builds character.

It doesn't. It builds calluses, lots and *lots* of calluses. Which I suppose gives my palms more character, now that they have little white seeds planted at the root of each finger.

The hours of sweeping and the calluses are all worthwhile.

Someday, Grandfather will teach me the ancient art of onmyōdō, which will give me power over the yokai demons and onryō ghosts who threaten our way of life. For a girl who has spent her days in the unwanted company of nightmares and monsters, my greatest wish is to be able to banish them at will. Despite my near-constant pleas, Grandfather says I will begin my training at twenty-one, when I become old enough to formally inherit the shrine. For now, he focuses on my martial arts training and lets me observe rituals and business transactions, greet patrons, and, of course, *sweep*.

As the sun drops toward the horizon, a chill creeps into the air. Patrons wave to me as they exit the shrine, on their way to warm homes and hot meals. Some will return to work, no doubt. The shadows lengthen and the place empties of everyone, except for the priests, my sister, and me.

I'm tidying the gatehouse when I spot something small sitting under the first torii gate.

Curious, I descend the grand staircase, taking the steps two by two. A small origami fox sits at the bottom of the staircase, alone. When I pick the fox up, a child starts singing a folk song in the distance, her voice carried by the wind:

"*Kagome, Kagome . . . circle you, circle you . . .*"

My bracelet grows warm. I glance over my shoulder, expecting to see Ami giggling behind one of the gateposts. She graduated from children's kancho-style mischief at five. Now six, she's seen enough variety shows on TV to have learned a more sophisticated style of pranking.

"Ami?" I ask. No answer. Tree branches click in the breeze. The air tugs the loose hairs at the nape of my neck, and the small of my back prickles. My body senses something's off, but my mind can't figure out what. "Hello?"

The stone steps lie empty, but I feel as though a thousand eyes have turned on me, their gazes brushing against my skin, my hair, and my chest. Fear uncurls against the base of my spine, something eyeless and primal. I back away and whirl, running up the steps, through the gatehouse, and toward the shrine.

The origami fox pricks the inside of my palm as I reach the top. I double over, panting. When I look over my shoulder, nothing waits in the torii gate below. I tell myself there isn't anything odd about finding a piece of origami at a Shinto shrine. It's an offering, not a warning. At worst, it's a child's prank.

It's fine. Everything is fine. I tuck the origami fox into my pocket. The sun slides ever farther down the sky, glittering through the tree branches.

Twenty minutes later, I finish sweeping the main courtyard. As I head back to the office to change, a little flash of white catches my eye. I pause and gasp: a second origami fox sits on a large, flat stepping-stone near the pond's edge. Had I missed this second fox earlier? No, I'd have noticed something so obviously out of place.

The breeze clangs through the wooden ema boards on racks nearby. I jump, my pulse ringing like Grandfather's old landline phone, and then roll my eyes at myself. I pluck the fox off the stone to carry him back to the office. It is, after all, just a bit of folded paper I can cage inside my fingers.

In the distance, cars rumble and honk, and the trees filter people's shouts and laughter down to a comforting hum. Beneath it all, the child's song continues: *"Kago no naka no tori wa . . . the bird in the cage . . ."*

Closer now.

"Ami?" I halt and turn in the courtyard. "If this is another prank, I'll make you walk *yourself* home tonight! In the *dark*!"

Giggles echo through the shrine. With a *tsk*, I slip my hand into my pocket, expecting to feel the paper's sharp points prick my fingers.

But my pocket is empty.

The first fox is gone.

THREE
Fujikawa Shrine

Kyoto, Japan

I stab my hand into my pocket, rooting around, my breath catching. *Did Ami somehow steal it from me?* No, that's impossible. My sister may be many things, but a cunning thief isn't one of them. *Something is wrong.* The knowledge chills me from the inside out, as if my bones have turned to ice. I need to find Grandfather.

Now.

I start across the courtyard. Grandfather takes his evening tea at the shrine's teahouse, no matter the time of year. He says he finds beauty in every season, and upon reaching his age—he's robust even at seventy-five—each month feels as fleeting and bittersweet as cherry blossoms.

As expected, I find him sitting on the teahouse veranda,

watching koi dance under the pond's clear surface. He still wears his regular shrine robes with black hakama, cradling a cup of tea in his weathered hands. His hair, which used to be black as the deepest part of the midnight sky, is now the color of the moon—silver white and glowing in the last embers of daylight. He looks up as I approach, smiling.

"Good evening, Kira," Grandfather says.

I bow to him, then rest my broom against the teahouse's low fence. "Hello, Grandfather. How is your tea?"

"Never mind the tea," he says as I join him on the veranda. "Do you hear that voice on the wind? Something is amiss today—other shrines in the area are reporting that yokai are swarming their streets. We are lucky so far, but there have been reports of violence in the north."

"Not too lucky," I say, offering the origami fox to him. Grandfather frowns. He sets his teacup down, then plucks the tiny fox from my hands. "I found this at the shrine's main gate. I put it in my pocket, only to lose it minutes later. . . ."

I trail off, unnerved by the look on Grandfather's face. The lines on his forehead multiply and deepen, the shadows drawing inky lines in his skin. Dread drops into my gut. He turns the tiny fox in his hands, examining it from every angle.

"Here is a lesson in onmyōdō for you," he says, pinching the fox's tail between his thumb and forefinger and holding it up. "This is a *shikigami*, a sort of servant that both onmyōji exorcists and yokai use in rituals. I did not summon it, and its magical resonance does not feel familiar to me."

"What does that mean?" My voice shudders over those words.

Grandfather holds up a hand, asking me to be quiet.

The wind kicks up again, whispering, *"Itsu, itsu, deyaru . . . when oh when shall we meet . . . ?"*

My bracelet flares white-hot, so bright and quick, it tricks my nerves into thinking the links have frozen. I grip my wrist in pain.

"Listen carefully," Grandfather says as he rises to his feet. "Go directly to the house, collect your sister, and hide in the cellar under the Seimei motomiya."

"What are you talking about?" I whisper. "Why?"

He removes a stick of incense from a nearby ceramic dish, then touches its burning tip to the shikigami fox. As the flames eat the shikigami's paper feet, Grandfather says, "Go. Do not leave the cellar until I come to find you. There are powerful protective wards in the motomiya. They will keep you safe."

Fear tastes like copper and bile on my tongue. My scabbed knees ache as I stand. "Grandfather—"

"Do not argue with me, Kira! *Go.*"

I turn on my heel and leap off the veranda, running down the teahouse path and grabbing my broom. Grandfather lives in a modest house on the shrine grounds, one that shares a garden with the priests' dormitories. The Seimei motomiya—or small shrine—stands on the very edge of his garden and property. It's the last original building on the site. The place honors our most famous ancestor, Abe no Seimei, who was the most talented onmyōji astronomer, magician, and exorcist of ancient Japan.

I jog onto the main path. On my right looms the shrine proper: the main hall, courtyard, and ponds beyond; straight ahead, obscured behind a high hedge, are Grandfather's house and the dormitories.

Something screeches in the darkness. The sound drags itself across my skin, sharp enough to leave welts. I halt. The shriek seems to come from the front of the shrine, and echoes across the deepening night. Men shout. Someone screams. Fear makes my head feel too light, as if it could float away like a festival lantern. The path blackens. I clutch the broom's handle to my chest, and my heart beats fast and hard against my ribs.

The shrine is supposed to be protected from malevolent yokai, I tell myself. *It's supposed to be safe.*

A sound clicks behind me, like a cicada but louder. The noise rattles inside my bones. I whirl. Behind me, a funnel of conjured shadows stretches across the air. A yokai crawls from the weblike strands and steps onto the shrine grounds. The beast has the head and torso of a beautiful woman, her hair styled as intricately as any geisha's . . . but the rest of her ends in a nightmare. She is half-woman, half-spider. Her eight elegant legs step in concert, and her claws click like knives against the cobblestones. The eight eyes in her face look like gashes, their insides burning bright as the embers of a fire.

It's . . . it's a jorōgumo.

I didn't even think those were real.

Her abdomen bobs behind her, strands of silk descending from her spinnerets. She hisses at me, then strikes.

"No!" I scream, swinging my broom like a baseball bat. The bristles slam into her left cheekbone. Her head snaps to one side. Something cracks in her neck. The jorōgumo staggers back, her growl rumbling like deep, shackled thunder.

Dodging past her, I sprint toward the shrine's assembly hall. I scramble onto the veranda, slipping on the wood and catching myself against the outer wall. The yokai leaps after me with a shriek, drawing my attention backward. Moonlight glimmers on her abdomen, and on the sickled ends of her feet. She looks like a scream made flesh.

I push off the wall and run. I make it ten steps, maybe more, before a rope of spider silk snares my ankle. It yanks my feet out from under me. I crash down, broom clacking to the wooden floor. As my heart pounds in my throat, I flip onto my back, snatching my broom. The yokai approaches. She keeps my tether taut, wrapping her silk around one hand. The veranda groans under her weight.

She lunges for me.

I lift my broom with a cry, jabbing the handle into her chest to hold her off. Her cheeks split and open like a set of glistening crimson leaves. Hot saliva drips off the needlelike teeth embedded in her flesh, splattering over my chest and face. It smells of bile and coppery blood.

She leans in closer, her weight pressing the broom's bristles into my gut. I grit my teeth, pain flickering across my vision in bright red bursts.

"What do you want?" I gasp.

She grins at me, but it's just a sick approximation of a smile. "Isn't it obvious, little priestess? You have a yokai's sight—can't you sense the weakening of the sun? Can't you feel her getting colder, darker?"

"Yeah," I say, grimacing at her smell. "And it's called *winter*—"

A shadow darts in on my left. Air hisses as a blade winks in the darkness, slicing into the back of the jorōgumo's neck. Her jaw falls open in shock. Great splatters of blood hit the ground. The jorōgumo becomes boneless, collapsing beside me, the life gone out of her. Her claws slice into the veranda, leaving great red wounds in the wood.

With a shriek, I scramble away on my knees and palms.

"Useless creature." A shadowy figure spits on the corpse. "I ordered you to leave the girl alone."

I know that voice. I've heard it ringing in the shrine's halls, even when it wasn't louder than a whisper. The white peaks of his fox ears almost glow with unearthly light. Black bloodstains spread across his kimono. If Shiro channels sunlight with his laugh, then his elder brother, Ronin, can funnel darkness with a look.

His gaze fills my whole soul with dread.

"W-what's going on?" I whisper, shocked to see the katana in his hand. The blade glows with a muted gray light, like a lightbulb coated in grime. Kitsune don't use katana—it's not possible to cast an onmyōdō spell while holding a sword, and magic is a kitsune's specialty. I blink fast. "I don't understand, h-how did you—"

"Ronin!" someone shouts behind us. I turn, surprised to see Shiro standing on the path behind us, his face and chest splattered in blood. The inky fluid drips from the tips of his fingers, which end in long, sturdy claws. Shiro's voice sounds lower, rougher, as though he's shifting deeper into his yokai form, leaving his human elements behind: "Let Kira go."

"I'm not going to hurt her, brother," Ronin snaps.

"I can't trust anything you say," Shiro says. "You've betrayed us *all*."

Ronin stares Shiro down. "I don't expect you to understand—"

"Don't pull the manga villain card on me," Shiro spits. "You're getting people killed!"

A sob hitches in my throat, drawing the brothers' attention.

"Get out of here, Kira," Shiro says, shifting his gaze back to his brother. "I'll deal with Ronin."

He doesn't need to tell me twice. I turn and run, nearly tripping over my own feet. Strange, dark lumps now line the shrine's paths, blood spreading like inkblots under their lifeless forms.

You're getting people killed!

Another sob burns in my throat.

Please be safe, Grandfather, I beg him in my head. *I need you to be safe.*

I sprint up the path to Grandfather's house and throw the front door open. "Ami!" I shout. "Ami? Where are you?" I find my sister's homework forgotten on the kitchen table, and hear sobbing coming from one of the cabinets. Ami whimpers as I open the door, looking up at me, blinking. Snot trails from her nose and crusts around the top of her lip.

"Kira?" she asks in a voice so small, it sounds even younger than her six years. No matter how annoying she may be, she's still my little sister. Seeing her frightened breaks something inside me. "What's going on? Are there terrorists attacking the shrine?"

How does a six-year-old know about terrorists? And how am I supposed to answer her question? I can't tell her *monsters* are attacking our family's shrine—for one, Mother would never forgive me. Two, it sounds crazy even to my ears. The shrine is supposed to be warded. Protected. *Safe.*

"Something like that." I take a knee beside her. "Grandfather wants us to hide in the motomiya till they stop. We need to go, okay?"

She nods, wiping her nose with the back of her hand. I pull her to her feet. Staying low to avoid being seen from the house's numerous, darkened windows, I lead my sister out of the kitchen and into the entryway.

Shoes—Grandfather's and Ami's—sit neatly against the wall. I glance down, realizing that in my panic, I forgot to remove mine upon entering the house. The offense makes the knot in my gut draw tighter.

"Hurry," I whisper to my sister. Ami slides her feet into her shoes, fat tears still rolling down her face. "Don't make a sound once we're outside, understand?"

"Okay," she says, sniffling.

"One, two—" I mouth the word *three* and open the door. I keep hold of my sister's hand as we step outside. The sky looms so dark it swallows all light, including the stars. I don't know if the yokai have enchanted the sky somehow, or if the stars have turned their faces away from us.

The grounds lie silent. I guide Ami past the front of Grandfather's house, keeping to the shadows under the eaves, listening for footsteps. We slide past the topiary bushes without being spotted or followed.

The motomiya stands apart from the rest of the shrine, hidden in a copse of trees. The wooden structure is about thirty feet by fifteen, with a clay tile roof and a checkerboard lattice on the outer wall. A shimenawa rope hangs over the door lintel, denoting the motomiya as a sacred place. With Ami in tow, I slip through the open doorway and then tiptoe across a floor that sings like a nightingale. I give the altar inside little more than a cursory glance.

Hurry, I hiss to myself. Kneeling, I run my hands over the floorboards, wincing as wooden slivers prick my skin. I flinch when my hand brushes up against the corpse of a dead mouse. Swatting the bones away, my fingers locate the right wooden knot. I slide them back toward my knees, counting the number of boards. One. Two. *Three.*

I dig my fingernails between the third and fourth boards,

drawing up a secret, sawtooth trapdoor. A breath of chilly, arthritic air puffs out to greet me. I shepherd Ami down the steps first, slip in behind her, and carefully lower the trapdoor over my head. It settles into its frame with a groan.

We huddle on the steps under the door. Only the faintest bit of light ekes through the floorboards. The rough steps were cut from stone many centuries ago, and their chill leeches the warmth from my body. The air here smells of mold and decay, almost like a tomb.

"Kira?" Ami whispers. "W-what's going on?"

"Shush," I whisper, wrapping my fingers around hers. "We have to stay quiet down here. Understand?"

Ami nods against my arm, her cheeks as wet as my own. We hold very still. Long minutes pass. My knotted nerves begin to unravel. Perhaps the demons won't find us here, hidden inside the motomiya, under a layer of protective wards older than the stones themselves. This shrine is a special place, one that may have been blessed by Abe no Seimei himself. Its power is ancient. Formidable. When the rest of the shrine burned down five centuries ago, only the motomiya remained untouched.

For a few moments, I allow myself to believe we're safe . . . until another shout rings from the garden outside. A scream cuts off mid-breath, strangled into a wet, whistling sound. Cringing, I squeeze my eyes shut and clap my hands over Ami's ears. She pulls one of my hands off, stubbornly. She hates to be treated like a child, even if she's acting like one.

A voice sings through the garden, winding down to us. It no longer sounds like a child's voice, but one that cracks like bones being burned. The sound rasps over my skin:

"Ushiro no shoumen daare? Who is behind you now?"

The air grows thorny, filling the shadows with sea urchins' spines. Static crackles in my ears, raw and electric, as the light between the boards flickers, fights, and finally dies.

Heavy footsteps scrape the floorboards overhead. The yokai's stench slips into my nose, heady as plums rotting in the summer sun. A bit of dust rains between the cracks in the floor, catching in my hair and eyelashes. My bracelet burns so hot it sears my skin. I bite my tongue to keep from crying out; I don't dare move, not even to slip the bracelet off. If the creature finds us, we have no place to run.

The storage area under the motomiya isn't much larger than the small shrine itself.

Tap-tap. The rap of claws echoes through the cellar. Ami trembles and wraps her arms around my waist. My head whirls, and I silently chant a prayer Grandfather taught me, which stops my vertigo for a few breaths.

Tap-tap, in the middle of the shrine floor.

Tap-tap, by the altar.

Tap-tap, near the trapdoor.

"Ibaraki-sama, lord of ogres," someone says. Despite the wheeze of his breath, I would recognize the timbre of Grandfather's voice anywhere. He sounds like he's badly injured. My heart squeezes at the thought, but at least he's *alive.*

Ibaraki, I think, biting down on the tip of my tongue. *Why does that name sound familiar?*

Grandfather continues: "You have come down . . . from the mountains . . . but for what purpose?"

"Don't pretend you're stupid, priest," the ogre says. "You know why we're here."

"I . . . most certainly . . . do not . . . ," Grandfather rasps.

"Lies!" The creature spins. "You have hidden the last shard of a holy sword in this place for five centuries. My master, the demon king Shuten-doji, has recovered all the pieces but one. Where is the last shard of Kusanagi no Tsurugi, sword of the Sun Goddess?"

"This shrine . . . has been rebuilt many times . . . ," Grandfather replies. "Everything . . . lost. You . . . must . . . go."

The yokai growls, but not in the way a wolf might. This sound gets mangled with a scream. It rakes my soul over sharp spikes, deflating my courage. The floorboards squeal as the monster charges forward.

Grandfather shouts the first syllable of a kuji-in exorcism mudra.

Another vicious shriek rends the night.

Silence seeps out in the aftermath.

The floorboards jump when something heavy hits them. I startle, clapping a hand over Ami's mouth. Her small whimper dies under my palm. Grandfather groans. Blood drips through the floor, spattering my knees and scalp, cooling on my skin. When

I squeeze my eyes shut, but tears leak out. I can't hold them back, not when the mixture of horror, pain, and shame cuts so deep.

I thought my worst enemy was Ayako.

I was wrong, wrong, *wrong*.

"We will find the last shard," Ibaraki says. "The next full moon will rise as a blood moon, weakening the Sun Goddess's power over this world. When that happens, my lord Shuten-doji will return to this mortal plane to make the Light suffer for the oppression of our people."

Grandfather's answer dies with his final breath. Tears prick the corners of my eyes. I'm listening to my grandfather's last moments, and there's nothing I can do to save him. If Grandfather could not defeat this demon, what chance do I have?

The yokai's steps crunch over the flagstones outside, fading into the shadows.

Ibaraki. I sear his name into my memory, repeating it over and over again. *Ibaraki killed my grandfather.* The thought turns into a cold, hard kernel of hate inside my heart. *Ibaraki killed my grandfather, and his master is Shuten-doji.*

I will make them pay for their crimes against me, my grandfather, and this shrine. But first, my sister and I need to survive the night.

Several minutes shudder by. Five, ten maybe, with no sign of the yokai. Police sirens roar in the distance. Releasing Ami, I open my eyes and wipe my cheeks with the backs of my hands. I place my palms on the trapdoor over our heads, gasping when something pricks my palm. It's softer than a shard of wood or a nail, and doesn't break the skin. Reaching up, I tug a small object between the boards. I run my fingers over its sharp, bloodied corners and gasp when I realize what I'm holding.

It's the shikigami fox, soaked in my grandfather's blood. And somewhere in the distance, I hear the yokai singing:

"Kagome, Kagome. Kago no naka no tori wa . . . circle you, circle you. The bird in the cage . . ."

The yokai's voice fades into the police sirens. I crush the little fox in my fist, its points breaking the soft flesh of my palms. My bracelet stops burning. It's all I can do to keep from screaming until these walls collapse and bury me in my grief and shame.

Kagome, Kagome. We are the birds in the cage.

And the monsters will come for us.

FOUR

Fujikawa Shrine

Kyoto, Japan

I hurl the crushed shikigami fox to the ground. "C'mon," I whisper to Ami. "We should go."

"Kira?" Ami whispers. "Are you sure? Where's Grandpa?"

"I think he's . . . he's not well," I say, because how am I supposed to explain to a six-year-old that our grandfather has been murdered by a *monster*?

"What was that voice?" Ami asks. "I-it felt like it was scratching the insides of my head."

"I wish I knew." I give the trapdoor a heave, but it doesn't budge. Blood drips between the boards and spatters on the stone steps. I cringe as it strikes my cheeks. It's still warm. "We have to go, okay? I'll answer your questions later, I promise."

"Okay," she whispers, though I'm not sure it's a promise I can keep. For now, my grief will hide behind the twin forces of my shock and terror. Once I get Ami somewhere safe, I can process my pain and choose my next steps. But until then, we need to survive. Using all my strength, I push up on the trapdoor, pressing my back into the boards. The hinges scream and protest. Grandfather's body rolls off with a heavy thud.

The door blocks the worst of Grandfather's injuries from view, though his arms and legs are angled in crooked shapes. My heart jolts. Not every part of him appears to still be . . . *attached*. A black pool stretches across the floor, puddling in the deep scores left by the ogre's claws. The meaty air feels too warm. My stomach lurches.

In the distance, police sirens cruise closer.

I swallow hard. This violence may be my last memory of Grandfather, but it doesn't have to be Ami's.

"Close your eyes and hold my hand," I tell Ami. We start up the steps and she stumbles, blind. I tug her up the last step and pull her against my side, shielding her from Grandfather's corpse.

My sister and I creep out of the motomiya. Though I can't see them, I can hear police officers shouting at each other, their voices harsh. Hurried. I wonder if I am condemning them to the same fate as the priests, should the yokai have lingered in the wake of the attack . . . but there's nothing I can do to save them. My warning would fall on deaf ears. What could I possibly say in a police investigation? That my family's shrine was attacked by yokai, and that those yokai were searching for a sword that was *supposed* to be kept in a shrine hundreds of miles away?

What do you say when the truth sounds like fiction?

"Where are we going?" Ami asks in a small voice. "What about Grandpa?"

"Grandpa wants us to run, Ami," I whisper, biting my lip to hold in my tears. "No! Don't open your eyes yet. Hold on."

Ami and I sneak around the small shrine. Our footsteps crunch in the pebbles and dry leaves. A shout goes up. I freeze, fearing the police have spotted us, but no. They're calling for backup, ambulances, and aid. They must have found the priests' mangled bodies, not my sister and me.

My sister sniffs, but follows me obediently. I lead her toward the back gate, the one hidden in a high hedge. It's so old, only my family knows about it. It groans as I tug it open, twigs snapping off and pattering against my arms and chest.

"Okay," I say, "you may open your eyes."

Ami's eyes snap so wide, their whites seem to glow in the darkness. When I try to tug her into the thicket, she digs in her heels, leans back, and pulls at my arms with both hands.

"No, no," she cries. "What if there are monsters in there?"

I can't help but wonder the same. For Ami's sake, I steady myself. "I thought you weren't afraid of monsters?"

"I-it's dark now." She sniffles, rubbing her free hand under her nose. "And I still hear that voice inside my head. . . . Kira, it won't stop—"

"Hush." Kneeling, I press my palm to her mouth. "Listen, the only other way out of the shrine is through the front gate, which would mean we'd have to cross the shrine grounds. The shrine isn't safe right now, Ami. We need to get you out. *Now*."

Ami shakes her head so hard, she flings tears. "I'm scared."

"Me too, okay? Can you be brave with me?"

She nods and grips my hand fiercely. We fight our way through the brush, using my phone's flashlight to push back the shadows. I shove the branches away from my face with my hands, glad for my bandaged palms. Twigs grasp at my clothing with knobby fingers. I beat a path open for Ami, sneezing as the dusty air fills my nose. Bits of leaves and broken-off branches drop past the collar of my kimono, and something wriggles against the small of my back. Sap sticks to my skin. I grit my teeth against it all.

"Kira, there's something in my hair!" Ami cries.

"Shush!" The sound barely escapes my lips when a barbed feeling curls around my spine, down my limbs, and pierces my gut. Something clicks and growls behind us. I startle, and my phone slips from my grasp and crashes into a large stone. There's a glittery *clink* of breaking glass. The flashlight snaps off, plunging us into deep darkness. Ami sobs.

I stumble out of the bushes, dragging my sister behind me. "Come on," I whisper to her. The bushes shiver and whisper with otherworldly force.

We run.

The road curves around the back of the mountain, dropping

down into the city after a half mile. I urge Ami on, faster. We pass a bakery, a curry house, and a gas station. Two bus stops blur by, plastered with glossy photos of idols and actresses, before my muscles fill with fire and burn down my will to go on. My lungs feel like they're full of phlegm and hunks of dirt. I don't breathe, I hack.

My sister stops and collapses on a curb. Snot has clotted under her nostrils again. I hand her a battered tissue from my pocket. She takes it without looking up at me. I double over, hands on my knees.

"Come on, we're almost home," I tell her softly, straightening up to watch the shadows around us. Nothing moves, but the prickly sensation in my stomach doesn't go away, either. I tug my sister back to her feet. We jog another few blocks before we reach our house.

Our family lives in one of the city's older districts, where the rough-hewn stone walls have stood for centuries. Many of the homes, while new, are built to resemble the structures of a more ancient Japan. Our house sits atop a small hill, behind one of those fat stone walls. My family has owned the land for many generations, but my parents built the elegant home on the hill. Lights glow from within the windows. Father's study lies dark. Our parents might not be home.

I take a few moments to knock the twigs from Ami's hair and straighten her pigtails and school clothing. She's trembling. I shake the debris from my own hair, and then retuck my kimono.

There's nothing to be done about the blood. It's splattered all over my shrine robes. I rub at a red splotch on Ami's face—at least she doesn't know she's wearing her own grandfather's blood. No, that horror is mine to bear, and mine alone.

Our grandfather is dead. As my adrenaline wears off, those words echo in the hollowed-out chambers of my heart. His blood hardens to scabs on my kimono. Our family's shrine has been defiled by demons, our trust betrayed by a kitsune meant to protect us. I have lost much of what I love because of Ronin and his yokai allies; and while I'm not certain what I should do *yet*, that offense cannot go unanswered.

Ronin. Ibaraki. Shuten-doji, I think, listing their names in my head so I don't forget. *You will pay for your crimes.*

"When you go inside, make sure you don't skip your evening bath or Mother will scold me again," I tell Ami as I punch the buttons for the code on the garden gate. My fingers shudder on the keys, making them difficult to press in the correct order.

She sniffles. "But Kira, I'm so tired. . . ."

I silence her with a look. *As if I'm not?* No matter what happened tonight, I'm the elder sister. My word is law. I realize Ami's only six, but she can't go to sleep wearing dirt, bug carcasses, and her own grandfather's blood.

Her legs shake as we climb the steps to the house. I snake an arm around her waist, supporting her the rest of the way.

"Grandpa's not going to be okay, is he?" she asks quietly.

"No, Ami, he's not," I say. "I'm sorry."

She tries to keep her lips from quivering. In the rush to escape, I haven't spent a moment thinking about what we're going to tell our parents. Anything but the truth, I suppose. I doubt I'd hear anything but the same tired responses, anyway:

Yokai aren't real.

They don't kill people.

It's all in your head.

All lies people tell themselves to ignore the hairs rising on the backs of their necks. Their guts know what their minds dismiss: that evil isn't always human, but it's always hungry. While terrorist attacks are rare, I'm certain what happened at the shrine will be labeled as something like domestic terrorism by the local authorities. They'll never catch the *real* monsters who did it.

That's my job.

"I'll deal with your clothes," I say at the door. "When Mother and Father come back, tell them you didn't see anything. We ran away before anything bad happened, okay?"

"But Kira—"

"You didn't hear anything, either," I tell her, maybe a little too forcefully. She shuts up and turns her gaze down, tears glittering on her lashes. At least Mother and Father will put less stock in anything Ami says. They'll write off the supernatural as figments of her imagination, a scaffold to help her cope with the terrors she experienced at the shrine. What other choice would they have? They don't see the world the way I do.

Ami and I take off our shoes in the lowered genkan entryway.

From here, I can see our older brother, Ichigo, hunched over his laptop in the darkened living room, his back to us. University papers and books pile across the table. I doubt he thought to turn the room's lights on as the sun set. Ichigo gets . . . *absorbed* in his work.

"You're late," Ichigo says. He doesn't turn around, the word *again* implied in his tone.

"There was trouble at the shrine," I say, ushering Ami into the hall.

"Trouble?" Ichigo's fingers stop clacking on his keyboard. He pauses, cocking an ear in our direction while still looking at his screen. I'm never worth more than half his attention. "What kind of trouble?"

"Grandfather got us out before we saw anything," I say, not bothering to mask the tremor in my voice. "Ichigo . . . I think people died."

Ami looks up at me, chin quivering. If she realizes I'm lying, she doesn't contradict me in front of our brother.

Ichigo's chair creaks as he turns in his seat. Dark circles wax like moons under his eyes. "You look like hell."

"We . . . um, had to crawl through the back hedge to get out," I say, explaining away my appearance.

"Did you alert the authorities?"

"We heard sirens."

After a long moment, Ichigo sighs, removes his glasses, and rubs the bridge of his nose. "And Grandfather?"

My tears well up again, and I blink fast to keep them at bay. I look away and shake my head. "I . . . I don't know if he's okay."

"Well, there's nothing I can do about it now, not if the police are already there," he says, picking up his cell phone. "I'll text Mother to let them know something's gone wrong at the shrine. Take care of Ami, would you? I have an important paper due tomorrow."

Ichigo sends a text and turns back to his work, fingers flying over his keyboard, *clack-clack-clack*. I wish he would see me for once, see my disheveled hair and the blood on my clothes, and ask me what happened. I wish he would come over, give me a hug, sit on the couch, and talk to me. I wish he would *listen*. *See* me. *Understand* me the way Grandfather could, rather than weighing me with a look and dismissing me when he found me wanting.

I should tell him Grandfather's dead, but the words stick in my throat, stiff and unyielding. If I tell him I listened as our grandfather was murdered, Ichigo will want to know how; and if I tell him the shrine was attacked by spider-legged yokai demanding a famous sword, he'll be on the phone with my parents in minutes, complaining that I'm telling stories again. *The yokai are mythical creatures, Kira*, he'd say. *And even if they weren't, why would they be interested in a dingy little shrine like ours?*

Our family's shrine isn't dingy, I think, before realizing I'm arguing with him in my head.

"I should . . ." I hesitate, feeling like a stranger in my own home. "I'm going back to the shrine to check on Grandfather and help the police. But first, I'll get Ami-chan into bed."

"Good," he says without turning, the way Mother sometimes does. "That would be helpful. Though I'm certain Grandfather is already getting the help he needs—I can't imagine you would be anything more than a bother."

His words crush crystals of salt into my heart. He doesn't say, *Let me go with you*, nor does he thank me. My brother and I are bound by blood, but little else.

"Good night, Ichigo," I say, and guide my little sister toward the bathroom. He doesn't answer me.

He doesn't even look up as we pass.

FIVE

Fujikawa Family Home

Kyoto, Japan

After disposing of Ami's dirty clothes, I trudge upstairs to my bedroom.

My mother is a fierce traditionalist, insisting upon old-world details in our home: the tatami mats on the floor give off a sweet, grassy smell. The walls gleam like eggshells, bisected by centuries-old, cracked wooden beams. Though my parents built this house, they used materials reclaimed from century-old machiya houses in Kyoto, so everything in this place seems to have long memories. This house may have been home for my whole life, but now it feels uncomfortable, foreign. My world has shifted. Shattered. The aged stairs groan underfoot, but their voices no longer sound familiar. When I reach the top of the stairwell, I turn right, slipping into the bedroom that has long been mine.

My room is simple: Western-style hardwood floors and furniture, with a bed covered with a teal duvet. My desk slumps under a pile of books. I share a sliding shoji wall with Ami, which means I've never had much privacy. My sister throws those doors open whenever she pleases.

But for the next few, precious minutes, my sister will be in the shower—water already hisses from the bathroom down the hall. I close my bedroom door, turn, and lean against its wooden surface. This might be the only time I have to mourn privately, at least for a little while.

A trembling starts in my fingertips and leaps to my hands. Tectonic plates of grief shift inside me, shaking me to my core. I was a child when the Sendai earthquake hit Kyoto, but I remember how the sidewalks looked that day—hundreds of tiny cracks opened in the pavement as the ground buckled. The holes looked like mouths, shrieking without voices. At the time, I had thought the world was ending, that the earth would rip itself apart and swallow me whole in the process. Now I almost wish it had.

I open my mouth in a silent cry, crumpling under the weight of the pain. Even if the shrine hasn't been destroyed, it was Grandfather who was always my home. Unlike my parents, my grandfather understood that I didn't suffer from an "overactive imagination." I'd inherited his ability to commune with the divine and the demonic, an ability passed down through generations of Fujikawa men and women, along with the shrine. Grandfather gave me the direction and guidance my parents couldn't, because they can't see the world he and I do. No, *did*.

The yokai won't come looking for us here—we have no swords belonging to famous goddesses in this house—but there's no escape from the monsters in my own mind. I will never be able to scrub the stain of Grandfather's blood from my skin, not the memory of it, at least. Nor will I be able to tear the sounds of his last breaths from my ears.

A shadow falls across my bedroom window. Startled, I glance up, my fear clanging through my veins like the tolling of suzu bells. A boy crouches on the roof. The small peaks of his ears twitch in the breeze. His eyes glitter like stars. Reaching out, he places one hand on the window. The tips of his fingernails scrape against the glass.

Shiro—he's alive.

"Let me in?" he says through the glass, throwing a nervous look over his shoulder. "Please? Ronin's sent those psycho spider girls after me."

I'm relieved to see that someone else survived the attack, especially the boy who may be able to explain Ronin's betrayal. I push myself up from the floor, wiping tears from my eyes with the backs of my hands. I cross the bedroom, lift the window's latch, and then slide the pane back. Shiro steps down into the room, immediately closing the window behind him and locking it tight.

"Thank the gods you're okay," he whispers. Blood darkens his forehead and left temple like a glistening red blossom. He reaches out, cradling my cheeks in his palms. The heat from his body warms the chilly space around us. I turn my face up to his, surprised by the gentle tug in my chest. I'm shocked by how much I'd like to lean into him. After everything I've been through, I almost crave physical comfort. "I panicked when I couldn't find you or Ami anywhere outside the shrine."

"We're both okay." I step back and out of his range, not ready for these feelings, especially not right now. "But Grandfather . . ."

"I know," Shiro says, turning his ears down. "I'm sorry."

"Why would Ronin do this to us?" I ask. "Why betray everything he was sworn to protect?"

"I don't know," Shiro says, sliding his hands into his pockets. "The Kusanagi is no average sword, and Ronin's new 'friends' are yokai who have allegiances to Shuten-doji—"

"Shuten-doji? He's supposed to be *dead*," I say, dropping my voice and glancing at my bedroom door. Shuten-doji is one of the Three Great Evils, an ogre-king who rampaged through Kyoto's countryside, killing maidens and causing havoc. The hero Yorimitsu defeated him in the first century and buried his head at Oeyama.

"Shuten-doji's been killed a time or two, yeah." Shiro wipes his brow with the back of his hand, smearing blood across his skin. "But it's not enough to kill his body—he's more powerful than your average demon, so you've gotta destroy his *soul*, too. And someone's obviously trying to resurrect him on the night of the next blood moon."

"You think Ronin is trying to resurrect Shuten-doji?" I ask.

"I can't be sure what Ronin wants. This isn't like him," Shiro says. "But my mother might know. If I catch a late shinkansen train to Tokyo, I should be able to request an audience with her tonight."

"You need to request an audience," I say, hoping the sarcasm in my tone conveys that I'm not asking him a question, "with your *mother*."

"If you and I have one thing in common," Shiro says with a sigh, "it's *mommy* issues—"

But he pauses, ears swiveling toward the bedroom door. He puts a finger to his lips as my brother calls out: "Kira?" My thin bedroom door muffles Ichigo's voice. Every cell in my body stiffens. "Who are you talking to?"

Motioning at Shiro to be quiet, I go to the door. Cracking it a few inches, I peer out at Ichigo. One look tells me that I have interrupted my brother's studies, and he isn't pleased with me.

"Mother and Father are on their way home," Ichigo says, eyeing me up and down. He frowns. "Is that *blood*?"

"I'm just grabbing pajamas for Ami," I say, the lie rolling easily off my lips, as if Shiro himself had planted it there. "I must have been talking to myself out loud. I'm sorry for disturbing you, brother."

Ichigo scrunches his face when he sees the flaky red splotches on my kimono. "I thought you were going to go check on Grandfather at the shrine?"

"I'll be on my way soon," I say.

"Fine," he says by way of goodbye.

I close my bedroom door, releasing the breath I hadn't realized I'd been holding. As Ichigo's footsteps thump away, Shiro shifts out of the room's shadows. "And I thought *I* had a terrible relationship with my brother," he whispers.

"You still win *that* contest," I say.

"Yeah, you're probably right." Shiro makes an awkward attempt at a grin, but the expression looks as fake as it must feel. It falls off his face. "You can't go back to the shrine, Kira. Not tonight."

"I know." I shake my head, pushing away from the door. "But it's the best place to start looking for answers."

"Well . . . you could come with me," Shiro says.

"To *Tokyo*?" I scrunch up my nose. "I can't just run off like that. What would my parents think?"

"Your ancestral shrine was just destroyed by one of your family's ancient enemies, and you're worried about what your parents think?" Shiro asks, frowning.

"You don't know my parents."

"That's true, but they can't be more terrifying than the yokai."

He *really* doesn't know my parents.

"I suppose the Fujikawa Shrine's last kitsune guardian relocated to a shrine in Tokyo," I say slowly, mulling the idea over. "He may be able to help us. Plus, my parents trust him."

"I remember meeting him. Older guy, nine tails, good sense of humor?" Shiro asks.

"Goro. He was the shrine's kitsune protector for almost seventy years." Goro's shadow used to loom as large as Grandfather's did—he was my protector, confidant, and friend. I missed him terribly when he left, especially when Grandfather replaced him with the Okamoto brothers.

"Then we'll find him, too," Shiro says. "Though I can't say my mother will have all the answers, or any at all. She's not fond of . . . your kind."

I lift a brow. "My *kind*?"

"Humans," Shiro says. "Especially the ones able to see our world as it really is, like you."

"Benevolent kitsune shouldn't have any issues with Shinto priestesses," I say.

"Which is a true statement based on a false assumption," Shiro says with a dark grin. "My mother is no kitsune, and *benevolent* is probably not the best way to describe her. She was born a lady, but she was also born a witch. She adopted me when I was a kid. You'll see."

She sounds wonderful. I frown. "This is probably a stupid idea. . . ."

"Those are the best kind." Shiro opens my window, drawing a deep breath through his nostrils.

Are you sure about that?

"Come with me," he says, extending a hand to me, palm up. "I can't promise you answers, but it will be an adventure."

If I'm going to understand what happened at the shrine

tonight—and more important, *why*—I'll have to go out into the world and seize them for myself.

I clap my hand into his. "To Tokyo," I say.

He grins. "To Tokyo."

SIX

Shinkansen Train to Tokyo

Japan

Two hours later, our shinkansen train speeds out of the city, leaving Kyoto's twinkling lights behind. The tension in my spine finally loosens. I'm seated beside the window, with Shiro in the middle seat beside me. Like most trains in Japan, the shinkansen train is impeccably clean and quiet, with nothing but the gentle *shush* of the rails against the tracks to disrupt my thoughts. I lean back into my seat with a sigh, watching the dark countryside rush past.

In the window, the shadowy girl looking back at me isn't dressed in a priestess's hakama and kimono anymore, but in skinny jeans, mint green flats, and a formfitting hoodie with cat ears on the hood. Once Shiro and I reached Kyoto Station, we purchased new clothes from the CUBE mall inside, changed in the public rest-rooms, and ditched our bloodied shrine robes in separate rental lockers. I called Mother from Shiro's phone while we waited for the train, reading lies off Shiro's lips. I assured her that I was fine, but had an urgent matter to take to Goro in Tokyo. My little lie hides a huge, frightening truth.

Shiro and I aren't on the run. Not exactly. But my mother wasn't thrilled to hear that I was en route to Tokyo.

Plus, I *sort of* hung up on her.

"You okay?" Shiro asks.

Do I look anything close to okay? I half laugh and shake my head. "No. A hundred times *no*."

"Yeah, me neither," he says, reaching out and placing his hand atop mine. I glance up at him, surprised to see an honest, raw ache in his eyes. "Your grandfather made me feel like I belonged some-where. It's been a long time since I felt like I had a home."

"Grandfather is good at that," I say, and then I pause and turn away, staring instead at my reflection in the train's dark windows. "Grandfather . . . *was* good at that."

Shiro's hand tightens on mine, then releases. Our train hurtles through the darkness, leaving what Grandfather *was* ever farther in the past. He will not be waiting for us when we return to Kyoto. I won't find him tending his garden in the springtime; nor will he chide me for forgetting to tend to my family's kamidana shrine. I'll never catch him drinking sake and snickering at retro manga on lazy summer afternoons; nor watch as a rare smile breaks across his face during a Shichi-Go-San festival for the neighborhood children.

He's gone.

The ghostly girl reflected in the window begins to cry. Silent tears spill down her cheeks. I turn away from Shiro, wishing I could tell the girl that losing her grandfather was a survivable event. I wish I could tell her that the hole he left in her life wouldn't suck all the light from her universe.

But at sixteen, I'm still five years away from being old enough to legally own the family shrine. The ownership, no doubt, will revert to my mother in the meantime. Mother has no love for the place, and Father has made it clear that he's grown tired of being one of the Fujikawa Shrine's chief benefactors. I'm not sure the shrine can survive without his support.

Who will help me cleanse and purify the shrine? Who will help me mourn our dead, raise money to repair the damages to the structures, and hire new priests? Not my parents. And on top of it all, I left my schoolbooks and notes in the shrine office, which means I won't even be able to study for my exams on Monday. Grandfather's death may buy me a few condolence days, but how does someone explain to her teachers that one of the Three Great Evils will be resurrected in her front yard in a month's time?

Short answer: she doesn't.

"Hey," Shiro says to me, pulling me out of my thoughts. "I'm here for you, okay?"

"I'm sorry, I'm so sorry," I say, brushing the rest of the tears off my face with my sleeve. "I'm embarrassing you."

"Hardly," Shiro says in a gentle tone. "Fujikawa-san deserves to be mourned."

"That's true . . . just not in public," I say with a dark half chuckle. "I don't want to make anyone on this train uncomfortable."

"You won't," Shiro says, popping up from his seat and looking to the fore and aft of the train car. "Nobody's sitting close, and nobody's listening."

"Well, then I don't want to make *you* uncomfortable."

"You could never," Shiro says, eyeing the woman heading down the train's center aisle with a food trolley. "But I've found grief is easier to handle on a full stomach, and the trolley hostess has ekiben. You hungry?"

The thought of food makes my stomach squelch. "Not really."

"Here's the thing—you and I are sort of on the run," Shiro says, lifting a hand to flag down the attendant. "Ronin's yokai may try to follow us to Tokyo. We may have to avoid the police, depending on whether your parents decide to cover for you. Eat whenever you can. Doesn't matter if you're hungry. *Eat.*"

"Sounds like you've done this before," I say.

"Yeah, kind of," he replies. His gaze seems far away, as if he's looking through time at a memory that still aches.

Before I can press him for an explanation, the hostess approaches with the food trolley. She offers us a shallow bow. We order several ekiben—bento box meals made specifically for train riders. I choose an ekiben containing artfully arranged rice, sautéed salmon, a tamagoyaki omelet, and vegetables. Pink and white tofu flowers accent the meal, making it almost too pretty to eat. *Almost.* Each part of the meal enjoys its own little compartment, beautiful, organized, structured. I wish my life made as much sense.

The moment I remove the ekiben's wooden lid and the scent of vinegared rice hits my nose, my stomach growls. I haven't eaten since lunch.

"Itadakimasu," Shiro says, grinning at me. It means *let's eat* and is customarily said before meals. He presses his palms together and bows his head over the food. The normalcy of the act comforts me. Rituals and cute tofu flowers can't heal the loss of my grandfather or the shrine, but they do dull a little of the pain.

"Itadakimasu." I'm not quite able to return Shiro's smile, but I'm grateful all the same.

We eat in silence, listening to the musical whir of the train as it rushes down the tracks, carrying us ever closer to Tokyo. With the hour approaching nine o'clock, it's not surprising to find the train so empty—we'll be arriving in Tokyo well after midnight. Shiro promises me that his mother is "more active at night," whatever that means.

"Tell me something," I say as I poke at a piece of tofu with my chopsticks, trying to decide if I'm still hungry enough to eat more. "Why do the yokai think a shard of the Kusanagi is hidden in the Fujikawa Shrine? It's a part of the Imperial Regalia belonging to the Emperor, which I thought was stored at the Atsuta Shrine in Nagoya." Honestly, I didn't know the sword had been shattered into pieces in the *first* place. None of the stories say anything about that.

Shiro picks up a piece of octopus with his chopsticks. "The sword in Nagoya is a fake."

"Excuse me?" I say.

He pops the tentacle into his mouth and chews, thinking. "So in the first century, there was this emperor named—"

"Sujin, I know," I say. "Because the Imperial Regalia confers power on our emperors, Sujin had copies made to protect the originals. At least one set of copies was thrown into the sea when the Taira clan lost the Battle of Dan-no-ura. Another was stolen in the fifth century by a Korean monk, or so the story goes. But the Imperial Family still retains the originals."

"You know your history," Shiro says with a wry smile. He pushes his half-empty ekiben box across his fold-down table, offering it to me. "Octopus?"

"No, thank you."

He slides it back, plucks out another piece of fish with his chopsticks, and tosses it into his mouth. "Anyway, once the copy of the Kusanagi was recovered, the Atsuta priests refused to let anyone see the copies or the real Imperial Regalia. Why?"

"Historical records aren't clear," I say.

"*Why*, Kira?"

"Because . . ." I gasp as the idea hits me. "Because it wasn't the *copy* of the Kusanagi that was stolen, but the real thing?"

"Exactly. All the stories are just that—stories," Shiro says, replacing the cover on his ekiben, setting it down on the empty seat beside us, and reaching for a second box. "During the last blood moon, like, five hundred years ago, *someone* thought it would be a good idea to break the sword and send the pieces to shrines all over Japan. The Fujikawa Shrine must have received one of them."

"Sounds like a good idea to me," I say. "There are thousands of shrines—it would take ages to find them all."

"But not forever," Shiro says. "Shuten-doji now holds all of the pieces but one."

I press my palms against my ears, mostly in jest, and squeeze my eyes closed. "So Shuten-doji needs one more shard of the Kusanagi no Tsurugi to reforge the blade," I say slowly, as if I don't really want to hear the answer.

Shiro dips his head in a nod. "Yup."

I drop my hands in my lap. "If he finds it, he'll use the sword to kill the Sun Goddess, Amaterasu, thus bringing an eternal night down upon Japan."

"And . . . y'know . . . ," Shiro says, flattening his fox ears against his skull, "the rest of the world. . . ."

Understanding steals over me slowly, drawing the light out of my soul. I recall the demon's parting words at the shrine: *The next full moon will rise as a blood moon, weakening the Sun Goddess's power over this world. When that happens, our lord Shuten-doji will return to this mortal plane to make the Light suffer for the oppression of our people.*

"We need to go back," I say, throwing my napkin into my bento box, tossing my manners aside, along with my better sense. "We only have a month, Shiro. We need to get back to the shrine, to stop them from—"

"Kira, listen," Shiro says, placing a hand on my wrist. "Shuten-doji's yokai fled as soon as the police arrived. It's safe, at least for now, and you and I need allies. We need my mother, and we need Goro, okay? We can't face Shuten-doji alone."

I suck in a breath. He's right.

At least I hope he's right.

SEVEN

The Red Oni

Tokyo, Japan

By the time we step out of the labyrinth of Tokyo Station, darkness still crowds the sky. The city's lights gild the undersides of the clouds. I grew up in a large city, but Kyoto isn't Tokyo.

Tokyo boasts ten thousand distractions. Candy-colored lights dance along every building in sight. The streets swell with people. Skyscrapers soar overhead. The residents here are fashionable and cosmopolitan; a lot of the young people on the streets look like idols. While I love Kyoto for its grace, beauty, and the wisdom in the city's bones, Tokyo makes my heart thump. I could lose myself here, disappear in the masses of people and the colors, and forget what happened at the shrine. At least for a few minutes.

"I don't see anyone following us." Shiro scans the area as we head to the nearest subway station. "That's one small thing to be happy about."

"Don't be too happy just yet, there are a lot of yokai around," I say, searching the crowds on the street. One woman reaches up to scratch the back of her head. When she turns, I glimpse the glistening lips and teeth of the second mouth embedded in the back of her skull. She's a futakuchi-onna, a yokai woman with two mouths. A faceless noppera-bo catches a cab. Spherical hito-dama glow around an elderly woman's shoulders, protective and bright. Every creature goes about their individual business, ignoring Shiro and me.

We take a train to the Shibuya district, then turn away from the city's glitter and glow, moving down dark alleys and into a seedier area. Litter swirls across the sidewalks here. Black wads of flattened gum add age spots to the concrete. Trash cans spew their contents, stinking of rotten meat and urine. The stench isn't helped by the narrowness of the streets—buildings huddle together, their awnings stretching like sagging wings overhead. Men whistle at us. Shouts echo off the buildings' faces. Sirens, too.

Finally, Shiro stops in front of a building cast in bruised light. I pause beside him, reading the sign hung at a crooked angle above a dancing, horned yokai figure: *The Red Oni*.

Oni are ogre yokai, and Shuten-doji is their most famous leader.

The wind swirls around me, yanking at my clothes. Hugging myself, I rub one hand up and down my arm, wondering when it got so cold out here. My bracelet prickles with heat. "This seems like a stupid idea," I say.

"The bar's a little . . . over-the-top, yeah?" Shiro says, tapping his index finger on the tip of my nose. He inclines his head toward the door and pushes it halfway open for me. "But I promise, Mother isn't allied with Shuten-doji."

"You didn't think your *brother* was allied with him, either," I say, tucking my hair behind my ears, and not a little nervously.

He frowns. "I know, but this is the best chance we've got. C'mon."

The inside of the bar is unlike anything I've ever seen before—a graffiti mural swirls across the walls, showing a reclining, bare-breasted woman with a snake's tail where her legs should be. In the bruised, red-and-violet light, her tail's tip curls, beckoning me closer. Overhead, twisting tree roots grow through the ceiling, reaching for the bar's patrons like clawed hands. Tiny tree spirits cling to the gnarled branches, rattling their heads like dried gourds. Liquor bottles glow behind the bar, their colors jewel-like in the diabolical light.

Entering the room feels like walking into a solid wall of water. I choke on liquor-laden air, hardly able to breathe with the increased spiritual resonance in the room.

The moment the door closes behind us, everything halts.

Every conversation, every movement, everyone falls still, despite the bass throbbing through the place. Kuchisake-onnas stare, grinning with their wide-cut mouths and their spike-sharp teeth. A dodomeki's hundreds of eyes swivel in his skin, each one of them narrowing as it focuses on me. Almost a hundred yokai have crammed themselves into this tiny space. Their gazes make me feel like I'm standing naked before them all.

To anyone else, this would look like a normal dive bar in the heart of Shibuya—one full of ambitiously fashionable people, perhaps, but nothing supernatural. The few true humans in the bar don't seem to realize they're surrounded by monsters, or have any clue what's about to happen to them. Perhaps they're too drunk to sense anything is amiss in the first place.

A hiss slips among the patrons, skittering into my ears on thin, spidery legs:

That girl can see us.

No, she must be wearing a glamour. Ask her who made it for her, it's fetching.

That's no glamour, I swear!

Don't be silly—

It's true!

She shouldn't be here, we're supposed to be safe here.

After what happened at the shrine, these whispers make my stomach shrivel like a persimmon left to rot. I never imagined the yokai feared us humans as much as we fear them. Or perhaps they fear us more—some of modern Japan has stopped believing in yokai, but the yokai never had the privilege to stop believing in *us*. Not all yokai may be evil, but most don't consider themselves allies of Amaterasu, either. To some, I will look like the predator, the exorcist, a danger.

To others, I look like *prey*.

I wrap one hand around Shiro's elbow, whispering, "Where are we?"

"Standing on the outskirts of hell," he says under his breath. "You know how I'm always telling you to relax?"

You say it so often, it's almost a catchphrase. "Yes?"

"Do that, but stay alert," he says, and takes me by the hand as he leads me into the bar. I follow Shiro through the crowd, scowling when someone tries to trip me. Whispers of *priestess* sizzle in my wake. Snarls and growls snag my bones. The yokai draw away from me, as if brushing up against me might burn them to ash.

The bartender turns toward us, drying a mug using a hand towel. She looks human enough, but as her body moves away from us, her head remains stationary, balanced on a sinuous, snakelike neck. She's a rokurokubi, or a "pulley neck." The creatures are found in brothels and are fond of drinking lamp oil, according to the old tales.

"You know the rules, kid," the bartender says to Shiro, tilting her chin toward me. "The girl isn't welcome here."

"We have important business with Lady O-bei," Shiro says. "Is she seeing supplicants tonight?"

Supplicants? I wonder.

The bartender nods at a lantern overhead, one lit with tiny red fireflies, all of which are beating themselves stupid against the glass. Bug corpses fill the lantern's bottom third. "Her Ladyship will be unhappy to learn that you've brought a miko into our midst."

"Mother will live," Shiro says.

"An odd choice of dying words," the bartender says with a frown. She motions to a serving girl with white antlers branching off her temples. "Go, then. Koemi will announce you to the Twilight Court."

As we follow the girl toward the back of the bar, Shiro falls into step with me, taking my elbow. "Nothing will be what it seems, once we're on the other side," he whispers in my ear. "Not even to eyes like ours."

"What are you talking about?" I ask.

"Death," he says. "Yomi. Hell. Whatever you want to call it, we won't be in the land of the living anymore."

Before I can ask what he means, the antlered girl leads us up a precarious set of wooden steps. The stairwell is so narrow, it forces Shiro and me to walk single file.

When we reach the landing, I find myself caught between two glowing hallways. On my right, the corridor appears to stretch into eternity, red light splattered all over the walls. The left hallway stretches just as far, its carpet and doors stained with a violet glow. Shrieks, groans, and cries filter through the thin walls. I'm not sure whether they're made in pleasure or pain, but they turn my cheeks scarlet.

A third hallway lies straight ahead, drenched in shadow. We venture into the dimness, and the shape of a torii gate materializes. Dry leaves crunch underfoot, startling me. *Where did all these leaves come from?* They stir in the dank wind blowing through the gate.

The antlered girl pauses at the gate's threshold, bows to us, and disappears without a word.

"You're sure about this?" I ask Shiro.

"Nope," he replies, straightening his leather jacket. "But there isn't a better place to start looking for answers. Ready?"

"Not at all," I say. "Let's go before I lose my nerve."

We step through the torii gate, making sure to take the left path. Just in case.

Light seeps through the shadows, leaving me half-blind. I squint, stepping into a large, airy courtyard that glitters like something out of the old tales. An enormous Japanese maple tree grows at the center of the room, its branches growing through the ceiling's open space. Its fiery, red-orange leaves dance in a breeze I can't feel. Tiny spherical hitodama float among its branches, illuminating the tree from within and setting its colors aflame. Moss covers the ground, boxed in by wooden verandas and shoji screens that lead to other rooms. It's an impossibly large space, worlds bigger than it appeared from the outside. The air here feels different in my lungs. More substantial, almost, as if I'm breathing in ghosts. Electricity crackles along my skin, making all the little hairs stand on end.

I straighten and turn, taking in the beauty of the place. *This is Yomi?* I wonder. Who knew hell could look like heaven?

A woman sits on a veranda on the opposite side of the room, surrounded by a court of yokai. With her moon-pale skin, chrysanthemum red lips, and sculpted hairstyle, she has all the beauty of a classical geisha, yet no human could hope to attain this level of physical perfection. She laughs at something one of her courtiers says, her voice bright as a pealing bell.

Who is she? I wonder. *Is that Shiro's mother? She's not a kitsune.*

I follow Shiro off the veranda, across the wide courtyard, and under the spirit-lit tree. The small ornaments in the woman's hair chime as she turns her head to look at us. She rises and conversation ceases. All eyes turn in our direction.

"Leave us," she says, pressing her painted lips into a thin line. "All of you."

A golden kitsune rises from her seat in the court. "But Lady O-bei, we shouldn't leave you alone with—"

"I can handle a human *girl*, Minami," O-bei snaps. "Don't be a fool. Go."

The yokai withdraw from their seats. Silent. Obedient. Some of them fade straight into the shadows; others disperse across the room, slipping behind the room's elegantly painted shoji screens or disappearing down corridors. The golden kitsune, Minami, is last to leave. She pauses at the threshold of an open shoji door, glaring at Shiro before she turns away with a flick of her tails. The door slides closed on its own, hitting the wooden jamb with a loud *thwack!*

O-bei moves down from the veranda and into the mossy courtyard, her gaze fixed on Shiro. Her furisode may be the most magnificent kimono I have ever seen, its colors a cascading purple ombré that starts as lavender at the shoulder and falls into bruised eggplant by her feet. Embroidered butterflies shimmer on the fabric, decorating the entirety of the kimono's long train.

Shiro bows as O-bei approaches us, and, not wanting to appear rude, I do the same. As she moves, the butterflies flutter their silver-thread wings, scattering across the silk. She presses her fingers together in an upside-down triangle in front of her obi, and her hitodama descend to float around her head and shoulders. Their light makes her look otherworldly. Dangerous, too.

It takes me several seconds to realize my mouth's hanging open. I close it, before noticing the small brown stain on the front of my sweater. Standing next to this creature, I must look like a fool.

"So," O-bei finally says, puncturing the silence. "You've come a very long way to tattle on your elder brother, Shiro."

"To tattle on him?" Shiro says, his brow furrowing. "No, Mother, I came to you because Ronin broke the oath he swore to Amaterasu. His actions got many people killed."

"And since when has that been a problem in this house?" O-bei asks, arching a brow. "Death is the family vocation, my child."

"It's *your* vocation," Shiro snaps. "Not mine."

O-bei's pout turns into a close-lipped smile. "And now it is also your brother's."

A beat of pure silence rolls out around us.

Shiro growls from the bottoms of his lungs, low and guttural. When he curls his upper lip, his incisors look sharper than before. "Ronin would never forsake his heritage to become something like *you*. We came here to ask for your help, not to hear your lies."

"Shiro, you wound me," O-bei says, reaching up to rest a hand on Shiro's cheek. She stands several inches shorter than him, so she reaches high to touch his face. Her kimono's sleeve slides back, revealing pale skin with blackened veins beneath. "There is no greater calling in all of Yomi than to usher mortal souls into death."

O-bei's words strike my mind like a gong. I'd thought she might be some sort of yokai, perhaps a kitsune who preferred a fully human form, or even a futukuchi-onna. But O-bei Katayama is no mere yokai.

"You're a shinigami," I say, and my voice shakes with the words. "You're a death god."

"*Goddess*, yes," O-bei says, barely taking notice of me or my shock. Instead, she looks up into Shiro's eyes. "Ronin has chosen to join me in my work. Who am I to deny him the right to be my successor and heir?"

Shiro trembles with barely restrained rage. "He swore an oath to the Goddess. . . . He was one of her priests. . . ."

"As was I, many centuries ago. Our kind are sometimes made in that fashion," O-bei says, stroking Shiro's cheek with her thumb. He growls and steps away from her touch, flattening his ears against his scalp. "Everything I do, my darling boy, I do for my children, my family, and my people. The Twilight Court cannot sustain itself without human hosts. And if Shuten-doji succeeds in his old mission, well, my people will starve."

"Ronin was *with* Shuten-doji's monsters tonight," Shiro snaps.

"I know," O-bei says, pointing a finger in Shiro's face. "It has taken me *decades* to earn the trust of Shuten-doji's general, Tamamo-no-Mae. Don't you dare interfere with my plans to destroy them, no matter how opposed you may be to my methods."

Anger swells in my breast. Over the last twelve hours, this world has tried to convince me that I am powerless, unwanted, unloved. And now I'm told that my grandfather's murder was just a political power play? Among *monsters*, no less?

O-bei continues, "It will be our power, not our principles, that will save us in the coming war, Shiro. Remember that."

"You're wrong," I say.

O-bei turns her head in a slow, deliberate way, considering me out of the corner of her eye. Her very gaze chills the air around me.

"Perhaps we haven't been properly introduced," O-bei says. "I am O-bei Katayama, Lady of the Twelve Dread Wastes, the August Granter of Wishes, and the Keeper of the Mortal Souls of Kyō. And you should know, girl, that I am *never* wrong."

It's strange how, in certain moments of sheer stupidity, fear can give way to fury.

"What is power without honor?" I say, balling my fists so tight, my fingernails bite into my flesh. "You stole my loved ones from me. You desecrated my home, and made the sacred profane for your wars—"

"Kira," Shiro says, a note of warning in his voice.

"Which means you now owe me a debt of honor, *Lady* Katayama," I say, ignoring Shiro. "You took something from me in exchange for nothing, and if you think I will easily forgive that debt, you're wrong."

The word *wrong* echoes through the empty courtyard.

Wrong.

Wrong.

Wrong.

One by one, the hitodama lights hovering over O-bei's head wink out. Little by little, the glow seeps from the room, till the shadows draw close and my bracelet burns my wrist.

"Wrong?" O-bei turns to me, slowly. Black veins branch across her throat, over her jawbone, and up her cheeks, as if her blood had been pumped full of sumi-e ink. Her brilliant, kaleidoscopic eyes darken into ebony mirrors, and the kernels of her teeth now have an onyx gleam.

Beside me, Shiro sucks in a sharp breath. He holds up his palms, placating, apologizing. "Mother, please, Kira didn't mean it, her grief is making her say things she doesn't understand—"

"You think I am *wrong*, Kira Fujikawa," O-bei says, cocking her head, examining me. She pulls the ornaments from her hair, dropping them to the ground. They tinkle like bells as they strike the soft earth. When she shakes her hair loose, a thousand dark-winged butterflies spill from between the strands. The tiny creatures flutter around her in a great cloud. They stir up an icy breeze that bites into my cheeks.

"You think I owe you a debt of *honor*." O-bei thrusts out her right hand parallel to the ground. A pale katana materializes in her palm, its blade reminiscent of the one Ronin carried at the shrine. The metal glows with the dull, ashen light of a cloudy day.

Shiro and I both step back. He eases in front of me, shielding me with his body.

"Then allow me to take one more thing from you," O-bei says, her voice no longer a musical, courtly sound, but the woven litany of a thousand wails. "Your *life*."

Her butterflies rush at me, enveloping me in a dark, velvet-winged wind. With an unholy shriek, O-bei leaps up into the air, the room's shadows unfurling around her like a set of great black wings. She draws her katana up in both hands, pointing its glowing tip at my chest.

O-bei dives toward me.

Someone screams.

Instinct kicks in. I throw my hands up in vain, crossing my wrists in front of my head. I expect the blade's chill to slice between my ribs, to stop the beating heart in my chest. To steal the soul off my lips.

The sword's tip collides with my raised wrists. Pain sends white-hot sparks crashing down my arms.

And light—radiant, golden light—explodes around me.

EIGHT
The Red Oni

Yomi

The light blinds me from all directions, as if I've fallen inside the sun. The brilliance burns away my pain, my exhaustion, and my fear.

Is this death? I wonder. Perhaps death isn't nearly as horrible as its harbingers; perhaps it is only this sweet release, this newfound buoyancy, this wholeness now coursing through my being. I close my eyes and wish to melt into this glow.

But the light fades, leaving me encased in a glittering golden shield. I glance up, finding O-bei's sword lodged in the shell, inches away from my head. The charms on my bracelet glow bright as noonday sunlight. A trickle of blood slips down my wrist. Several of O-bei's butterflies now rest on my shoulders, opening and closing their wings, basking in the soft light emanating from my clothing.

I . . . I'm not dead.

At least I don't think I'm dead.

I step back, lowering my shaking hands as the light sinks into my skin. It suffuses my soul with its warmth, drawing with it memories far older and more ancient than I have the right to remember. The tips of my fingers burn with light. I blink twice to clear the illusion from my eyes, and realize we're not alone.

The Twilight Court has reassembled itself on the verandas—some of its members now prostrate themselves, kneeling with their foreheads pressed into the floor. Others regard me with wonder or terror, their mouths agape. On my left, Shiro lies dazed on the ground, squinting at me and shading his eyes with one hand.

How long was I standing in that light?

Several yards away, the kitsune Minami helps O-bei back to her feet. O-bei staggers, wiping a trickle of eggplant-colored blood off the corner of her mouth with her sleeve. She leans on her kitsune for support, her clothing in disarray, her eyeliner creating long, melted trails down her cheeks. The darkness in O-bei's veins fades as she catches her breath, leaving only smooth, pale skin behind.

When she straightens, she lifts her wretched gaze to mine.

"No wonder my sons refuse to let you die, Fujikawa," O-bei says. "You are descended from Abe no Seimei, the greatest exorcist and onmyōdō practitioner of the Heian period. Who knew that so many generations later, his kitsune mother, Kuzunoha, would still be protecting his line?"

Shiro rises from the ground, tripping over his own feet as he stares at me. As my shield dissipates, O-bei's sword falls to the ground. The blade turns to mist before striking the mossy floor.

"Kuzunoha will not allow me to kill a member of Seimei's line," O-bei says flatly. "A pity. But if you have the protection of a spirit like Kuzunoha, it means you may be useful in the coming war."

"I want nothing to do with your wars," I say, spitting the last word out of my mouth. I can't trust her, not when she was willing to attack a guest in her own home. Not now, not ever. The creatures of Yomi aren't subject to human mores, and that's why I have no faith in them.

"You don't have a choice in the matter," O-bei says. "Your shrine harbors the last shard of the legendary Kusanagi no Tsurugi. In one month, Shuten-doji will rise with the blood moon. Either we ally to fight him, or he will destroy us all."

"Then why work with his lieutenants?" Shiro asks through gritted teeth. "Why send Ronin into Fujikawa Shrine, backed by Shuten-doji's thugs?"

"I am not obligated to discuss my strategies with you," O-bei says.

"It'd at least be nice to know where your loyalties lie, *Mother*," Shiro snaps. "Especially since you kept me in the dark about your plans for Ronin, defiled the shrine I swore to protect, and just tried to kill my friend *in front of me*."

Are we friends? I glance sideways at Shiro. It's been so long since

I've had a proper friend; I haven't really made any new ones since I transferred to Kōgakkan. But Shiro may be the last person I can trust in this world, and if that doesn't count as friendship, I'm not sure what does.

"Watch your tongue, youngling," Minami growls, drawing closer to O-bei. Protective, almost.

"I don't answer to you," Shiro says, a growl rumbling in his chest.

Minami bares her teeth at him. "I see shrine life hasn't taught you to respect your elders."

"And I see you haven't lost your taste for licking the soles of my mother's shoes," Shiro retorts.

"Why should I listen to a fox kit with no tails—"

"Enough! Both of you," O-bei snaps. The kitsune glare at each other across the courtyard, their bodies taking a predatory lean, muscles taut. But despite the palpable tension between them, neither attacks. *And I thought my family was difficult to get along with.*

"We do not have time for your bickering," O-bei continues. "I have endeavored to kill the beast known as Shuten-doji for hundreds of years, and I will *not* have the three of you thwarting the last fifty years of hard work with your foolishness! Am I understood?"

"Yes, O-bei-sama," Minami says with a bob of her head.

"Yes, Mother," Shiro echoes, but with more bite.

O-bei glares at him. "The Twilight Court's efforts to stop Shuten-doji's resurrection have failed. Our last recourse is to destroy him in both the mortal realm and in Yomi, which will be no easy task."

She turns to me. "In short, you and I are in the unfortunate circumstance of needing each other, Fujikawa."

"If you need my help, it will come at a high cost," I say.

"And what might that be?" O-bei asks.

"You rebuild the Fujikawa Shrine and restore the honor of my family's legacy," I say. "I know you cannot bring my grandfather back, so I at least expect you to honor the site he gave his life to protect."

O-bei taps her chin with her finger, considering my proposal. "I could send my people to protect the Fujikawa Shrine, under the auspices that we are looking for the shard for Shuten-doji. Minami, you will oversee the shrine reparations. Assemble twenty of your best craftspeople and leave for the Fujikawa Shrine at dawn."

"Very well, O-bei-sama," Minami says, though she glares at me.

O-bei continues, "We will make the Fujikawa Shrine the site of our last stand—"

Shiro groans. "How fantastic. Wonderful plan, Mother."

"Would you prefer Shuten-doji's own yokai to patrol the shrine until he rises with the blood moon?" O-bei says, lifting an eyebrow. Both Shiro and I shake our heads. "I thought not. I will repair your shrine to make amends, Kira Fujikawa, but I will not commit the Twilight Court to your war without a good-faith effort on your part."

"Meaning?" I ask.

"I will need your assistance with . . . a delicate diplomatic matter," O-bei says.

"Here we go," Shiro says, mopping his face with his palm.

If O-bei is annoyed by Shiro's impudence, she makes no sign. "There are two ways to kill a creature like Shuten-doji: One, through the use of a holy blade like the Kusanagi no Tsurugi. Or two, through the power of a cabal of shinigami. Seven of them, to be exact."

A cabal? I shoot a sidelong glance at Shiro. He squeezes his eyes shut tight and wrinkles his nose, as if he's just bitten into a lemon.

"Find seven shinigami for me," O-bei says. "And I will help you destroy your demon."

Shiro sneers. "Do you and my *dear* elder brother count as part of the seven?"

"Perhaps," O-bei replies. "Depending on the success of your recruitment efforts, of course. So what say you, Fujikawa? Do we have a deal?"

I wish I could discuss this transaction with Shiro, because I sense deceit behind O-bei's pretty words. She's basically given me a contract with the fine print written in a foreign language. I glance sideways at Shiro. He flicks one of his ears back, but doesn't meet my gaze. Worse, exhaustion nips at me. My back muscles ache from standing ramrod straight in O-bei's presence. A tension headache has built itself up behind my eyes. My body has endured too much over the last few hours. Here in Yomi, I'm not sure time even *exists*. On one hand, it feels like Shiro and I have been here for a matter of minutes; on the other, an eternity.

Even in this state, I'm not sure I have much choice in this situation. Shuten-doji is rising, and while I'm not sure how Shiro and I will recruit shinigami to our cause, doing *something* is better than doing nothing. We can't fight a demon god on our own. At least not on the timetables fate has given us. A month's time isn't enough.

I don't have to trust O-bei to *use* O-bei. We don't need to be friends, just temporary allies, each using the other for her own ends.

"All right," I say. "If you help me protect the Fujikawa Shrine, Lady Katayama, I will help you find your shinigami."

O-bei smiles. I can't help but think her lips curve like a harvest sickle, its blade ready to reap souls instead of rice. "A wise decision. Should you find me my shinigami, Kira Fujikawa, I promise you will have the full might of the Twilight Court to assist you in this war."

With that, O-bei snaps her fingers. The entire court disappears, leaving Shiro and me alone in the dusty bones of the Red Oni's attic. Silence and darkness, sudden, unexpected, and horrible, settle into the piles of dead leaves around my feet. Music throbs through the floorboards. A few hitodama bob around the building's old rafters, providing meager light. A chill douses the air, sneaking up my sleeves and leaving me shivering.

I turn to Shiro, who runs his hand down his face in exasperation.

"How difficult will it be to convince other shinigami to help us?" I ask him.

"Would you prefer the pessimistic or realistic answer?" he asks.

"Let's start with realistic."

"Nearly impossible," Shiro says. "You see, Mother . . . *sort of* offended a powerful shinigami clan a few years ago."

"Wait, there are shinigami *clans*?" I ask, blinking.

"Yeah, and they sort of have this treaty with Shuten-doji?" Shiro says, wincing. "As in, the shinigami clans won't interfere with his kingdom, so long as they're not subject to his rule."

My mouth drops into a little *o* shape. "How many of the shinigami belong to a clan?"

"Almost all of them."

I slide my hands into my hair and count backward for a few seconds, breathing through my frustration. "Somehow, I think I've managed to make this worse."

"It's not your fault, Kira. C'mon," Shiro says, turning away from me and walking toward the torii gate. "Ronin and I have a room here, at least. We should get some sleep."

Shiro leads me to a small, tidy room away from the Red Oni's tumult and noise. After the day I've had, the room's tatami mat flooring and sweet, grassy smell comforts me and reminds me of home. Yellow light falls from a single square-shaped chandelier hanging from the ceiling. A tokonoma alcove sits on the right side of the room, displaying an ornamental scroll and deadwood bonsai. The tree's white bark almost glows in the low light.

Straight ahead, two shoji doors yawn open, revealing a small sitting nook with a table and chairs, perfect for tea. Behind them, darkness turns two sliding glass doors to mirrors. I catch sight of my reflection and sigh. I look every ounce as exhausted as I feel.

"Will O-bei mind if I stay here tonight?" I ask.

"Nah. She allows far worse than you to stay in the ryokan," Shiro says, shooting me a cheeky grin. I make a face at him, narrowing my eyes and scrunching up my nose.

Shiro laughs. "We've got extra nemaki in the drawers beside the alcove." He pulls a futon bundle out of the closet. "I thought about going to the baths, but honestly? I just want to sleep. Today's been . . ."

"Heartbreaking?" I interject. "Earth-shattering? Apocalyptic? The absolute worst?"

With a long sigh, he rubs the back of his neck with his palm. "Yeah, all of the above."

Crossing the room, I slide one of the larger drawers open to find the nemaki—light lounging and sleeping kimono often worn in ryokan inns and bathhouses. The fabrics are decorated with intricate blue-and-white designs and are tied with a woven belt.

Shiro steps outside while I change. We switch when I finish. I stand in the hallway, soaking in my surroundings, which are reminiscent of a more ancient time in this country's history. The shoji doors have been crafted with actual washi paper. The lacquered wood floors gleam underfoot, suffused with the hallway's warm light. It's an entirely different world from the bar downstairs, or the brothel on the other side of the building—quiet. Warm. Everything about this place tells me I should feel secure here, but I doubt I'll ever feel safe anywhere, ever again.

I lean against the wall with a sigh. My body feels heavy, as if there are weights tied to my fingers and nose and eyelids; but my soul feels hollow, as if all the important bits of me have been scraped out and burned. I close my eyes, but all I see are the frantic final moments of Grandfather's life.

"Mrow?"

Startled, I glance down, pressing one hand to my mouth. A massive cat sits at my feet. He—at least I'm guessing it's a *he*—has a mousy brindle coat, which is mostly red with long, thin cracks of black. A large patch of fur is missing from the top of his head. One large pink scar cuts across his left eye, which can't be bothered to be the same color as the right one. His left eye is yellow as a harvest moon, his right the bright blue of a crisp winter sky.

But the strangest thing of all: the cat has *two* tails, which means he's not a *cat* at all, but a nekomata. A spark of magical teal fire burns at the tip of each tail. He might be the ugliest cat I've ever seen.

The nekomata growls at me, as if he heard me call him *ugly* in my head.

"Oh, I apologize," I say to the yokai. "It took me a moment to realize you were more than an ordinary cat!"

Shiro slides the door open, poking his head into the hall. "What'd you say, Kira?"

Before I can answer, his gaze zeroes in on the nekomata. His eyes widen. Shiro grabs me by the wrist, tugging me into his room so fast, I trip and land on one of the neatly made futons with a muffled thud.

He slams the door closed behind us.

"What's wrong with you?" I snap at him, pushing myself up to my knees. "That nekomata looked friendly enough—"

A deep growl interrupts us, one that rolls through the room and makes the washi paper panels in the door vibrate. Shiro reaches over to the light switch and snaps it off. The light from the hallway filters through the door, and the silhouette on the other side . . .

What is that?

It's not the shadow of a house cat, but of a feline twice the size of a *tiger*. The nekomata's fur bristles along its neck. Its dual tails switch back and forth. It rises on its hind legs, putting one massive paw on the fragile door.

"Oni-chan," Shiro says through the door. "You can't eat this one, she's a guest of Mother's."

Another growl rumbles through the air.

"Listen," Shiro says to the cat yokai, "Mother needs this girl to find some shinigami, okay? If you kill this girl now, there will be nobody to find shinigami for Mother, and she'll be angry with you. And you know what Mother's like when she's upset."

Oni-chan drops back to all fours, making a strange half-growling, half-whimpering noise.

"No, you can't eat her *after* she's done looking for shinigami,"

Shiro says, shooting me a look that says, *You see what you've done?*

"How is this my fault?" I whisper.

"You're a Shinto priestess," Shiro says. "You should know better than to talk to an unfamiliar nekomata!"

"Pretty sure I've talked to *worse* today."

"Fair point." Shiro turns back to the screen. "Oni-chan, if you promise to leave the girl alone, how about I take you to that ramen place you like tomorrow, eh? The one with the open hibachi?"

Oni-chan shrinks a bit and cocks his head. "Mrowl?"

"Okay, okay, we can go to the shrine with the good yakitori, too," Shiro says, rolling his eyes. "But *no* people-eating, are we clear?"

The cat chuffs, blowing out a breath against the screen. I guess that means yes, because the cat shrinks back to house cat size. Shiro turns the light on with a sigh.

"Oni-chan has one last stipulation," Shiro says as he opens the door.

"What's that?" I ask, lifting a brow.

Shiro frowns. "He says he gets to sleep on your futon tonight."

My gaze falls on the demon cat sitting in the hallway.

I swear he's grinning.

NINE

The Red Oni

Tokyo, Japan

The next day, I awaken in unfamiliar surroundings with noonday sunlight streaming across my face. I sit up with a start, and the creaks in my bones and in my heart and in my soul remind me where I am:

I'm in Tokyo.

Sleeping in an inn made for yokai.

Last night, my family's shrine was desecrated by demons.

My grandfather is dead, and I must ally with the shadows to avenge his murder.

Today, I wake to a world that is forever changed. Even the shape of the sunlight looks wrong, dimmer somehow, as if my filters have shifted and left me looking through a dirty lens. Grief weighs so heavily on my chest, it's almost hard to breathe.

Wait. That's not just grief—*it's a cat.*

I sit up. Oni-chan slides down into my lap. The cat growls at me, paws flailing in the air as he tries to right himself. He rolls over onto his pudgy belly, claws extended, and struggles through the deep pockets of bedding.

"I thought cats were supposed to be graceful?" I ask with a grin, pushing the comforter away to help him fight his way through the blankets. In the daylight, Oni-chan may be even *uglier* than he appeared last night. But I prefer his charms when they are house cat size.

Shiro is gone, his futon stowed in the closet. I kick off my comforter and rise, surprised to see how high the sun hangs in the sky. A small breakfast tray waits on the table by the window. I peek under the lids of the bowls to find natto, warm white rice with seaweed, miso soup, and a small piece of fish. As the smells waft into the room, Oni-chan comes to sit at my feet. He meows, licking his lips and bedraggled whiskers. I hand him a piece of fish, which he gulps down with little ceremony and no thanks.

A note lies beside my breakfast tray, left atop a slim black cell phone. It's from Shiro, and it reads:

Good morning, Kira! I hope you like natto—this place only serves traditional breakfasts, so I grabbed as many things as I could carry. I've gone to run an errand for Mother, and I should be back in the afternoon. We'll start looking for shinigami then.

Also, I've left a spare cell phone for you to use, since yours broke. You might want to call your mom, since she won't stop calling me now.

There are women's showers in the public baths. If you want to get dressed, just use the wardrobe you used last night. Think of the thing you'd like to wear, and it should appear in the cabinets when you open them. Nice, right? Don't ask me how it works—you won't like the answer.

I fold the note over my index finger, glancing at the wardrobe. It looks entirely ordinary—just a black-lacquered chest with golden doors, with a crane in flight painted on its left-hand side.

Setting Shiro's note down, I go to the wardrobe and imagine black skinny jeans. No, not just jeans . . . but jeans from the best brands in Japan, like Studio D'Artisan or Samurai. Clothing Mother would *never* allow me to buy. My parents are well off enough, but they're frugal and fashion isn't a top priority for them.

I take hold of the door pull, draw a breath, and pull the cabinet open.

A pair of black jeans sits on the shelf inside.

With a small shriek, I slam the door closed and hop a few steps backward, nearly tripping over my futon. On the other side of the room, Oni-chan lifts his head to snort at me, then goes back to basking in the sun. He thumps his tails against the ground in annoyance.

"That's not how wardrobes work in the real world," I say to

him. He glances up at me, blinking slowly as if to say, *Stupid girl—my world is obviously as real as yours.*

I suppose the cat has a point. If his world *weren't* real, I'd be spending today with Grandfather at the shrine, not preparing to search all of Tokyo for shinigami on behalf of Lady O-bei Katayama, Granter of August Wishes and Royal Pain in the Rear End.

After I bathe, I spend fifteen minutes settling on something to wear: black tights, mini-length jean shorts, a fitted button-down shirt, and an overlarge army jacket—an outfit like those I've seen fashionable girls wearing on the streets of Tokyo. I text Mother, letting her know I stayed with Shiro's family overnight and will be heading to see Goro this afternoon.

Kira! she replies within seconds. *Call. Me. Now.*

I'm sorry, Mother, I reply. *But I'm on a train, and it would be rude.*

Then call me the moment you disembark. The police need to speak with you immediately—

A knock rolls across the door. "May I come in?" Shiro asks.

"Yes," I say, pulling my jacket over my shoulders. The fabric feels fresh and crisp against my skin. I slide my phone into my pocket, putting Mother out of my mind for now.

Shiro slides the door open and steps inside in stocking feet. He looks sharp: a long-sleeved, slim-fit tee hugs his muscular chest, and he's paired it with jeans and mussed hair. Looking me up and down, he gives me a grin. "You figured out how to use the wardrobe."

"Can I take it back to Kyoto with me?" I ask, checking my hair in the mirrorlike depths of the framed artwork on the wall.

"I can't imagine we'd get it on the shinkansen." Shiro's smile brightens, chasing all the shadows out of my soul. I cross the room to be a little closer to him, and to all that light and warmth.

I join him by the door, leaning one shoulder against the plaster wall. "Where'd you go this morning?"

His smile drops off his lips. "Mother wanted me to pick Ronin up from the train station."

"And you didn't kill him?" I ask in deadpan. "That's a shame."

"Don't think I didn't want to," he says through clenched teeth. He balls his fists, the tendons popping out in his neck. "I couldn't even look at that bastard, not after everything he's done. You lost a grandfather last night, and I lost a brother. He's forgotten the face of our birth mother. His tails are gone. *He* is gone."

I open my mouth to respond, but can't find the right words to say. Maybe there aren't any, really, that can fix this kind of grief. Reaching up, I cup one of his cheeks in my palm.

"I'm sorry," I say. Those are the only words I can think of, but at least they're true.

"Me too." Some of the anger drains out of him, softening the angles of his face. "Why choose death over life?"

"I don't think there's an easy answer to that question, no matter who's asking it," I say, stroking his cheekbone with my thumb. Shiro shifts closer, bringing our faces just inches away from each other. My breath catches, and I go still. My heartbeat thumps in the tips of my fingers, and I wonder if he can feel it on his cheek.

But before he can kiss me, something shatters near the breakfast table. I startle. Oni-chan hops off the table, headed for the puddle of natto on the floor. The cat slurps soybeans off the shell of a broken bowl.

"You're a rude cat," Shiro says with a little laugh. Oni-chan growls at him before polishing off my breakfast.

"I wasn't that hungry," I say, lifting one shoulder in a shrug. While Shiro and I couldn't have been in Yomi for more than twenty minutes, we lost almost six hours in the real world. My body still hasn't adjusted for that fact. "We should get going, anyway. The day's already half-gone."

"Where do you want to start?" Shiro asks.

"The Kanda Shrine," I say, turning toward the door. "Maybe Goro will know how to get us out of this mess."

TEN

Yoyogi Park

Tokyo, Japan

Goro no longer works for the Kanda Shrine.

The Kanda priests tell me it's been months since Goro was reassigned to the Meiji Shrine in the heart of Tokyo. It's a more prestigious assignment, yes, but the fact leaves me feeling hollow inside. A small seed of doubt sinks into the darkest soils of my mind: Why did Grandfather keep such an important detail from me? What harm would it have caused for me to know Goro was now at the Meiji? And what else did Grandfather neglect to say? Did he think we had more time, even with a blood moon looming?

It hurts to know I'll never have answers for any of these questions.

"The Meiji's right in the middle of Yoyogi Park," Shiro says as we head toward the train station, Oni-chan trotting at our feet. "We can look for shinigami while we're there. Two birds, one stone."

"It's already getting late," I say, shielding my eyes as I look up at the sky. "We might have another three hours of sunlight, and another day will be gone. We've barely started, and we're already running out of time."

"We still have a few good hours to look," Shiro replies. So we take a train. Two. People shoot looks at the ugly "cat" peering out of the crate beside me, but say nothing. I'm used to people staring at me, and Oni-chan seems unconcerned with the opinions of mortals.

After finding Oni-chan his yakitori skewers, Shiro and I begin our search in Yoyogi Park—a sprawling, 130-acre park at the heart of the Shibuya district. Here, the trees stand so tall they block out most of Tokyo's skyscrapers. Wide walking paths snake through the trees, skirt ponds, and crisscross the lawns. On weekends, subculture groups gather in the park: not just cosplayers, but rockabilly enthusiasts, martial arts clubs, jugglers, and more.

As we walk in, a girl group dances to a Twice K-pop song. College-aged men toss a baseball around on the lawns, while a mother chases her laughing toddler down the path. Everything looks so *ordinary*, so . . . normal.

Well, everything except for the boy with the fox ears and the two-tailed demon cat walking on his hind legs and eating yakitori skewers. I'm not sure what other people see when they look at Oni-chan, but I know they don't see the foul-tempered, manner-less creature *I* see. The one who, for some reason, has taken an instant liking to *me*.

We pass a group of schoolchildren playing *Kagome, Kagome*, and I shudder. I'll never be able to hear that tune again without thinking of Grandfather's blood on my skin, or remembering the way his last breath wheezed from his chest. I hear so much dark-ness in the song now. Darkness and death.

"You sure we're going to find shinigami here?" I ask Shiro, scanning the crowds. "Shouldn't we be looking in a place that's a little more . . . maybe like the Red Oni?"

"Meaning?" Shiro asks.

"Someplace more . . . I don't know, magical?" I say, frowning at the word because it's not exactly what I mean. The Red Oni is more than *magical*, it's . . . "Otherworldly."

"Shinigami are drawn to human crowds," Shiro says. "Busy street corners, hospitals, bars—the more accident-prone a place, the better."

We wander down a manicured path, beneath tree canopies edged in autumn reds and oranges. "But how do they know when it's someone's time to die?" I ask.

Shiro shrugs. "Shinigami see both the mortal realms and Yomi at once. When it's time for a mortal to die, they . . . *flicker*. Or something. Mother never talks about what she does in detail. I guess she thinks it's tacky."

"I'm surprised she cares," I say, frowning as a scruffy, unleashed dog wanders a little too close to Oni-chan . . . or maybe a little too close to his yakitori. The yokai cat hisses and swats at the dog's nose, then throws an empty skewer at the canine as it scurries away, whimpering.

"While she can be ambitious, vain, and *definitely* murderous"—Shiro smiles at a child as she scampers past us—"Mother does care for the welfare of her people and the Twilight Court. And I think—in her own twisted way, at least—for me."

I cock my head at him. "I thought you hated her?"

"No," he says with a firm shake of his head.

"Even after everything she's done?"

"She took Ronin and me in when our birth mother died. Besides, I'm not sure you're in much of a position to judge," he fires back, nudging me playfully with an elbow. "Your relationship with your mom sounds messy, too."

I sigh. "You know, Grandfather once told me that my mother used to love the shrine, and now—"

"Look," Shiro says, pointing at a young businessman lingering on one of the park's arched bridges. He wears a suit of solid black, but the fabric looks like it's edged in twilight. A cloud of gray butterflies whirls around him, the tips of their wings trailing bright moonlight. With his slicked-back hair, high cheekbones, and skin as smooth as glass, he's just as beautiful as O-bei.

"Do you see the butterflies around him?" Shiro asks under his breath. "Those are the souls of the dead."

Before the attack on the Fujikawa Shrine, I doubt I would have paid any attention to this man. Today, I can see him for what he is: *shinigami*. Death incarnate.

He's exactly what we're looking for.

The shinigami watches a small boy playing by the riverbank. The park's river moves swiftly past its shores, deep enough to drown someone so small. The intensity of the shinigami's gaze, the sheer *focus* of it, makes my fear roil. I've already seen the terrifying truth behind the human facade, but I refuse to be cowed.

"Let's talk to him," I say, walking toward the bridge without a plan.

"Wait, Kira!" Shiro says, grabbing for my wrist. He misses. I step onto the bridge, and its wooden planks shiver beneath my feet. The shinigami lifts his hands. The boy wobbles, stumbling closer to the water's edge. He's so small, no more than three or four years old.

"Excuse me?" I ask the shinigami. "Sir?"

The shinigami's gaze snaps to me.

He drops his hands.

I release a breath I didn't realize I was holding.

The boy's mother calls his name, and he toddles away from the river's flank. My relief slips out of me on a sigh. The shinigami's lip curls.

"How are you able to see me, *girl*?" He spits the word *girl* as if it's made of poison.

I bow deeply. "My name is Kira Fujikawa. This is the kitsune guardian of the Fujikawa Shrine, Shiro Okamoto," I say, gesturing at Shiro, who has managed to catch up to me. "We're on an errand from Lady Katayama—"

"Ha, as if I'd help *Lady* Katayama in her foolish quest to become queen of Yomi," he says, turning away. His butterflies swirl around him in a tornado of silver. "Get out of my sight."

O-bei wants to be queen of Yomi? I pause for a second, exchanging a glance with Shiro. This wasn't information O-bei had offered to me herself; and it makes me wonder how much of a pawn I've become in this game of yokai.

Either way, someone still needs to stop Shuten-doji. I can't do it alone.

"Please, sir," I say, starting after him. "My family's shrine was attacked two nights ago. If we can't find help from a few shinigami, we will not be able to defeat Shuten-doji, and the world will—"

He whirls on me, murder in his slate-gray eyes. "Do you think I would stoop to help a *human*?" He spits on the ground. "Betray my own people to serve a mortal's interests? *Leave*, before I decide you'd look better as a butterfly."

Both Shiro and I bow again. When I rise, I watch him walk away, his patent-leather shoes striking the bridge's planks like gunshots. Oni-chan jumps up onto the bridge bannister, twitching his tails and shooting a judgmental glare at the shinigami's back.

"Did you know your mother wants to be queen of Yomi?" I ask Shiro without looking at him.

Shiro sighs.

"I'll take that as a yes," I say, watching the little boy skip across the grass with his mother. Oni-chan begins washing his face, apparently unconcerned with our failure. "Will O-bei be a better queen than Shuten-doji is king?"

"I suppose she might be." Shiro's ears slant at forty-five-degree angles.

I'm not comfortable with the question mark in his tone, but addressing it now will only distract us from our goal—recruiting shinigami. I don't know enough about the politics of Yomi to know whether helping O-bei is a mistake; for now, I file the information away to ask Shiro about later.

"Fine," I say to him, knowing our situation is anything but *fine*.

We make our way to the Meiji Shrine slowly, searching the entirety of Yoyogi Park. By the time the sun touches the horizon, we've been rejected by three more shinigami: an old woman carrying butterflies on her parasol, a fashionable girl who wears her souls strung in a necklace, their wings struggling for purchase against her silken blouse; and a round-bellied, red-faced man whose brown moths tremble as he shouts at us. For every thousand human souls I see, at least one shinigami hovers on the edge of our spaces, waiting for the opportune moment to strike. But none of the shinigami want anything to do with humans, outside killing them. And nobody wants to work with O-bei Katayama.

Nobody.

The shadows stick to our shoes as we stroll into the park's dense forests, headed for the shrine. Darkness falls over the forest floor. The treetops make black blots against the sky. Every few yards, I spot another massive spiderweb hanging between the trees, each spun by a jorō spider the size of my thumb. The last of the light limns the delicate fibers of their webs, making them glitter like gold. I'm not certain whether the phenomenon is natural or *super*natural.

"We need to hurry," Shiro says, looking at the spiderwebs. The tone of his voice tells me he's trying to sound casual and failing. "Something's not quite right about this place—"

A song curls under the park's ambient noise, one I hear with my soul, not with my ears.

"Kagome, Kagome . . ."

The small hairs at the back of my neck rile. Shiro lifts his head and scents the air, cursing under his breath. I scan the area, looking to see if any yokai lurk in the shadows of the park's massive trees. I see nothing. No one. Even the pedestrians on the path have disappeared. My bracelet remains cold against my wrist, the one consolation.

"Shuten-doji's spies must have followed us," I whisper.

Shiro puts a hand on my lower back. "Word gets around fast in Tokyo."

"Where's Oni-chan?" I whisper, looking around. The little demon cat appears to have faded into the shadows, for he's no longer at my feet. "Oni-chan?" I whisper. "Oni-chan!"

Shiro growls. "Of course he wanders off the *minute* we need him—"

The song lifts again, closer now. *"Circle you, circle you . . ."* The tune crushes salt into the wounds in my heart, and I shudder at the fiery sensation that sears through my chest.

"Do you know where the Meiji Shrine is from here?" I whisper to Shiro.

"No, but I think I can sense where it lies," he says, pushing his bangs out of his face. "C'mon!"

We run. The asphalt path stretches and ducks through the shadowy forest, with no end in sight. We run till my heart burns and my lungs feel like they're going to pop like balloons. We run till the shadows fill in the spaces between the trees. Till my legs feel like they can't take another step. Till the soles of my feet ache.

A torii gate comes into view, standing like a sentinel against the growing darkness. It towers over the path, and the golden medallions on its lintel glow like cats' eyes.

Shadows congregate beneath the gate, swirling around a young woman in a crimson furisode. Her footsteps make no sound, and while everything about her appears human, there's a certain sort of *wrongness* about her that sets my teeth on edge. Maybe it's the infant wail carried on the wind, or maybe it's the strange way the lower half of her kimono moves, almost as if something beats the fabric's insides with tiny fists. Her face seems to be almost . . . *fluted.*

No, not fluted. The creases running up and down her flat,

ovular face aren't slits at all, but *eyes*. Eight of them, all shaped like pea pods and glowing like tiny stoplights in the dark.

She's a jorōgumo. And she's blocking the only path to the Meiji Shrine.

Shiro and I halt.

"What do you want?" I shout at her.

The woman smiles as she advances, revealing several rows of jagged teeth. "The Master has heard there are flies who wish to challenge his authority," she says. Her voice is more hiss than hum. "We have come to end your insurrection before it can begin."

Other yokai women emerge from the shadows around us, their alabaster faces glimmering with hellish light. I turn, watching them multiply: two becomes four, then four becomes six. They wear furisode in a rainbow of pain, reds and blues, purples and blacks. One wears silk in the off-white color of broken bones; another, the seeping yellow of pus. I'm drawn to and repulsed by them in equal measures.

"You serve Shuten-doji?" Shiro asks.

"*Yessss.*" The affirmation comes in stereo, echoing from the many mouths around us. The sound worms under my skin and chews its way into the seat of my spine.

"Then *you* are the ones guilty of insurrection," Shiro says. "And your *master* should fear the retribution of Amaterasu-omikami for his insolence."

The jorōgumo snicker, their voices winding around Shiro and me like a dense web. Words like *stupid little kitsune* and *light-dwellers* and *fools* reach into my ears. Their derision sticks to my skin, heavy and wet. They step forward, circling us tighter.

"My Lord and Master has come to liberate my people from the tyranny of the light." The red jorōgumo throws off her furisode, gaining height as her glamour falls away. She's naked beneath and human only to the waist—she dances nimbly on eight spindly, sleek spider legs. Her white flesh quivers in the low light. Muscular. Strong. These yokai are different from the ones that attacked the shrine, more evolved, more poised.

More powerful.

Fear laces every muscle in my body, making them tighten and clench. My brain's shouting *move!* at me, but flight isn't an option. The trees around us wink with endless glittering, ruby eyes. It's impossible to tell how many jorōgumo lurk in the woods; but we'd never be able to outrun them all.

Either we fight, or we die trying.

"Your day, light-dweller," the red jorōgumo says, lifting her clawed hands as she stalks toward us, "is *over*."

But just as she lunges toward us, a high-pitched scream echoes from somewhere beyond the tree line. Shiro throws a protective arm in front of me. As the sound gurgles and throttles, the jorōgumo halts and turns her slender head.

"Yui?" the red jorōgumo asks, frowning. A susurrus answers from the forest, the sound of many voices whispering,

Yui?

Sister?

Yui, where are you?

She is no more.

Can you feel it?

Yui is no more.

I turn my head, keeping track of the other yokai on the path—but they are not paying attention to me. They shudder on their spidery stilts, easing sideways, looking nervous. Shiro and I inch closer to each other. I wish the claws extending off Shiro's fingertips were a comfort, but they look so small against an army of so many.

"Yui! . . . Was that you?" the purple jorōgumo asks.

A small object comes hurtling out of the trees. It slams into the red jorōgumo's chest, leaving a fresh crimson smear of blood across her skin. She scuttles backward with a shriek, her gaze fastened to the basketball-shaped object on the ground.

Wait . . .

Is that hair?

I stumble back before my mind makes full sense of the horror on the ground before me, this head without a body, ripped so savagely from her shoulders. The hellish glow has gone out of the jorōgumo's eyes, and yet they still seem to stare up at me. Her mouth still rings around an unfinished scream. The white of her throat ends just a few inches under her chin, bits of shredded meat gleaming in the fading light.

"No," the first jorōgumo says, and the depth of the sadness in her voice surprises me. The jorōgumo lowers herself to retrieve her sister's head, scooping it off the ground in both hands, tears flowing from the corners of all eight of her eyes. "What has happened to you?"

As she stoops down, I spot eyes glowering in the bushes behind her. Each eye is as big as my fist. No, *bigger*. The left eye appears cloudy, as if injured once upon a time. One eye gleams yellow, the other blue.

"Kira," Shiro whispers, barely louder than an exhale, "when I say run, you *run* to the Meiji Shrine, do you understand?"

I nod, but barely. He twists a single index finger around mine and squeezes as if to say, *I'll be right behind you.*

A growl guts the air. Before the jorōgumo can react, a massive cat leaps from the woods, slamming into the red jorōgumo. The two figures tumble forward, a flash of white fangs, singed, brindle-black fur, and spider legs. The creature's claws run crimson red as they tear into the jorōgumo's flesh. Her screams punch into my eardrums like sharpened pencils.

Shiro shoves me toward the torii gate. *"Go!"*

I can't leave him. "But I—"

The blue jorōgumo charges at me from my left, throwing off her kimono with a shriek. My fear has grown through my feet and rooted me to the ground.

"Dammit, Kira!" Shiro says, pushing past me. He snaps his fingers, summoning a ball of fire that burns like a miniature sun. When he pushes his hands out in front of his torso, the ball follows his fingertips, floating overtop them. He moves his fingers in intricate patterns, and it looks like he's tutting a spell. A spout of white-hot foxfire erupts off his fingertips, leaping toward the jorōgumo and catching fire on her skin. Each flame looks like a tiny foxtail.

The jorōgumo burns as quick as tinder, the fire licking up her arms and back and catching in her hair. Her screams echo and snap as she tries to beat the flames down with her hands.

Behind us, a roar cracks the asphalt underfoot. I clap my hands over my ears, but before I can turn around to see what's behind me, Shiro grabs me by the upper arm.

"Go. *Now*," he says, his skin starting to glow with ethereal light.

"Shiro—"

"You can't fight them, Kira! Just go!"

Without another word, I turn and run through the first torii gate. Full dark has settled along the path. The heels of my boots strike the ground, loud as horses' hooves. Behind me, screams and shrieks snap at each other's throats like dogs. Up ahead, small lights twinkle like fireflies through the trees.

You can't fight, Kira.

My eyes blur. I wipe my lower lids with the sleeve of my coat as I run.

You. Can't. Fight.

A second, more formal torii gate sits at the end of the road, marking the entrance to the shrine grounds. And safety.

Fifty feet from the torii gate.

Then twenty.

I don't even hear her sneak up behind me.

A loop of spider's silk catches me around my torso. The leash snaps taut, yanking me off my feet. I slam into the ground. The breath gets skinned straight out of me. I try to wiggle free, but manage only to get more of the silky stuff stuck to my jacket.

As I struggle, someone chuckles at me. I roll onto my side, only to see the jorōgumo in the yellow furisode walking toward me. Thousands of jorō spiders crawl out of the forest foliage, until the very ground seems to undulate on their black-and-yellow backs.

Everything inside me collapses. *Not like this*, I tell myself, watching the small spiders form a sea of glittering eyes and twitching legs around me. My bracelet burns with fire as they draw closer.

The yellow jorōgumo limps toward me. Splatters of blood cover her face and torso, and there are long gashes in her left side. She pauses a few yards away, giving her lasso a rough, cruel tug. The spider silk tightens around my body till I can barely breathe.

"My sisters are dying because of you, girl," she says with a hiss. The jorō spiders advance. One crawls up my shoe and onto the flesh of my calf. I kick it off, but two take its place, crawling over my boots, up my thighs, over my abdomen, and inside my jacket. I shriek as the first set of fangs tears past my tights and into the flesh of my leg.

The yellow jorōgumo gives the lasso another yank. "For that, my children will devour you slowly, bit by agonizing bit."

Another jorō spider sinks its fangs into my ankle. I bite my tongue, not willing to give this demon the pleasure of hearing me whimper. It is harder to ignore the spider that nips my abdomen, and I squeeze my eyes shut to handle the pain.

Just a little closer . . . , I think, shaking my head to dislodge the spiders crawling over my cheek.

"My, my," the jorōgumo says, easing another step forward, letting her guard down, "you are a proud one, aren't you—"

Before she can strike, a shadow drops from the trees with a great *whoosh*. A glint races through the spider-woman, slicing through her from the crown of her head to the bottom of her thorax. Slowly, the bisected parts of the demon shift and open like two gory petals. The monster's viscera hit the ground with a wet slap. The little spiders scatter, disappearing into the shadows as fast as they came.

A man in white lands a few feet away, dark blood dripping off the edge of his sword. His hat tumbles down after him, revealing two white fox ears sticking out of his long, silvery hair. Nine bushy white foxtails cascade from his backside.

He turns.

It's Goro.

ELEVEN
Yoyogi Park, Meiji Shrine
Tokyo, Japan

"What are you doing here, Kira?" Goro asks as he cuts my spider-silk bonds off me. He helps me to my feet. "Your mother said you'd come to Tokyo, but you should be at home, behind the protective wards I wove into your parents' house!"

"Protective wards can't help me now," I say, my voice trembling. "Didn't you hear . . . about . . . ?"

Grandfather.

Just thinking the word triggers a sob in my gut. It hits my lungs, rising through my chest like a tsunami. I throw myself into Goro's arms, overwhelmed by the swell of emotion. He hugs me back, his embrace so fierce it's almost as if Grandfather himself is here. Almost, but not quite.

Goro puts a hand on the crown of my head. "I know. The Grandmaster phoned this morning."

"I'm sorry," I say through my tears. "I'm so sorry I couldn't save him."

"Don't be," Goro chides me gently, releasing me to arm's length and taking my shoulders in both hands. "I knew Hiiro better than anyone, and he would have been happy to trade his life for yours. And if there is a blood moon on the rise, not even *I* could have stopped Shuten-doji's beasts. Do you understand?"

"I know, but—"

"No *buts*," Goro says. "There is nothing you could have done, not as you are. If you want to survive the blood moon, you will need to become better, hmm? Stronger than me, stronger than your grandfather. You must prepare for a future that honors Hiiro's sacrifice."

I sniffle, then manage a short bow.

"Kira!" Shiro jogs down the path, drawing our attention. A regular-size Oni-chan runs beside him. Shiro spots the oozing jorōgumo corpse on the ground and halts, his attention snapping to Goro and me.

"Thank you, Goro-sama," Shiro says with a bow. "I regret that my failure to protect Kira forced you to intervene on her behalf."

"Nonsense, young kit," Goro says with a smile. "That's the most action these old bones have seen in decades. Come. I will have my acolytes deal with the mess we've left. The three of us have much to discuss. But"—Goro points to Oni-chan—"you will have to wait outside, nekomata. I'm sure you understand."

Oni-chan growls and flattens his ears, but Shiro kneels and chucks Oni-chan under the chin with a knuckle. "Be good, and there will be an entire yakitori *stand* in your future, got it?"

"Meow?" Oni-chan twitches his dual tails, his eyes bright with mischief.

"Okay, okay," Shiro says, rising to his feet. *"Deal."*

Goro chuckles. As he heads down the path to the shrine, he says, "You shouldn't make deals with nekomata—that cat has two more tails than you."

Shiro blushes so bright, it's obvious even in the shadows. "I-I, I mean I should say that I—"

"Come," Goro says, turning down the path. "It is a perfect night for a good cup of tea."

Shiro mutters to himself as we follow Goro. One of the elder kitsune's great, hoary white ears swivels backward. His smile turns into a wolfish grin. He leads us under the main torii gate and onto sanctified shrine grounds. The shrine's slatted wooden fence seems so flimsy; but I remind myself it isn't a shrine's fences or walls keeping the demons out in the first place. The purity of these grounds keeps most yokai away.

Or at least it should.

We step into a courtyard lit with traditional stone lanterns. Their orange flames dance brightly, transferring their warmth to my spirit. The gentle light illuminates the Meiji's wooden walls and the turquoise-colored tiles along the roof's gables. In comparison to other shrines I've seen, the Meiji Shrine has an understated, quiet magnificence to it; while it doesn't have the Heian Shrine's brilliant colors or Fushimi Inari's vermilion gates, this shrine rivals them easily. It's a perfect place to enshrine the kami of Emperor Meiji and Empress Shoken. Their presence brings me peace: the tension seeps from my muscles, and the pain from my spider bites eases. For the time being, Shuten-doji's minions cannot harm me.

"I've never been to the Meiji Shrine before." I keep my voice low as we pass the shrine's other priests and miko. "It's beautiful here."

"I enjoy it," Goro says, motioning for us to step off the veranda and cross a small street. "But it will take time for Tokyo to feel like home. I lived in Kyoto for more than a hundred years; it is the land where the gods walk, and I used to be able to hear their voices on the wind if I listened hard enough. Tokyo is far too busy for that."

We follow Goro to a private apartment on the shrine grounds. He taps a security code into a slatted, pine wood screen, and then slides it open for us. The garden beyond isn't large—no more than ten by ten feet—but life bounds from every corner of the space. Large fronds and flowers spill from clay pots, all of which look hand-thrown. Goro used to be an avid potter, and it looks like he has continued his craft here in Tokyo.

"Tea?" Goro asks as we step into his genkan entryway to remove our shoes.

"No, thank you," I say.

"Oh, but you *must* have tea," he says, ushering us into his kitchen. Even at a shrine as grand as the Meiji, the priests' living quarters are modest and simple. "It will be wonderfully restorative after an old-fashioned fight with the yokai, hmm? I've received a Sencha leaf from a friend at the fox preserve in Shiroishi. I was waiting for company to try it."

Shiro and I settle at the kitchen island, sitting in stools as Goro fills a metal kettle with cold water. I decide not to dither with small talk: "What did the Grandmaster tell you about what happened at the Fujikawa Shrine?" I ask him.

"The Grandmaster is unclear about the night's events." Goro shoots a playful yet somehow reproachful glance at Shiro. The younger kitsune flattens his ears and drops his gaze, as if in apology. "Apparently, the Okamoto brothers have yet to make a full report. Where is Ronin? I've heard he's quite meticulous, so I'm surprised he didn't call the Elders straightaway."

Shiro sucks in a breath. "You don't know?"

"Kitsune know many things, but I'm not a mind-reader," Goro replies, measuring out a heap of tea leaves. I can smell their sharp, spicy scent from where I sit. He sets the leaves down, and when he lifts his gaze, I swear he looks ages older than before. "Tell me he wasn't lost in the attack?"

"No," I say. "Not exactly."

"But Ronin is not here with you." Goro's gaze slides to Shiro, who turns his face away. "Ah, so he has taken your mother's offer to become her heir. That news brings me great sadness. I expected better from Ronin."

"How did you know about that?" Shiro asks. "I thought nothing leaked from the Twilight Court—Mother kills anyone who speaks to outsiders of her plans."

"When you grow into your power, Shiro, you will understand," Goro says, resting his hands on the kitchen island. His aged hands look like Grandfather's did, wrinkled and brown, like the strongest roots of an old tree. "You will know things about people, simply by looking at them. Just as I can see Kira has made a foolish deal with Lady Katayama."

I flush. "I thought you said you weren't a mind-reader!"

"And I am not, but the truth is plain on your face." Goro chuckles, turning to gather three handmade teacups from his cupboard. "What sort of quest has she sent you on? Has she asked you to gather songs from nightingales and weave them into silk so fine it feels like a breath of air? Or perhaps she wants you to fetch her a ruby from Amaterasu's own crown? Does she have you taking the beaks off tengu in Okinawa, or locating the very snow that birthed a yuki-onna?"

"She wants shinigami," I say. "Seven, to be exact, to help us protect the Fujikawa Shrine."

"*Seven* shinigami," Goro says, clucking his tongue. "Seven to fight a rising demon lord, more like. A full cabal of them. My goodness, Lady Katayama *is* ambitious, isn't she?"

"Do you think it will work?" Shiro asks.

Goro sets the teacups down in a line. "Perhaps. Though I don't think you have considered all the implications of this scheme,

Kira. A shinigami's role in this world is to reap the souls of the living. They are death's messengers, and therefore impure. They cannot be allowed to step foot on sanctified shrine grounds."

"But the shrine's already been defiled," I say, thinking that Goro's right about one thing—in Shinto, death is unclean. I can't have both shinigami *and* Amaterasu's holy protection of the shrine. "I won't consecrate the Fujikawa Shrine again until after we have destroyed Shuten-doji."

"This is foolishness, child." Goro frowns, tapping the island with impatient fingers. "Shinigami are broken creatures. They reap the souls of the living to keep themselves from withering into oblivion, because the life force of the souls they gather can sustain them, at least for a time."

"You mean the butterflies?" I ask, thinking of the shifting, winged patterns on O-bei's kimono. "Shinigami feed on the souls they reap?"

"No, not quite," Goro says. "The souls are eventually released and allowed to pass into Yomi. It's more of a . . . symbiotic relationship, in which a soul helps to sustain the shinigami in exchange for protection during their transition into death. You can't trust these creatures to help you destroy a demon. They have no motivation to help you."

"I'm not sure I have a choice," I say.

"You always have a choice," Goro chides me.

"Who else could I possibly turn to for help?" I ask, spreading my hands wide. "Many people believe the yokai are fairy tales made to frighten children, not a reality hunting them from the shadows. These days, most human *priests* can't even see the yokai anymore."

"I agree that the world is not as it once was," Goro says, "and that many people no longer believe as they once did. But that doesn't mean death itself is your only recourse."

"Well, I'm open to suggestions," I say. I won't deny that I'm frustrated.

My words draw a heavy sigh from Goro. "I didn't say I had any, at least not off the top of my head. Perhaps the Grandmaster would know how best to approach this situation?"

"With all due respect, Goro-sama, no," Shiro says, crossing his arms over his chest. "*Hell* no. If we go to the Grandmaster and his council, we'll be stuck in an endless cycle of bureaucracy, meetings, and pointless hand-wringing. And while I don't agree with everything my mother does, I can trust her motivations."

"Can you really?" Goro asks. "You two may think you're clever enough to use Lady Katayama for your own ends, but she has been manipulating people for a thousand years. I don't trust her." Goro shoots me a dark glance, which I interpret to mean *and neither should you.*

"She wants Shuten-doji dead, just like us," Shiro replies.

Goro lifts a single, bushy brow.

"That's good enough for me," I say.

Goro sighs again. "Very well. But I can't imagine your grandfather would approve of this plan."

"No," I say softly. "I don't think he would, either. If we knew where the hidden shard of the Kusanagi no Tsurugi was, we might be able to do things differently—"

"Bah!" Goro says, waving a hand. "Its presence in the Fujikawa Shrine is a myth, nothing more."

"That 'myth' got my grandfather killed," I say. "Can you be sure the shard isn't in the Fujikawa Shrine?"

"No, but even so," Goro says, "nobody's seen the thing since the sword was broken some five hundred years ago. Finding a shard of the Kusanagi is an impossible task."

"I've been given a few of those lately," I say with a sigh. Shiro places his hand on my shoulder and gives it a gentle squeeze. "You don't happen to know any shinigami looking for work, do you?" I ask with a self-deprecating smile.

"No, not really." Goro clucks his tongue. He's thoughtful for a moment. Steam begins to curl from the kettle's lip. "But when your grandfather was young, we used to find a shinigami drinking on the shrine's front steps after dusk. He never said much, and he was never drunk . . . but every time I saw him, I sensed deep, centuries-old waves of regret spilling from him. I suspect he was a priest at the shrine, long ago."

"Do you know his name?" I ask.

"Your grandfather nicknamed him 'Shimada,'" Goro replies. "He resembled the movie character, and Hiiro was a fan of Kurosawa's at the time. I haven't seen this man for many years . . . but there are tales of his like around Tokyo. Stories of a shinigami who dresses like he's stepped out of samurai-era Japan. He wears a red haori jacket—no, blue? I will search for him tomorrow, while you scour the city for anyone who might be willing to help. And as for you, Kira—"

The teakettle shrieks, startling me.

Goro grins. "We should probably call your mother."

TWELVE
Shibuya District
Tokyo, Japan

Two nights later, our luck hasn't managed to grow good fruit. No matter how hard we try, Shiro and I haven't managed to recruit a single shinigami. We have no problem *finding* them, of course. Death gods stalk every neighborhood in the city. We see them in train stations, cafés, parks, street corners, and shops. They haunt the hallways in hospitals and follow elderly couples onto buses. But none of them are willing to help us.

Goro hasn't fared better. No one in Tokyo has seen the shinigami he remembers so fondly, nor does any clan have a record of him.

"You weren't kidding when you said this was going to be impossible," I say to Shiro, pulling my coat tight against an icy evening breeze. Shiro and I are waiting for a bus back to Shibuya—after being attacked by yokai in Yoyogi Park, Shiro and I try to limit our searches to the daylight hours. It's difficult to waste time at the ryokan when each sunset brings us closer to the blood moon . . . but like Goro always says, *You can't save the world if you're dead.*

The bus stop itself provides no shelter from the weather, and the snowflakes tumble down in clumps. It's so cold, I'm starting to consider taking shelter in the laundromat behind us. The yellow light streaming from its windows looks cheerful and warm.

I shift my weight to the other foot, shivering. "How many times were we rejected today? Eight? Ten?"

"Thirteen," Shiro says, blowing into his cupped hands to keep his fingers warm.

"Let's hope we can find shinigami in Kyoto, then," I say. With Goro's help, I talked Mother into allowing me to stay in Tokyo for a few days. Goro told her I should recover in Tokyo, under the watchful eyes of the priests at the Meiji Shrine. Mother believed him and gave me till Wednesday to return home. That's the day after tomorrow, so we're running out of time. "I'll have less time to look in Kyoto, though—school will take up a lot of my day."

"Kira, Kira, always with her head in a book," Shiro says, teasing me lightly.

I wrinkle my nose. "I don't have a choice. If my grades drop, I'll lose my place at Kōgakkon and my parents will be *really* upset with me." Though I admit, my time at Kōgakkon hasn't been everything I'd wished it to be. My last high school wasn't as prestigious, but I hadn't been bullied there. Plus I had a few friends. Sort of.

A bus pulls up to the stop. It almost seems to exhale as its doors open. Shiro and I move aside for the passengers trying to board. "On top of that, Goro says I need to start learning onmyōdō."

"I thought you *wanted* to learn onmyōdō?" Shiro says.

"I do, but a month isn't enough time," I say, kicking the snow piling up near my feet. It wouldn't be this cold back in Kyoto, at least not yet. I don't like the feeling of winter nipping at my nose, reminding me that our time is drawing shorter with alarming speed. We have less than four weeks till the blood moon rises. It isn't enough time—not to find shinigami for O-bei, nor to pack a lifetime's worth of magical training into my skull. I won't be enough against Shuten-doji, not alone. With shinigami at my back and Shiro at my side, perhaps we'll stand a fighting chance. *Maybe.*

I don't like living with so many maybes. In everything else I've done in life, good preparation has assured success. But in this case, I can prepare all I want and still lose the whole world.

The snow falls harder. Flakes get stuck in my lashes. I shelter my forehead with my hand, my fingertips naked and tender from the unexpected cold snap. Clouds overhead suck the remaining light from the sky. The snow blurs the glow from the lampposts. It's close to seven o'clock, and several businessmen wait at the bus stop with us, along with an elderly shopper or two. Nobody has properly dressed for a snowstorm; nobody was expecting it—*especially* not the weathermen.

"Do you know any shinigami in Kyoto?" I ask Shiro, peering at the oncoming traffic, hoping to see a bus on its way. I stamp my feet to get my blood pumping through my toes, which are barely more than tiny blocks of ice stuffed into my shoes.

"Not any we'd want to work with," Shiro says.

"We're sort of desperate," I say. "Aren't we?"

"Not *that* desperate," Shiro says, narrowing his eyes by a sliver. "Not yet."

"Even if we could just convince *one*, I'd have hope that this crazy plan might work—"

A horn screams, startling Shiro and me. My gaze snaps to the center of the road, where a bullet-gray van skids sideways across the icy asphalt. The driver behind the wheel struggles to regain control of the vehicle. The tires turn helplessly against the physics of ice and snow.

The van careens straight for the bus stop.

Before I can scramble out of the van's path, Shiro yanks me backward. I stumble and slip. We become a tangle of arms and legs on the slick pavement, until the world tilts at ninety degrees and I slide backward. Horns blare. Metal shrieks. Glass shatters. People scream.

I tumble and slide till I collide with something solid, straight, and cold. The impact claps the breath from my lungs. Pain sparks hot, like a poker being jammed into my shoulder.

The street falls silent.

When I open my eyes, I'm smashed up against the laundromat's glass windows. Inside, several middle-aged women point to something outside; I think they might be laughing at me. But then my head begins to clear, and I realize the emotion on their faces isn't humor.

It's *horror.*

I sit up. Shiro's propped up on one arm, cradling his forehead with his free hand. It takes my eyes a few seconds to focus. The twisted metal and broken glass don't compute. A vehicle has lodged itself between the awning and the metal bus route map. Tongues of orange fire lick the busted-up hood of a van. One yellow blinker still signals psychotically, throwing its yellow light over the chaos on the sidewalk. Behind the spiderwebbed windshield, the driver of the van slumps over the wheel. He's not moving.

I see the blood next. The stuff splatters across the sidewalk, as if someone took a giant bottle of sumi-e ink and smashed it against the ground. It fans out from the epicenter of the crash, where—

No, I think, my mind unable to accept the scene in front of me. My blood chills. Every hair on my body stiffens.

A man is wound up in all that glass and metal and oil—a man who wasn't lucky enough to scramble away in time. He now lies crushed between the bus stop and the van. Several of his bones are broken into wrong angles. Glass protrudes from between several of his ribs, and his blood drips from his body, its heat hissing against the snow. His silver hair glints in the low light, and his round-rimmed bifocal glasses lies several steps away. A smudge of blood stains the cracked left lens.

His primal cry tears into the air. The sound seems to have claws sharp enough to rend my heart in two. I scramble back until my back hits the laundromat's windows again. Tears spring to my eyes. Everything inside me screams to *look away, you baka!* But I can't, I can't, *I can't.* I should help him, somehow—but what am I supposed to do?

Shiro kneels in front of me, blocking the horrific scene with his body. As he whispers something, my gaze wanders out into the street, where three cars have piled up near the center median. An injured woman screams for help, clutching an unconscious child in her arms, her crushed passenger-side door hanging horribly ajar. Traffic has come to standstill, save for the blaring horns and the distant, high-pitched ambulance wails.

The snow still falls, serene and soft, as if it hasn't noticed hell has descended on this street.

Reaching out, Shiro takes my chin in his icy fingers and turns my face back to his. His mouth forms words, but I'm too distraught to make sense of them.

"Kira," he finally says, his voice breaking through the buzzing in my ears. I watch the woman in the street, looking down at her child and bouncing him in her arms. He still isn't moving. Shiro persists: "Kira, you need to listen to me and do exactly as I say, okay? Take a deep breath. There, good. Now take another. Look at me."

I meet his gaze and hold it.

"Good. Keep breathing," he says. "In your head, I want you

to name something you can touch, something you can smell, and something you can see, okay? Can you do that for me?"

I nod and force myself to anchor my mind to the present—to feel the grit on Shiro's fingertips, to shiver at the coldness of the ground beneath me, to smell the oil and blood in the air, and then to count the amber flecks in his unusual eyes. Today, there are twenty. Yesterday, there were seventeen . . . though I don't recall counting them, not then. *When did I count them?* I draw in a breath and find I'm steadier, even as the injured man's agonized moans shake the chords of my heart.

"He must be s-someone's grandfather," I say, my breath breaking out of me in short, tight puffs.

"Don't think about that," Shiro says, scooping me into his arms.

"W-we sh-should help him."

"You're in shock, Kira," Shiro says, kicking the door to the laundromat and carrying me inside. The light seems too bright, and I squeeze my eyes shut and turn my face into his chest. "And even if you weren't, there's nothing we can do to save him."

"But we . . . shouldn't we . . . Grandfather . . ."

"He's not your grandfather, I promise," he says, setting me down on top of a rumbling clothes dryer. Its warmth seeps through my wet clothing. From this angle, I'm not able to see the bus stop outside, save for the traffic stopped in the road. At least ten onlookers have taken refuge inside the laundromat. Some peer out, shading their eyes with their hands. Others have cell phones pressed to their ears and are talking to emergency responders in low, urgent tones. They bow to people on the other line, unseen.

In the back of the laundromat, far away from the chaos, a father distracts his small child from the scene with a Pokémon toy; the comforting smile falls off his face whenever the child isn't looking.

Amid it all, a chill murmurs through my bones and bleeds into my soul. Shiro must sense it too, because we look up in synchrony. By now, my soul recognizes death before my head does. Its arrival changes the barometric pressure around me. My ears pop. Even my heart slows in my chest, as if yielding to the power of the creature outside. Death has a spiritual resonance, and I've learned to listen for its call.

I slide off the dryer without a word, heading for the exit. Bells jingle over my head as I push past the door. The outside wind whips the warmth from my clothing. I look up and down the sidewalk, and then at the scene before me.

A figure in a slate-gray kimono and black hakama pants stands beside the dying man, the edges of his red haori flitting in the wind. Snowflakes gather on his conical sugegasa hat and broad shoulders. A host of onyx-winged butterflies surrounds him, clinging to bloodied glass and bent metal, their wings so dark they seem to absorb all visible light. Each butterfly must be the size of my palm, if not larger.

That's no man, I think, awed as I watch the shinigami place his hand on the dying man's head, his gesture gentle. Reverent, even. The bells on the laundromat door clang behind me. Shiro appears at my side, placing a hand on my back and whispering, "Whoa."

The shinigami unsheathes his katana. I hadn't even noticed the blade. "Wait," I whisper. "Should we . . . I mean . . ."

"No," Shiro murmurs, putting an arm around my shoulders. He hugs me tight. I press my hand to my mouth. Tears warm my bottom eyelids. The bracelet tucked inside my sleeve begins to glow, suffusing me with sunlight.

If anyone else at the scene can see the shinigami, they make no sign.

With great care, the shinigami inserts the tip of his blade into the dying man's forehead, between the brows. The katana ripples, its blade turning to mist. Its cloudy light softens over the man's skin.

The man's mouth falls slack. The tension in his muscles releases, and his body rests against the van's engine. His eyes, once bright with pain, turn to glass.

The shinigami reaches up and closes them. As he draws his katana from the dead man's head—leaving no physical mark on the corpse—I spot a small lump on the blade's back side. It looks like a piece of hardened amber, brownish black in color and rough-hewn.

No, not a lump, I tell myself. *That's a cocoon.*

The shinigami breaks the cocoon off his sword and sticks it under the brim of his hat. Sheathing his sword, the shinigami makes two quick, precise hand gestures over the body, and then he turns.

"That's him, the shinigami in the red jacket," I whisper, pushing Shiro away. "He's the one we've been looking for."

"Kira, *wait*," Shiro says. But I've already started up the sidewalk, following the shinigami away from the chaos at the bus stop.

"Shinigami-sama?" I ask a bit timidly, hurrying after him. My boots slide on the icy sidewalk. "Excuse me? Shinigami-sama? May I have a moment of your time?"

He pays me no mind. I take a chance, betting on my instincts.

"Shimada!" I shout.

The shinigami stops in the snow, standing so still that his clothes freeze.

"How do you know that name?" he half growls, turning his head to look at me. His eyes blaze under the shadows cast by his hat. Unlike the eternally youthful shinigami I've seen before, this man wears a weathered face, one that has seen countless sunsets. His eyes, however, glow from beneath the brim of his hat. Those eyes warn me not to mistake his compassion for the dying as kindness toward the living.

I've never seen another shinigami like him.

After several long moments, he tugs his hat down to conceal his face.

"It is not your time," he says, turning away. "You are none of my concern."

I chase after him, the words scrambling off my lips. "I-I'm the granddaughter of Hiiro Fujikawa, former high priest of the

Fujikawa Shrine. Please, I mean no disrespect, but I'm certain that you are the only one who can help me."

"Your family name is Fujikawa?" he asks, walking faster.

I nod, scarcely able to breathe. I hold my hands out at my sides to keep my balance.

"That's unfortunate for you," he says, pulling his hat down farther. "But I can't help you. Nobody can."

"Try," I say, reaching out to take hold of his sleeve. The fabric feels so cold, it burns. "I'm told you left regrets behind at the Fujikawa Shrine—"

Shimada moves faster than I can think. He stops, mere inches from me, so close that his hakama pants strike the side of my leg. It takes a full second for my brain to register the icy spark of pain at the side of my neck.

His tanto knife nicks my skin. A hot drop of blood slides into the hollow of my throat. The pain near my jugular vein makes me suddenly, horribly aware of each heartbeat. The only thing I dare move is my eyes—I meet his gaze with defiance.

If I so much as slip on the ice underfoot, I'm dead.

"You know *nothing*," Shimada says.

"That's not true," I whisper. One of his butterflies lands on my shoulder. "You're an agent of death, and yet respected by the oldest kitsune I know. It is said you follow no clans, so you must not need protection from the yokai. Not like the others."

He narrows his eyes.

"But I need *you*," I say through my teeth. "Because there's a blood moon set to rise over Kyoto, and when it does, Shuten-doji will tear my family's shrine apart to find the last shard of an ancient blade. If we don't stop him, he will use the blade to destroy everything good and holy in this world."

"*Tch,*" Shimada says, but he lowers his knife. "The miseries of the human world do not concern me."

"Maybe not," I say, touching the small wound at my throat. I take my hand from my neck, extending it to him. Crimson blotches stain the tips of my fingers. Another butterfly lands on my hand. Then two. "But you can't pretend the Fujikawa Shrine doesn't mean anything to you, not now."

His gaze falls on my hand, then slides to the light emanating from my bracelet. "What is that?" he asks, pointing at the light.

I tug back my sleeve to expose my bracelet's metal links. "It's a family heirloom, one passed down to me by my grandfather."

When I look up, Shimada looks . . . *younger*, somehow, in my bracelet's light. Time hasn't carved so many lines in his face, and he wears priestly robes resembling the ones Grandfather once wore. I see the shimmer of wonder in his eyes, rather than wells of deep hatred.

He pulls his hat down, blocking his face from the light. But-terflies collect on his hat and shoulders, shaking snow from their thick, velvety wings.

"I need time to consider this," Shimada says, turning away. His butterflies take flight, filling the air with undulating shadows.

My breath catches. "But Shimada-sama, I don't have time—"

"Three nights." He halts but does not turn back to me. "*If* I choose to help you, I will appear on your shrine's steps on the eve of the third night."

Before I can say anything else, he disappears into a cloud of black mist and seeps into the cracks of the sidewalk. I glance sideways at Shiro, openmouthed.

"Well, you heard the man," Shiro says, sticking his hands in his pockets. "I guess we'd better get back to Kyoto."

THIRTEEN
Tokyo Station

Tokyo, Japan

On Wednesday—almost a week after the shrine was attacked—I find myself in Tokyo Station, headed home. My company includes two kitsune, one angry nekomata, and *zero* shinigami. We won't know if Shimada has joined our cause until tonight. I've fretted over him so much these past two days, I've chewed my bottom lip raw. My grief over losing Grandfather hasn't helped matters any, either. I feel guilty having wasted so much time in Tokyo with such laughable progress.

Tokyo Station may be one of the largest train stations in the world—it's a sprawling, massive underground complex with tentacles snaking all over the city. It's no small wonder that Goro, Shiro, Oni-chan, and I get lost in the place twice. It does nothing for my nerves, which are already frayed.

"I should have rented a car," Goro grumbles, slipping his hands into his voluminous sleeves. While Shiro buys shinkansen tickets to Kyoto, Goro and I wait for him outside the security gates. Oni-chan growls from a crate sitting at my feet. I'm not sure which creature is grumpier: the elderly kitsune or the nekomata.

"Hush," I say to Oni-chan, taking a knee by his crate. "They won't let you on board unless you're in there!"

"You are brave, scolding a nekomata like that." Goro grins, flashing teeth. But before I can sass him, his grin drops away and he lifts his head. His gaze narrows, focused on a point behind me. Oni-chan snarls again, thrashing in his crate.

I get to my feet, expecting to see an enemy stalking us through the crowds. I'm even less pleased to spot Ronin in the terminal. When our gazes touch, he stops in the middle of a busy thoroughfare. The masses of train riders give him a wide berth, as if the crowd senses the blood on his hands and the darkness in his heart. The light that once emanated from his skin has dimmed. The sacred foxtails he bore with pride have vanished, as have the ears that marked his kitsune heritage. Ronin's transformation into shinigami has already begun, and the goodness has gone out of him. He wears a finely tailored cobalt velvet suit and tie. With his platinum hair styled over one eye, he looks like a pop idol. Women stare, openmouthed. So do men.

I suppose even death looks beautiful, sometimes. But its beauty is a lie.

Shiro rejoins us, balancing a tray of coffees in one hand. He shoves his wallet into his back pocket with the other, the corners of three small shinkansen tickets tucked between his teeth. He hands me the coffees, takes the tickets in one hand, and swears when he sees his brother.

"What's Ronin doing here?" I spit, clutching the coffee tray. My mood is now as dark as Oni-chan's. The cat hisses, butting his head against the side of his crate.

"Oi," Shiro says, stepping in front of me as Ronin approaches us. "What do you want?"

"Mother sent me to keep an eye on your progress," Ronin replies. He looks Shiro up and down and sneers, as if unimpressed by Shiro's dark jeans, leather jacket, and T-shirt.

"We're doing exactly what she's asked of us," Shiro says. "You don't need to be involved."

"Relax, dear brother. I'm only here to look after Mother's interests. She's already sent a crew ahead to fix Kira's precious little shrine." Ronin reaches around me and takes a coffee from the carrier. Shiro grabs his brother by the wrist, the motion so quick, I don't even see him move. The stitching in Shiro's jacket strains, his back muscles flexing to keep Ronin held in place. Shiro glares. Ronin smirks.

"You are no longer a kitsune, *dear brother*," Shiro says under his breath. He digs his nails into the flesh of Ronin's arm. Ronin's smirk twists into a grimace of pain. "And it shows."

Ronin drops the coffee. The cup hits the floor and bursts open, splashing hot liquid over the toes of my boots. Shiro shoves his brother back, forcing him to stumble. A small, dark part of me enjoys watching Shiro put Ronin in his place. I know I shouldn't, but I do.

I look to Goro. He keeps his arms crossed over his chest, watching the brothers argue, but makes no move to intervene. As Ronin straightens his coat, I take a step forward to say, "Enough."

"This isn't your fight, Kira," Ronin says, never taking his eyes off Shiro.

"You're right, it's not," I reply, "but I'm ending it anyway. Follow us to Kyoto if you'd like, Ronin, but know this—you are forbidden from stepping foot on the Fujikawa Shrine grounds again."

Ronin turns his head. "Excuse me?"

"You heard me." Before he can argue the point, I pick up Oni-chan's cat carrier, pluck a ticket out of Shiro's hand, and walk toward the security line. "You'd better hurry if you want to come with us. The train's leaving soon."

I settle into an aisle seat as the train pulls away from the station, Shiro at my side. Goro sits in the single seat across the aisle, looking around the train car with curiosity. To my eye, it's not much to look at: an eggshell-white interior with large cube windows and a burgundy carpet underfoot. Shiro sprang for Gran-class seats, however, which are roomier than their economy counterparts. There's enough room for Oni-chan's crate by my feet. The cat growls as I set his carrier down.

Ronin seethes two rows behind Goro. If I turn my head a few degrees, I can see him from the corner of my eye. I consider asking Shiro to switch places with me, but if I move I'll have to listen to the brothers argue all the way to Kyoto.

"How long is the trip again?" I ask.

"Three and a half hours," Shiro replies. "It'll be a good time to practice your mudras and tuts. Goro's right, you're getting your-self into enough trouble. You should learn onmyōdō, even if you only master a spell or two for now. Let's see how fast your fingers can go, hmm?"

"What does speed have to do with spellcasting?" I ask.

"You need to be able to tut in your *sleep*," Shiro says, moving his fingers through the Nine Celestial mudras, or the Kuji-in, with ease. "Rin, Pyoh, Toh, Sha—"

"Show-off," I say, as he turns to me and performs the mudras without looking at his fingertips.

"C'mon, do it with me," Shiro says, elbowing me playfully and steepling his index fingers into Rin. I mimic his hand motions, and together we say, "Rin."

Shiro knits his fingers into the next mudra, Pyoh. With his hands pressed together, his middle fingers move over his pointed index fingers and curl down to touch the tips of his thumbs. He does this without thinking; I very much need to look at my hands and sculpt them into the proper position.

"For mortals," Shiro says, slipping into the Toh mudra, easy as breathing, "these mudras are an aspect of esoteric Buddhism. They symbolize the forces of the universe, and how all the elements are united against evil. But for people like us"—Shiro performs a mudra I don't recognize, followed by a cut quick through the air with two fingers—"well, they're magic."

The tips of his fingers catch fire. It dances along his skin without burning him. Shiro grins at me, and then shakes it off.

"But *I'm* a mortal," I say.

"A mortal who carries the blood of Abe no Seimei in her veins," Shiro says.

"He lived a very long time ago," I say softly.

He runs a knuckle down the side of my face, leaning closer. "And yet it seems that his mother hasn't forgotten your line, not through all these centuries. Who knows, maybe you have enough kitsune blood to cast foxfire, even—"

Something smacks into the window beside us. Shiro and I both jump. I smother a scream with my hands, not wanting to disrupt any of the other passengers in the car.

A heavy *clunk!* echoes against the train's roof. We all look up. There are at least ten other passengers in our car, all of whom startle from their seats, asking variations of *What was that?* Others peer out the windows, shielding their eyes from the mid-morning sunlight.

"We've got company," Ronin says, getting out of his seat.

Shiro looks at the other passengers. "Get out of the car!"

"What?" one of the passengers asks. "Why?"

Before Shiro can answer, the connective tissue between the

train cars splits open. Light stabs through the wounds. A torrent of white silk moths spills inside, their wings beating against the train car's glass doors. My mouth falls open.

"Go!" Shiro shouts at the other passengers. "Just go!"

The others flee as the glass doors shatter inward. The moths flurry through the car like snow, rushing toward us. Soft, fuzzy bodies slam into me, chalking up the air and making it harder to breathe. I hold my hands up to block my face. Someone shoves me backward, toward the window, and I nearly trip over an armrest. The other passengers shriek, fleeing out the other side of the car to safety.

Goro speaks a single word in a language I don't recognize. A shock wave slams into the train car, shoving the moths away from us. They scatter like autumn leaves, driven forth by strong winds.

Metal whistles through the air, its screech halted by a sharp *clap*. I look up, barely able to see Goro standing several feet down the aisle from me, the blade of a katana stoppered between his palms.

A woman in a white kimono wields the sword.

No, she's not a woman, *she's a* shinigami. One with more butterflies than any death god I saw in Tokyo. Her hair's done up in a simple chignon. Her beauty is like the edge of a sharp sword— best appreciated from a distance.

Shiro pushes me behind him, putting his body between me and the shinigami's blade. Oni-chan growls at my feet. He sinks his claws into the crate walls, making it buck and rattle. Ronin steps into the aisle behind this new intruder, one hand on his sheathed sword.

"Stand aside," she says. "My orders are to kill the girl." Her gaze hits me like a blade between the ribs. I try to gasp, but I can't suck the air in. My lungs feel like they've popped in my chest.

"Who are you?" Goro asks. "I know most of the shinigami in Yomi, but I've never seen your face before."

The Shinigami in White narrows her eyes. "It doesn't matter who I am."

"I disagree," Goro says. "For I've heard stories of a shinigami who serves Shuten-doji as an assassin, one who dresses in white so that the blood of her victims may stain her garb. It is said she keeps every kimono."

One corner of the Shinigami in White's lips twitches upward. "Do they also say that she displays the patterns from her favorite kills in her home?"

"No," Goro says, returning her wicked smile with a grimace. "But I'd believe it."

"You are surrounded, lady." Ronin draws his sword. "The only blood that will be staining your kimono today is your own."

"Is that so?" the Shinigami in White says with a short laugh. She lifts a hand, beckoning to the moths that cover almost every nearby surface in the train car. They beat their wings and rise. "Let's see you try to land an attack on me, *child*."

Her moths envelop her in a cyclone, and then explode outward in a swift-moving cloud. Blades clang. Goro swears, then grunts in pain. Shiro scrambles into the aisle, shouting, *"No!"*

I drop between the seats. As the moths thunder overhead, I reach down and open Oni-chan's crate door. The cat darts out with a yowl. To my right, the sounds of a struggle reach through the drumming wings. Another shout rocks the train car, clearing the moths from the air; but this time, the voice belongs to the Shinigami in White. I rise, white moth dust speckling my shoulders and everything else in the car. My allies are cocooned in pill-shaped, silken white sacs. One sac writhes on the floor in front of the Shinigami in White. Hands press against the springy wall, from the inside, and I swear I hear Shiro shouting, "Run, Kira!"

And go where? I ask him in my head, easing back as the Shinigami in White turns toward me. *There isn't anywhere to run on a train!*

I scramble to remember the spells Shiro taught me, but all I can think about is the shinigami's katana plunging into my gut, or feeling my heart stop beating around that blade. Fear scatters everything I've learned to the dark corners of my brain.

The Shinigami in White now wears three deep scratches on one cheek. They ooze droplets of black-red blood, each making a little rosette on the shoulder of her white kimono. "You little beasts have caused more trouble than you're worth," she says, narrowing her eyes. She brings her blade level to my chest. "Stand still, now, if you want to die without pain. Even my precision has its limits . . . as does my patience."

She tenses for an attack, but just before she springs, her eyes grow wide. The reflection of a massive cat ripples across the train's tinted windows.

Even I flinch when Oni-chan roars, the sound exploding through the car as if it were a drum struck by one of the gods. The Shinigami in White takes a step back.

It's just the distraction I need.

Memory surges through me. Dropping down to one knee, I tut the symbol for Rin. All my pent-up fear roils, bubbling over into my heart and making my fingertips tingle. I shove my hands forward. Fire explodes off my palms, tearing through the air in the form of crimson flames. Heat billows against my face. The moths burn, and if I weren't so shocked, I'd marvel at them twirling through the air on cinder-edged wings. The flames chew through the cocoons that hold Shiro, Goro, and Ronin.

Gray ash and black smoke linger in the flames' wake.

"Whoa," I say, turning my palm over, marveling at my unblemished, unbroken flesh. My hand pulses with heat, several degrees hotter than the rest of my body, as if my blood's turned to napalm. *That was . . . that was so . . . whoa.*

The Shinigami in White straightens. Smoke stains her kimono. "They said you are a clever girl," she says, lifting her blade. "But not clever enough—"

Shiro grips the Shinigami in White's throat with clawed fingertips. Rubies of blood appear at each pressure point. "Drop it," he growls. "Or we'll see how much blood I can get on your kimono."

The Shinigami in White sneers. "As if you could ever best *me*, boy."

She hisses a spell and bursts into a cloud of moths, disappearing through the train's broken window.

"Dammit!" Shiro says, turning to slash a nearby headrest with his claws. Stuffing leaks out of the tears in the fabric. His chest heaves with each wave of his fury.

"Well, everyone's alive," Goro says with a sigh, picking moth silk off his clothing. Oni-chan, now back to his regular size, leaps up onto the back of one of the seats. He begins washing his face with a paw. "I suppose we'll call that a victory for now."

"But what about the train?" I ask, gathering Oni-chan into my arms. He turns into putty, but still twitches his tail as if annoyed. Everything is charred, blackened, burned; my allies, at least, look only a little singed.

"We'll blame the damage to the train on a gas leak," Ronin says. "Or some equally dull mortal fear."

I shake my head, incredulous. "But there aren't any gas lines aboard this train—"

"It won't matter," Ronin says, sliding his katana back into its sheath. "Mortals will believe anything I wish them to believe."

Oni-chan hisses at me as I ease him back into his crate. *After everything I've done for you?* he seems to say.

It's going to be a long ride to Kyoto.

FOURTEEN
Kyoto Train Station

Kyoto, Japan

I step off the shinkansen train in Kyoto, anxiety rising. I have faced demons, death gods, and more danger than I ever could have dreamed of surviving—but none of it terrifies me as much as the prospect of my parents' wrath.

"On a scale of one to ten," Shiro says, hopping onto the platform after me, "how pissed are your parents going to be today?"

I doubt numbers could describe my parents' ire. Their fury won't be like a firework, but more like an asteroid plummeting to Earth, one that slams into the surface and chokes the atmosphere with dust. Their anger will linger long after the brightest parts of it have burned out, as will their shame. It couldn't have been comfortable for them to explain my disappearance to the authorities, my teachers, their friends, or the rest of our family. And while Goro's intervention may have bought me some time, it did *not* buy me their forgiveness.

"My parents are very traditional, and very conservative," I say, setting Oni-chan's crate down on the ground as we wait for Goro and Ronin to disembark. "From their perspective, it looks like their daughter ran off to Tokyo with a boy."

"I'm not a *boy*. I'm a kitsune shrine guardian," Shiro says with a sniff.

"They don't know that," I say.

Ronin steps off the train with a short laugh. "And can you really call yourself a kitsune, brother, when you've yet to earn your first tail?"

"I'd rather be tailless than dead," Shiro fires back, snatching Oni-chan's crate off the ground.

As Goro joins us on the platform, he sighs. "You are both fools, hmm? What is done is done, and arguing about it won't help matters."

Ronin turns away from us. "I've made reservations at the Nishiyama Ryokan. Have my things delivered there, won't you?"

With that, he disappears into the crowds on the platform.

"By the gods, I hate him sometimes," Shiro says. Oni-chan growls in his crate. I'm not sure if the little demon agrees with Shiro or if he's just hungry. I'm betting on the latter. It's *always* the latter with him.

As we exit the terminal, my nerves balloon. A thousand different conversations cascade through my head, each one of them ending in embarrassment and humiliation for me. And the look on my mother's face does nothing to help my confidence.

"That's them right there," Shiro says, recognizing my parents from across the station. He waves, then falters. "Your mom looks, er . . . *happy* to see you."

My parents wait in the station's entryway, backlit by the chilly sunlight outside. Mother's lips move, but the space between us swallows up the sound. Now Father turns his head and spots me. He looks even less pleased. Both are dressed for a government function—Father in a conservative black suit and Mother in a gray kimono with a pale pink obi. Mother's formal manner of dress tells me exactly what kind of government function it was—*important*. Which means I'm interrupting something. Perhaps there were memorials held in Grandfather's honor today, many of which I will have missed.

Great.

My parents take me straight home, where I endure their interrogations first, then the police's. I doubt I helped the case much: like Ami, I told the police that Grandfather hid my sister and me in the small shrine's cellar. We saw nothing and heard only screaming. Like Ami, I lied.

But what am I supposed to say? That my family's shrine was desecrated by demons hell-bent on obtaining the last shard of a legendary sword? That my grandfather was murdered by a demon lieutenant of Shuten-doji? That I'm currently recruiting death gods to try to save my family's shrine? *No.* Even after everything I've endured, those answers sound improbable even to *me.*

Once the police are gone, Mother's mood teeter-totters. She's usually so reserved with me—she only hugs Ami and keeps her kind words for Ichigo—but twice now, she's reached for my hand, seemed to remember herself then and withdrawn it. Nothing hurts worse than the promise of love, retracted. My mother has never loved me the way she loves her other children.

We don't argue until I ask to stay at the shrine until the new year.

Father turns to look at me, expressionless. He makes a dark silhouette while standing near the garden windows, keeping his hands clasped behind his back. Mother and I kneel on cushions around the chabudai—a short-legged table used for dining, working, or studying. She shifts her weight, and the lines in her brow deepen. She looks at my father before she says: "I don't think that's wise."

It's a polite way of saying *absolutely not.*

"There should always be a Fujikawa at the family shrine," I say, wishing I could tell them my real reasons for wanting to stay there. The yokai have attacked me three times now—if I live at home, I worry my family could become targets, no matter how many magical wards protect the house. Instead of saying these things, I insist, "It's tradition."

"I'm not sure you can handle the responsibility, Kira," Mother says, lifting her chin. "When you went to Tokyo on 'shrine

business,' you left me with the odious task of explaining your disappearance to the authorities and your school. I know you wanted
to grieve, but running to Goro-san was *not* the answer."

"You embarrassed your mother and me," Father says, his attention trained on the gardens outside. An unspoken warning *again*
lingers in his tone.

"I'm sorry," I say, performing a polite bow to my mother. Shame
hooks into my back and tugs downward, making my shoulder
blades ache. "I didn't intend to make you worry, or to embarrass
you or Father. I only wanted to do what was right, and to honor
Grandfather's memory."

"And yet you were not here for his wake." Father scoffs, shaking his head. "This is why I did not want her spending so much
time with your father, Midori. The man has filled her head with
folklore, rather than facts and figures."

"Grandfather taught me Shinto, not folklore," I say, balling
my hands in my lap. It's hard to keep my tone even, especially in
the face of Father's dispassion for the family shrine. He will never
understand what the shrine means to me, even if he is family;
Father doesn't *want* to understand.

Mother purses her lips, casting her gaze to the floor. The tension tightens between us, so taut I could almost reach out and
pluck the air like a shamisen string. Mother used to be a priestess
at the Fujikawa Shrine. Grandfather required my father to take
her family name when they married. Mother was an only child,
and Grandfather insisted that the shrine remain in the Fujikawa

family. From my grandparents' stories, I know Mother left the shrine days after I was born. Nobody will tell me why. Nobody wants to discuss the events that turned me into my parents' cursed child, an outcast in my own home.

The only place I have ever felt comfortable is the Fujikawa Shrine. I intend to return there, and to *stay* there.

I rise from the chabudai table, step back, and kneel in seiza position. I place my hands on the floor, making a triangle with my thumbs and forefingers, and bow forward. Custom requires I hold the bow for the space of two blinks, then straighten gracefully.

When I sit up, I meet my mother's gaze. "Mother, allow me to honor our family's past by preserving our shrine for the future."

This time, Mother doesn't look to Father—this choice belongs to her. I suspect she knows I'm lying about the attack on the shrine, my trip to Tokyo, Goro, all of it; there's a glimmer of regret in the deep, black mirrors of her eyes. I've lived with this woman for the sixteen years of my life, and yet my mother has always been a mystery to me.

Seconds pass. Mother inclines her head in a nod. "Very well. You may stay at the Fujikawa Shrine through the end of the year, so long as you maintain your grades and do not shame your father and me any further. You are to listen to Goro and respect him as you would me. Am I clear?"

"Yes, Mother," I say, bowing again. My hair slides forward, hiding my smile.

"Good," she says, rising from her seat.

Both my parents leave the room without another word.

I don't arrive at the Fujikawa Shrine until late in the afternoon.

The torii gate at the bottom of the shrine steps leans to one side, its hashira poles propped up with wooden bolsters. Shadows curl against the stairs. I shiver as the temperature plunges. While the trees that line the shrine's steps are evergreen, I can see the tops of the shrine's maples, their bare, skeletal fingers reaching toward the sky.

Part of me doesn't want to climb these stone steps. I'm not ready to see the rest of the destruction, not yet. So many memories linger in this place: brilliant festival days, when people from all over the city would come to watch me dance; serene moon-viewing parties and sunsets spent with Grandfather; the gentle smiles of the other miko; quiet afternoons spent sweeping the cobblestones; and the gentle laughter of children, feeding the koi in our ponds with their parents.

I can't let one nightmare ruin a lifetime of good memories. But today, I'm already weary straight down to the depths of my soul. I spent the better part of the afternoon getting scolded, then ignored by my parents. While I don't blame them for being angry with me—I shamed and terrified them by running away—I wish we could have spent one moment together, honoring Grandfather at the family kamidana. Grandfather deserved at least that much from us.

I pluck a piece of blue-and-white police tape out of the bushes near the torii gate. With a growl, Oni-chan leaps out, startling me. He jumps up to try to catch the tape in his claws. I dangle it for him, laughing as he wiggles his rear end and springs. He snatches the tape away.

"How are you able to walk on shrine grounds, little demon?" I ask him. He cocks his head at me, and then I remember that this ground is no longer sacred. Under my current plan, the shrine won't be rededicated until the last day of December, in a special oharae ceremony that will purify this place.

That is, of course, assuming any of us survive that long.

Still carrying the tape in his mouth, Oni-chan bounds up a few of the shrine steps and stops, looking back at me as if to say, *Aren't you coming?*

With a small smile, I start up the stone steps. My suitcase wheels bang on each ledge, useless. Oni-chan trots ahead of me, flicking his dual tails.

As the shrine comes into view, my spirit dims. Silvery webs still cover half the buildings, making it seem like the gods have stretched a funerary shroud over the main hall. The verandas are curtained off by sheets of leaves caught in cascading webs. Spongy green scum covers the pond, and a thick layer of leaves rests atop the cobblestones. Shadows gather in the courtyards, and I wonder what might be watching me in the growing darkness.

I expected the destruction, even braced myself for it—but nothing could truly prepare me to face the wounds my enemies left on my home.

I am surprised, however, to see buildings framed in neat steel scaffolds. A massive dumpster sits in one of the courtyards, full to the brim with the shrine's broken bones. Someone has started reconstruction, and from the looks of it, they've been at it for several days now. Perhaps O-bei Katayama intends to keep her promises and will make restitution for her crimes.

It doesn't matter what she does, I think. *She'll never be able to bring back Grandfather.*

"Hello?" I call out, as much to hail the kitsune as to break the oppressive silence. Nothing moves. "Shiro? Goro? Is anyone here?"

No answer.

I set my suitcase down. The breeze rustles in the treetops, making their bare branches creak. Turning, I glance back down the front steps, and the memories of *that night* come crawling back to me. I imagine children singing *Kagome, Kagome* in the distance. Pain pricks my palm, and when I turn it over, the places where the paper fox shikigami pierced my skin begin to bleed. I take a step back. Icy talons grasp my heart.

A black butterfly lands on my outstretched hand, feather light. It laps the blood from one of my cuts.

It's sunset, I realize, looking up.

Sunset on the third day.

Darkness gathers on the shrine steps, drawing the heat from the air. The butterfly launches itself from my hand, fluttering down the steps as shadows form into twin poles and a lintel resembling a torii gate. In the space beyond the gate, I see the steps of the Fujikawa Shrine descending into a darkness so deep, it chills my soul.

A man in a conical hat steps through the torii gate. Shadows burst from his clothing like dust. Black butterflies—*hundreds* of them—spread out like a flock of crows, blacking out the sky.

He's here. I press my hands to my chest, afraid my heart might break through my rib bones and leap down the steps.

Shimada tips his hat up. I bow to him. When I rise, I'm surprised to see another figure coming through the torii gate. A girl appears beside him, one who doesn't appear much older than seventeen or eighteen. She's dressed in black samurai armor studded with sharp, silver spikes. Her hair's short and braided to her scalp. The sinuous braids follow the curves of her ears, and she wears black gauges in her earlobes. The armor leaves her arms exposed, allowing me to see the butterfly tattoos beating their wings under her skin. Some of their wingtips lift off her body, leaving ghostly contrails in their wake. Tattoos are taboo, and I don't think I've seen someone with a real one before.

There isn't just one shinigami standing on my front doorstep, but *two*.

"Shimada-sama," I say, bowing again. "Welcome to the Fujikawa Shrine."

Peals of laughter bounce up the steps, chasing away any dignity I might have afforded my guests.

"*Shimada?*" the female shinigami asks, snorting at him. "Is *that* what you've asked them to call you?"

"You will have to forgive Roji, Fujikawa-san," Shimada says to me, closing the shadowy torii gate with a wave of one hand. "She had no manners in life, and death hasn't improved her any."

"Hush, you," Roji says, punching Shimada in the shoulder. "I know you've missed me."

"In a manner of speaking," Shimada replies, resting one hand on his sword.

"So *this* is the girl, eh?" Roji says, turning her attention on me. She scratches a spot under her earlobe and looks sideways at Shimada. "Another Fujikawa with a demon problem, surprise, surprise."

"I figured you would be the most . . . *empathetic* to her plight, Roji," Shimada says with the ghost of a grin. "So be empathetic."

"Empathy isn't my strong suit," Roji says, starting up the stairs toward me. "Killing, on the other hand? Well, there aren't many in this world or the next who are better at it than *me*."

Death's aura clings to her, so sweet and cloying I can almost smell it like incense. Something in her gaze sends a shock wave of fear through my system. She reaches the top of the steps, popping my bubble of personal space. I step back, forgetting I'd left my suitcase a pace behind me, and crash into its side. I tumble to the ground. Pain echoes through my palms—now scraped again— and a sharp blade of rock stabs into my left ankle. I push myself up on my hip, my hair hiding my reddened cheeks from sight.

Roji crouches down in front of me, resting her wrists on her knees. "I didn't mean to frighten you, baka," she says with a grin, and then offers me a hand up. I look down at her outstretched palm—her skin so pale it could be the color of paper. I put my hand in hers, surprised to find her touch cold. Stony.

She helps me to my feet. Shimada joins us at the top of the stairs.

"*This* is the girl you want wielding the Kusanagi?" Roji asks, jerking her head in my direction.

Shimada nods. "It would consume us with fire. The kitsune do not fight with anything but their magic and their claws. That leaves the priestess."

"*Me?*" I ask, almost choking on the word. "But I-I don't know anything about fighting with a sword!"

"Don't worry, kid." Roji grins and claps me on the shoulder. She gives me a small shake, even as I bristle at the word *kid*. "That's where I come in."

FIFTEEN

Fujikawa Shrine

Kyoto, Japan

The next morning, I'm awakened by Roji.

Rudely.

"Get up!" she says, slamming the guest room door open. "We don't have time to waste with sleep!"

I sit up, blinking at the bedside clock. "Roji-san, it's five o'clock in the morn—" A yawn overtakes the rest of what I mean to say.

"And?" she says, putting her hands on her waist and tapping a bare foot. She's dressed in a white crop top and loose, flowing black pants. The top shows off her abdomen, which is covered with the myriad branches of a cherry tree tattoo. Inky butterflies waft across her pale skin. While the tattoos are a work of art, it's hard to call them beautiful. Not when each butterfly represents a life taken.

"Shuten-doji isn't coming *today*," I say, sliding my legs out from under Oni-chan. The cat grumbles at me, yawns, and hops off the bed. "What do you want?"

"To train," she says, snapping her fingers at me. "If you're going to be ready to face the demon god in three weeks, I can't have you tripping over your own feet."

"But we don't have a single shard of the Kusanagi," I complain.

"The shards are Shimada's problem," Roji says, crossing the room and throwing off my comforter and sheets. "You're *mine*. Let's move—we've got a lot to cover before I lose you to that mortal school garbage."

I can't help the irritation that sparks in my chest. I stayed up late last night preparing to go back to school—the police returned my schoolbooks, and most of my teachers emailed me my missed assignments. I need to complete a substantial amount of makeup work by next Monday, four days from now. Honestly, the task feels as impossible as learning kenjutsu swordsmanship by the rise of the blood moon.

"Fine." I groan, swinging my legs off the bed. My toes touch down on the cold floorboards. "Just let me get dressed, okay?"

Roji doesn't move, keeping her arms crossed over her chest.

"Are you going to watch me change?" I ask, feeling anger catch fire in my chest.

She lifts a brow, grinning at me. "Would you like that, or . . . ?"

"Get out," I half shriek, half laugh, grabbing a pillow from the bed and tossing it at her. She catches it easily. When she throws it back, the force of the pillow slams into my torso, pushing me down on the bed.

"Hey!" I say, sitting up and rubbing the tip of my nose. "You didn't have to throw it so hard!"

"No, I didn't *have* to," Roji says with a laugh. "But I *wanted* to, ha!"

Something tells me it's going to be a long three weeks.

After I change into a set of gym clothes—leggings under my shorts with a loose-fitting hoodie—I walk downstairs to Grandfather's kitchen. I'm greeted by all the best breakfast aromas: miso soup, grilled salmon, and daikon pickles and rice. My stomach rumbles. I pull my hair into a messy bun at the top of my head. One of Shimada's black-winged butterflies dances around a light fixture.

In the kitchen, Goro is at the stove, tending to pieces of fish and sautéing vegetables. Shimada sits at Grandfather's dinner table, nursing a mug of tea. *Hold on, shinigami drink tea?* Neither he nor Shiro looks up as I enter—they're absorbed in reviewing maps of the Fujikawa Shrine. The maps are made from paper as thin as an old man's skin and their edges curl up like scrolls.

"Good morning, Kira!" Goro says with a smile, drawing my attention. "Would you like something to eat before you join Roji?"

"You approve of this plan?" I ask. "The one where I, a girl with almost no martial training, kill a demon king *with a sword*."

"Of course!" he replies, handing me a bowl of miso soup.

"With. A. *Sword*," I repeat, as if he hadn't heard me the first time.

"And?" he replies. "Do you expect me to put a holy blade into a shinigami's hands?"

"We don't *have* the Kusanagi no Tsurugi," I say.

"At the moment, no," Shimada says. I turn, and he gestures to the maps on the table. "The blade of the Kusanagi was shattered from tang to tip, and its fifty-two pieces were scattered across Japan. Fifty-one of those pieces have been located by Shuten-doji's forces."

"And the last piece is here?" I ask him.

"Hidden so well, it's survived centuries of attempts on your family's shrine," Shimada says. "It's almost as if Seimei himself has hidden it, eh?"

Shiro grins and winks at me. I roll my eyes.

"This is getting ridiculous," I say, fishing my chopsticks out of a kitchen drawer. I brought my favorite pair from home, the wood coated in smooth red lacquer. They were a gift from the teacher who helped me prepare for my Kōgakkon entry exams. While my father taught me to value hard work over luck, I could use a little good fortune in the coming weeks. Especially today. I bump the drawer with my hip, closing it gently.

"This is how we *win*," Shimada replies as I join them at the kitchen table. "Goro-san says your grandfather never told him your shrine had a shard of the Kusanagi no Tsurugi—did Fujikawa-san ever make any mention of it to you?"

I shake my head, plucking a cube of tofu out of my soup and popping it into my mouth.

Shimada looks back at the maps. "In that case, we may need to try to summon his spirit—"

I nearly choke on my tofu, covering my mouth with one hand to hide a cough. "You can *do* that?"

"Yes," Shimada says, flicking a small crumb of tofu off one of the maps with disdain. My cheeks burn with shame. "I can do that if I must."

Glad to see I'm making a positive impression on our new guests. I eat my soup quietly, picking out the best bits of tofu before lifting the bowl to my lips. The salty, oniony broth wakes up my taste buds, and the warmth braces my spirit. Good, I need some strength to face the day; I'm anxious about joining Roji for training—I usually like to have more time to prepare for things like this so that I don't look like a fool. That's not an option, not now.

Once I've finished my meal, I wash my dishes, thank Goro for breakfast, and head outside into the dark, chilly morning. Night still drenches the shrine. The moon wanes in the sky—after Shuten-doji, time is my next greatest enemy. Some of the shrine's buildings have been destroyed, and their bones reach up into the night, their edges glazed in moonlight. I shiver, realizing I can't feel the presence of the kami here anymore. These grounds have been desecrated; if I'm ever to restore them, I must learn to fight an enemy as ancient as memory.

Despite the early hour, hammers bang and buzz saws growl.

Floodlights focus their beams on the main shrine, where Minami's team appears to be repairing the roof. Two kitsune stand atop the building, silhouetted by the bright lights, going over a set of building plans. I spot Minami on the ground, talking to a small group of yokai. I wave as I pass. She scowls. I don't care if she doesn't like me—she's rebuilding the shrine, and that's what matters.

As one of the largest buildings on the Fujikawa Shrine's grounds, the assembly hall has been used for various community gatherings. It functions as a waiting room for those planning to worship at the main shrine. It's still mostly intact, barring some damage to the verandas on the western side.

This morning, the hall serves as a makeshift dojo.

I slide off my shoes at the door, leaving them outside. The front doors are open to the morning chill. Roji lies on the gleaming wood floor, hands under her head, an ankle propped on the opposite knee. All the furniture has been pushed against the eggshell walls to make enough space for practice.

"It's about time," Roji says. Two wooden bokuto rest by her side. Practice swords. They look just like steel katana, except that they're made from a smooth, blond wood. Roji performs a kip-up, leaping to her feet. She tosses me one of the weapons, which I manage to catch but barely. The tip of the sword swings down and makes a hollow *thok* sound against the wood floor.

Roji knocks my bokuto's blade with her own. "You ever used one of these before?"

I shake my head. Grandfather provided me some with hand-to-hand martial training, but we never had the time to do any sort of kendo or kenjutsu.

"Yeah, I can tell by your grip." Roji swings her bokuto down so fast it whistles through the air, knocking the wooden sword out of my hands. My bokuto clatters to the floor, the impact leaving my hands stinging.

"Hey!" I cry, shaking my hands. Roji laughs, but there's no malice in the sound.

"Lesson one," she says, sliding a foot under the tip of my bokuto, kicking it into the air, and snatching it with no small degree of style. She delivers the wooden sword to me, handle-first. "When your life depends on the sword, your sword depends on your grip."

I take the bokuto in both hands this time, mimicking Roji. Pivoting, I fall into step beside her.

"Your left hand provides the power, and your right hand the precision," she says, pointing to my hands in turn. "While it may seem counterintuitive, you'll want to keep your grip light up top. Hold the sword with your middle, ring, and little fingers."

I relax the tension on my pointer finger and thumb. The grip feels . . . unstable at best. "Won't I drop the sword if I try to block a heavy blow?"

"Sure, you can worry about that—if you're an actress in a samurai movie," Roji says, setting her bokuto aside to rework the positioning of my left hand. "Actual combat isn't flashy, and striking your opponent's blade is a surefire way to break your own. You're better off relying on quick thinking and superior footwork to exploit the weaknesses in your opponent's defenses, thus allowing you to disarm or destroy them."

We spend the next hour developing my footwork, including stances, slide steps, and shuffles, all done while maintaining a proper grip on the bokuto. While Roji makes the movements look effortless, my arm and back muscles begin to ache before long. The one-pound bokuto hadn't seemed heavy at first . . . but Roji snaps at me if I let the tip fall below my knees. I've yet to perform even one practice swing, but my body already complains from the effort.

However, I refuse to acknowledge these pains out loud. I don't wish to seem ungrateful. Not only does Roji's presence mean I have two shinigami committed to my cause, but she's teaching me how to defend myself against the yokai, too. It's what I've always wanted, even if the packaging isn't ideal.

As we stow our bokuto in a closet for the morning, my muscles burn with exhaustion. I won't be able to take a break anytime soon—classes start at eight-thirty and end at three-fifteen. Afterward, Shiro and I will spend several hours searching Kyoto for more shinigami. And then I'll return to the shrine, help O-bei's people with their repairs, and try to get a few hours of homework in before bed.

In manga, the hero responsible for saving the world generally gets a free pass on real life . . . but I don't live in a manga world. The real world keeps moving forward, despite the danger it's in.

I step outside, taking a deep breath of the morning air. The night has already started draining into the west. The last of the stars glitter overhead.

"Hey," Roji says, joining me on the veranda. "I can't tell you things are going to be okay, kid. But if you have to go down, you might as well go down fighting."

I don't reply right away. Roji picks a small scab off her arm and flicks it away. Her tattooed butterflies make lazy loops around her biceps; I've never noticed before, but the tattoo ink varies greatly in intensity, as some of the butterflies have begun to fade from her skin. Others are so new, their black-blue coloration glimmers like wet ink. Several small, butterfly-shaped welts decorate her shoulder, as if she took new souls and pressed them straight into her flesh.

I wonder what color my wings would be, if she wore my soul on her skin.

"Encouraging others isn't one of my strong suits," Roji says with a chuckle. "But I hope you know we *are* here to help."

"Thank you, Roji-san," I say with a bow of my head. "I'm sorry, I'm just . . ."

"Overwhelmed?"

"Yes, that."

"I don't really remember what that feels like," Roji says, leaning against the balustrade and looking toward the pond. "Emotions aren't something we shinigami really feel. But if you remember one lesson from me, it should be this—every situation in death or life is easier to handle if you keep a good grip on it."

"Easy to say for a master," I reply.

Roji grins. "I guess you'd better be a quick study then, eh?"

SIXTEEN

Fujikawa Shrine

Kyoto, Japan

An hour later, I hurry downstairs dressed in a clean school uniform. Kōgakkon's dress code doesn't change—no matter the weather—so I've put on thick black tights under my pleated skirt to keep out the chill. I've also opted to wear a long sweater under my blazer, one that ends a few inches above my hemline and keeps my skirt looking trim. I haven't had time to replace my school bag, so I've borrowed one of Mother's leather carryalls.

The aromas of breakfast still linger in the kitchen; otherwise, everyone's left for the morning.

Everyone, that is, except Shiro.

I find him in the kitchen, leaning against one of the countertops, reading something on his phone. He's styled his hair for once, keeping his long, reddish bangs swept to the side of his face. He looks up with a wolfish grin. Or perhaps it would be better to say *foxish*.

"What do you think?" he asks me, stretching his arms wide to show off his outfit. His clothing, however, catches my attention only insofar as that white shirt strains across his muscular chest. "Do I look the part of earnest high school student Shiro Okamoto?"

"You're going with me?" I adjust my bag's strap on my shoulder, cocking my head at him. "To *school*?"

"That's the plan," he says.

"Security won't allow you on campus unless you're a student," I say.

"I guess it's good that I'm enrolled then, isn't it?"

My mouth drops open. "*How?* Have you even taken an entrance exam? Have you even *been* to school before—"

"Kira," he says with a laugh, placing a finger on my lips. "Rules are for *mortals*."

I tug his hand away. "You're going to embarrass me. I'm already struggling to save face there."

He takes my hand and turns it palm up, exposing the old scabs on my palms. "You may have already lost that battle," he says gently.

I look away. The pain of the past still throbs under my skin.

"Listen, I don't mean to embarrass you," Shiro says, covering my palm with his other hand. "But bullies are the least of our worries. We've been attacked by Shuten-doji's followers three times, and I couldn't live with myself if I wasn't there for a fourth. I promise, I'll follow your lead and try not to stand out, okay?"

It's hard to deny him anything, especially when he's so earnest.

"Okay," I say. "But we'd better get going—you don't want to be late for your first day."

When Shiro and I arrive at school, the other students' whispers tiptoe around us. They range from the mundane to the extraordinary to the downright rude. Some of the students have pity in their voices, saying I've been in mourning for the past week. Other people theorize that the yakuza attacked my family's shrine and I was held hostage while my family scrambled to pay the ransom money.

The girls stare at Shiro, whispering to one another, hiding giggles with their hands.

Who's that new boy? they whisper, making sure their voices are loud enough to hear. *Is he a bodyguard?*

Maybe Fujikawa really did *get kidnapped by the yakuza.*

Her parents don't have enough money for a ransom, baka.

They try to tease apart the nature of our relationship in sideways glances, measuring the inches between our bodies. I spot at least one girl hiking her skirt up a little, and another sliding some gloss on her lips—breaking school rules for a boy they've never even met. They sneak flirty glances at Shiro, but he ignores them.

The boys size him up, shooting him cool glances across the

hall. On occasion, one will give him a short uptick with their head as if to say, *Hey.* I try to pay them no attention, ignoring the worst of the lies. Compared to me, their worlds are so small. I am the girl who consorted with death itself and lived; I have fought demons, outmaneuvered a death god, walked in Yomi, and befriended a kitsune. It's hard to be cowed by gossip now that I've accidentally set fire to a train car full of demonic butterflies.

I am forever changed, forever different, forever set apart from my classmates.

As Shiro and I step into homeroom, my teacher, Mifune-sensei, beckons to us. She rises from her seat as we join her at her desk.

"Welcome back, Fujikawa-san," Mifune-sensei says with a gentle, condolence-filled smile. The adults, at least, are cognizant of the depth of my loss. "I take it that this is Shiro Okamoto, the . . . family friend who will be joining us for the rest of the term?"

"Indeed," Shiro says with a quick smile and charming bow.

"Very well," Mifune-sensei says. "For now, please take a seat next to Fujikawa-san. We should get started."

The school day passes without incident, though it leaves me anxious. I'm behind in all my classes. Several important exams fall right before the next full moon—the blood moon—so I'm stressed. If I fail to keep up with my studies, I'll lose my place at Kōgakkon . . . and then I'd have to change schools *again*. While I may not like some of the students here, Kōgakkon *is* one of the best private schools in the country. If I graduate from this school and have top-notch entrance exam scores, I'll be able to attend any university I want, at home or abroad.

Shuten-doji's already taken so much from me. I won't let him have my future, too.

Shiro excels at playing the dutiful student, going so far as to answer Kurosawa-sensei's most difficult physics questions. He can speak English and perform complex mathematical equations in his head. Shiro wasn't kidding when he claimed kitsune are clever—Kurosawa-sensei delights in stumping his students, but even *he* wasn't able to get the better of Shiro.

"Don't worry, you'll catch up quick," Shiro says as we help clean our homeroom's chalkboards after school concludes. Cleaning the school is a daily ritual all students engage in, no matter their status. "I can tutor you, if you'd like."

"There's just so much to do," I say, wiping the rest of Mifune-sensei's last lecture off the board. "I've missed at least three exams and a paper, and I should have started my bunkasai Culture Day project last week."

He wrinkles his nose. "You're too hard on yourself. Everyone's willing to give you some extra time, Kira."

"I doubt Nakajima will be so . . . understanding," I say, blowing out a breath. The class president of homeroom 3-A, Emiko Nakajima, has high expectations for this year's Culture Day. Every fall, Culture Day festivals are held in schools all over Japan. These events are often open to the public and aim both to demonstrate the skill and talent of an individual school's student body and attract new students to its ranks. And at a school as prestigious as Kōgakkan High School—where parents are often well-known members of Kyoto society—Culture Day is very, *very* important.

Or at least, it used to be.

"All these things seem so meaningless now," I say, arranging pieces of chalk into dotted lines along the blackboard's railing. "After everything we've been through, worrying about a school festival seems silly. How am I supposed to take everyday life seriously?"

Shiro reaches out, smearing a little white chalk on the tip of my nose. I make a face at him. Bad move—I breathe in dry chalk dust, which forces a sneeze from me. He chuckles.

"Hey, you don't have to take life too seriously," Shiro says, tipping my face up with a knuckle under my chin. "Things are going to be okay."

"I'm not so sure," I say.

Shiro steps closer, running his thumb along the edge of my jaw. One of his knees bumps mine. He grins. "Then I'll tell you things are going to be okay until you believe it."

"It won't be easy to convince me," I say. "You might run out of breath."

"Challenge accepted," he says, leaning in.

Footsteps clatter in the hallway. A blush flares across my cheeks. Stepping back from Shiro, I grab my cleaning cloth and go back to scrubbing the chalkboard. Not two seconds later, Mifune-sensei steps into the room.

"Are you two almost done?" she asks. "If so, I'd like to lock up."

"Yes, Mifune-sensei," we say in tandem. As we put away our cleaning implements, a stream of students comes in to grab their things, before moving on to school clubs, cram schools, or afternoons spent at the arcade with friends.

Shiro and I, however, will spend the afternoon in a very different manner: searching all of Kyoto for shinigami.

I step into the school's main courtyard, headed for the gates. The midafternoon chill slides up my skirt. I shiver, clutching my books to my chest. The school's white-faced buildings tower over Shiro and me, blocking the worst of the breeze.

Ayako and her friends congregate around their favorite bench, sipping hot drinks from the vending machines and giggling. One of the girls—I think her name is Nanao—points at me, and the group turns to look like a pack of hungry wolves. Ayako steps forward, her sights set on Shiro, her mouth making a perfect little *o* shape. When she realizes Shiro and I are looking at her, she slips behind a mask of cool indifference.

Shiro places a hand on my lower back, protective and familiar, sending a clear signal to the other girls that I won't be such an easy target anymore. Ayako's eyes narrow, but I turn away from her, unafraid.

Maybe having Shiro around won't be so bad after all.

SEVENTEEN
Fujikawa Shrine

Kyoto, Japan

By the following Monday—ten days after the first shrine attack—Roji's predawn training sessions start to take their toll. My body aches, muscles pumped full of lactic acid, caffeine, and fear. Exhaustion hangs on me like a weighted blanket. I've been up till midnight every night this week, catching up on homework, helping Shimada search for the shard of the Kusanagi, or answering Minami's endless questions about the Fujikawa Shrine.

Any time I want to complain, I turn my eyes up to the sky. Some days, the ghost of the moon is there, haunting me, watching, waiting. It's grown so thin, it's nearly disappeared into the sky.

I yawn as Shiro and I leave Kōgakkon for the day, covering my mouth with the back of my hand. A few snowflakes flutter from low-hanging silver-bellied clouds. One lands on my forehead like a cold kiss.

"You need to get more sleep, Kira-chan," Shiro says as we turn onto the sidewalk.

When did I become your -chan? I think, but bite the words back. It's not like I've given Shiro a reason *not* to use that endearment. "Tell that to Roji, my teachers, and Shuten-doji," I say, adjusting my scarf to hide my lips and nose from the wind's bite.

"Nobody on that list will listen to me," Shiro says, blowing on his hands to warm them. He refuses to use the gloves I bought him yesterday, even if the cold turns the tips of his fingers bright red. "Least of all Roji."

I laugh. "She wants to add afternoon training sessions to my schedule." I take my umbrella out of my bag. I open it, and the wind immediately fills its belly and tugs it skyward. "I told her I can't, not until we find more shinigami."

Without a word, Shiro takes the umbrella handle and holds it over our heads. He leans in close. My cheeks burn so hot with embarrassment, I don't need my scarf to keep my face warm. I look around, checking to make sure nobody has noticed. Public displays of affection—even simple ones—aren't proper, and I would feel bad if I made someone else uncomfortable. Plus, any of my parents' friends might see us, which would infuriate my mother. I've sworn to her that Shiro and I aren't dating.

A middle-aged woman motions at us, clucking to her teenage daughter; but otherwise, nobody's looking our way.

Shiro leans his head on mine. "You know what I think?"

"I'm a priestess, Shiro, not a mind-reader," I reply.

He chuckles good-naturedly. "You'd be happier if you stopped worrying about what other people think of you."

I nudge him off me. "There are rules to being human, you know. Most times it's just easier not to break them."

"Easier, but far less fun," Shiro replies, flattening his ears in mock frustration. "I thought human girls liked sharing an umbrella with handsome boys?"

"Oh, I never said I didn't *like* this," I reply, drawing a grin out of him. "And whoever said you were handsome?"

"Just about *every* girl at your school," he says, grinning at me. "Have I mentioned I have *great* hearing? I can hear them swooning through the walls, *'Oh, Shiro!'*"

"Ugh, gross, they can have you!" I say with a laugh. Now that I'm standing this close to him, I admit it feels good to be noticed, to be *seen* by someone. Especially when that someone is *Shiro*.

We reach the shrine. As we step past the chain link fences, Shiro tugs me behind one of the large *KATAYAMA BUILDING CORP* signs. It's snowing harder now, and big, thumb-size flakes dance in circles across the ground. The cold blows straight through my tights. I shiver. Hooking one finger around my scarf, Shiro tugs it down, stroking my cheek with the back of his finger. His touch sends sunshine racing through my body.

"I don't understand why humans have so many rules," he whispers.

"Don't you?" I say, tilting my face up to his. "I thought kitsune were supposed to be clever."

"We are *terribly* clever," he says, wrapping his arm around my waist and pulling me flush against his body. He's warm. I place a hand on his chest, bracing myself. "But that doesn't mean there aren't any mysteries left in the world."

His fingers dig into my wool coat, gathering me as close as he can. I stand on tiptoe. My blood rushes through my heart and floods my head, making me dizzy. His lips brush mine, tentatively, and he smiles.

"Is this okay?" he whispers, so close our foreheads touch.

But just as I'm about to say, *Kiss me already, baka!* my umbrella flies upward. A large drift of snow dumps down on our heads. "Hey!" I cry. The snow tumbles into my scarf, getting into the warm nooks and crannies and freezing me immediately. Cursing, I take a step back and glance up.

A blue-skinned oni perches on a crumbled bit of masonry wall. He clutches the top spindle of my umbrella in one hand, holding it just out of Shiro's reach. He looks familiar, but I've never seen an ogre this close before: his fangs are stained a urine-yellow color, his skin is pockmarked, his beard scraggly and unkempt. His body odor might be even uglier than he is—a mixture of three-day-old tuna and sweat-stained laundry basket. Despite the cold, he's half-naked, dressed only in a loincloth made of tiger fur.

The ogre makes a kissy face at us, snorting.

"Kiku!" Shiro shouts, grabbing my umbrella back from the

demon. He hands it to me. "Get out of here!"

"You know this *thing*?" I ask Shiro, gesturing at the ogre.

"Unfortunately," Shiro says, eyes narrowed. "Your grandfather always asked me to shoo him away from the shrine."

Kiku wipes his nose with his dirty wrist. "I hear you idiots are gonna fight Shuten-doji. I want in."

"What?" I ask, furrowing my brows. "You're an ogre. Shuten-doji is your *king*."

"I don't bow to no king," Kiku says, spitting on the ground. "Especially not that old bastard. I wish he'd just stay dead."

"Wait, why?" I ask, surprised to find that I care.

"Because!" Kiku roars. "And *because* is a good enough reason for you!"

"*Because* isn't a good enough reason for anyone," I say flatly.

"Fine!" Kiku says, crossing his arms over his chest. "Give me something to do to prove myself, then."

Shiro rolls his eyes. "I don't know, how about you bring us a golden peach from heavenly Takamagahara? Or pluck a feather from the robe of a holy tennin, or some other equally crazy, impossible task?"

Kiku blows out a breath. "Those are baby quests!"

"Then bring me the shards of the shattered Kusanagi no Tsurugi," I say jokingly. "And we'll let you fight with us."

Kiku's eyes grow wide. "Oh, the girlie wants the sword, eh? The shiny bits of sword?" The ogre grins.

Shiro glances at me. "Do you know where Shuten-doji keeps

the shards of the Kusanagi no Tsurugi, Kiku?"

"Of course! I will bring you the sword," he says, hopping off the wall. "And when I do, you will let me help you kill Shuten-doji!" He whoops, loping off into the snow.

"Well, that was, uh, interesting," Shiro says.

"I didn't think he'd take me seriously."

"Did we just send an ogre off on an epic quest?"

I wince. "I think so?

"Don't worry about it," Shiro says. "Kiku may be an oni, but he's mostly harmless. C'mon, I'm in the mood for some ramen. There's a good place just up the street, if you're hungry?"

"Ramen sounds *great*," I say with a smile.

Shiro's favorite ramen shop lies a few blocks away from the Fujikawa Shrine. The building is machiya-style, with elegant wooden lattices over the windows and a fabric drape—known as a noren—hung in front of the door. Golden light melts through the windows. Parting the noren with one hand, I step under the restaurant's eaves. My stomach rumbles.

Inside, the warmth seeps into my pores and burns the cold away. The umami scents waft around us, bold and inviting; and the gentle conversation from other guests wraps me up in a warm, comforting embrace. Like many ramen shops, this restaurant is so small, it can probably seat only ten or fifteen people at a time. There are a few cozy wooden tables, plus space at the bar.

Shiro and I settle at the bar. From where we sit, we can watch the chefs cooking in the kitchen. They're both dressed in black polo shirts, burnt-orange aprons, and matching kerchiefs to hold back their hair. One noodle chef acknowledges us with a big grin, then shouts, "Hey, look who's back! I haven't seen you in ages, how you been, kid?"

"Heihachi-san," Shiro replies to the noodle chef with a toothy smile. "It's been too long. You heard about what happened at the shrine, right?"

"I did. What a shame." As he walks toward us, he dries his hands on a kitchen towel. He's not an imposing man—he stands just an inch or two taller than me. He's stout and barrel-chested, with a clean-shaven face and his long hair tied in a bun. "Glad to see you're all right. You want your usual?"

"Yeah, but this is Kira-chan's first time. Give us a minute?" Shiro asks, sliding a double-sided, laminated menu across the bar. The tips of our fingers touch, and a bit of static jumps from his fingers to mine. I look away, embarrassed.

"Kira-*chan*, huh? She's cute," Heihachi says with a wink at Shiro, which only makes my blush burn brighter. "I'll be right back, then," he says.

Before I can stammer out a response, Heihachi turns and heads toward a back room, where he yells, "Are you done with those vegetables yet, Haruto?"

He's through the door and out of sight before I can hear the answer.

"I like this place already," I say, making sure to dip my words in sarcasm.

"Heihachi's a tease," Shiro says with a smile. "Nothing more."

"How often did you come here?" I ask Shiro. I've never heard him mention this place before, and honestly? I suppose I don't know very much about Shiro as a *person*, outside of shrine life. He's not a stranger, but if I were asked to name any of his favorite things—colors, foods, et cetera—I know I couldn't.

Shiro leans into the countertop, folding his arms in front of him. "Often enough. Ronin hated the company here, so it was the one place I could go and be sure he would leave me alone."

"I didn't know he was following you around," I say, incredulous. ". . . Why bother?"

"Mother never trusted me the way she trusted Ronin," Shiro says with a shrug.

I make a face. "That *can't* be a bad thing." After all, O-bei asked Ronin to give up his *natural life* to serve her as a shinigami. While I understand that kitsune, yokai, and shinigami operate on different moral planes than do humans, what Ronin did to the Fujikawa Shrine isn't acceptable under any moral code.

Except O-bei's, of course.

"I know you see her as a monster," Shiro says, interrupting my thoughts. "But Mother . . . I know she's not good, but she's not all bad. . . . She just is what she is."

"If you're trying to be philosophical," I say dryly, "you're failing."

"Okay, let me explain it this way," he says, pausing for a second as a waitress brings us glasses of water. He smiles at her in thanks, and then continues, "My birth mother used to serve Lady Katayama in the Twilight Court."

"Like Minami serves her now?" I ask.

Shiro nods. "My mother died when I was young, leaving Ronin and me orphaned. Lady Katayama could have sent us away; instead, she took us in. Gave us a home. Loved us, in her way."

"And then she asked one of you to give up his life and become a shinigami," I say under my breath.

"That too," Shiro says, scratching himself behind the shell of one ear. "It's harder for humans to accept the fact that we are all made of darkness and light—there's not a lot of middle ground with your kind."

"There you go again with the *your kind* business," I say, flipping my menu over to look at some of the items on the back. "You sound like your mother when you talk like that, you know?"

Shiro opens his mouth to reply, but before he can get a word out, Heihachi bustles over. "So! Has your girlfriend decided what she wants?" he asks with a cheeky little bow.

My eyes widen, panic fluttering in my chest. "I-I'm not his—"

"We'll both have the tonkotsu," Shiro says.

"Shiro!" I cry.

"Good, good." Heihachi looks at me, then back at Shiro, his grin so wide I hope it makes his cheeks ache. "Don't worry, miss, we make a good one here! I'll be right back," he says, rapping on the bar with his knuckles.

As Heihachi turns away, I glare at Shiro. If we were alone, I might even hit him on the shoulder, but I don't want to draw attention to us. Shiro has managed to embarrass me *twice* today, and I'm not keen on a round three.

"I can order for *myself,* thank you," I say.

"Tonkotsu *is* your favorite kind of ramen," he says. "Am I wrong?"

I don't know *how* he knows I like tonkotsu, but it makes me feel like he has an advantage in our relationship. I *tch*, pulling my phone out of my bag. "I hate that you know all these things about me. I barely know anything about you."

"You know my family's crazy," he says.

"True," I reply. "But that doesn't say much about *you*. I suppose you take a perverse delight in embarrassing me publicly?"

"You make it so easy," he says with a laugh. "What do you want to know? My favorite color, or maybe my blood type?"

"I'm not interviewing you for an idol profile, silly," I say, setting my phone down. "Hmm . . . tell me why you wanted to become a shrine guardian."

"I respect O-bei, and maybe even love her in my own way," Shiro says, leaning back in his chair, "but I didn't want to spend my life in her service."

"I can respect that," I say softly.

Movement draws my attention to the kitchen. A tiny white moth flutters down and lands on Heihachi's shoulder. He brushes it off, nonchalant, but it leaves behind a sprinkling of dust on his shirt. The tiny creature flies toward the pendant lamp overhead, dancing around the hand-blown glass bulb.

I look harder at the man. *It's just a coincidence*, I tell myself. *A shinigami wouldn't hide in plain sight as a noodle chef.*

. . . Right?

The white moth follows Heihachi all over the kitchen. He bats at the thing if it gets too close to the food, but it seems like Heihachi's putting in the effort only for our sakes.

I lean close to Shiro. "Is your *friend* Heihachi a shinigami?"

"Maybe," Shiro says, a grin tweaking one side of his lips.

"Why haven't you tried talking to him before?" I whisper fiercely. "It's not like he doesn't know about what happened at the shrine."

Shiro leans his forearms on the counter. "I haven't asked him, because unlike other shinigami—"

A ball of fire explodes in the kitchen. Glass shatters, men shout. Heat billows toward us, searing my skin. I stumble away from the bar, nearly tripping over my own feet. One of the chefs rips a burning kerchief off his head. Hurling the fabric to the ground, he stamps the fire out. Heihachi grabs a fire extinguisher. A plume of white smoke billows from the extinguisher's mouth.

A cat leaps through the extinguisher's cloud with a yowl. He lands on one of the hot grills, not bothered by the heat, and snatches a piece of chicken in his jaws. Steam rises off his paws. When our eyes meet, I swear he's grinning through the mask of white flame retardant he now wears.

I'd know that face anywhere. Those mismatched eyes. *Those scars.*

"Oni-chan!" I cry, racing up to the bar. "What are you doing here?"

"Catch that cat!" Shiro says, leaping over the counter. When Shiro dives for him, Oni-chan rockets off the grill, bounds off Shiro's shoulder, and lands on the bar. The nekomata slips on the lacquered surface, knocking our chopsticks and condiments to the ground. Before he can leap away, I scoop him into my arms.

"Bad kitty," I say, taking the chicken breast out of Oni-chan's mouth. The cat makes a grab for the meat with his paws, flattening his ears against his skull, beating his tails against my abdomen with a growl. The sound makes his body wind up, tight as a coil. I set the pilfered chicken on the countertop, then cradle the cat against my chest. It keeps him from getting any purchase against my body.

Cursing, Shiro rights himself. He rubs a set of red welts on his forehead, left behind by Oni-chan's claws. "For heaven's sake," he says, checking the tips of his fingers for blood. "You could have just asked!"

Oni-chan makes a sound that's somewhere between a meow and a crow, as if he's pleased with himself for causing so much trouble.

"Is that cat yours, Kira-chan?" Heihachi asks, setting the fire extinguisher down with a metallic *thunk*. The tiny, feather-headed moth now clings to the top of his bun, shaking.

"Sort of," I say, trying to keep hold of Oni-chan, who has become a wild, bucking, clawed thing. Even if Oni-chan isn't *technically* my cat, I still feel responsible for his actions. "I am *so* very sorry, Heihachi-san. We'll pay for the damages."

I try to bow deeply, but with Oni-chan in my arms, my attempt is anything but graceful. The nekomata growls at the deepest point of my bow. As if I needed any more embarrassment today, both Heihachi and Shiro break into peals of laughter.

"There's no need to reimburse me for the damages," Heihachi says to me, once he catches his breath. "I think you have enough to worry about, Kira-chan."

Maybe it's the gentleness in his tone. Maybe it's because for the last week, I've shouldered the blame for everything that's gone wrong. Maybe it's the pressure, maybe it's the fear. Maybe I'm just too exhausted for even one more thing. But I drop Oni-chan to the ground and cover my face with my hands, trying not to care that my fingers smell like chicken grease, cat fur, and copper.

I don't just cry; I *sob*.

"Oh no!" Heihachi cries. "What did I say? I'm so sorry!"

"Nothing, Heihachi-san," Shiro says, putting an arm around my shoulders. He pulls me into a hug, tucking the crown of my head under his chin. "It's been a rough week."

"I'm sorry," I say between each sob. "I'm sorry, I'm so sorry—"

"No more apologies," Heihachi says, shooing away his employees. He motions to a booth. "Come, come. I will feed you, and you will feel better, hmm?"

As Heihachi fetches us bowls of tonkotsu ramen, I wipe a mess of cat fur and tears off my cheeks. Shiro's right, it's the best I've ever tasted and it *does* make me feel better. The pork broth has the right amount of bite, and the umami flavors dance across my tongue. Even Oni-chan gets his own bowl. Heihachi tells us that he makes the noodles by hand each morning, a practice that has been in his family for centuries.

A white moth lands on the edge of a serving tray, antennae twitching. It's a small, delicate creature with a furry gray body and speckles on its wings.

"Heihachi-san," I say, setting my chopsticks down beside my bowl. "That isn't an ordinary moth, is it?"

"No," he says with a small, sad shake of his head. "She isn't."

She? I wonder.

"I've heard about what you're doing," Heihachi says, coaxing the moth to climb onto his fingers. "I would pledge myself to your cause, but I'm afraid I wouldn't be much help."

"Why not?" I ask.

"I don't kill," he says, cupping the moth in his hands. "Not since this little one. She and I have a bargain, hmm? We keep each other safe."

"You wouldn't have to kill anyone, Heihachi-san," Shiro says.

"Except Shuten-doji," Heihachi says softly. "That's what a cabal of shinigami does, right? It doesn't just destroy a being's physical body, but its soul as well?"

I glance sideways at Shiro. He clenches his teeth but doesn't reply.

So I do.

"Yes," I say. "The plan is to destroy Shuten-doji, body and soul, and stop the darkness he wishes to draw over the world. I wish to avenge my grandfather's life, and protect the shrine that my family has tended for generations. We could use your help, Heihachi-san."

Heihachi blows out a breath, pushing his hat off his head. His gray-white moth launches itself in the air, beating its wings in front of his face. He extends his index finger to the moth, which hops over his finger and flicks its antennae at him, agitated.

"Sana seems to like you," Heihachi says, running the tip of his finger down the moth's back. "You've won her over, and if you have her support, you will have mine as well. I won't lift a sword, but I can lend my strength to the cabal rites."

I press my hands together in front of my sternum and bow. *Three.*

EIGHTEEN
Fujikawa Shrine

Kyoto, Japan

When Shiro and I arrive home from school on Tuesday, we find not one, not two, but *three* shinigami in the main office, discussing battle plans with Goro.

Everyone looks up as we enter the room, which has been turned into a makeshift headquarters. Maps cover every horizontal space, held in place by mugs, stacks of wooden ema plaques, and tissue boxes. Black butterfly dust hovers in the air. Shimada's butterflies cling to the rafters. Heihachi's small white moth, Sana, flutters among them.

Shimada stands with Goro by the largest table, pressing two knuckles into the tabletop. Roji slouches in a swivel chair on the opposite side. Heihachi leans against another table, his back to the door.

"Shiro-kun! Kira-chan!" Heihachi says, turning as we walk in. "It's so good to see you both!"

He's here. A shot of relief courses through me.

"Thank you for coming, Heihachi-san." I bow to everyone. "I'm grateful to see you here."

Heihachi returns my bow. "It is an honor to serve with such distinguished shinigami."

"That's right," Roji snorts, propping her boots up on the table. "I'm a *distinguished* lady."

"Hardly," Shimada says, shoving her feet off his desk. Roji snickers as her boots thump on the floor. "I'm glad the two of you have arrived. Shiro, will you and Roji please show Heihachi-san around the shrine this afternoon?"

"Me?" Roji says, taking a knife from her pocket and flipping it open. She snaps it closed with a flick of her wrist. "And pray tell, what is your lordship going to do while we peasants labor in the fields?"

"Our efforts to find the shard by hand are failing," Shimada says, gesturing to Goro and me. "We must try another method."

"Like?" Roji asks, flicking her knife open again.

"We need to speak with the shrine's last head priest," Shimada says, turning to me. "Perhaps your grandfather will have the information we need."

"You want to summon my grandfather's spirit?" I half whisper, awed and thrilled. I would give anything to have the chance to see Grandfather again, even if it's only to say goodbye.

Shimada nods. "The sun will be setting soon, and its last light may help to draw a priest to my side. Show me where your grandfather died."

With an excited shiver, I follow Shimada and Goro from the office and into the main courtyard. The sun drops in the sky, leaving behind peachy splashes of orange and red. The late autumn chill stings my skin and sucks the warmth from my bones.

I lead them through the shrine, passing a crew fixing the cracks in the haiden's walls. O-bei's people rise at dawn to work on shrine repair and fortifications—I've grown accustomed to the sound of banging hammers, shouting foremen, and beeping machinery. O-bei has kept her promise to me; if I can manage to find a few more shinigami, I'll be able to return the favor.

The motomiya still has the ghosts of police tape clinging to it. I tug a bit of blue tape away, taking splinters of old wood with it. A black spider crawls across one of the beams, and I recoil, remembering the sound of the jorōgumo's feet slicing up the verandas. Inside, the shadows have already settled in for the night, making themselves comfortable among the offerings at the altar.

Shimada steps inside and draws a deep breath. "The death is fresh," he says.

"Ten days now," Goro says, halting beside me. He places a comforting hand on my shoulder, but it trembles. "I am sorry, Kira, but I should not take part in this ritual. Will you forgive me if I excuse myself?"

"Of course," I say.

Shimada kneels on the floorboards. He glances over his

shoulder at me, then inclines his head. I step inside and kneel beside him.

"Close your eyes," Shimada says. "You shouldn't watch this part."

I do as he says. Closing my eyes, I listen to his chanting, which is done in a language I don't recognize. Its words can't possibly belong to this *earth*.

His voice grows stronger, bolder, as the room chills. Gooseflesh prickles along my forearms. A ghastly energy fills the room, one that digs into my shoulders like cracked fingernails and drags itself down my spine. The small hairs at the back of my neck lift and ache as if they are being plucked out, one by one.

My next inhalation is a shudder, not just a breath.

"Hello, wanderer," Shimada says. I open my eyes, expecting— no, *hoping*—to find Grandfather there. Instead, a different specter flickers into sight before us.

I gasp and shrink back. *"Grandmother?"*

The old crone's missing her lower half—intestines dangle from her rent body in ramen noodle–like loops and clumps. Half her face is crushed, deforming her eye socket. Her brow and eyelid are stripped away, leaving her eyeball naked. Grandmother's been dead for several years, after someone pushed her off the station platform and into the path of a moving bullet train. Or so the story goes. I never saw the body . . . or what was left of it, apparently.

"Sit up straight, Kira!" she commands. "How many times have I told you it's rude to stare?"

"Yes, Grandmother." My spine obeys, snapping straight and rigid as a katana. My eyes finally settle on the space above the crown of her head, so it appears I'm looking *at* her. If she senses I'm not giving her my full attention, she'll scald me with her words. "I'm sorry, Grandmother."

Grandmother turns her gaze on Shimada. "And who are you? One of my husband's lackey priests? Or another poor beggar taken in by the shrine?"

"Not exactly," Shimada says with a grin. "Your granddaughter calls me Shimada."

"You're ugly," Grandmother tells him.

"Well, Fujikawa-san, death isn't kind to any of us," he replies.

Grandmother glares at him for a moment. I open my mouth to defend him, to talk Grandmother down, to say *anything* to salvage the situation . . . but to my surprise, Grandmother bursts into laughter.

I don't think I've heard Grandmother laugh before. *Ever.*

"Who knew a shinigami could have a sense of humor, eh?" she says. To my horror, I think she tries to *wink* at me. Her rent eyelid makes it only a third of the way across her eyeball. She plucks at a strand of her intestines. "On a scale of one to ten, how awful do I look? We don't have mirrors in this realm, you know. Not like I can see for myself."

There aren't words to hide the truth, so I turn my eyes down to the ground.

"Must be bad." Grandmother cackles, flinging her intestines at my face. I duck, but they pass right through me, misty and cold. "That's why Ichigo's always been my favorite grandchild—he tells the sweetest lies. Well, what do you want, anyway? I suppose it must be something awful, Kira, if you've enlisted the aid of a shinigami."

"It is urgent," I say, focusing on a chunk of hair still clinging to her head. "We need to talk to Grandfather, if he's available."

"Hmm," she says, scratching what's left of her belly. "So Hiiro's dead, then?"

Fear strikes a fierce chord in my chest. I exchange a glance with Shimada. "Yes, for more than a week now. . . . You haven't seen him?"

"He hasn't come to greet the Elders yet," Grandmother says. "Which means he hasn't managed to cross over, the old fool. Just as directionally challenged in death as he was in life."

"That's not unusual," Shimada says to me. "Time moves differently in Yomi, and souls will sometimes linger with their shinigami for the space of many human months."

"What would happen if Grandfather's soul wasn't reaped by a shinigami?" I ask. "I was there when he died, after all. There was no shinigami to help him."

Shimada slides his hands into his wide sleeves, as Grandfather used to do. "Shinigami would have been drawn to the shrine in the wake of so much death. Someone must have intercepted your grandfather's soul."

"That's not what I'm asking," I say, balling my fists in my lap.

"I want to know what happens to human souls when they are *not* reaped by a shinigami."

"You know the answer to that question, priestess," Shimada says.

I do, but I want my fears to be articulated so I know they're real. Someone must have found my grandfather's wandering soul. Someone must have given him respite, and sheltered him until he was ready to accept his death. I hope he and all the other priests here at the Fujikawa Shrine are guarded by someone wise, kind, and noble. I hope someone like Shimada found them, each and every one.

Because if Grandfather's soul was allowed to wander, he most certainly would become yokai. My heart breaks over the mere *idea* of Grandfather being forced into such a wretched state.

"Don't worry about that old prude, Kira," Grandmother says with a rusty chuckle. "Unless there is a demon that enjoys giving *lectures*, your grandfather is too high and holy to become a yokai."

"If he is not here"—I suck in a breath and steel myself, pushing away my fears for now—"might there be someone else Shimada-sama and I can ask about the missing shard of the Kusanagi no Tsurugi, sword of the Sun Goddess?"

Grandmother rubs her chin. "So, that's what you're after, eh? What would you want with that thing?"

"We need it to strike down Shuten-doji, once and for all," I say.

Grandmother's eyes open wide in shock—or at least as wide as they are able without tumbling from what's left of their sockets.

"Shuten-doji? Even I know the horrors of that name—what sort of trouble have you gotten yourself into, child?"

"Kira inherited her place in this," Shimada says. "She deserves no blame for the conflict ahead."

"And you've taken it upon yourself to help her, Lord Death?" Grandmother says with a scoff. "Do you think yourself a hero?"

Shimada doesn't reply right away, nor does he flinch under Grandmother's critical gaze. "I have my own mistakes to make amends for, Fujikawa-san."

"And what happens if you find this shard, eh?" Grandmother asks. "You can't slay a demon with a sliver of a sword, you'd need the whole thing!"

"Exactly," Shimada says, arching a brow. "If we can find the shard hidden in the Fujikawa Shrine, our next step would be to steal the remaining shards back."

"From Shuten-doji?" I ask.

"Who else would we steal them from?" Shimada asks.

"Hmph," Grandmother says. "Very well, then. I will go consult with the other ancestors and see if they know anything about your precious sword. Don't move. I'll return shortly."

Grandmother dissipates into the air. Shimada and I do as she says, not even chancing conversation. Minutes pass. The longer I sit like this, with my feet tucked under my seat bones, the more the tips of my toes begin to tingle. It was barely noticeable when I was distracted by conversation; now it's all I can think about.

I'm not sure how long we wait for Grandmother to reappear;

but when she does, she comes as quickly as she went. All the contempt has been drained from her, leaving only the chill of death in its wake.

"They say they cannot tell us where the last piece of the Kusanagi lies." Grandmother toys with the edge of her kimono sleeve, twisting it, fretting. I'd get lectured for playing with my clothing like that; but Grandmother's so agitated, she doesn't even realize her eye has popped out of its socket again. "They say that information was passed down through the generations, from one high priest to the next. Because we are not high priests of the Fujikawa line, they refuse to share the location of the last shard with us."

"If we can't find the last shard, the Fujikawa Shrine will burn," I say. "Just like it did five hundred years ago. Is that what they want?"

"Don't get salty with me, girl!" Grandmother snorts hard enough to suck her eyeball back into place. "I'm just the messenger. I don't make the rules."

"Can we speak with the Elders?" I ask, rising to my feet. "Surely, we could make them see reason—"

"These are the spirits of men dead for centuries, Kira," Grandmother says, shaking her head. "Tradition means everything to them, and they do not see the world the way you do."

I shift my weight. "Well, if *we* can't find the shard, perhaps Shuten-doji won't, either."

"Once Shuten-doji returns to this realm, he will never cease his assault on your shrine until he has what he desires, or until he is dead," Shimada says gently, rising too. "Your only option is to destroy him."

"We can do that with a cabal," I say.

"Assuming we have enough shinigami for one," Shimada says. "Failing that, we can slay his physical vessel again and force him back into Yomi for a time. But you will only burden tomorrow with the problems of today."

"As this family has done for centuries," Grandmother says. "Listen, shinigami—I do not want my granddaughter to have to fight this monster for the rest of her days. I will intercede with the family Elders on your behalf, *but* . . ."

My heart lifts in my chest, beating a little faster. "But?" I ask.

Grandmother peaks what's left of her eyebrow. "I want better offerings made on my behalf at the family kamidana. You've ignored it for months, Kira. How can you expect help from your ancestors if you've failed to remember them?"

Dropping to my knees, I bow so low my forehead nearly touches the ground. "I'm sorry, Grandmother. I'll remedy the family kamidana immediately, and care for it daily."

"See that you do," Grandmother says. "And as for you, shinigami—*if* the Elders are willing to impart their wisdom, I will find you in the realms of the dead."

"Very well, Fujikawa-san," Shimada says. "Thank you."

Grandmother inclines her head a few degrees. "Just don't hold your breath. All the dead have left are traditions, and they cling to them like caged monkeys that have been given grapes. Good luck."

As Shimada and I step outside, the evening chill wicks the heat from my clothing. I pause on the motomiya steps and look up to the sky, where a handful of stars have already opened their eyes. The last of the day glows faintly blue on the horizon, every minute hurtling us closer and closer to the month's end. The waning moon now looks like a grimace.

We've been running out of time since the night Grandfather died.

"This fight keeps getting more and more complicated," I say with a sigh.

Shimada chuckles. "You chose to meddle in the affairs of the gods."

"As did you," I say.

Shimada tips his hat back to gaze at the night sky. "You and I are too honorable for our own good."

"You'd think that would be a compliment," I say.

"I have taken hundreds of thousands of dying souls under my wing. I have eased the suffering of men and women dying on the battlefield; I have stood beside executioners, walked into the depths of prisons, and held children weak with starvation. Eventually, all lives end," Shimada says, stretching an index finger into the air to provide a perch for one of his black-winged butterflies. "The dead cling to tradition because we have forgotten what it means to breathe. We can afford to be rigid, unchanging—something that, by definition, the living cannot be. But honor means very little in Yomi."

"Then why do you still practice it?" I ask. "Why come here to fight my demons?"

Shimada launches the butterfly in the air. "By protecting others, I save myself."

"Save yourself from what?" I ask, furrowing my brow.

Shimada does not answer me immediately; nor does he look at me. After a few moments of silence, he steps off the veranda, heading through the shrine's courtyard. "I'm going out to reap," he says without looking over his shoulder. "I will see you tomorrow, Kira. Please make sure Roji doesn't kill Heihachi-san before we can put him to work. She is good, but she doesn't suffer kindness."

"Wait, Shimada-sama," I cry.

He disappears into the shadows, leaving me to wonder what a death god might fear.

NINETEEN
Kōgakkan High School

Kyoto, Japan

Within days, the snows come for real.

I usually love the cold season, especially at the shrine's high elevation, where snow hushes everything with a thick white blanket. In winter, the shrine's eaves glitter with icicles, and the world smells pristine and pure.

But today, the fog creeping through the shrine fills me with a deep sense of foreboding. My anxieties shook me awake before my alarm, and I spent the morning worrying about everything from the upcoming Culture Day festivities to Shuten-doji to the scuff on my favorite shoes. Anxiety likes catching me alone and unawares. It's been worse lately, especially as the second week comes to a close.

Shuten-doji has become an obsession; I fall asleep reading articles about him on my phone, and sometimes catch myself humming *Kagome, Kagome* in the shower.

I've never laid eyes on him, and yet I see him everywhere. Every time I spar with Roji, I sense Shuten-doji's gaze on me. When I search for the missing shard with Shimada, Shuten-doji seems to inhabit every shadow. No matter what I do, he's there. Watching. Waiting.

"You okay?" Shiro asks as we walk to school. "You've been quiet this morning."

"I'm fine," I say, shooting him a thin smile.

"Liar," he says, and reaches out to take my hand. Normally, I'd try to pull away from this sort of gesture in public; for now, I crave the reassurance. I walk a little closer, letting our long coats hide our hands from sight. He squeezes my hand. I squeeze back.

The snows have hushed Kōgakkan's grounds. Students hurry across the quad, tucked tight into their coats, heads down. Umbrellas dot the outdoor areas like winter flowers. Inside, students shake snow from their hair and brush the icy flakes off their shoulders. And everyone comments on the strange depth of the December cold.

Despite my sense of foreboding, the day feels unremarkable. One class drags its feet by, stumbling into the next. My teachers blare on. Students take dutiful notes around me. On days like this, it seems crazy that everyone around me remains so blissfully unaware of the dangers barreling toward us.

There are days I wish I was like them, and days I'm glad not to be.

After school, Shiro waits for me outside homeroom, where Hotohori-sensei asked me to stay behind to discuss my grades. Rather than lecture me while I remain in my seat, she and I lean against her desk, staring out at her empty classroom. While all my teachers are excellent, I sense that Hotohori-sensei really cares about me as a person.

I'm worried about you, she says.

You always seem tired these days, but today, the burden seems greater than usual.

I'm concerned your grades may slip if this continues much longer.

Is there something I can do to help you, Fujikawa-san?

I wish I could tell her what's going on in my life, but honesty won't help either of us. She's right that I'm tired all the time: if I'm not at school, I have a sword in my hand. If I'm not training with Roji, I'm working on learning my mudras with Shiro or Goro. If Shiro and I aren't out looking for shinigami, I'm holed up in my bedroom doing homework.

As much as I try not to complain about my situation, I'm exhausted. Plain and simple.

When I emerge, Shiro's leaning against the wall outside, alone. He looks up at me. "Everything okay?" he asks, twitching one of his ears.

"Okay enough," I say. Hotohori-sensei wasn't wrong to pull me aside—my grades have inched downward, though not by much.

I'm fighting hard to keep my head above water, so it doesn't help to have my failings pointed out. Then highlighted. And underscored.

We head down the stairs. "I don't know how you stand it," Shiro says, pinching the bridge of his nose between his thumb and forefinger. "Day in and day *out*, listening to someone blather to you about things you should already *know*."

"What do you mean, things I should already know?" I ask as we head out the door into the quad. The world feels chilly as an icebox. An arctic wind blasts the school grounds, and I button my woolen peacoat against the cold. "I mean, I might be *good* in school, but it's not because I already *know* these things."

"Humans," Shiro says with a *tsk*, shaking off the cold. "I don't know how your kind have survived so long without inherited memories."

"We have those," I say smugly. "We just call them stories."

"Yeah, but you aren't *born* with those stories in your head," Shiro says, sidling a little closer, blocking me from the worst of the wind. "I remember things that happened to my ancestors. The stuff they knew. Mathematics. Languages. History. Art. We . . ."

But he trails off, his eyes widening. He's looking at something on my shoulder.

"What's wrong?" I ask, glancing down.

A white moth alights on my peacoat. It opens and closes its wings, the tips of which are frosted with ice crystals. Its fuzzy body looks soft to the touch, its antennae bushy as tiny pipe cleaners.

It has a little white furry ruff around its head, as if outfitted for winter.

But I know better—moths hibernate through Kyoto winters.

This isn't a living moth.

The sound of steel against scabbard rings through the courtyard. I look up.

The Shinigami in White stands inside the school gates, blocking the main exit. Her moths spiral around her in a snowy cyclone, terrible to behold. She's still clad in her white kimono, but it's accentuated with a white fox fur ruff. Shiro sees the fur and curls his upper lip.

She sees Shiro's expression and grins. "A gift from Tamamo-no-Mae, General to Shuten-doji the Endless," she says, stroking the fur. "Though I should like one in red as well."

"What do you want with us?" My voice is little more than a terrified whisper.

"You know what I am here to do," she says, lifting her sword. She levels the blade at my chest. "I have been commanded to take your life. I am sorry to do so before your appointed time, priestess, but I must do as my master commands."

"Apology not accepted," Shiro says with a growl. Shoving his palms forward, he performs an impressive set of tuts, summoning a glittering, brilliant torii gate made from light. Strange runes twine in ribbons around its hashira poles. Before I can ask Shiro what's going on, he grabs me by the hand and plunges us through. The light settles over my skin, crackling and popping till it renders me translucent as a ghost.

"Fox invisibility." The Shinigami in White sniffs, scanning the courtyard with eyes as sharp as knives. "How utterly predictable. You may be able to hide from me, but you'll never be able to escape. Not for long."

We're . . . invisible?

Shiro presses his hand into the small of my back, ushering me toward the school. The Shinigami in White dashes to the place she last saw us standing, swinging her sword in an arc. The blade whistles through the air, making the snow flurry around her. I shudder to think what it would do to my flesh.

"Where are you, little birds?" she asks in a lilting, patient voice.

The Shinigami in White blocks the only way out of the school. There are doors out the back of the building, but to use them, we'd need a key card from one of the school's staff members. If we want to escape, we'll have to lose the Shinigami in White in the warrens of Kōgakkan's hallways.

Shiro must agree. He pauses a few feet away from one of the school's large, double-wide doors and tuts a mudra I don't recognize. In an instant, the air in the courtyard seems to detonate, blowing all the doors to the school open with a loud metallic *bang!*

We sprint inside. The Shinigami in White scans the courtyard, trying to ascertain which of the doors we went through. Shiro takes me by the hand. I follow him into the school.

"How long will the invisibility last?" I whisper.

"A few minutes, if we're lucky," he says, looking for an open classroom. "I've never used my invisibility magic on two people before. I doubt we'll get out in time—the school is well-fortified. We should hide and call the others."

We jog down a hallway, finding every classroom locked for the day. Desperate, I try the door to the teachers' office, relieved to find it open. We slip inside. The office is empty, except for old Araki-sensei snoring over her desk. She startles awake as the door clicks behind us, her glasses askew, a bit of drool drying on her chin. I'd laugh if our lives weren't in danger.

While she gets up to make coffee, Shiro and I sneak to the back of the room, passing the other teachers' desks. We step into the coat closet at the back, careful not to make a sound. The dark closes around us. Shiro and I tuck ourselves behind a large cluster of flags in the corner, and under a set of moth-eaten, musty winter coats. Neither of us dares speak, but Shiro's hand finds mine in the dark. He squeezes tight, and I squeeze back.

The minutes stretch so long, they might as well be hours.

"Hey!" Araki-sensei, her voice muffled by the closet door. "Who are you? What are you doing in here? Is that a *sword*?"

I press my lips together, praying silently that the Shinigami in White doesn't harm Araki-sensei.

"Be quiet, woman," the Shinigami in White says. Her wooden geta sandals click on the linoleum floor. Getting closer.

No, I whisper in my head. *No, no, no. Turn around, go away.* My palm grows sweaty in Shiro's hand.

"Only authorized personnel are supposed to be in the school after hours," Araki-sensei says. "I'm calling the police."

"Very well," the Shinigami in White says. "See how much good it will do you."

There's a loud *ding!* like the sound of one of the school's old phones being smashed against the floor. Araki-sensei shrieks, so high and piercing, it makes my blood's temperature drop. I shut my eyes and bite my lip to keep quiet. All the memories of the night Grandfather died rush back at me, taunting me from the closet corners.

Coward!

Your grandfather's dead because of you!

Everyone will die because of you!

The shinigami's voice breaks through the closet door again: "Get out, or I'll kill you."

A weeping Araki-sensei must comply with the demand, because the door to the teachers' office slams a few seconds later.

Click-clack.

The Shinigami in White's steps draw closer.

Click-clack.

She takes her time, rummaging through the room.

Click-clack.

A shadow falls over the line of light on the floor. I hold my breath, my heart bashing itself against my ribs.

The door opens.

I can't see the shinigami's face, nor any part of her besides the hem of her pale kimono. A single moth lands on her toe. I wonder if it can see me, shrouded in musty school flags and shadows, or if

Shiro's spell has worn off or worn down.

After several torturous seconds, the shinigami closes the door.

I don't breathe again until the office door closes, too. Then Shiro and I slump together, our shoulders touching. We don't risk so much as a word. He leans down and presses a kiss into my hair, breathing in deep. It'd be romantic if I weren't so terrified all my insides were about to become my outsides.

My phone rumbles in my pocket. Cursing in my head, I yank out my phone and check the messages.

It's from Roji: *Send me your location now—we'll open a torii gate for you. O-bei's here and she says your life is in danger.*

I drop her a pin of my current coordinates, then type back to her. *There's a shinigami here, at my school—*

A white moth flutters down and lands on my screen. Its little pipe-cleaner antennae twitch as if to say, *Caught you.*

"Oh no," I whisper, fear gripping me.

"Move!" Shiro kicks the closet door open. He darts out first, looking right, then left. "Hurry," he says, offering me a hand. We race past the teachers' desks, papers fluttering in our wake, to the big bank of windows on the far wall. I throw the latch on the closest one, but it's painted shut. Wire mesh tempers the glass pane. Shiro punches the window, but it doesn't shatter.

"Try the other ones!" I whisper fiercely, hurrying to the next window and fiddling with the lock. None of them budge. My heart pounds in my throat, and I beg the latches to move. "Can you use the door-opening spell again?!"

"That's an air pressure spell!" Shiro shouts. "It won't work on—"

The door to the teachers' office explodes open. A cloud of white moths swirls into the room, heralds of my would-be killer. I spin, putting my back to the wall of windows.

"Enough!" the Shinigami in White shouts. "You die, *now.*"

"I don't take orders from dead people!" Shiro shouts. A plume of fire explodes through the room, roaring over the desks and setting their surfaces alight. The Shinigami in White leaps through the flames, brandishing her blade. Shiro dodges her first swing, then counters her second by grabbing a desk and flipping it upright. The Shinigami in White's sword slams into the wood. Papers, lamps, staplers, and wire baskets roll off the desk's surface, bouncing off her shoulders and body, and then crashing into the floor. The shinigami shrieks with rage, trying to wrench her sword free.

With a shout, Shiro throws his shoulder into the desk. It topples over with a crash, trapping the Shinigami in White from the hip down. She claws at the wooden desk, her sword just out of reach. Shiro won't be able to hold her off much longer, not without help.

And that's when I spot the sasumata. Every school in Japan has a set of these polearms—they look like long, blunted pitchforks. I grab two from the wall rack and rush across the room, tossing one to Shiro. He snatches it from the air, leaps onto the desk drawers, and slams the sasumata's prongs around the Shinigami in White's torso and upper arms. She swears and struggles, but Shiro keeps her trapped against the floor. When she tries to tut a spell, I leap forward, capturing her right arm against the desk's back flank.

Shiro looks up at me and grins. "You're getting good at this."

"I guess that's one way to put it," I say with a grimace. The Shinigami in White grabs my sasumata with her free hand. I lean my full weight on the pole, engaging the calf muscles in my legs. I'm holding her, but barely.

"Now what will you do?" the Shinigami in White asks us. "Keep me captive till the room burns down? Or hope your mortal police arrive in time to save you?"

"Please, Yuza darling," someone says from the hallway. "Do you really think I'd let you kill an ally of the Twilight Court?"

I turn. O-bei stands in the doorway with a smirk. Even in the world of the living, she looks every bit as ethereal as she did in Yomi—her furisode is made from black silk patterned with glowing white chrysanthemums and shaded with the red shadows of butterflies. She wears her hair in an elaborate updo, and when she steps into the room, her delicate hair ornaments twinkle and ring.

"Damn you and your lies, Katayama," Yuza—the Shinigami in White now has a name—wheezes from the ground.

"I sent my son to stop you the first time," O-bei says, strolling to my side. "But since you are so very persistent, I thought a personal visit might be more . . . impactful?"

O-bei knew about the train attack, and she didn't warn us? I shoot a dark look at Shiro. He narrows his eyes, but otherwise, his expression is unreadable.

"I'll kill you all," Yuza snaps.

"I see you are succeeding in that goal," O-bei replies, sounding bored.

Yuza hisses, but she's interrupted by the sound of heavy boots in the hallway. "Did you find them?" Roji calls. She pokes her head into the teachers' office, her eyes going wide when her gaze lands on Yuza. "By the gods, is that *Yuza of Osore*?"

"Indeed," O-bei replies.

Roji blinks. "Whoa. Do you want me to kill her?"

"Oh no," O-bei says, and her smile looks positively crocodilian. "No, no, my children. She comes with us. I have plans for our dear Yuza-san, the Black Blade of the Iron Palace."

Yuza closes her eyes, her face a mask. Even to my ears, O-bei's pronouncement sounds like a fate worse than death.

TWENTY

Fujikawa Shrine

Kyoto, Japan

The wee hours find me slouching over history homework, but I find reading about war while *preparing* for one is an exercise in frustration. It's hard to focus on the present when the future keeps tugging on my ear. My gaze drifts to a book sitting on the corner of my desk—a battered library copy of otogi-zôshi stories, legends from old Japan.

Sticking my pencil in my bun, I set the book of legends on top of my textbook. The old pages cough dust in my face. I sneeze, wiping water from my eyes as I turn the pages. It doesn't take me long to find the tale of Yorimitsu, the hero who last slew Shuten-doji. The book includes an illustration of Shuten-doji at Oeyama: his massive, crimson-red ogre's head dominates the page, his mouth open in an eternal cackle. Black smoke billows where his hair should be, and—

A knock sounds at my door, startling me. Shaking off my nerves, I swivel my desk chair toward the door and say, "Come in!"

The door swings inward. To my surprise, Shiro stands on the other side. He leans against the jamb, holding up a pair of Kit Kats. "I saw your light in the window and thought you could use a break," he says by way of explanation. "So I ran down to the twenty-four-hour konbini. Raspberry's your favorite, right?"

"Um, yeah." I slide my glasses off my face, suddenly conscious of my polka-dot pajama bottoms and loose-fitting tee. "How'd you know?"

"Easy," he says with a shrug. "You always picked it when we were in Tokyo."

"Oh," I say, setting my glasses down on the desk. I pull my legs up, sitting cross-legged on the chair. It was one thing for Shiro to be in my sleeping space while we were in Tokyo, because we didn't have any other choice. Back at O-bei's inn, he and I danced around each other's privacy, knocking more often than we needed to, and excusing ourselves to the balcony whenever necessary. Shiro *had* taken perverse delight in removing his shirt in front of me, which never failed to burn a blush into my cheeks.

It was one thing for Shiro and me to share neutral territory— but even if this is a guest room, it's still my private space in Grandfather's house. The implications of him being in here could shift under my feet like quicksand. Perhaps I'm as old-fashioned as my mother, but it just feels like it means something to invite a boy into my bedroom. Especially *this* boy.

K-dramas promised me that love was something that hit you out of the blue, like a star falling from the sky. Perhaps it felt that way for him; but for me, it crept up on little fox feet, slow and quiet, as if it didn't want to startle me.

"So . . . ," Shiro says with a sheepish grin. "Can I come in?"

After a moment's hesitation, I nod. He crosses the room and sets the chocolate bars on top of the illustrations of Shuten-doji—one raspberry, the other green tea. Kit Kats are often gifted to students before exams . . . or, I suppose, to Shinto shrine maidens about to attempt a military coup against one of the country's most reviled demons.

With every breath I take, the blood moon gets a little closer to rising. We are not ready. Shimada and I still don't know where the final shard of the Kusanagi lies. We have three shinigami pledged to our cause—five if you count O-bei and Ronin, I guess, but they won't stay if we don't manage to complete the cabal of seven.

What's more, *I* am not ready. No matter how much training I complete with Roji, I won't be a master by the time the blood moon rises.

"Kitto katsu," Shiro says softly, which means *you're sure to win* in Japanese.

"I don't know about that," I say.

He glances down at my reading material, leaning against my desk. "And reading horror stories about Shuten-doji will help?"

"You know I like to be prepared."

"*Over*prepared," he says with a grin.

"Only when I can't afford to fail." I rise from my seat, slide the Kit Kats off the library book, and close it. "But I don't feel like I'm doing enough, even though I spend every waking moment getting ready for the blood moon. The pressure of trying to balance everything is just . . ."

I pause, not sure I can articulate how I feel without crumbling.

"It's intense," Shiro says, wrapping his pinkie finger around mine.

"Yeah," I say with a sigh.

He rests his cheek on the crown of my head. I turn my face toward him, drawn by some force I can't quite name. Our noses bump. I giggle. A Kira of any other moment would be mortified to make that sound, but it draws a happy sigh from Shiro. I suppose it can't be all *that* bad.

"Can we finish what we started under the umbrella?" he asks, running his thumb along the line of my jaw.

I ball one of my hands in his shirt. "You mean before we were so rudely interrupted?"

"By an irritating oni."

"So long as you'll still owe me a kiss under an umbrella . . ."

A faraway scream rolls through the shrine, startling us both. Shiro pushes himself away from the desk, his muscles tensed, ears pricked in the direction of the sound.

"What was that?" I whisper.

"It sounded like a woman screaming," Shiro says.

"Well, I know that much," I say, trying not to roll my eyes.

Shiro puts a finger to his lips as another shriek slips inside the house. "Stay here. I'll go find out what's wrong."

"Are you kidding me?" I say, crossing my room. I grab a pair of skinny jeans from the dresser. "I'm not staying behind, not when someone is *screaming* in my shrine."

"You'll be safer if you stay—" But he stammers to a stop as I shuck my pajama bottoms off, my underwear hidden by the length of my T-shirt. He stares, and for once, it's *his* turn to blush.

"You mind?" I ask, stepping into my jeans. "It's not like I have time for propriety, here."

He faces the wall, chuckling to himself as he wipes his palms on his thighs. I button my jeans, tuck the front of my shirt into my waistband, and grab a sweatshirt from my closet. I toss it on as we head downstairs. Shiro opens the front door. I slip into a pair of flats, and then I follow him out into the darkness.

The night stands at attention, cold and still, as if it shares our fears. We pause for a moment, listening. My breath clouds around my face. Another cry pierces the air, and Shiro takes my hand. We plunge through Grandfather's wilting gardens, following the screams to the motomiya.

When we reach the small shrine, my gaze falls to the trapdoor. It yawns open, the darkness inside perfect. Complete. A woman's wail creeps up from the cellar.

I start for the door.

"Kira!" Shiro hisses at me, grabbing for my hand. I shake him off, entering the small shrine and easing onto the cellar steps. At the bottom, a small amount of light struggles across the floor. My ears pick up a guttural voice, one that drags through my belly and leaves me quivering. Its tongue—unrecognizable, foreign—sounds hard-edged and cruel, as if its speaker has a mouth full of nails.

Shiro follows me down.

The air grows colder as my feet hit the cellar's dirt floor. The darkness runs thick, barely broken by the meager hitodama spheres bouncing along the ceiling. I breathe in through my nose. The dry, dusty air stings my nostrils and throat.

The shinigami have collected here like shadows. Heihachi turns to me as I enter—he's hovering closest to the door. His moth beats her tiny wings in alarm, fluttering over his shoulder. The others are crowded in a loose semicircle around one corner of the room: Shimada stands at the center apex, his face grim, his hands tucked into his sleeves. O-bei is at his side, her heart-shaped mouth drawn into a thin line; Roji has her fists on her hips, and a fifth person stands with his back to me. Despite his ashen-white hair, it takes me a second to recognize him.

Ronin.

"What are you doing here?" I say, charging into the cellar, Ronin in my sights. "I told you to stay away—"

A shriek stops me. A woman in a dirty kimono kneels on the floor, shackled by her wrists and ankles. The gray metal reminds me of the shinigami's blades—it glows with the light of a cloudy day. She peers at me through a snarled curtain of hair, the irises of her eyes swallowed by her pupils. Looking at her pokes holes in my sanity.

"Yuza?" I whisper.

She lunges at me, screaming. Oily tears leak down her cheeks, staining her skin. In the chilly light of her chains, she looks like a vengeful ghost. She strains for another moment, neck tendons popping, before she lets out a mournful sob and collapses to the floor.

"What are you doing to her?" I ask. My revulsion puts my anger on ice.

"Nothing," O-bei says, stepping close and placing a hand on Yuza's head. Yuza growls. "Shuten-doji's followers have cursed this one, and they now try to call her home. You must understand, Kira, we needed the talents of five shinigami to subdue her."

"You should have come to me for permission," I say through my teeth. O-bei always sets them on edge.

O-bei croons at Yuza, turning the other shinigami's chin up and stroking her cheek. "Had I waited but one more moment, this one would have broken free and had a knife at your pretty throat—"

Yuza shrieks like a police siren. Her body contorts, neck snapping back at an impossible angle. She collapses to the floor, reaching out to me with a shaking hand. I step back, right up against Shiro's chest. He places his hands on my upper arms, bracing me.

Even O-bei recoils as she screams again. Heihachi shudders. Only Shimada remains impassive, unmoved.

"Can't you help her?" I ask them.

"No," Shimada says gruffly. "Though I want to be clear: should we fail to destroy Shuten-doji, the shinigami in this room will share Yuza-san's fate. Her curse may pass, but our torment will be everlasting."

"We will not fail," I say, though I feel helpless watching Yuza struggle. If I can't protect one shinigami, how can I expect to save *seven*?

"There is one thing I could try . . . hmm," Heihachi says, breaching the ring of shinigami to crouch at Yuza's side. She swipes at him with one hand, but the malice in her attempt is overcome by her frailty.

"May you know peace, sister," Heihachi says, pressing his thumb to Yuza's brow. His small moth balances on his knuckles.

Tendrils of smoke rise from Yuza's flesh. It swirls around her face, funneling toward Heihachi and sliding into his nostrils, his tear ducts, and his ears. He gasps in pain. Yuza's breathing slows, and the tightness in her limbs eases. She collapses to the floor, drawing in a deep, jagged breath.

Heihachi's face pales, growing so gray I wonder if it will crumble like ash. A black tear bubbles from the corner of one eye. He wipes it away with a finger.

Yuza coughs, then gazes up at the shinigami. "Fools . . . my master . . . will find me . . ."

"You're quite welcome," Heihachi says, cupping his struggling moth in both hands. He rises, wavers, and allows Shimada to brace him for a moment. Roji places a hand on his lower back, brows knotted. Heihachi looks like he might collapse without their support.

"What did you do to her?" Shimada asks.

"I drew out as much of her pain as I could bear," Heihachi says, opening his palms. His little moth, Sana, flutters up and tucks herself inside his collar. "Not all power comes from a sword, Shimada-san."

"Neither does all death," Shimada replies.

Heihachi says nothing to this, but bobs his head in a short, tired bow.

Shiro and I move aside, giving Shimada and Roji the space they need to escort Heihachi from the cellar. Exhausted, Heihachi drags his feet, kicking up dust and exposing a small, white object near the bottom of the steps.

I cross the cellar, wondering what lies in the dust.

"I want Yuza guarded constantly," O-bei says behind me. "If not by one of you two, then by Minami."

"That's a lot of work," Shiro says, rubbing the back of his neck with his palm. "Especially when Kira and I still have shinigami to recruit."

"Surely you can dedicate a mere eight hours a day, brother," Ronin says. "After all, what else is a tailless kitsune good for?"

As the brothers bicker, I kneel by the stairs and pluck a bit of folded paper from the ground. I dust it off, and my heart sinks. *It's the shikigami fox.* Its bloodstains have dried to brown, its edges now blunted. I rise. Any malevolence it once had is gone now, but I'm going to burn it all the same. No magic, either. Just me and a match, simple physics, and some ash.

I turn to leave, but Ronin calls me back: "Kira, wait—can we talk?"

My hand tightens around the shikigami, crushing it in my palm. I pause and turn, feeling the weight of the room's attention on me. O-bei, Ronin, and Shiro make a strange family, two death gods and a kitsune. Yuza now leans against the wall, her face hidden by her hair, and sleeps.

Ronin steps forward. Shiro moves to intercept him, placing a hand on his chest. The brothers glare at each other, but Ronin eases back.

"May I apologize?" Ronin asks, breaking his brother's gaze first. I'm not certain if he's asking for permission from me, or Shiro.

Ronin is further gone than he was at the train station—he moves with a shinigami's grace, as if his muscles and bones are no longer subject to gravity. He looks older, too, though maybe that's just the effect of his tailored suit and tie. He would look like a salaryman, were it not for the death in his eyes.

Maybe he thinks words can absolve him; but no matter if you're living or dead, a true apology needs to be made with your whole soul. And Ronin no longer possesses one.

"While I'm grateful to Lady Katayama for the work being done on the shrine," I say, "*sorry* doesn't bring my grandfather back."

"Kira . . ." Ronin says.

"Does this mean you're staying?" I ask O-bei.

She nods.

"Fine." I walk out of the cellar, alone.

TWENTY-ONE
Fujikawa Shrine

Kyoto, Japan

The next morning, Shiro and I sit at the kitchen table before school, practicing my onmyōdō mudras. Goro busies himself about the kitchen, cleaning up from breakfast and drinking tea. Oni-chan sits on the stove, noisily destroying the rest of our leftovers. The morning news blares from the front room, and outside, the sounds of shrine reconstruction bang on.

"Zai!" Shiro says. I fan my fingers out, palms down, with only my thumbs and index fingers touching. When I glance over, Shiro's hands already form a perfect Zai mudra.

I almost completed the Zai mudra before him. *Almost.*

"You nearly beat him that time, Kira-chan," Goro says with a chuckle. "You're getting quicker."

"Not quick enough," I say, grinning at Shiro.

"Shiro, you should teach Kira to properly empower her mudras for use in battle," Goro says, and then drains his teacup. "I won't be here at the Fujikawa Shrine much longer, and I'd prefer she *not* blow up any more train cars in my absence."

"Really?" I say, sitting up straighter. Learning onmyōdō—*real* onmyōdō—has been a dream of mine since I was old enough to know that humans could wield magic against the yokai.

Goro nods. "We empower the kuji-kiri by filling it with our intentions. In battle, we may use mudras to strike down our enemies or shield our allies. It will take practice, but you seem like a quick study."

My heart glows. It's not often I receive praise from an elder. In celebration, I begin tutting the mudras in order: *Rin, Pyoh, Toh* . . .

"Maybe a little *too* quick, for a human," Shiro adds, looking me up and down. "Are we sure she's human? Roji says she's been picking up her sword training with unnatural speed as well."

"She's human," Goro says, pouring himself another cup of tea. He sets the kettle back down on the stove. "Do you see any trace of yokai in her, boy?"

"Hmm," Shiro says, looking me over, tucking one side of my hair behind my ear. "She does lack proper ears, it seems. Even half-breeds have some point to them." He flicks the top edge of my ear.

"Hey!" I say, playfully batting his hand away. "There's *nothing* wrong with my ears!"

Shiro responds by flicking his fox-shaped ears back and forth.

"Show-off," I say, pretending to grumble about it.

"Sorry," he says with a sheepish grin.

"You can make it up to me by teaching me how to empower my mudras," I say with a smile.

"Oh, right! To empower a mudra, it's not enough to think of its name," Shiro says, folding his fingers into the Rin position. "You need to think about what that mudra *means* to you. If Rin is fire, what does fire *mean*? Is it a cozy fire on a chilly winter's evening, or is it an all-consuming inferno? Your intent determines the force of your cast.

"For example, if my intention is to summon a small flame— say, no larger than a bit of candlelight—I get this." Shiro pushes his hands out, setting one of his index fingers alight. A tiny fox forms from the flames. It crawls onto the tip of his finger, wrapping its fiery tail around his knuckle. "Try it."

"*Not* in the house," Goro says, setting his teacup down. "Learning such control is the work of years. *Decades*. Take it outside."

"I barely have weeks," I say.

"We'll practice," Shiro says, gripping my hands as I go to perform a Rin mudra.

"One question, before you go," Goro says, not fooling anyone with his faux-casual tone. "I saw Ronin emerge from the motomiya this morning. I didn't realize you'd invited him back to the Fujikawa Shrine, Kira."

"*I* didn't," I say, snapping my fingers in annoyance. "Lady

O-bei thinks she has the authority to do whatever she wants here."

"I warned you about her," Goro says. "That woman looks out only for herself."

"That isn't true," Shiro says.

"You keep trying to convince me your 'mother' isn't a monster," I say, making air quotes around the word *mother*. "But she keeps living up to my low expectations for her."

"I have proof," Shiro says.

"Is that so?"

"C'mon," Shiro says, pushing back from the table. "There's something I want you to see."

Shiro and I leave Grandfather's house and head for the priests' dormitory. In the distance, I hear O-bei barking orders at someone over shrine fortifications and spells.

I glance sideways at Shiro. He clears his throat but says nothing.

The priests' dormitory isn't large—most of Fujikawa Shrine's priests lived off-site, with their families or roommates. No more than ten or twelve priests could live on shrine property, and our dorms were never more than half full. Grandfather occasionally loaned the rooms to homeless men who needed a warm room on a cold night, or to traveling priests who needed a safe place to stay. I've offered the rooms to the shinigami, but they don't seem to have much use for sleep. Or, for that matter, a defined personal space.

We remove our shoes in the dormitory's genkan, then step past the noren curtain that shields the interior from view. I step up into the main hall, the wood floor worn smooth from years of use. Shiro leads me past a communal room—currently empty—and the bathroom and shower facilities. His dorm is the last on the right, the one with a ding in the wood beside the knob.

Shiro's bedroom isn't just neat—it's *precise*. His bookshelf is sorted first by topic, then by author; his bedding makes a perfect cube against one wall; and there isn't a speck of dust in sight. While the room is no larger than the one I have at my parents' house, it has a lovely view of one of the smaller gardens and half of a pond. My jealousy blossoms. What I would give for a little room like this, here at the shrine. That dream lies within my grasp, technically; but my parents could snatch it away at any instant, or on a whim.

"I like this place," I say softly, crossing to the window. A small porcelain lucky cat chime hangs from the frame—I tap it, making it ring. "There's good energy in this place."

"I've been happy at the Fujikawa Shrine," Shiro says, opening his closet and removing a dusty, battered box from the topmost shelf. I turn from the window, curious. He looks over at me. "I hope I can stay for a long time, Kira."

It's a simple statement, and yet it makes the air pressurize around me, like I've stepped outside just before a storm breaks over the city. Since the attack on the shrine—maybe before, for him—we've danced around naming whatever exists in the space between us. I tell myself that it's not proper, that a shrine maiden shouldn't fall for her shrine's protector; and I tell myself that I don't care. I'm constantly torn between the rules I should abide by and what I want.

He beckons me over, removing the lid from the box. Inside are photographs—hundreds of them—mostly of kitsune that I don't recognize.

"What's this?" I ask him.

"My family," he says, sitting on the floor. "My *actual* family."

I kneel beside him as he spreads the photos in an arc around us. I don't know any of these people, but a few of them bear a passing resemblance to Shiro, or to Ronin.

"When I was little, I begged Mother to tell me stories about my parents," Shiro says, placing his hands on his knees. "I think the asking may have hurt whatever heart she had left, because she'd always insist *she* was my parent. But she didn't have these magnificent ears." Shiro bounces his index fingers up along the outer ridge of his fox ears. I laugh.

"Most of all, I wanted to know about my mother," Shiro says, reaching for a more recent picture of a woman with seven tails, her hair and fur as red at Shiro's. He rubs its edge with his thumb, smiling. "I was really little when she died—maybe three or four? She used to make charms for O-bei, and I would nap on her tails while she worked."

"That sounds cozy," I say. "And if she had seven tails, she must have been very powerful, and very wise."

"It seems Ronin takes after her in that regard," Shiro says. I can taste the bitterness in his words. It must ache, knowing that Ronin had not one but *two* kitsune tails at Shiro's age, only to throw his birth family's legacy away for his adoptive mother's power.

"Tell me something?" I ask.

"Anything."

"If you had been the elder brother, and O-bei had asked you to become shinigami instead of Ronin," I say, leaning into his side, "would you have done it?"

"No," he says, and the word is hoarse, and painful. "I would never do anything that would hurt you or your grandfather. O-bei may have raised me, but Fujikawa-san gave me a home."

"Who's the wiser brother, then?" I ask.

He swallows hard and doesn't answer me.

TWENTY-TWO

Kōgakkan High School

Kyoto, Japan

At school the next day, all anyone talks about is the fire in the teachers' office.

As Shiro and I walk into homeroom, my guts churn. If my parents find out that I was involved with the fire *in any way*, the freedoms I enjoy at the shrine will end. Shiro's invisibility spell must have saved us in more ways than one, because I don't hear anyone whispering our names in the halls.

Araki-sensei—the teacher who saw Yuza in the teachers' office—speaks of a woman in a white kimono but is unable to identify her. Nobody can. And nobody will, because she's chained up in my shrine's motomiya. As far as the authorities are concerned, Yuza of Osore doesn't even *exist*.

Just before Shiro and I leave for the day, I run to the restroom to fix my shirt, which became untucked while we were cleaning the windows. It looks lumpy under my sweater, and I don't want to be caught on the street looking so rumpled. It wouldn't be respectful to my school.

As I straighten my skirt in a stall, a giggle steals past my door, followed by a sharp *shush!*

I pause. "Who's there?" I call, but nobody answers. It isn't possible to see past the stall door, which has no gaps at the top, sides, or bottom. I'm completely sealed in, with no way of knowing who's waiting on the other side, or why. I left my phone in my messenger bag in our homeroom, which means I can't just text Shiro, either.

"Hello?" I say.

No answer. No surprise, either.

"Look," I say, summoning up as much of Roji's swagger and O-bei's authority as I can muster. "I don't have time for stupid drama today. You have five seconds to walk out that door. Stay, and I'll make sure you leave this place bleeding."

I'm half bluffing, but I'm counting on Ayako and her girl goon squad to lose their collective nerve. Fights are won and lost in hearts and minds. All I need to do is make the girls doubt themselves, and I win.

"Five," I say.

The rubber sole of a shoe squeaks against the floor tiles.

"Four," I say.

A whisper creeps into my stall, a small, scared thing.

"Three," I say, injecting boredom into my voice.

The outer bathroom door slams once, and hard.

"Two." I click the lock on my stall door.

"One."

Someone giggles on the other side of the door. "Like we're afraid of *you*, Kira."

I narrow my eyes, shifting into that sense of preternatural calm I've developed via sparring with Roji. "Time's up," I say softly.

I kick the door so hard, it flies open and smacks one girl in the face. She shrieks. I don't see who I've managed to hit. As the door rebounds, I grab its side and step out of the stall. Nanao Miyamoto slouches against the bathroom sinks on the other side, clutching her gushing nose.

Nanao is one of Ayako's favorite little monsters. The girl sees me and shrieks, dropping to the floor and crawling under the sinks. Bloodstains erupt across her white blouse like gory fireworks.

"I warned you," I say, turning to face three other girls, including Ayako. Three of them now bear yokai parasites, which no doubt drove them to try to harm me today. The blood moon grows closer, emboldens the malicious yokai. "But no, you're too foolish to listen when someone tells you to back off."

I turn on the other girls, who back toward the main bathroom door, clutching one another. The girl on Ayako's left—I think her name is Haruhi—trembles and trips. The other girls shriek in collective alarm. In mere seconds, I've shifted the balance of power in this room. These girls thought they were going to come in and gorge themselves on my misery, fear, and pain. I almost pity that their souls are so empty of meaning that they need to turn their anger on another person to feel whole.

Almost, but not quite.

"W-we saw you," Ayako says. "The day of the fire! We saw you and your weird boyfriend disappear from the courtyard."

"Did you?" I ask. "That sounds an awful lot like a made-up story, Ayako. The kind that just might *put a dark mark on our sterling reputation* here at Kōgakkon." I say those words with absolute venom, hoping she remembers the ones she spoke to me that day.

"That's Ayako-*senpai* to you," Haruhi snaps.

"Not anymore," I say, cocking my head at an angle like I've seen O-bei do when she's openly mocking someone. "The honorific *-senpai* confers respect. And I don't see anyone worthy of my regard in this room. The four of you have done *nothing* but torment me since I arrived at Kōgakkan, but that ends today."

"You can't speak to me this way," Ayako says, hate swirling in her gaze. "You know who my father is, and what he'll do to you if—"

"Have you ever stopped to consider the shame you'd bring down on *your* family, Ayako?" I ask, narrowing my eyes. "Attacking the granddaughter of the recently deceased head priest of a local shrine, *tsk*. What would your father say, were he to be informed of your behavior?"

Tears hover in the corners of Ayako's eyes, betraying her embarrassment. And her fear. I try not to feed on those emotions, or to pull any enjoyment from Nanao's sobs. This isn't about vengeance—this is just a petty schoolyard feud, one that's wasting my time and energy.

"You would *never* tell," Ayako says.

You're right, I won't, but only because tattling is for children. "Go, Nanao," I say to the girl beneath the sinks. "Tell the school nurse you tripped and fell. It would be shameful to admit the four of you lost to the school outcast, now, wouldn't it?"

Nanao crawls out from under the bathroom sinks, blotting blood off her lips with her sleeve. She stumbles toward her friends, shooting a frightened look at me. Haruhi takes the girl under her arm.

"Nobody will believe she tripped," Ayako says with a sniff.

"They absolutely will," I say, holding up my palms, showing Ayako the pink-skinned scars left over from our last violent encounter. "They've been believing that lie for ten whole months."

"This is your fault, Ayako," Nanao says in a wheezing, nasally voice. Her lower lip has started to swell, too, and blood-tinged saliva oozes off its puffy edge. "I-if I end up with a disciplinary action on my record, I'll *never* get into Tokyo University—"

"Oh, shut up," Ayako says, holding the bathroom door open for Nanao. She turns to me. "This isn't over, Kira."

"Now you're hurling lazy threats?" I ask, putting my hands on my hips. "It's absolutely over. If you come after me again, you'll be bleeding next."

Ayako's face flames red. She slams the main bathroom door so hard the walls shake.

When they're gone, I brace myself against the sink and dry heave. Not because I'm afraid of anything Ayako can do to me—I know what real monsters are capable of now—but more so because that showdown dumped more anxiety into the pit of my belly. But try as I might, I can't vomit up an emotion. I'm empty.

I wash my hands, then my face. Lifting my gaze to the mirror, I watch rivulets of water run down my cheeks and drip off the end of my chin. Sometimes it soothes me to watch the physics of my world—sometimes, they're the only parts of it that still make sense.

After drying my face, I use some toilet paper to clean Nanao's blood off the floor. I regret hitting her so hard; judging by the amount of blood on the floor, she probably walked out the door with a broken nose.

Then again, if she'd heeded my warning, she wouldn't have gotten hurt in the *first* place.

As I exit the bathroom, I find Shiro waiting for me outside, a grim smile on his face. He has my bag slung over one shoulder.

"I was going to interfere, but it sounded like you had the situation under control," he says, handing me my bag.

"It would've been weird for you to be in the girls' bathroom anyway," I say in a deadpan tone, making it clear that I'm fine but fed up with this place. "Let's get out of here, we have shinigami to find."

TWENTY-THREE
Fujikawa Shrine

Kyoto, Japan

That evening my parents come to the shrine.

It's the night of the new moon, and lately, Roji has been dragging me into the assembly hall for practice. After all these weeks, I've begun to enjoy the feeling of the wooden bokuto sword in my hands. The blisters at the roots of my fingers have hardened into calluses, and the once-soft muscles in my arms, back, and abdomen have grown accustomed to the sword's weight.

"Oi!" Roji says, keeping a brisk pace. "Move your arms like you mean it!"

We stand with our feet spread hips' distance apart, raising our wooden swords over our heads in a practiced, methodical way. *Up, down. Up, down.* We begin our warm-up with thirty of these exercises, which seem simple in theory. After weeks and weeks of training, they still make my muscles blaze with the effort.

"I'm not the sloppy one," I say, not a little breathlessly. "You're not even paying attention to your footwork!"

A knock interrupts us. We turn. Three dark figures crowd the assembly hall's door. I pick Goro out first, mostly from the silhouette of his ears. It takes me a half second longer to recognize my mother.

I swear under my breath. Mother steps into the hall in her stocking feet, looking tidy in a wool peacoat and black slacks. Father follows her inside, still dressed in a dark suit and tie. No doubt he's just finished work for the day.

As for me? Well, I look like a mess—baggy clothing, my hair askew, and my skin flushed and sweaty. Mother lifts a brow as she scans my outfit. If disapproval could take a human shape, it would probably look like my mother. Pursed lips, prim peacoats, and a middle-aged perfume I can smell from ten feet away.

"Mother. Father," I say, performing a polite bow. I don't need to ask why they're here—it's apparent from the quiet fury in Mother's eyes.

"May I have a moment with my daughter, Miss . . . ?" Mother says to Roji, and I watch my mother squirm as she realizes she doesn't know the names of the people I "work" with.

"I'm no *miss*," Roji says, but she nods. "You want to keep that?" she asks, gesturing at my bokuto as she walks backward toward the door. I toss it to her with a small grin, my attitude belying the anxiety gnawing on my guts. I promised my parents that I wouldn't shame them any further, and yet here I am. Busting girls' noses in the bathroom and setting the teachers' office on fire.

. . . I really hope they didn't hear about that last bit. I tuck loose strands of my hair behind my ears, trying to make myself more presentable. I'm failing, no doubt.

When Roji and Goro are gone, Mother wastes no time with small talk. "You hit Nanao Miyamoto in the ladies' restroom today."

"Proper girls don't start fights at school," Father says.

"I didn't start that fight," I say, resting my hands on my hips. "But I wasn't going to be the one bleeding at the end of it, either."

"You broke Nanao's nose," Mother says. "Do you have any idea how embarrassing this is for our family? Her father is a business associate of ours, Kira! Did you consider how this would impact our relationship with him?"

"No," I say with a shake of my head. Of *course* my parents show up to the shrine once their business relationships are threatened, and not before. "I was thinking about survival. Do you know what happened the last time Ayako and her friends cornered me? They *beat* me."

Mother turns her face away, sucking in a sharp breath.

I continue, "They pushed me to the ground, kicked me in the chest, and pulled my hair. What was I supposed to do today? Let them hurt me?"

"No," Mother says, sweeping both hands down as if to push

the idea away. "But it was still wrong to lower yourself to their level and shame the family as a result. You're likely to be expelled from Kōgakkan for this, Kira."

"Fine," I say, knowing it's anything *but* fine. Mother gasps. "Why should I attend an institution whose students have so little honor?"

"Because Kōgakkon is one of the best high schools in Kyoto"— Father's voice rises—"and it is a privilege to attend the institution."

I hold up my hands, showing my parents the pink scars that hug the bottoms of my palms. "Is it a *privilege* to be pushed to the ground, Father? To have my dignity stolen from me, day after day, as my entire class shuns me?"

Mother presses the back of her hand to her lips and looks away. My father remains expressionless, but I can see the muscles in his jaw flexing. He's frustrated. My parents came here to collect a rebellious daughter and march her back home in shame. Now that I've shattered their assumptions, they scramble to deal with an unexpected complication: I *have* broken my promise to them, but not because I'm wild or rebellious. I acted in self-defense.

"I know you're here to bring me home, but I can't leave the shrine. Not now," I say. Not with a waxing moon hanging over my head like an executioner's blade.

"You don't get to make that decision, Kira," Mother says softly.

Before I can argue further, a faraway scream reaches my ears. I turn away from my parents, cocking my head toward the sound, and listen hard.

"What was that?" Mother asks. I hold up a hand, asking for silence. It can't be Yuza—she stopped screaming in pain after her first night here.

Footsteps pound the veranda outside. The door wrenches open, and Roji sticks her head inside the room. "Kira, we've got company."

"What kind of company?" I ask.

A second cry pierces the walls, closer now.

"Let's just say they're not here for tea," Roji replies with a smirk.

"What's going on?" Mother demands, but I'm already running across the room. "Kira!"

"Stay here!" I shout at my parents. Roji pushes the door open as I rush outside, then slams it in my wake. "Is there really an emergency, or are you just getting me out of a lecture?" I ask.

"Oh no, the yokai are here," Roji says, tutting a quick spell over the assembly hall's doors to keep them locked tight. My parents bang their fists on the glass, calling my name. Roji grins, jerking her head in their direction. "Lovely people, your parents."

"Don't start," I say.

She tosses me a blade. I pull an inch of it out of the sheath and catch a glimpse of my reflection in the glittering metal. Live steel.

"Don't kill yourself with it," Roji says, jerking her head toward the back of the shrine. "Better yet, don't kill *me* with it."

"You're already dead," I say.

"And I don't want to be more dead!"

"What's going on?" I ask as we jog around the assembly hall.

"Shuten-doji decided he wanted Yuza back," Roji says. "He sent a few of his little friends to get her."

"How many?" We jump off the veranda and into the small courtyard.

"Enough to matter," Roji replies.

I follow Roji, my heart pounding in my chest. My grip on my katana feels slick with sweat. Fear closes clawed fingers around my heart; I remember a night like this, not long ago, when Shuten-doji's creatures came and took everything from me. The shrieks and screams I heard that night come shooting back like bullets that tear into my courage.

I'm not the girl who hid from her grandfather's killers.

Not anymore.

As we pass Grandfather's house, several dark, spidery shapes race past, headed toward Yuza's cellar prison in the motomiya.

"I'll get the jorōgumo," Roji says, and then points to something on the wall above us. "You take her!"

I glance up. A shadowy yokai hunches on the stone wall, her icy eyes burning with hate. Her once-beautiful face has a melted quality to it, as if her flesh had liquefied and then refrozen. A yuki-onna, or at least she *was* before she was burned.

The yokai makes a pained, gurgling sort of sound. She leaps from the wall, clawing at my face.

I take a step back, out of her range. Just like I would while training with Roji. The yuki-onna tumbles to the ground, glaring up at me through the mess of her half-burned hair. Something within me spurs me onward—this hot rush of adrenaline, maybe, or my brain screaming *kill or be killed!* with the decibel level cranked up. Gripping my sword, I step forward and thrust my blade into the demon's chest. Bone and flesh and muscle resist my katana. I shove it in harder, feeling the way the blade's sharp edge grinds against her rib bones.

The yuki-onna's death rattle echoes up the sword, through the hilt, and tremors into my arms. She collapses around my blade, boneless, bloodless. Her body blows away, snowflake by snowflake, into the wind.

I release a deep, shuddering breath. Horror seeps into my bones like the slow creep of cold up one's spine.

I took a life.

Or at least, I took an existence. It doesn't matter that I killed her in self-defense, or in defense of the shrine; the realization still hits me full-bodied and hard. Somehow, taking her life has only made mine emptier.

I yank my sword from her body. Roji circles back to me, her white shirt stained cherry red. Unlike me, she wears the blood of our enemies comfortably, almost as if she doesn't even notice it's there at all. I heave, nausea rising in my gut like a wave.

"There's nothing good about killing," I say to her, breathless.

"No, there's not," Roji says. "That's why being a shinigami is a *curse*. But we can talk about regret later. Let's move."

I follow her to the shrine's motomiya, throwing an uneasy glance over my shoulder. Nothing stalks us, save for the swirling snow. The shrine grounds lie oddly silent. No screams rend the air. The clash of steel doesn't echo through the night. But smoke curls like dragons' tongues over the tops of the buildings. It scratches my throat like sandpaper and burns in my tear ducts. I rub one eye with a knuckle, but it serves only to spread the pain.

We sneak around the back side of Grandfather's house, keeping to the shadows by the garden's outer wall. Roji moves like a cat, sinuous and silent; the snow doesn't even crunch under her bare feet. The breeze tugs at the loose, short strands of her hair—this is the first time I've seen her without her signature braids.

She halts at the garden's edge, motioning for me to halt.

At first, I'm not sure why we've stopped; but then I hear a soft shuffling, the clack of bone, and a soft, sad exhale. I turn my head, looking left. The sounds seem to be coming from the motomiya, which is hidden beyond a hedge. Roji glances back at me, mouthing, *Be ready.*

I nod at her, even though I feel anything *but* ready. I slide my hands into position on the katana's hilt—my right hand tucked against the sword's guard, my left gripping it by the base. Roji taught me to grip the sword primarily with my index and pinkie fingers, keeping the middle fingers more relaxed. But I can't help but grip the sword like a lifeline, as if letting go would mean a fall to my death.

Roji pushes herself off the wall, heading for the motomiya. I follow her close. The small shrine emerges from the shadows, its boxy sides and sloped roof darker than anything else around it.

Yokai corpses litter the ground, their blood draining into the cracks between the cobblestones. With every drop of blood spilled here, I swear I feel the shrine's bones ache. I count ten—no, twelve— dead. Limbs twitch, but nothing struggles to get back up.

I step into the shrine, peering down into the cellar. Even now, I sense the malevolence leaking out of the very boards of this place, as if the memory of what happened here couldn't be burned away. What's more, I can't be sure whether it's my own discomfort speaking, or something true. Something real. Something *evil*.

In this light, the bloodstains on the floorboards look black.

Roji follows me inside.

Something stirs behind her, shifting into view.

Roji must see the look on my face.

She whirls.

I scream.

With a roar, a giant oni charges at us. He has a crimson face and a wild mane of matted black hair. He swings his bone-studded club off his shoulder, shattering one of the small shrine's pillars. I turn my face away as the wooden shrapnel zings past my face.

Roji responds faster: "Retsu!" she shouts, making a one-handed mudra and shoving it outward. The air around her seems to heave, slamming into the ogre and staggering him. Roji takes advantage of this opening, rushing forward and slamming her shoulder into his meaty chest, pushing him out of the small shrine.

"A little help here, Kira?" she shouts at me.

"Oh, right!" I say.

Roji rolls her eyes.

I dart out of the small shrine as the ogre lurches back to his feet. The ogre stands larger than most men—even taller than Shimada—and has thick, heavy muscle cording his arms, legs, and back. In a one-on-one match, I doubt I could take him; luckily, I'm not alone.

He grins at me, chuckling under his breath. "How happy my lord will be when I bring back not only his prized assassin, but his favorite enemy."

"You should never assume a girl wants to go home with you," I say.

The ogre says, "Ha!" and rushes toward me. I sidestep to the right, his club whistling past my head.

Roji charges in, ducking his backswing and striking at his side. She misses, dancing a step or two out of range; the ogre slams his fist into the space she was occupying a breath ago. I step forward, driving my sword through the ogre's left calf. He howls in pain and grabs for me. I drop down, while Roji takes her sword and drives it through his gut.

A trickle of blood slides from the ogre's mouth as he collapses to his knees. Roji draws her sword from his body as he gurgles, his eyes rolling up into his head. He hits the ground.

Roji extends her hand to me. "Not bad, kid. You learn quick."

I grin, clapping my hand into hers. She pulls me to my feet, and together we back away from the ogre's corpse.

"Whoa, are you okay?" Shiro says, popping up through the

open trapdoor in the motomiya's floor. "I thought we'd already cleared the grounds, I'm sorry!"

"We're fine," I say. "Is Yuza still down there?"

"Yeah, we have her secured," Shiro replies, stepping onto the motomiya's veranda. He frowns at the broken pillar, picking a toothy sliver out and dropping it on the ground. "Shimada and Goro went to check the shrine's perimeter, and my mother's gone to help the kitsune—"

A gasp interrupts him. Shiro's features go rigid, guarded, as his gaze zeroes in on someone behind me. *Oh no*, I think as I turn, my spirits in free fall.

Mother steps from the shadows of the veranda. Before her lies the unmistakable corpse of a slaughtered oni, a twitching garden of dead jorōgumo legs, and a wayward daughter bearing a bloodied blade. The demon blood spattered over my clothing isn't doing me any favors, either.

I start toward her. "Mother, I—"

"This was not the life I wanted for you, Kira," she says, stepping down from the veranda. I halt. "This was the life I tried to protect you from."

"You *knew*?" I ask, anger hitting me like a hot poker. "You knew it wasn't all a lie? You knew about the yokai, and Grandfather . . . Can you see past Shiro's glamour?"

Mother says nothing—she merely holds my gaze with her dark one.

"*Why?*" I say, my voice edging close to a sob. "If you know, why have you left me to bear this burden alone?"

"This world was never my world," Mother says. "Not the way it was your grandfather's, and not in the way it's now yours. I thought I could shelter you from it, tell you it was a lie, that your eyes deceived you . . . but I was wrong."

She doesn't apologize, but the sorrow in her voice doesn't sound manufactured, either. I press her harder: "Mother, the shrine is in danger. *We* are in danger. There is a blood moon rising, and—"

"I can't help you, Kira. I never had your talents," she says with a shake of her head. "Though I will allow you to remain at the shrine until the new year. Make your grandfather proud—he was always so very fond of you."

Mother turns away, heading for the shrine gates.

"Mother, wait!" I say.

She pauses, looking back at me.

"Did Grandfather ever mention that our shrine was hiding a piece of the Kusanagi no Tsurugi?" I ask.

Mother frowns. "Why should we have a piece of the Imperial family's holy sword? Isn't that being held in Nagoya?"

"I suppose so," I say.

When she is gone, Shiro puts his arms around me. I lean against his chest, and he rests his chin on the crown of my head.

He doesn't say anything.

He doesn't need to.

TWENTY-FOUR
Kōgakkon High School

Kyoto, Japan

On Monday morning, Shiro and I find that December has unleashed an even deeper chill. Winter winds bite my cheeks, and ice slides under the soles of my shoes. The moon has become a low-hanging thumbnail in the sky, now growing more full by the day. In a little more than a week's time, the blood moon will rise and our war will begin in earnest.

I'm surprised to see the family car waiting on the street, engine idling. Mother steps out of the vehicle, her mouth set in a grim line. "Kira," she says by way of greeting. She refuses to acknowledge Shiro, not even with a polite *hello*.

"Good morning, Mother," I say, pausing on the front steps. "What are you doing here?"

"Kōgakkon High School has agreed not to expel you, on one condition," Mother says, her words going up in a plume of fog.

"Oh? And what's that?" I ask.

"You are to make a formal apology to Nanao Miyamoto and her parents," Mother says. *"Today."*

"That's it?" I ask, looking for the conceit, the trap, the hidden condition inside my mother's words. I've spent so much time in the world of monsters, it's difficult to accept anyone's intent at face value anymore.

"I met with Miyamoto-san, Nanao's mother, on Saturday," Mother said. "I made sure she was aware that you believed you were acting in self-defense. We are meeting in the principal's office this morning to deliver your formal apology."

Mother is . . . helping me? In her own self-serving way, I suppose. "You've left me no choice."

"Do you deserve one?" Mother says, her words as chilly as the breeze.

I sigh. While I have no desire to apologize to my bullies, allowing my parents to save face will keep them from complicating my life. "Fine, I'll apologize to Nanao," I say.

But before I join my parents in the car, I turn to Shiro. "I'll meet you at school, okay?"

"You sure about this?" Shiro asks, sticking his hands in the pockets of his slacks.

"Yeah," I say, flashing him a quick smile as I start down the steps. "See you in homeroom!"

He winks at me and waves, ignoring Mother's withering stare. Father says nothing to me as I slide into the backseat of his sedan. We don't speak on the drive to school. Mother doesn't chide me for my friendship with Shiro, nor do we talk about what happened at the shrine last Friday night. Instead, I'm forced to play out my apology to Nanao in my head, over and over again.

By the time Father parks outside Kōgakkon High School, sweat has dampened the back of my shirt. My heart squeezes each beat, aching as if I've just run a marathon. I don't want to kneel in front of my enemies and beg for their forgiveness, nor do I want to pretend that I'm sorry for defending myself. I'm not sorry, though I *will* be sincere. Unlike Ronin, I understand what an apology really means—it's a request to return to a more harmonious state, and a promise not to repeat the behavior in the future. If Nanao doesn't repeat her behavior, I'll never be forced to, either.

Once we arrive at school, I follow Mother and Father to Principal Ito's office. The room has warm hardwood floors and leather couches. Abstract sumi-e artwork decorates the walls. Pale, cloudy light drifts through the windows. One pane stands half-open, allowing a frozen breeze to slide into the room.

Principal Ito rises from behind his desk; he's a small, neat man, who seems almost dwarfed by the furniture around him. He smoothes the front of his suit, exchanging bows and pleasantries with my parents. Nanao and her parents rise as well, exchanging bows and subdued greetings. Our fathers engage in a bow-off, demonstrating their respect and humility, as well as acknowledging their equal status in the room. Their bows begin at the standard fifteen-degree depth and grow shallower with each dip.

When my gaze meets Nanao's, she touches the side of her bandaged nose and looks away quickly. While I've never been good about "reading the air," so to speak, there's nothing triumphant in her demeanor—Nanao looks as uncomfortable as I feel. I expected her to revel in every second of this, and to later spread horrible rumors about me. I even thought Ayako might be here to witness my public humiliation. But the only emotions I read in this room are shame and sorrow.

"Kira," Father says without looking at me. "I suppose you have something to say to Miyamoto-san and her parents?"

"Yes," I say, placing my hands on the tops of my thighs and bending forward till the tips of my fingers touch my knees. It's a very deep bow—seventy degrees with a straight back—the kind reserved for approaching shrine kami or very, *very* sincere apologies. "I apologize, Miyamoto-san, for injuring you and causing you physical pain. My actions were foolish, and I am sorry for any distress I have caused you and your family."

I rise. My parents repeat this process, except to Nanao's parents. Mother apologizes for raising such a mannerless daughter. I fight to keep my expression neutral, letting her words pass through me like sand through a sieve. Even when I resign myself to listening to her, it still grates.

"My daughter has assured me that she will not act so coarsely in the future," Mother says, and then dips into another, shallower bow. "I am grateful, Miyamoto-san, that you are not seeking her expulsion from Kōgakkon High School. Your generosity knows no bounds."

"No, Fujikawa-san, I should be apologizing for my own child," Mrs. Miyamoto says, bowing in return. "We can't hold your daughter entirely responsible for this situation, can we, Nanao?"

Nanao blinks fast, holding back tears.

"Nanao?" Mrs. Miyamoto insists.

With a hiccup, Nanao bows to me. Her perfect hair cascades over her shoulders, falling in two twin waterfalls on either side of her head. Her fingertips tremble on her knees. I'm so shocked and confused, it takes the full two beats of her bow for me to regain a neutral, open expression.

"I must apologize, too, Fujikawa-san," she says, keeping her eyes downcast. "I recognize that my actions may have given you the wrong impression of me and of my family. In the future, I will try to be a better classmate and member of Kōgakkon's esteemed student body."

Principal Ito clears his throat. "I expect this will end the hostilities between the two of you. Exemplary students must strive to promote harmony among their classmates. Should any additional altercations occur, you can expect swift and decisive action from me. Am I clear?"

"Yes, Principal Ito," Nanao and I say in concert. We bow to the principal. Nanao sniffles, desperately trying not to lose more face.

I pity her—it should be *Ayako* here, bowing and apologizing for the harm done. Nanao may have played along, but Ayako pulled all the strings.

I bid my parents goodbye at the door and head to class, glad that Nanao and I don't share a homeroom. And maybe, just maybe, Nanao will stop Ayako and their friends from tormenting me further. Admissions to Tokyo University are so competitive, Nanao won't be able to afford a demerit on her record, much less an expulsion. And now that Ayako and her crew have seen that I can fight back, well . . . I don't really expect them to come after me anyways. I've killed a demon with these two hands.

I keep my head up through the school day, ignoring the whispers and rumors swirling around me.

The fox does not fear the mouse.

TWENTY-FIVE
Fujikawa Shrine

Kyoto, Japan

Two nights later, Goro asks me to take a tray of food to Shiro. "It's his turn to guard Yuza in the motomiya tonight, hmm?" the older kitsune says. "He shouldn't go without something to eat. You two came back late from your shinigami hunting."

Our failed *shinigami hunting*, I think with a sigh. We haven't managed to find another willing shinigami since Heihachi, and time is running out. The moon waxes more full by the day. By now, the shinigami of Kyoto know who we are, and they know what we're looking for—and not one of them wants anything to do with *us*. From Gion to Arashiyama and every neighborhood in between, help is hard to find.

We've had no better luck locating the missing shard of the

Kusanagi no Tsurugi—it remains just as elusive as the shinigami.

I carry a tray of grilled fish, potato stew, and brown rice to the motomiya. I've already eaten, but the food still smells heavenly. I squeeze out the front door, waddle across the garden, and tiptoe down the motomiya's stairs. Shiro sits on the bottom step, playing a battle royal game on his phone.

"Goro sent dinner," I say, sinking down beside him and balancing the tray on my knees.

Shiro puts his phone aside. "That man is divine." He takes the tray from me, his stomach rumbling.

The motomiya's cellar isn't large, perhaps ten yards by ten. A naked lightbulb hangs over the door, rigged up with extension cords. Its hard light chases spiders and other creeping things into the cracks of the walls. Old, rusted tools line the edges of the room—some of them look like they predated Grandfather. Dust coats everything in a thick blanket. Nothing here has been touched in more than a lifetime.

Yuza sits in a corner, watching us with the same curiosity that a caged tiger has for schoolchildren. Her kimono, once white, has now taken on the cellar's rusty, drab brown. Two moths still cling to her sleeve. One hasn't moved since I entered the room.

"You sure you want to be down here?" Shiro asks. "It's pretty cold."

Translation: *I know what this place means to you.* Grandfather's blood still stains the motomiya's floorboards. All these weeks have dulled my grief, but not my desire for revenge. I will always miss

Grandfather. But I will not allow the shrine to fall to the monsters who killed him, not while I still draw breath.

"I'll be okay for a little while," I say, warming the chill from my fingers by tutting them through the nine major mudras. They feel more comfortable now, as if I'd spent my life training to use them, rather than a few short weeks.

Shiro picks a potato out of his stew, popping it into his mouth. "Let's work on empowering your mudras," he says, setting his tray aside and scooting closer to me. "You still need practice."

"Lots and lots of practice," I reply.

"Little Miss Overachiever," he says with a grin.

"*Hardly!*"

The shinigami shifts her weight in the corner, saying nothing. Her gaze unsettles me; while she sits across the room, I almost feel like she's staring at the back of my neck, waiting for an opportune moment to strike.

I tut the mudra Rin, focusing my mind on a candle's flame. My fingertips catch fire, just like magic. As I shake the flames off my fingers, a light flashes across the cellar's dirt floor.

Shiro and I look up. "What was that?" I ask. Even Yuza frowns and sits up, her gaze riveted to the middle of the room.

"Do the mudra again, Kira," Shiro says. So I steeple my fingers together in Rin, thinking of candle fires winking like cats' eyes. Fire bursts along my fingertips. White light dances across the floor, illuminating a familiar shape in the dust. The image burns itself into my retinas. When I close my eyes, I see it transposed on the backs of my eyelids.

I gasp, pushing up from the stairs. "That was a Seimei pentagram." It would make sense if his magic lingered here—this motomiya is the only surviving building from the original shrine. These stones, this dirt, everything here is *ancient*. The wood has been replaced throughout the years, but the stones have stood since Seimei's time.

"No," Yuza says, shifting her weight. "*That* was a seal."

"A seal?" I ask.

"Think of it as a sort of lock"—Shiro snaps his fingers—"or like a password. It can be opened if you know the right combination."

"Or in some cases, possess the right bloodline," Yuza says with a chuckle. "The seal was not responding to *your* magic, boy."

If I were going to hide the shard of a sacred sword anywhere, I think, *it would be in a place like this.*

"How do we open it?" I ask.

Shiro lifts a shoulder in a shrug. "I suppose you could try standing on the pentagram and casting the mudra for clarity? Or awareness?"

"Let me find it first. . . ." As I walk toward the space, I place my hands back in Rin and light my fingertips on fire. The ground blazes around me, and the pentagram appears under my feet. I almost laugh in surprise, watching in delight as a white ring of light encircles me. Characters—many of which I don't recognize—burn up through the dust. My bracelet glows with bright fire.

I look through the light at Shiro. He stands on the other side of the wall of light, openmouthed. I beckon to him as the disk of light begins to turn underfoot, like a key turning in a lock.

The ground disappears under my feet.

I don't even have a chance to breathe.

Shiro shouts my name as I fall into darkness. I plummet ten yards into frigid water, hitting the surface like a thunderclap. Air bubbles buffet my body. The cold slaps me next, shocking my skin. Panicked, I fight my way to the surface, shrieking as I bump against a bloated rat's corpse. My other hand brushes against something solid, slimy, and soft. I shudder, jerking my hand away. I try not to think about all the diseases currently crawling over my skin, and wipe the water from my eyes. I kick hard to keep myself afloat.

Shouts and echoes of *Kira!* make their way to me. I turn my head toward the sound. I can't see Shiro's face—the brilliance of the light up above casts everything else in shadow. Down this deep, the glow from my bracelet puts silver caps on the water's ripples. I can't see anything else.

Where am I?

"Kira!" Shiro shouts. "Kira! Are you okay?"

"I'm alive!" I shout back, splashing around and trying to find purchase with my toes. I think I'm in some sort of well, one that reeks of sewage and rot. I pull a chunk of algae out of my eyelashes, cringing.

"What happened?!" Shiro shouts back.

"I think that's my line!" I say, churning the water with my legs. "Can you please do something? Get me out, maybe?"

"On it," he says. A rope's silhouette bobs over the well's lip. Its frayed edges reach for me like an outstretched hand. The line comes up several feet too short. I try to climb the slick well stones to reach the rope, but slip and tumble back into the water.

"Hold on," Shiro shouts down to me. "I'll find something else!"

"Hurry," I call back. "It's freezing down here."

I tread water, hoping—no, *praying* that Shiro hurries back. My teeth chatter, and every muscle in my body feels leaden. Slow. Something brushes up against my leg. I shriek, paddling away. It's impossible to see anything beyond the oily black surface. Wishing to stay quiet and still, I put my back to one wall and focus on staying afloat.

The links of my bracelet grow warm. Its light spreads through the water, but struggles to penetrate deeper than a half foot or so. I hold my bracelet in front of me, especially when I think I catch a bit of movement at the light's edge.

"Hurry, Shiro," I whisper. *"Hurry."*

Yuza starts to laugh, but the well's slick walls twist the sound into something otherworldly. "You'd best be careful, priestess. I don't think we're alone—"

A hand slides around my ankle. I look down, catching a glimpse of cratered eye sockets in a bare skull. A torn gossamer shroud holds the skeletal spirit's bones together like translucent flesh.

I scream, kicking the yokai in the face. It drags me under. I panic, scrabbling for purchase, looking for a handhold to stop this descent into darkness. My fingernails scrape against slick stone.

The creature drags me into blackness so thick, it compresses my limbs and tries to force its way into my mouth and nose. I jam my heel into the yokai's shoulder, but its bony hand grips me tight.

The yokai slams me into the well's rocky floor. I hit so hard I cough, expelling the rest of the air inside me. The bubbles race into the darkness. My ears pop. As the creature wraps its fingers around my neck, my hands scrabble for something, *anything*, that I can use as a weapon. Shiro's fire spells are useless underwater. I have no sword, nothing to use to run the beast through.

I'm going to die.

My lungs burn, vision flashing red. Everything within me screams. Airless. Voiceless.

I'm going to die.

Then I see it—a toothy bit of light in the darkness, a spear of sun in the depths. Desperate, I draw my legs up and kick the monster in the chest. On the second kick, I snap one of its wrists and manage to push free. The yokai grabs my hair. I jerk away, tearing strands from my scalp. I struggle toward that light. Reaching. The water no longer feels cold. My lungs cry for air. I kick and fight and stretch and reach.

My fingers bump against a hard, smooth sliver. It burns to the touch. When I grip it, the sharp edges slice little mouths into my skin.

The yokai yanks me backward. When it tries to sink its fingers into my throat again, I stab at its torso. At its arms. At any bony part of it that comes too close. Each blow leaves a dash of light on the yokai's bones, until my weapon sinks into something soft. Something fleshy.

The yokai screeches, the sound earsplitting and haunting under the water. I yank the shard out, but the motion's sluggish. A sheet of exhaustion falls over my body. Muscles refuse to respond. My eyes close, even as I fight to keep them open.

I breathe the water in, as if I have become a fish. My mind darkens, my body ready to slip into this dark abyss. I feel a pressure, a lightness. Buoyancy. I don't know if my eyes are open or closed. Every part of my body goes numb.

I let go.

When I wake, I find myself wrapped in a cocoon of comforters. I cough, still able to taste the well's grime on my lips. My head throbs.

"You're awake."

I turn my head, surprised to see sitting Roji at my bedside. She leans forward, resting her elbows on her knees. "For a little while there, I thought I'd be turning you into a butterfly, kid."

"What"—I cough again, trying to sit up—"what happened?"

"Don't sit up, you nearly drowned," Roji says, propping her bare feet up on my bed. Oni-chan mews, getting up from my side and hopping onto her lap. "You were attacked by a kyokotsu in a cursed well. You're lucky that boy's so blindly in love with you, he was willing to jump in and dredge you out. Damn fool."

I'm not sure who she's calling *fool*—Shiro, or me. Or both.

"Shiro's not in love with me," I whisper, turning my face toward the ceiling. The words sound like a lie.

"I don't know what else to call it, then," Roji replies, scratching Oni-chan behind one ear. "It's easy to forget what something like *love* feels like after a hundred years or more."

"We're friends."

"I'm dead, not blind."

"You just said you don't remember what love feels like!"

"Doesn't mean I don't remember what it *looks* like," she says with a *tch*.

Fine, I'm not arguing about my love life right now. "Is Shiro . . . ?"

"He's okay," Roji says. "He and Goro are currently purifying the well—"

I sit up, my memories crashing back. "The well! I found something down there, something sealed under a Seimei pentagram, and I, I . . . Did I bring it back up with me?"

Roji chuckles, taking a silk-wrapped object off my nightstand. "Oh yes, you did. Shimada left this with me, because he knew you'd want to see it."

I sit up straighter as she unwinds the raw silk and exposes a long, thin piece of metal.

"Is that what I think it is?" I whisper to her.

She grins. "Put your hands out, Kira Fujikawa. Palms up."

I extend both my palms. Roji rests the metal shard—silk and all—in my hands.

The metal catches fire—no, it catches *light*. It blazes in my tiny room, and when I look up at Roji, I see her differently. Her tattoos are gone, as are the gauges in her ears and the cynicism in her eyes. Her hair runs down her back in a long, straight sheet; and the cut of her kimono seems different, the fabric more natural and home-spun than I'm accustomed to seeing. Her hakama are miko red.

"It's the last shard," I say softly. "Finally."

And the girl Roji once was, many, many centuries ago, smiles.

TWENTY-SIX

Fujikawa Shrine

Kyoto, Japan

On the Friday before the blood moon rises, I go through the motions of a normal day: I have breakfast with Goro, who will retutn to Tokyo later this afternoon; I train with Roji, who gives me a few new bruises; and I go to school with Shiro. We secretly tuck our hands in his coat pocket, letting our fingers lock together on the way home. It's the last day of school before winter break—at least I won't have homework while I'm trying to save the world.

Shiro and I spend most afternoons looking for more shinigami, but today, we head home to say goodbye to Goro. By the time we arrive at the shrine, Goro waits at the top of the steps with Shimada and Roji. A small suitcase sits at his side.

"Goro!" I call, racing up the stairs. I'm in better shape now, and running up the steps leaves me exhilarated, not winded. I throw my arms around the old kitsune, who chuckles and places his hand on the crown of my head. "I'll miss you," I say softly.

"Your grandfather would have been so proud of you, Kira," he says as I pull away from his embrace. "Trust Shimada-san and Roji-san, they are good souls"—he smiles at them—"for a couple of dead people."

"I don't know about *good*," Roji says, scratching the side of her nose. She grins at Shimada, who crosses his arms over his chest and looks unamused. He's particularly good at that expression, his eyes narrowing by a few degrees, their irises flashing like flint. If I didn't know him better, I'd be frightened. Perhaps I still am.

"As for you," Goro says, turning to Shiro. He places a hand on the younger kitsune's shoulder. "It is not often that Amaterasu tasks one so young with a responsibility like this, but you are up to the challenge. Trust yourself."

Shiro bows to Goro. As Goro takes hold of his suitcase, he takes one final long look at the Fujikawa Shrine, and then at us. "When the darkness finally comes," he says with a deep bow, "may the Goddess watch over you all."

"And may she watch over you." I bow to him, and then watch him descend the stairs. He will take a train home, where he will help the priests of the Meiji Shrine prepare for the blood moon. Most shrines will be bolstering their defenses this week, as Shuten-doji will be looking to weaken Amaterasu as much as possible.

Destroying her houses of worship is only the first step.

"I am sorry to interrupt," a voice says behind me. I turn, surprised to see Yuza standing in the gatehouse. Her shackles are gone. She stands before me, scrubbed clean of the cellar's filth and dressed in midnight black from shoulder to hip to hem. Her hakama pants swing like bells in the breeze. Like the other shinigami, she wears her kimono folded right side over left—only the dead wear their kimono this way. "But Lady O-bei wishes to discuss our next move."

Yuza looks so different from the monster that wanted to take my life. "Yuza," I say, turning toward the gatehouse. "You're free."

"Not until Shuten-doji is dead," she replies coldly. "He stole decades from me, and he will pay dearly for that."

"Does that mean you're joining us?" I ask, hope bubbling up in my chest.

A hint of a smile touches her lips. She turns. "Come, we have much to discuss."

I glance at Shiro, mouthing *Six!* at him. Counting O-Bei and Ronin, of course. If we can manage to recruit one more shinigami in the days left before the blood moon, we'll have a chance at destroying Shuten-doji. And not just for now, but for *good*.

We convene in the shrine office, which has become a flurry of activity. Yuza joins O-bei at the desk, as does Shimada. O-bei pores over maps of the shrine. Roji drops into a nearby chair. Ronin's at the window, his back to us, hands folded behind him. Heihachi leans against one wall, playing with his little white moth. Shiro and I sit on the edge of an unused desk, our hands close, pinkie fingers barely touching.

The butterflies, with all their wings in different shapes and colors, flutter around our heads. When I turn my face toward the ceiling, the dust from their wings coats my lips and slips into my nose. I sneeze.

"We have less than a week till the blood moon," O-bei says, tapping a long, crimson fingernail on the maps. "My people tell me the shrine fortifications will be complete by then, but we have yet to find a seventh shinigami." Her gaze hits me so hard, it seems to pierce my soul.

"We will find a seventh, Lady O-bei," I say, lifting my chin. I'm not about to be cowed by her, not anymore. Shiro and I have spent most every afternoon searching Kyoto for shinigami. We've managed to recruit six total death gods to our cause, which feels miraculous. However, all our weeks of hard work will mean *nothing* if we can't manage to find another shinigami. We need seven for a cabal. Only seven can slay the demon.

"See that you do," O-bei says. "You must understand, I have destroyed my relationships with the Iron Palace for you and this shrine—"

And your ambitions, I think to myself, but even I can read the air well enough to know I shouldn't say those words aloud.

"—And if we fail now, Shuten-doji will enslave us and slay the mortals," O-bei says, her voice rising. Several of her butterflies whisper across the silk of her golden kimono, as if upset by her tone. "He will likely hunt down every member of my court, and your family as well, Kira."

A shudder starts at the base of my spine, worming its way through my vertebrae and into my skull. On one hand, I know O-bei might be using my family to manipulate me into doing what she wants; on the other, I've seen Shuten-doji's cruelties. I refuse to subject my family, my friends, or this world to his rule.

We must defeat him, no matter what it takes.

"If you wish to succeed," Shimada says, rubbing the stubble on his chin with one hand, "we should take the remaining shards of the Kusanagi from Shuten-doji."

"And how do you propose we do that?" O-bei asks sweetly, lifting a brow. "Shall I send my armies to his front door and demand the shards back? Or perhaps you and I could raise Shuten-doji's last and most infamous murderer from the grave? One mortal man shouldn't be a problem, not for you and me."

O-bei smiles, but there's no warmth in the expression. I can't tell if she's teasing Shimada, or challenging him.

"Don't be melodramatic," Shimada says. "A group of us could break into the Iron Palace and retrieve the sword. These are oni— mere ogres, dangerous and stupid in equal measures. They aren't gods."

"*Most* of them aren't gods," Roji mutters.

"Are you suggesting a *heist*?" O-bei says with a little laugh. "My dear, we have five *days* till the blood moon rises. How could we possibly infiltrate the Iron Palace in that time frame?

Tamamo-no-Mae is no fool. It would take months of planning, curating assets, stealing maps and securing key posts—"

"I'll do it," Yuza says.

The room falls so quiet, I can almost hear the soft, feathery beat of the butterflies' wings in the rafters.

Everyone turns to Yuza.

She continues: "I served that *beast* for decades, and I know every corner of the Iron Palace. Nobody should go but me."

"That might work," I say. If I could face down the blood moon with seven shinigami at my back and the Kusanagi in my hands, I could be reasonably sure of our success. *Reasonably.* O-bei's people have been fortifying the shrine not just for an attack, but for a *war.*

"It's a terrible idea," O-bei says flatly.

"Why?" Annoyance snaps in my chest. "Shouldn't we do everything in our power to defeat Shuten-doji?"

"And run the risk of stretching ourselves too thin?" O-bei replies, gesturing to the map. "We have days left before the blood moon. Our resources are not endless."

I hop off the table, preferring to face O-bei on my feet. "So send *one* solider in," I say, gesturing at Yuza.

"Absolutely not," O-bei says. "It's far too great a risk—"

"As if taking on Shuten-doji here at the shrine *isn't* a risk?" I snap.

"Do not interrupt me, girl," O-bei says, the last word more growl than grace. "It is one thing to take an intelligent risk, and another to squander precious soldiers on unnecessary maneuvers."

"It's not *squandering lives* if we succeed," I say, my temper flaring. "Letting Shuten-doji control a major advantage makes it look like you *want* him to win."

O-bei blanches. The color seeps out of her eyes, leaving them pale as moonstones. I bite back my anger, knowing I've let things go too far. "I'm sorry, Lady O-bei," I say with a short bow. "That was unfair of me."

She lets my apology hang in the air for a beat, and then moves on as if I never lost my temper. "Time moves differently in Yomi," O-bei says, smoothing her hands down the front of her kimono. "Spending hours in Yomi costs days in the mortal realm. And if we were to lose a shinigami in the endeavor . . ."

O-bei trails off. Roji punctuates the silence by flicking her butterfly knife open and closed. Heihachi stares at the floor. Neither Shiro nor Ronin has said much since our conversation began. Shiro stands quietly beside me, running the back of his thumbnail over his lower lip, lost in thought.

"Let us send Yuza in," Shimada says, knocking once on the desk. "I understand your concern, Lady O-bei, but I do not wish to leave this battle to chance. If Kira"—he gestures to me—"wields the sword, victory is far more likely."

O-bei turns her glimmering eyes on Shimada, narrowing her gaze. She takes a step toward him, sizing him up, cocking her head to one side. "And why are you so keen on retrieving the blade, hmm? You, the shinigami without a name? What drives you to demand . . ."

But her eyes widen, her lips curving into an *o* shape. Her gaze slides to Roji, and she asks, "Ah, I think I know what's happening here—you were bearers of the shattered blade, weren't you? I heard everyone involved in that act was punished, but I didn't know you were turned into *shinigami*."

Roji turns her face away with a *tch*. Shimada says nothing.

"So much for your noble hearts," O-bei says, covering her mouth as she snickers. "You are both here to settle an old score."

"As are you," Shimada says.

"Wait," I say, looking back and forth between Shimada and Roji. "What's Lady O-bei talking about?"

"Ancient history," Roji says, snapping her knife shut. The click echoes in the silence that follows. "And I'm not keen on giving any of you a lesson. I'm out."

Roji pushes out of her chair and leaves the room, letting the door slam in her wake. I look to Shimada, but he shakes his head.

"It's a long story," he says. "A long, tragic story."

I cross my arms over my chest. "We have time—"

"Time is the one thing we *don't* have," O-bei says.

"That, and the rest of the Kusanagi," Shiro mutters under his breath.

O-bei looks at him, long and hard, until Shiro bows his head. "If I allow Yuza to attempt this, she must leave tonight. Otherwise she may not return before the blood moon rises. Kira, I would like to send you with her."

"What?" Shiro and I say in tandem. Only I ask, "Why me?"

"Because Yuza will need someone to feed to the oni if things go badly," O-bei says, and when she sees the look on my face, she laughs. "That was a joke, Kira."

"You've always had a marvelous sense of humor, Mother," Shiro says darkly. Ronin chuckles, casting a glance over his shoulder.

"Some types of magic need two sets of hands for the working, and I can't spare anyone else here," O-bei says. "Either you go with Yuza, or we abandon this plot altogether."

She's left me no graceful exit from this situation, not if I want Yuza to attempt to steal the shards of the Kusanagi. I'm caught between my love for the shrine and the terror of following Yuza into Yomi.

Yomi is death, but the shrine is my life. This is my one and truest home.

"Fine," I say, looking to Yuza. "Let's go steal a sword."

"If Kira's going, so am I," Shiro says.

"No," O-bei says. "We are not risking anyone else on this little excursion, especially you. I need you to remain behind and search for the final member of our cabal."

"Then send me in her place," Shiro says. "Kira can keep looking, and I'm the better onmyōji—"

"No," O-bei says, her tone making it clear she won't brook any arguments. "If this sword is so important to them, let these fools try to steal it from the demon god."

Yuza and I are to leave at sunset. I head home to change my clothes, but my feet carry me to the motomiya instead. The small shrine sits in the growing shadows, alone and forgotten. But forgetting the night Grandfather died will be impossible, I think. Even if we win—even if we manage to bring the sword back—I will never forget the blood that was spilled here.

The boards still sing when I step inside. I kneel on the stained floor, pressing my palms into the wood until it bites into my skin. The pain distracts me from the wounds in my heart. And then I lean down until my forehead touches the ground.

"I'm scared, Grandfather," I whisper to the boards. "Is it all right to be frightened?"

I sit up, but no answer comes. I am not a shinigami—I cannot call out to the dead.

"Your sacrifice will not be forgotten," I say with a shiver. "Not today, not ever. You gave your life to save mine, and in return, I will fight to protect this place till my last breath. Even if I have to venture into the land of the dead."

I'm not sure how long I sit in the small shrine—long enough, at least, for the evening to curl into the room and rest its head on my shoulder. Just before full dark, Shiro finds me. I hear his footsteps first, and then a deep inhalation, as if he's scenting the air. There's a pause, as if he's processing everything that's happened here, as if he can remember the way the blood rushed out of Grandfather's body from the scent alone.

Shiro drapes his jacket over my shoulders as he sinks down beside me, then pulls me under one arm. "You don't have to go, Kira. Mother's just being terrible. As usual."

"No, she's right," I say, with a shake of my head. It knocks loose a tear, which I wipe away. I steady myself with a breath. "We're going to need those shards if we can't find a seventh shinigami—maybe your mother will accept the Kusanagi instead."

"I knew you'd say that." He frowns, reaching into his pocket. "So I made you something, just in case."

"Really?" I ask, scooting over to give him a little more space.

He tugs a tiny stuffed fox from his pocket. No larger than the height of my thumb, the little creature has red-tipped ears and a tail that curls over its back. I take it from Shiro, running my fingers over the fox's silken fabric, sensing the strength of the magic within.

"It's a special omamori amulet," he says, tucking a strand of hair behind my ear. "I've imbued it with some of the magic from my hoshi-no-tama—a kitsune's soul gem. I hope it brings you luck."

I look from the omamori to Shiro, and then back again, swallowing hard. Nobody has ever given me such a thoughtful gift, not in my whole life. Words fail me. I throw my arms around his neck. He gathers me close, holding me for a few precious, comforting seconds, before I pull away.

"Thank you," I whisper.

"Anytime, and anything you need," he says, letting me snuggle under his chin. "Always."

He holds me till the sun is gone.

TWENTY-SEVEN
Fujikawa Shrine

Kyoto, Japan

At dusk, Shiro and I join the others in the courtyard. Shimada stands with his back to us. Roji and Yuza both crouch a few yards away from him, tutting shadows into shapes. Smoke twists off their fingers, crackling like fire and forming twin hashira poles. A lintel forms atop them, completing a nightmarish torii gate. The space between the poles looks black as cats' pupils—not even the courtyard's floodlights can break darkness so deep.

The sight of it makes my heart thump. Shiro squeezes my hand, then tugs me to a stop. Pivoting on his heel, he blocks me from the group with his body. "I should go with you," he says, looking to the side and swallowing hard. When his gaze wanders back to mine, I can see the ache in him. "I can't let you walk into the Iron

Palace alone, not when Shuten-doji and Tamamo-no-Mae want you dead."

"You can't, you know you can't." I cup his cheek with one hand. "Even if Yuza and I manage to find the sword, our hours will be your *days*."

"I know," he whispers.

"Someone has to stay and look for shinigami." I take his fox omamori from my pocket, showing it to him with a half-exhaled laugh. "And at least I'll have your luck with me, right?"

Shiro gives me a thin smile, but his lowered ears tell me I can't comfort him. He leans his forehead on mine. "Promise you'll be careful?"

"I'll be more than careful." On an impulse, I turn my face up and press my lips to his. It's a short kiss—a chaste kiss—but it still sets a dark corner of my heart on fire.

I hop back from him, pressing my fingers against my mouth. I'm a little embarrassed, but not sorry. Once Shiro gets over his initial shock, he grins at me. Every cell in my body yearns to stay here with him, where at least the world around me is a known quantity. Once I step through that gate, a thousand things could go wrong—I'm putting my life in the hands of my would-be assassin. Yuza could betray me and hand me over to my enemies. Or something terrible could happen to her, leaving me stranded and alone in Yomi.

"Kira!" Roji calls, beckoning to me. "Time to get going."

"I'll be right there!" I call back, trying to ignore the wave of anxiety in my gut. I'm going. Not because I have something to prove to O-bei, or even to myself; I'm going because the Fujikawa Shrine is *my* responsibility. It wouldn't be right to ask someone to do something that I'm not willing to do myself.

"I'll see you in a few hours," I say, bobbing in a short bow.

"I'll see you in a few days." Shiro gives me one last, wistful hug. I soak up the moment of security and warmth. While I want to stay nestled here in Shiro's arms, I have a sword to steal.

Releasing him, I turn to face the gate. Looking at it, its poles seem to be whispers made flesh. The mere sight of it leaves a sick taste in the back of my throat, as if I've just gargled with stomach acid. My whole soul scrambles back as I step forward. I clench my jaw to keep my teeth from chattering.

"The portal will take you as close to the palace as we can get you." Roji hands me a tanto knife—a kaiken blade no more than eight inches long, and designed to be hidden in one's clothing. "Take this. I can't send you in with a sword, so a knife will have to do," she says.

"Let us hope you won't need it," Shimada says to me, slipping his hands into his kimono sleeves. "The goal is to remain unseen, unnoticed, and unremarkable. The more attention you attract, the more dangerous your task becomes."

Yuza unsheathes her sword, places its tip against her palm, and drives it through her flesh. I gasp, surprised to see the blade disappear into her hand. She removes her sheath and tosses it to Roji. "We won't be seen. We'll take the back alleyways to the palace and slip through the corridors as courtesans. Nobody pays attention to silly-looking women."

"Not unless they're hungry," Roji says, her tone implying that she isn't talking about food. She looks to me, asking, "You're sure you want to do this?"

No, I think. But "Yes" still pops out of my mouth. Roji's eyebrow twitches upward, but she says nothing.

"Good," Yuza says over her shoulder, stepping up to the portal. "Follow my lead." Darkness ripples around her body like water, then swallows her whole.

Roji gives me a little shove forward. "Hold your breath while you're going through, eh? It'll be more tolerable that way."

Clutching Shiro's fox omamori, I glance back at the others. Shiro lifts his hand in a small wave, giving me a forced smile. Roji grins, as if she's already picturing what my face will look like once I reach the other side.

"We will watch over your shrine, priestess," Shimada says, tipping his hat back from his face. "Go get the sword."

"Okay," I whisper. Taking a deep breath, I step into the portal's embrace. The darkness hisses in my ears. I lean in, the air fluttering across my cheeks like the edges of butterfly wings.

The floor drops out from under me. In the darkness, I lose all sense of orientation—up, down, right, or left. Every sensory organ I possess seems to shut down, leaving me panicking in a dark, floating void.

Then the world rushes back as fast as it left, the air roaring, my heartbeat pounding inside my skull. I'm falling, lights gleaming and tumbling around me, until I slam into a rough surface and skid. Pain spikes through my shoulder and hip.

I roll onto my back, finding myself in an alleyway. The shadows of ramshackle, Edo-era buildings rise on either side of me, their roof tiles undulating like the waves of the sea. They're juxtaposed with modern houses, the boxy angles in stark contrast to the more traditional, ancient lines of the others. In some places, lone buildings jut from the ground like broken teeth. Trash litters the ground, a shattered CRT tube television lies broken on its side near my foot, and a strange animal's corpse hangs by its neck from one of the eaves.

The stars don't shine overhead, nor the moon. Diffuse, dim light bounces off low-hanging clouds. Underfoot, the ground trembles. The air smells like strange herbs, a sickly-sweet scent that clings to the back of my throat. Spiderwebs cover the walls, long funnels of dusty web disappearing into cracks and under the eaves of some homes. No lights blaze in the windows. On the wall beside me, a hand-size spider crawls toward the roof. I can hear its body scrape against the plaster.

"Are you all right?" Yuza asks, crouching beside me. Her voice sounds different, louder and more melodious somehow, as if I'm picking up frequencies here in Yomi that I wouldn't in the natural world. "I should have warned you—the first crossing is always the worst."

I sit up. Grit from the road bites into my palms. "Where are we?" I ask, tucking Shiro's omamori safely into my jacket pocket.

"The old quarter of Oeyama," Yuza says, scanning the area around us. "Come, we must hurry. And keep that bracelet out of sight—the less attention we draw, the better."

Frowning, I tuck my bracelet inside my jacket sleeve. I follow Yuza through shifting intersections, losing track of our direction. We pass dumpsters and the drifters curled up beside them, nekomata cat fights, and hollowed-out cars. And the *graffiti*! I've never seen real graffiti in Japan. Trash crunches underfoot, everything from paper scraps and lost phone charms to hypodermic needles. The alleyways seem to draw garbage straight into their veins. Everything reeks.

We slip from the alleyways, ducking into a vibrant night market. Colorful lanterns bob in the air. Yokai hawk their wares from innumerable stalls, which feature a range of products (and *smells*) that I don't recognize. I see fruits and vegetables I have no names for, some that pulsate with strange light; anglerfish-like creatures laid out on ice; and I look away from a display of what appears to be human hearts for sale. I'm dizzy by the time Yuza banks right, taking us out of the market and into the backstreets.

She was right about one thing—we draw no attention. If anyone notices our passing, they make no sign of it.

"Here," Yuza whispers, halting in front of a nondescript building. She places her hand on the concrete wall. The air shimmers. Bright graffiti explodes under her palm, paint rippling up from the concrete surface. When the mural completes itself, it depicts a red torii gate surrounded by demons. The concrete inside the gate cracks, shudders, and collapses, revealing a hidden passageway. Once we step inside, the wall re-forms behind us.

Yuza tuts a spell, summoning a hitodana orb for light. The magic tugs at something inside me, almost like . . . a *memory*. Before I can invite the idea in and dwell on it, Yuza plunges into the rough-hewn tunnel. "This will take us straight into the palace storerooms," she whispers, moving like a shadow. "From here on, I speak for both of us. Understand?"

"Got it," I say, struggling to keep up and yet stay quiet.

We move fast, silent as the dead. The air smells mildewed and slightly sulfurous. I have to watch where I put my feet, because single steps and inclines appear out of nowhere. Air whistles through cracks in the walls, and more than once, the ground tremors from something unseen. I count enough steps to make up a mile, then two. The walls shift from carved rock to stacked stone. Up ahead, one of the wooden supports used to hold up the ceiling has failed, its spine cracked, edges toothy. I turn sideways to slip through the rubble.

Yuza stands on the other side, running her hands over the shattered stones. "Help me move these," she says. Together, we dismantle enough of the rubble to reveal an iron grate set into the palace's foundation. Yuza takes the grate, moves it aside, and then slips past. I follow her, emerging into a dark, cavernous room.

Keeping to the shadows, Yuza leads me through the towering shelves full of baskets of rice, passing large-bellied barrels intended for fermenting soybeans or sake. I turn one of my ears back, listening to the scuttling of mice.

Or at least what I *think* are mice.

As we move deeper, whispers crawl from the shelves. Wicker baskets rasp. Bolts of silk snicker. It seems we've woken the objects around us, and they're angry to find strangers in their midst. While it's no surprise that the objects in Shuten-doji's palace have become yokai in their own right, it's unsettling to hear them. Objects in this world—or my own—that exist for a hundred years or more earn their own consciousnesses. We call them tsukomo-gami, or "tool kami."

As we emerge into the storage room's foyer, Yuza halts. She stops me with her arm, nodding at something up ahead. Ten kimono stand in a circle, blocking our path to the door. Their sleeves hang parallel to the ground, almost as if they're on display without bodies, mannequins, or wires to support them. Malice ripples in the air, and it tastes like I've touched the tip of my tongue to a nine-volt battery. My bracelet burns hot.

"What are they?" I whisper.

"Nothing good," Yuza replies, her voice barely higher than a breath. "Stay here. I will draw them away from the door—"

But something crashes behind us—the sound slices into my ears, high and bright, almost like pottery shattering. I spin on my heel. A pile of Gigaku theater masks now lies half-hidden behind a shelf. Some of their faces splintered in the fall. Yuza steps away from me, casting her palm down toward the floor and then up across her torso. Her katana appears in a flash of light. We exchange an uneasy glance over the arc of her blade.

"The stuff on the shelves," I say, taking a step back. "I think it's alive. Er, *aware.*"

"Breathtaking spiritual insight, priestess," Yuza deadpans.

Before I can snap at her—or even cry out—silken kimono sleeves wrap their arms around me. They slide across my stomach, my throat, and my mouth, wrapping me up so tight that I struggle to breathe. Yuza's katana clatters to the ground. She claws the silk away from her face, but it surges forward again, closing over her mouth and muffling her swearing. When her gaze meets mine, her fury is so sharp I'm surprised it doesn't slice the silk into ribbons.

"My, my, what have we caught here?" a woman's voice asks. I glance up, fighting to keep my balance as the kimono draws itself tight around my knees and ankles. I gasp through the musty silk, because there's no way I *wouldn't* recognize the white-tailed kitsune standing before us.

"Minami." I scramble to make sense of her presence, wondering if O-bei has sent Yuza and me into a trap. *Why else would O-bei's favorite pet be here?*

"Imagine how pleased His Eternal Majesty will be when I return Yuza of Osore, Scourge of the Tsujimori." Minami grins, spreading her nine tails like a peacock's plumes. She's guarded by three pomegranate-skinned ogres, each brute larger than the last. "How the Master has missed you, Yuza dear."

Layers of silk hold down Yuza's reply.

"When I heard this plan, I saw an opportunity to prove my loyalty to the throne," Minami continues, turning her gaze on me. "O-bei is foolish for trying to deceive her betters, and you have no chance of defeating Shuten-doji in Kyoto. I do not wish to throw my life away on mortal concerns."

How could you have so little honor? I understand that Minami could easily betray me—we aren't friends—but O-bei? How could Minami betray the woman who freed her, fed her, *protected* her? I want to scream, but the kimono sleeves muffle anything I could say.

Instead, I work one hand behind my back, reaching for the knife stuck in my belt.

"Besides," Minami continues, flicking her tails as she turns away, "the gift of Shuten-doji's favorite assassin—and the descendant of one of his oldest enemies—will secure me a high place in his court. Seize them and bring them to my chambers. We'll bring them to the War Room after the council disbands for the evening. You might want to . . . *hurt* them a little. Otherwise, they may try to escape."

"How hurt?" one of the oni asks.

Minami pauses at the storage room door. "Break a few bones. Not anything in their legs or arms—the Master would be displeased if his best assassin was rendered useless to him."

My stomach feels like it has dropped through the floor. The ogres advance. Yuza looks at me, her eyes full of apology. I don't have time for apologies—two ogres will be in range of her in seconds. I need to move—*fast*.

The third moves toward me, slapping the palm of his hand with his mace. The ogre might be ten paces from me. He chuckles when I hop backward, pretending to lose my balance. I tumble to the ground with a grunt, loosening the knife at my back from its sheath. I strain my hand toward its hilt, fighting the cocoon of silk for each inch of space.

The ogre takes two more steps. He smells of stale beer and overcooked onions. The stench makes my eyes water, even as my fingers brush the knife's hilt. I'm so close—the tendons in my arm burn as I push the knife free.

Swinging his club high, the ogre charges with a shout. I watch the weapon's studded tip, calculating its arc. As the club comes whistling toward my head, I roll. A sharp pain slices into my lower back. I ignore it, using the force of my body to push the knife through the back of the fabric. The ogre's club slams into the ground with a heavy thud. Taking hold of the knife's hilt, I jerk it upward, tearing the silk. Its scream is barely more than a whisper; it sighs across my skin as the fabric slides to the floor. Boneless and dead.

The ogre lifts his club, peering at the cracked floor beneath. He cocks his head, confused. I rise, clench my knife between my teeth, and tut a spell by feel, not by training. I form a triangle with my fingers and thumbs, using my ring and pinkie fingers as bolsters. Envisioning an inferno, I slam my hands together, fingers threading. When my palms connect, they clap like thunder. My hands catch fire. The flames dance like foxtails across my skin, leaving me unharmed.

I take my knife from my teeth. The foxfire roars down its hilt, setting the blade alight. The ogre growls, narrowing his eyes against the firelight. Gripping the knife by the bottom of the hilt, I fling it at the ogre. Its tip slams into the meaty part of his shoulder, and the fire leaps into his unruly beard. The ogre drops his club with a howl. Stumbling backward, he tries to yank my blade from his flesh. But the damage is done—the flames eat him alive, racing across his shoulders and licking down his back. He screams, waving his arms and stumbling into the wooden shelves, spreading the fire as he goes.

He left my burning knife behind. It gleams in the growing firelight. While the other ogres watch him in horror, I snatch my knife from the floor and race to Yuza's side. It takes a mere second to slice the kimono off her, and one more for her to grab her katana.

With two smooth strokes, she beheads one ogre and disembowels the other. Their bodies hit the ground, reduced to sacks of meat. With a short squeak, I hop back from their corpses. Pools of blood grow under their twitching bodies, slick as oil and reflecting the flames.

"That was quite the trick," Yuza says, wicking the blood from her blade with a short flick of her wrist. "I owe you my life, Kira Fujikawa."

"Don't thank me just yet," I say, watching the fire pull down one of the large storage units. Little foxes dance in the flames, digging their fiery paws through burning baskets of rice, or racing one another through the lanes between shelves; they stick their noses in piles of silks and tear the spines from books. The heat billows toward us now, scorching my cheeks. "We have to get out of here alive."

"No doubt Minami's already gone to raise an alarm," Yuza says. "Can you cast that foxfire on command?"

I slide my knife back into its sheath, repeating the triangular tuts I made. When I clap my palms together, my hands catch fire.

"Burn this place to the ground," Yuza says, motioning for me to follow her. "Come, we must hurry."

We dash through the palace hallways. Fiery embers fall from my fingertips and spring up as foxes made of flame. They race alongside me, frightening courtesans out of our way and sending the guards scattering. Confused tengu pause and watch us fly past, then flee. There's no time to process my surroundings—I glimpse a garden courtyard, painted shoji doors, and massive suits of armor. We run so fast, my heart strains. My throat burns as if I'm breathing fire, too. Exhaustion pulls on my muscles and bones.

Yuza banks right, taking us into a lavish quarter with golden walls and an inlaid wooden floor. We burst into a foyer. The walls glitter—gold leaf and gems decorate towering murals of oni at war, torturing human beings, and wreaking destruction upon the world of the living. The oni love chaos, so it's no surprise to find these scenes on the walls of their treasure rooms.

Twelve real oni guard a golden door. Unlike the ogres we saw in the storerooms, these creatures loom with stately, straight-backed strength. But even as they stand at attention, wielding their golden naginata polearms, they wear necklaces of rotting hands. Their thick, coarse black hair has been braided with bits of gold-dipped bone.

I wonder if they take the hands of thieves who steal from Shuten-doji.

As Yuza and I skid to a stop, twelve heads turn in our direction.

"Yuza!" one shouts, his fury shaking the very ground. He storms forward, the blade of his naginata whistling as he palms it. Bones rattle in his braids. "You traitorous monster! You will pay for what you've done!"

"Not today, Ibaraki," Yuza says, a sick smile twisting her lips.

Ibaraki.

I know that name.

That was the name of Grandfather's murderer.

A bright rage fills me. Heat flares in my heart, pumping through my veins. My skin begins to shimmer, then glow. My enemies step back, shielding their faces with their hands.

"Yuza," I say with a voice that crackles like fire. *"Move."*

Flames burst from my fingertips. Their light's so bright I can't see anything beyond the foxfire, which leaps off my hands in the shape of a massive, nine-tailed fox. The fiery, golden creature crashes down upon the oni guards. The yokai scream, but even their voices are consumed by the flames' roar.

The fires die as fast as they came. Seconds later, I find myself on my knees, blinking stupidly at twelve piles of smoldering embers.

Did I . . . ? What just . . . ?

Yuza chuckles. "My, my, you *are* interesting."

I get to my feet. Yuza reaches over and taps my chin, reminding me to close my mouth.

"Ibaraki?" Yuza asks, lifting a brow.

"He killed my grandfather," I say, following her toward the golden vault door. I spit on what I assume to be Ibaraki's ashes.

"Ah, I see. He was a bastard, anyway," she says.

We approach the vault door. I catch my blurred reflection in its smooth, dark surface, and tug at one of the strange ears on my head. The vault doors are inlaid with white gems that glimmer like stars; as Yuza begins to perform intricate tuts, the gems glow bright. One by one, graceful arcs of light connect them, creating strange constellations across the vault's face. The ground trembles. The light shifts clockwise and a metallic *thunk!* echoes through the room.

Yuza frowns as the light sinks into the door, leaving behind deep scores. The metal groans as it retracts into the ceiling and floor. "One would think they would have changed the spells guarding their vaults."

"I'm sure they never imagined we'd try something like this," I reply.

Yuza only grins. We step inside. I'm not certain what I was

expecting from an ogre-god's vault, but this wasn't it—finely dressed skeletons lie buried by heaps of beautifully wrought armor, and some pieces look like they predate any era I have a name for. A mountain of scrolls takes up one corner of the room, some of which float in the air, independent of gravity. Weapons glimmer from large racks on the walls. There are strange chests with eyes where the locks should be, or clockwork birds perched in the rafters. No matter where I look, I find something wonderful, or something I wish I had more time to explore.

Yuza snaps her fingers. The vault doors groan closed. "Come," she says, heading into the vault. "We don't have much time."

We pass multiple doors cast in various precious metals. One door appears to have been carved from a slab of jade, and the next has the cloudy gleam of quartz. One door has been cast in bronze; but nothing steals my breath like the golden doors at the end of the hallway, lit by torchlight.

The doors stand at least fifteen feet tall. A woman floats at their center, dressed in a kimono fit for an empress. Her hair flows long and thick under a crown of sunbeams, and the clouds beneath her feet. In her right hand, she bears a sword. In her left, a jewel.

"Amaterasu," I whisper. Even Yuza pauses before the door, her expression awestruck, her eyes soft and wide. It takes me a moment to shake off my awe, or to reckon with the fact that we've found Amaterasu in such a dark place. "I should bow," I say quietly.

"Then do it quickly," Yuza says, glancing over her shoulder. "It won't take Shuten-doji's monsters long to reach us."

I fall to my knees, placing my palms on the floor before me, and dip low enough to press my forehead into the stone floor. For the first time in hours, peace floods my soul. I draw a deep breath. Everything I have done for the last three weeks—no, for my entire life—has brought me to this moment. My grandfather gave his life to protect the light in the world; and after everything that's happened, I'm no longer afraid to do the same.

I rise. Yuza steps forward and places a hand on the door. It responds to her touch, splitting down the middle and swinging outward. We step inside. Yuza gasps, drawing my attention to a pedestal at the center of the room.

An *empty* pedestal, one with the memory of a sword pressed into its silken cushions. My heart skips like a pebble across a pond, then sinks.

The Kusanagi no Tsurugi—*it's already gone.*

TWENTY-EIGHT

Fujikawa Shrine

Kyoto, Japan

"Where's the sword?" I whisper.

"Shuten-doji has collected the shards here for centuries," Yuza says, charging up to the platform. She slams a palm down on the cushion. A cloud of dust erupts around her hand. "Either he moved the sword before we arrived, or someone has beaten us to it."

"We should go," I say, glancing over my shoulder.

"Yes, yes, I am quite aware that Shuten-doji's little pests are at the gates," Yuza says, pressing her lips in a thin line. She tuts a few spells, opening a small torii gate. Beyond its hashira poles, I can see the courtyard of the Fujikawa Shrine glimmering.

Yuza gestures to the portal. "After you."

This time, I'm prepared for the shock of moving through the portal. I hold my breath, close my eyes, and wait to feel the real world materialize around me again. It takes a second. It takes an eternity.

I open my eyes to twilight. The sun has slipped behind Kyoto's toothy skyline. And a pregnant, not-quite-full moon hangs over my head. I turn my face to the sky, the adrenaline draining from my body. Despair—or something very close to that—takes its place. My limbs feel heavy, my bones leaden, my heart a block of pure ice.

With the moon that full, we can't have more than a day left. I can't face Shuten-doji without the Kusanagi no Tsurugi—I was so close to retrieving it, and yet all I brought back is shame.

Yuza steps through the portal, closing it with a quick tut. "Damn," she says, shaking her head.

"Do you think Shuten-doji moved it?" I ask her. My words sound strange—off, almost as if I've gotten water in my eardrums. I shake my head, rubbing one ear with my fingers.

"No," Yuza says. "We left within hours of making our decision. Minami wasn't acting under Shuten-doji's orders—otherwise, we would have faced his entire Royal Guard in the basement."

"You're sure he had it in the first place?"

"Of course," Yuza says. "I have seen the sword there before—"

"Kira!" Shiro shouts. Yuza and I turn. Shiro jogs toward us. While the relief is clear on his face, strain shadows the lower lids of his eyes.

Yuza touches my shoulder. "I am going to report to Lady O-bei. Hopefully the others have had more luck in securing a seventh shinigami."

As soon as she's gone, Shiro sweeps me into a hug.

"I'm so glad to see you're safe," he says, pressing his face into my neck. His breath tickles the hollow of my throat, making me giggle. "I've barely been able to sleep since you left."

"I'm fine, I promise," I say, laughing as he sets me down. "But I could . . . *do* things in Yomi, Shiro. I cast spells I'd never seen before, and turned fire into foxes that burned down half the Iron Palace."

He chuckles. "Where's your fox omamori?"

I reach into my pocket and retrieve the little white fox he made for me. The fox's little nose appears singed, but otherwise, it's in fine shape.

"You?" I ask.

"*You*," he says. "You're not kitsune, but you're related to one of the most famous kitsune who ever lived. Like any kitsune, you needed something to anchor that power—you weren't born with a hoshi-no-tama like the rest of us. But I can share a little of my power with you, at least for another day or two."

I clutch the omamori in one hand, then press my fist against my chest. Not long ago, I clutched a paper fox in my hand, one that became the harbinger of my nightmares. But this fox holds the key to my dreams.

"I can't repay this gift," I say.

"Why should you have to?" He folds me in a hug. I lean into the comfort and strength of his arms. His touch keeps my despair at bay and buoys my spirit.

"We didn't get the sword," I whisper, stepping out of his embrace. "It was missing by the time we reached the vault."

"I figured, from the look on your face," he says, leaning his forehead on mine. "Our luck hasn't been any better here, either."

"The blood moon must be rising tomorrow," I say, looking up into his eyes. "What are we going to do? We have no shinigami cabal, no holy sword. . . ."

"I don't know." He presses a kiss into my forehead. "All I can do is trust in the kami, and trust in you. We'll find a way to destroy Shuten-doji . . . somehow."

"I wish I had your optimism," I say.

"C'mon." He links his pinkie finger around mine and gives my hand a tug. "We should check in with the others—they're probably figuring out what our next steps should be."

Morale in the office isn't high: Kyoto's shinigami have fled the city. The shinigami clans have disavowed our mission, and they swear to kill any shinigami that lifts a sword against Shuten-doji. Worse, our small team of six shinigami can't handle the rising number of dead, restless spirits in Kyoto—and Shimada worries that Shuten-doji may call those spirits to his side during our last, desperate battle.

My heart aches. After everything I've done, I'm no closer to victory than I was on the night Grandfather died. It seems impossible to have gone so far, only to find myself standing in the same hopeless place I started in.

O-bei paces back and forth in the office, the butterflies on her kimono fluttering wildly over the silk. "We cannot turn back now—failure will spell doom for each and every one of us. There must be *something* we can do."

"We are out of time," Shimada says, leaning over the maps on the office desk. "Which means our only recourse is to create a seventh shinigami ourselves."

A heavy silence settles over the office. I lift my gaze to Ronin, who sulks in a corner. If he heard Shimada, he makes no sign—he just stares out the window at the rabbit in the moon. Shiro shifts his weight, uncomfortable. I wonder if his mother's calculating gaze has fallen on him, but I can't bring my twice-broken heart to look. I couldn't bear to lose Shiro, too.

"With who?" Roji asks with a snort, batting one of Shimada's butterflies out of her face. She pushes off the wall, stalking toward him. "Not sure you've noticed, but almost everyone in this room is *dead*."

"*Almost* everyone," O-bei says, and my skin crawls with the idea hidden in those two words. But when I lift my head, I realize she doesn't have Shiro in her sights.

She's looking straight at *me*.

"Go to hell," Roji says to O-bei. "Kira's done nothing to deserve this half-life."

"Except promise me *seven* shinigami," O-bei says with a lilt in her voice, as if the idea of taking my life and making me like *her* is delightful.

Fear doesn't grip me immediately—it creeps into my soul like ice overtaking a pond, starting from the outside and working its way into the deepest, darkest parts of me. I shiver, speechless and frozen. If someone touches me, I might shatter.

"Kira *is* trained to use a sword," Shimada says, but it seems like these words now cause him pain.

"Don't," Roji says, pointing a finger at his face. "Don't you dare start, too."

"Hush," Shiro says, holding up a hand. He cocks his head, ears perked and focused on the sounds coming through the walls. Even I can hear the ghosts of something outside.

Shiro moves away from me, heading for the office door. Curious, I round the back desk, following him. Shiro steps barefoot onto the veranda. If the cold bothers him, he makes no sign. I join him on the threshold, peering out into the darkness beyond.

A hulking figure stands in the courtyard, his broad, bare shoulders outlined in moonlight. He's stripped bare to the waist, and dressed only in a loincloth made from tiger fur. His long, dark mane hangs down his back in a series of knots and snarls. Two identical white horns branch off his forehead into curved points. He wields an oni's massive club and has a fabric rope twisted across his muscular chest.

I recognize him instantly, though it's been weeks since he's shown his face at the shrine.

"Kiku," I say, stepping out onto the veranda with Shiro. "What are you doing here?"

"I heard you went looking for a sword," he growls, untying the rope from around his chest. Slinging a makeshift bag off one shoulder, he holds it up in the air. Its contents clink together like shards of broken glass. "Too bad I stole it first."

I cover my mouth with my hand. I'd forgotten about our little exchange outside the shrine—it feels like an eternity ago.

"You?" O-bei spits, joining us on the veranda. The other shinigami emerge one by one, fanning out behind me. "Am I supposed to believe a blue-skinned *ogre*, a creature hardly fit to be a servant in the Iron Palace, managed to steal the Kusanagi no Tsurugi from his own *king*?"

"I have no king!" Kiku roars.

I place a hand on O-bei's arm, asking her not to interfere. She shoots me a look of disgust, jerking her arm away. I ignore her, stepping down from the veranda. The cobblestones feel like ice under my feet. I shiver.

"Several weeks ago, you came to the shrine asking to help slay Shuten-doji," I say, choosing my words carefully. If Kiku has managed to steal the sword—and this isn't a trap—I can't afford to offend him now. Reading the air may not be my strongest suit, but I think I've grown comfortable with the language of monsters. They seem to make more sense to me than people do, these days. "I told you that if you could prove yourself to my cause, I'd allow you to join us."

"Excuse me?" O-bei mutters.

Kiku nods with a *hmph.*

"So," I say to Kiku, "prove that you belong here, with us."

"He is not shinigami, Kira," Shimada says.

"If Kiku has brought the shards of the Kusanagi—*all* of them—I don't care if he's shinigami or not," I say to Shimada. "We'll have the weapon we need to slay Shuten-doji; otherwise, we're out of options."

"Not to mention out of *time*," Roji says.

Kiku sets the bag on the ground, then kneels. His big, clumsy fingers work to untie the knots in the lumpy, sweat-stained fabric. It appears to be an old sheet, twisted into a makeshift carryall, with knots to keep the shards from falling out. Dropping to one knee, I help him undo the package.

He shifts into a crouch. I loosen the final knot, then peel the fabric away. The moonlight glitters across thin, shattered spears of metal. I reach out to touch one of the pieces, and the whole pile hums with light. The shards closest to my bracelet glow the brightest. Even Kiku pauses, struck by the beauty of the sword's radiance.

I look up, dazzled by the light. "Why do you want to help us destroy Shuten-doji?"

Kiku regards me for a moment, sizing me up. Or perhaps he's weighing the costs of telling me the truth. Finally, he speaks.

"Shuten-doji killed my brother." Kiku's voice twists into knots tighter than the ones we just unwound. "I want my vengeance. Let me *fight*."

I know that feeling too well.

"You'll give me the sword if I let you stay?" I ask.

"Yes," he says, bobbing his head and shoulders.

"Fine, then," I say, bowing my head. I slide my hands under the fabric, then lift the shards and rise. I turn toward the shinigami. "When the blood moon rises, we'll fight that monster *together*."

TWENTY-NINE
Fujikawa Shrine

Kyoto, Japan

I have all the shards, but that doesn't mean I can make the Kusanagi no Tsurugi whole.

I carry the shards to the motomiya's cellar. Shiro and I work in silence to reconstruct the blade, communicating only in gestures and nods. O-bei paces back and forth, occasionally chewing on her thumbnail. I've never seen her look almost . . . I don't know, *nervous* before.

Kiku crouches near the well, too tall to fit in this space. Roji leans against one wall, watching O-bei pace back and forth. Shimada stands nearby, occasionally offering us a word of advice.

Slowly, we form what appears to be a very early and *very* rusty tachi. The shattered blade is almost thirty inches in length from tang to tip, not including its hilt.

But when I set the final shard in place, nothing happens.

"Now what?" I ask, looking at Shimada. If anyone would know how to fix the Kusanagi, it would be him.

"The blade was shattered with magic," he says. "Let's start there."

First, we try spells. When those fail, we attempt to console the shards with purification rituals. We spend the whole night trying everything we can dream of, and when dawn breaks, we carry the sword outside, trying to coax the shards together in the sunlight. Nothing works. And all my bracelet does is make the shards glow.

I call Goro for help, and he recommends a magical swordsmith in Narita. Shimada dismisses the idea, saying, "This is a sun-forged blade—no mortal fire will melt this metal."

I rub my face, exhausted physically, mentally, and spiritually. Every time victory looks close at hand, fate yanks it away again. With only six shinigami, we need the Kusanagi no Tsurugi whole again. If I can't find a way to reforge this blade by sundown, I may have no other choice *but* to give up my life. I've already tasted what it's like to end an existence—it left me dark and despairing. I'm not keen on spending the rest of eternity cursed to kill.

"Can we summon my grandmother?" I ask the shinigami. "Now that we have the shards of the Kusanagi, the Elders might be willing to help."

"It's worth a shot," Roji says with a shrug. "I'd like to meet the old bird—Shimada told me so much about her. You've been maintaining her kamidana better, yeah?"

"I don't think I'd have the courage to suggest it if I hadn't," I say.

"Nor would I," Shimada says with a grin.

Footsteps echo on the cellar stairs. Heihachi descends into the basement, befuddlement clear on his face. He leans into the room on the last step, one hand hooked on the wall, as if he doesn't intend to linger here. "Kira, there are some people here to see you," he says. ". . . I think they might be your parents."

"Ugh, that's the last thing I want to hear," I mutter, pressing my hands to my ears. "What are they doing here?"

"They have a great sense of timing, that's for sure," Roji says with a twinge of annoyance in her voice. "We'll get things ready for the summoning, Kira. See you in a minute?"

"Let's hope," I say darkly, following Heihachi up the steps. We part at Grandfather's garden, where I find my parents waiting at the gate. "Mother, Father," I say, performing a short bow to greet them both. "What brings you to the shrine today?"

And of all the days you could've picked, why did it have to be this one? I have a hundred and one things to do today, and *none* of them include a conversation with my parents. They're obviously here for a reason—and from the looks on their faces, it's not to say hello. Whatever news they've brought can't be as important as forging the shattered Kusanagi anew, or fighting off an ancient demon king.

"We need to talk," Mother says, judging me with a head-to-toe look. Her brows knit together, and that's when I remember I haven't changed my clothes since I got back from Yomi. I'm still wearing my enemies' ashes on one cheek, and there's blood spatter across my right shoulder.

"About?" I ask, rubbing my cheek with my sleeve.

"This is a private family matter," Father says. "We should go inside."

Great, I think. *That's exactly what I need, additional complications.*

I enter the garden gate's code and slide the door open for my parents. Once I've unlocked the front door, I step out of my shoes and head toward the kitchen.

Mother calls me back: "We're not going to be here long."

I halt in the hall. Both my parents stand in the genkan, shoes on. While I support their desire for a short visit, their reluctance to even remove their shoes alarms me. Mother frets with her hands, first grabbing her purse strap with one hand, then sticking her hands in her pockets, and finally clasping them in front of her.

"What's wrong?" I ask, looking between them. "Is someone sick? Did Ami get hurt at school? Or did the Miyamoto family decide I don't belong at Kōgakkon anymore?"

"No, no, nothing like that," Mother says, glancing up at Father for support, or perhaps for reassurance. Whatever she's looking for, Father doesn't pay her any mind. "I suppose it's best not to sugarcoat the issue. . . . Kira, I'm sorry, but I've chosen to sell the shrine."

It takes her words a full second to sink in—first, because I can't imagine the *Fujikawa Shrine* not belonging to a member of the Fujikawa family; and secondly, because everything I have done, every sacrifice I have made has been for the shrine. For our *family.* Grandfather's *blood* still stains the floorboards of the motomiya. How many nights have I stayed awake, counting the hours till the next full moon? How many times has my life been threatened, my body been injured, and my spirit bruised in the name of this place? And now my parents want to take it all away from me?

I want to scream, to lose my temper and let them feel the full weight of my fury. *How dare you?*

How dare you think you have the right to do this? To take this away from me? From our family, and every generation that comes after us?

And to my mother: *How dare you turn your back on everything we are?*

I don't say any of these things. What else is there to say? By this time tomorrow, an eternal darkness may coat the world because I have *failed.* Or perhaps I will have turned my back on life to follow our shinigami into the abyss.

"You understand, don't you?" Mother says, her voice like steel. "Your father and I . . . we don't want you to spend the rest of your life here, dealing with the problems of the shrine—"

"You mean *fighting monsters*, don't you?" I ask coldly. My parents flinch at the word *monsters.* "One day, perhaps you both will realize that I never had the privilege of leading another life. I never got to be *blind to these things*, do you understand?"

"Maybe you could try," Mother says.

"What, like *you*?" I spit, trying to control the fire on my tongue and failing. "I know you can see who and what Shiro is—I know you can see the yokai, at least some of them. And rather than try to protect me, you *abandoned* me. Just like you did the shrine—"

"Don't you judge me," Mother snaps. "You have no idea what I had to endure to bring you into this world! And now you're friends with . . . with something like *that*!"

"Some*thing*?" I say with an annoyed laugh. "Shiro is a *shrine guardian*, Mother! He's not a *thing*!"

"Kitsune are dangerous creatures!" Mother lifts her voice— I realize I've never heard her yell before. Nor have I heard her acknowledge the yokai before.

"So are the demons you left me alone with!" I shout back.

"That is *enough*," Father says. My mother and I fall silent. Mother drops her gaze, face red, ever the dutiful wife. Father continues, gently this time: "We already have several buyers interested in the property. I think it's time that you returned home. All this talk of ghosts and demons . . . it's not healthy."

I open my mouth to reply, think twice, and shake my head. "I am home," I say.

"He means *our* home," Mother says.

"I know what he means, and my answer is no," I reply, grabbing my shoes from the genkan. "Sell the shrine. You've already turned your back on our birthright, what's one more slight to our family's legacy?"

My mother gasps as if I've slapped her with an open palm. I shake my head, then leave them alone in the genkan. I head through the kitchen. My parents call my name. Shoes clatter on the genkan's wood floor. I step out the back door, letting it slam in the frame.

As fury tinges the edges of my world red, I disappear into the depths of the shrine gardens. The natural world has always given me a measure of peace—I need it more than ever now. I run my palm over the prickly top of a manicured shrub, which hasn't been tended since Grandfather's death. I take a deep breath of the crisp, chill morning air. A bird sings from the branches of an evergreen tree. Closing my eyes, I turn my face toward the sun. Her warm glow passes through my eyelids, a brilliant spot of red in the darkness.

I don't want to lose this world.

"Am I interrupting?" a male voice asks.

I open my eyes and turn.

Ronin stands near one of the high hedges, hands in the pockets of his tailored peacoat. He tries on a smile, but it doesn't fit him. Several teal butterflies cling to him, their wings gleaming in the morning sunlight.

"You're the last person I want to see," I say, turning my back on him. I start to walk away.

"That's harsh," he says.

I stop. "Are you here to bungle an apology, or to convince me that I should join you in death?"

"Perhaps a little of both," he replies awkwardly.

"Save your breath," I say. "Not that you have it to waste, not anymore."

I turn on my heel, knowing I would give my life to protect this shrine. I might even damn my soul if the blood moon were rising and the Kusanagi no Tsurugi still lay in shambles. But there are hours yet, and I still haven't spoken with Grandmother. I will find a way to forge the Kusanagi anew—somehow.

I walk away. It's not enough just to survive the night—I want to *live*, too.

Ronin doesn't follow me.

THIRTY

Fujikawa Shrine

Kyoto, Japan

The shinigami summon my grandmother's spirit to the motomiya, but they leave me alone to speak with her. Grandmother's soul no longer looks like a specter from my nightmares, and her once-tattered spirit now looks happy, well fed, and *whole*.

I gasp when I see her, and dip into a bow.

"You see what happens when you remember your ancestors?" Grandmother says, whacking me on the back of the head.

I rise from my bow. "I'm glad to see it's made a difference."

"And then some!" Grandmother replies.

We sit in seiza form on the floor of the motomiya. The morning sunlight falls through the open door, glitters on Grandmother's ethereal form, and bounces off the motes of dust in the air. The sun comforts the aches in my muscles and bones.

"You've been stirring up trouble," Grandmother says. "Sneaking into Yomi, stealing swords from demons, burning down half the Iron Palace—"

My face flushes. "I'm sorry, Grandmother, if my actions have brought shame—"

"*Shame?*" Grandmother says with a snort. "Are you kidding? This is the most entertainment the Elders have had in *centuries*! Everyone's talking about you, including your prudish Great-Aunt Michiru. I have to remind that old goat almost daily that you're *my* granddaughter, not hers!"

"Oh!" I say, covering my mouth with one hand to hide my surprise. ". . . If only my parents were so pleased with my actions."

"Ah, yes," Grandmother says, the mirth draining from her features. She leans forward to place her hand on mine. "I know it must be difficult for you to see, but your mother has a good heart. She only wishes to protect you."

"Then why did she let me believe she can't see the yokai?" I ask, fighting to control my tone. My anger is still too fresh and new, and it bubbles from the cuts on my heart. "Why abandon the shrine? Why leave me to battle this darkness alone?"

Grandmother squints at me, as if I'm a lens through which she can gaze upon the past.

"I think your mother knew about all this," Grandmother says after a quiet moment, gesturing to me, the motomiya, and maybe even Grandfather's blood on the floorboards. "While she was pregnant with you, your mother spoke of a golden fox spirit who visited her in her dreams. The fox told her that the child—a daughter—would face a great darkness. After you were born, your mother stepped down from her duties at the shrine. I think she wanted to change your fate, but fate is tricky, and you chose your path regardless of your mother's intentions. Children are wont to do that."

When I can't find any words, Grandmother pats my hand. "May I see the shards of the Kusanagi no Tsurugi?"

"Yes," I say softly. "Come, I'll show you."

We descend into the motomiya's cellar. The shards of the Kusanagi no Tsurugi glimmer in the low light, protected by magical wards both ancient and new. Grandmother floats forward, halting a full yard before the altar. She performs a deep bow.

"We can't find a way to reforge it," I say as we approach the altar. "I was hoping you might know how?"

"No," Grandmother says, shaking her head. "We are a family of priests and priestesses, not swordsmiths. But . . ."

"But?" I ask.

"In life, I had a handmade stoneware bowl, passed down to me by my mother, and her mother before her," Grandmother says, resting her hands on the altar's edge. "It was my most prized possession. The day I broke it might have been the worst of my life—I was inconsolable. But your grandfather took the shards and restored the bowl with gold. After that, the bowl was far more beautiful and far more precious to me."

"I'm not sure what mending pottery has to do with forging legendary swords." I realize that Grandmother is trying to help, but I was hoping for a less philosophical answer.

Grandmother shrugs. "My point isn't that you should fix the sword with gold, child. It's that our scars make us ever more valuable. Perhaps you must accept the scars on this sword—and the ones on your own heart—before it will answer your call."

"I wish I knew how to do that," I say, staring down at the fractured metal. "If I'm going to survive the night, I need this sword whole. I can't save anyone—not the shrine, not myself—without it."

"I know, child," Grandmother says with sadness in her tone. We stare at the shards in silence for a few moments, contemplating the fall of night. "Perhaps it is better not to be a hero. You must remember one thing about the heroes from the old stories—not all of them survive."

All through the day, I try to reforge the Kusanagi. All through the day, I fail. The closer the sun gets to the horizon, the more the pressure under my ribs expands. The shinigami come and go; Shiro takes laps around the well, rubs his face with both hands. I eat when Heihachi shoves a bowl of ramen into my hands.

No matter how much I try to make sense of what Grandmother told me, nothing happens.

As the sun sets, I gather in the main courtyard with Shiro, the six shinigami, the oni Kiku, and Oni-chan.

"This is madness," O-bei says, gesturing furiously at Kiku. Despite her misgivings, the shinigami are going to try to form a cabal with Kiku acting as their seventh. According to Shimada, ogres serve a similar function in Yomi—though their skills lie closer to *torturing* humans in death, rather than reaping their souls. While there aren't any guarantees, it's entirely possible that Kiku's spirit will withstand the cabal ritual. Maybe.

The closer the sun gets to the horizon, the more I tremble. I tell myself it's because of the cold, which has been creeping up on the shadows' backs; I tell myself I'm just afraid of the unknown. It's not because I fear death; no. It's not. *It is.*

But I am not the girl who cowered in a basement while a demon killed her grandfather; nor am I the girl who allowed herself to be tortured by bullies. That girl did not have calluses at the roots of her fingers from hours of sword practice. She did not have clothes singed from practicing her mudras. She had not yet stepped into Yomi, nor faced down a shinigami.

On a crisp fall evening, I left that Kira Fujikawa on a train platform back in Kyoto. Scared and shaking. When I returned, I was forever different, and forever changed.

I'm dressed in my miko's red hakama paired with a white kimono, with my hair pulled into a high ponytail. I carry a regular steel sword shoved through my belt. Even if I go to face my death, I'll make sure my enemies die with me.

Oni-chan lies at my feet. Shiro stands at my side. The shinigami (and their rogue ogre) convene in the middle of the courtyard.

Shimada appears to be explaining the process of creating a cabal to the others, his red haori fluttering in the breeze. Heihachi looks overwhelmed. Roji seems bored, picking at her fingernails. This is the first time I've seen her wearing armor since the day she and Shimada arrived. She catches me looking at her and makes a kissy face.

O-bei and Yuza are both dressed in all black—from here, they almost look like sisters. O-bei has opted for a kimono, coupled with a slender breastplate over her chest and an armored amice on her left shoulder. Butterflies scatter over the fabric in white thread. Yuza wears black hakama and a black kimono, looking poised. Deadly. On the other side of the spectrum, Kiku crouches on the ground, naked to the waist, his thigh and calf muscles bulging. He chews his thumbnail and spits something on the ground.

My hopes now ride on an ogre. If he fails, all is lost.

It's almost as if Shiro hears my thoughts. He puts an arm around my shoulders, pulls me close, and kisses my head. "It's going to be okay, Kira," he says. "This is going to work."

"We can't be sure," I whisper, watching the shinigami take their places. Their formation resembles the Big Dipper constellation, with Shimada standing in the place of the Pole Star. The Big Dipper, or Seven Stars of the Northern Dipper, has held significance in onmyōdō since Abe no Seimei's time. Those seven stars have long symbolized a ward against evil and, perhaps more important, divine justice.

Shimada hasn't told me much about this ceremony, but I

understand the significance of the formation nonetheless. The shinigami face the falling sun, performing a complex series of tuts I can barely follow, much less read.

Silence falls. As they cast the cabal spell, their shadows take on monstrous shapes. Their figures grow long claws and curling horns, shifting scales and seething fangs. I take a step back as Shimada's shadow reaches out of the ground, pressing its palm into the cobblestones. It releases a cry I hear with my soul, one that sends my courage scrambling away.

The butterflies lift from O-bei's kimono and scatter from Roji's tattoos. Yuza's white moths join with Ronin's blue-winged swallowtails; all of which are dwarfed by Shimada's black-winged behemoths. Thousands of butterflies and moths swirl across the courtyard, curtaining something dark, sickled, and horrible from my sight.

"What have we done?" I whisper, stepping back from the creatures that are rising from the darkness.

"The only thing we could do," Shiro says, bracing me. "Don't lose your courage now; the worst is yet to come."

Oni-chan growls, glaring at something atop the main hall. I follow his gaze. A woman stands on the roof's gables, watching the scene below her with distaste. She holds her nine golden tails in a great fan at her back, and her kimono—golden and glimmering in the last rays of sunlight—flutters in a breeze I can't feel. Her beauty is otherworldly, so perfect, I almost wish I could capture it in my mind.

I know who she is without having to be told: Tamamo-no-Mae, one of the great evils of Japan, herald of Shuten-doji. Fear grips me so hard and fast, I can't breathe. I can't move.

They're already here.

Tamamo-no-Mae lifts a conch shell trumpet to her lips.

The horn echoes through the shrine like thunder.

THIRTY-ONE
Fujikawa Shrine

Kyoto, Japan

Oni-chan roars in response. He leaps to his feet, growing to his full size in a bound. I place a hand on the cat's back, bracing myself. The coarse fur on his shoulders grows in fits and tufts around his crisscrossing scars. He wears a deep notch in one ear. When Oni-chan thrashes his twin tails, their fiery tips spit embers and hiss.

They're here.

Shiro pulls me close and kisses me.

The blood moon hasn't risen yet.

The horn sounds again, this time answered by the shouts of demons.

They're here.

The shinigami unsheathe their swords. With a great shout, Kiku swings his club off his shoulder and shakes it at Tamamo-no-Mae. The shadows that surrounded the shinigami sink into the cobblestones, clawing at the air as if drowning. For now, the cabal ritual has been broken. Our enemy is at the gates.

"Shuten-doji shouldn't be here!" I shout at Shiro. "The moon hasn't risen!"

"It's not him!" Shiro says. "It's Tamamo-no-Mae—they're here to interrupt the cabal. They have to kill only one shinigami to stop us, do you understand?"

I nod, fear gripping my throat so tight, it's hard to breathe.

"We'll hold them off here," Shiro says, his ears pricked forward as if tracking prey. "Take Oni-chan and collect the shards of the Kusanagi. We can't leave the sword unprotected."

"Okay. Be careful. Please be careful." I cup his cheeks between my hands, noticing the amber flecks in his eyes, the small freckle on his right cheek, and the way his bangs feather over his forehead at an angle. If I die tonight, I want to remember his face in my last moments.

"You too," Shiro says. "Go. *Hurry.*"

Oni-chan butts my hand with his head, making a sound that's more growl than purr. I step back from Shiro, wishing I could stay by his side. But Oni-chan leaps away. I scramble after the big cat, passing the main shrine, skirting verandas, and slipping past the priests' dormitories. The motomiya looms ahead, its eaves looking charred under a sunset-scorched sky and bloodied clouds.

Oni-chan trots to a stop outside the door. I scratch him behind one of his ragged ears as I pass, whispering, "Wait here, I'll be right back." He makes a rumbling noise in his chest, leaping up to the roof to watch for invaders.

I descend into the motomiya's empty cellar. The Kusanagi's shards glint on the altar, resting on a silk cloth. I pause before the altar, bow twice to the shards, clap twice, and then bow once more.

"Please," I whisper, keeping my palms pressed together in front of my chest, eyes closed. "If these shards have a kami to guard them, listen to my prayer. If there was ever a time to forge yourself anew, Kusanagi no Tsurugi, sword of Amaterasu-omikami, well, this is it."

When I open my eyes again, the sword remains in pieces—as does my heart. Our mission now hangs by a thread, and I need the Kusanagi no Tsurugi whole again. If something happens to the shinigami, our only chance of success lies with this blade.

Outside, Oni-chan roars. Something shrieks. Tossing a glance over my shoulder, I twist the shards inside the silk cloth, tying it off at both ends. I loop the makeshift bag over my back and then tie it in front of my chest. It won't hold the shards long, but it keeps my hands free.

A howl rocks the motomiya. I charge up the cellar stairs, emerging in time to see Oni-chan slam an ogre to the ground. With a jerk of his massive head, Oni-chan tears out the front of the oni's throat.

A second ogre shrieks, swooping toward Oni-chan's exposed back. I won't reach them in time with my sword—so I tut the mudra for Rin, funneling all my fury toward the ogre. I collapse my fingers inward, riding the rush of heat that surges through my body. A bright ball of fire blasts from my hands, soaring across the courtyard and striking the ogre. He stumbles, his knotted mane aflame, shrieking and drawing Oni-chan's attention.

The great cat pivots, snarling, blood dripping from his chin. He coils, muscles compressing like powerful springs, and pounces. His front claws gleam like razors. Oni-chan hooks them into the oni, then drags it screaming to the ground. I turn my face away. Bones crunch. Tendons pop. The courtyard falls silent.

As Oni-chan steps off the ogre's corpse, I catch myself wishing I could climb onto his back and run—he looks large and fast enough to carry me far from here. If the shinigami fail, I can't let the Kusanagi fall into enemy hands. And if I can't forge the blade anew, perhaps it would be wise to take its pieces and flee.

I stand in front of the motomiya, one thumb hooked under the strap of my makeshift bag. My other hand rests on the hilt of my steel sword. The shadows thicken around my feet. Blood pools from the ogres' chests and throats—it has the color of pitch in the growing darkness. Fear coats my tongue, coppery and electric. Oni-chan pads over and bumps my hand with his massive, scarred head. I scratch him behind one ear, looking toward the shrine gates, and shudder.

Shouts whistle through the shrine hallways like arrows. The

trees around me quiver, perhaps able to see the violence in the main courtyard. From where I stand, I can only hear the battle shouts and the clang of metal on metal; in the distance, something cracks like a gunshot.

It's hard to be brave when the monsters that haunt your past have shown up to destroy your future. I turn, looking at the stains on the motomiya's floorboards. Even after they've faded away, I will always be able to see them. I will never forget what Shuten-doji did to me, to this shrine, and to my grandfather.

Stepping back into the motomiya, I drive the tip of my sword into the bloodstained floorboards. I wrench the hilt sideways, prying up a sliver of wood, which I take and stick in my pocket beside Shiro's fox omamori. No matter what happens tonight, this is *my* shrine. This is *my* home. Even if I am afraid, I will defend this place till my dying breath.

"Come on, Oni-chan," I say, sliding my katana back into its sheath. "Let's go kill some demons, eh?"

I swear that big cat grins.

We race to the front courtyard, which has broken out in chaos. Kitsune move barricades—of the physical and magical varieties—into position to keep our enemy contained. I spot Kiku standing atop the main gate, swinging his great club and knocking oni off our walls. The shinigami must be in the fray—I can't see them from where I stand, but a cloud of panicked butterflies churns the air with their wings. There's no sign of Shiro, either. I need to find him. If we're going to fight to our last breaths for this shrine, we're going to do it *together*.

I need a better view of the battlefield, perhaps from the shrine's roof. It'll take too much time to fetch a ladder—which means I'll need to get creative. I spot some leftover scaffolding still attached to the haiden wall. Hurrying toward it, I grab a steel pole and climb it like a jungle gym. I pull myself atop the building. Oni-chan leaps to the roof in a single bound, looking at me smugly.

"Thanks for the help," I say sarcastically. He follows me as I run across the roof, his bulk cracking tiles as he goes.

From up here, I can see everything—we're outnumbered two to one, at least. Shimada and Roji hold off a knot of oni near the gatehouse. They're standing their ground, back-to-back. One ogre charges at Shimada with a naginata-style polearm; Shimada sidesteps the blow, but before he can land one of his own, the ogre slams a fist into the shinigami's side, staggering him.

The ogre does not see Roji, nor her blade, as she slices him across the abdomen.

Wincing, I scan the battlefield for Shiro, but spot O-bei next, surrounded by a phalanx of kitsune spellcasters. Ronin fights at their front, every bit as fierce as I'd imagined he would be. O-bei hasn't yet unsheathed her sword, preferring to sling spells at any yokai who dares come near her. As the ogres try to push deeper into the shrine, O-bei and her kitsune hold them back.

I spot Heihachi on the walls with Kiku, pushing down ladders, stomping fingers, and smacking ogres in the face with what *looks* to be an iron wok. And Yuza! She moves like a hawk through the hordes of yokai, slicing down anyone or anything that comes close.

And that's when I spot Shiro—on his own near the edge of the fray, battling a *massive* ogre. I bottle back a scream as the ogre swings his club, slamming Shiro in the torso so hard, it lifts him airborne. Shiro slams into the side of our ema stand, which explodes into a cloud of sawdust, splinters, and shattered prayers.

The ogre jounces his shoulders, swings his club like a baseball bat, and stalks toward Shiro. Going in for the kill.

"Shiro!" I scream, my voice hoarse. "Go, Oni-chan!"

The big cat roars, leaping off the roof and into the fray. Below me, the noise draws Ronin's and O-bei's attention. O-bei's mouth drops into a horrified little *o* shape.

"Kira!" Ronin shouts, pointing at something behind me. *"Move!"*

I spin on the ball of my foot, my hand on the hilt of my sword. A woman stands behind me, one whose beauty makes time slow down so it can gaze upon her face. Her hair shines like liquid sunlight, bound by a piece of silk near her waist. Two perfect, triangular ears sit atop her head, and a tiny crown of bright orbs hovers between them. Nine golden tails float behind her like sun-struck clouds, and her furisode flutters in a ghostly wind.

She bears no weapons, but Tamamo-no-Mae—one of the Three Great Evils of Japan—doesn't need steel to make me bleed.

"Hmpf," she says, scanning me from head to toe. "*You* are the girl who bested Ibaraki with a look? I am almost ashamed I ever gave any credence to his abilities. You, girl, are nothing more than a human *mutt*. Kuzunoha's blood has been diluted to the point of perversion."

"This mutt managed to set your precious palace on fire," I say, drawing my sword. The dying sunlight glints off its blade. "I'd be careful, Tamamo-no-Mae. Even mutts have teeth."

She disappears, drawing a gasp from me. Something yanks my hair around its fist, and Tamamo-no-Mae's lips brush the shell of my ear. She tugs me close. "Listen to me," she says, and her voice cuts into my head like a scalpel. Blood leaks out my ear canal and drips onto my shoulder. I grunt in pain. "I refuse to watch a mere *child* of sixteen summers destroy my work. When the blood moon rises, you will bow before Shuten-doji and hand him the sword that you have stolen."

"Never," I whisper. "I will *never* bow to you or your master—"

A shock wave slams into my back, sending me tumbling, head over heels, across the rooftop. My sword clatters away. A rib hits a tile at the wrong angle, and a *crack* resonates through my chest. I roll to a stop near the roof's edge. The Kusanagi's shards clatter against my back. As I push myself up on one elbow, I watch Tamamo-no-Mae advance. She's a black shadow, outlined by the setting sun, her nine tails blazing with bright fire. Long claws extend from her fingertips, each gleaming in the light. I try to breathe, but it's like someone's bound my ribs with silk. Each breath I draw feels too short, too shallow.

Get up, I tell myself. *Get. Up.*

My sword sits in the roof gutter several yards away. Out of reach.

"Little mutt," Tamamo-no-Mae says with a *tsk*. Streams of light swirl around her hands. "It is time you learned what a *proper* kitsune can do—"

A dark shape lands on the tiles between us, crushing them under its feet. Black silk flashes as the figure charges forward, silver sword absorbing the visible light.

I squint against the sunlight. At first I think it must be Yuza, but the figure isn't tall enough.

It's O-bei.

"Traitor!" Tamamo-no-Mae shrieks. "You will regret this deception, O-bei Katayama!"

"I doubt that very much," O-bei snaps, lunging forward. Tamamo-no-Mae dashes right, up the slope of the shrine's roof. She conjures a ball of foxfire in her fingers, sweeping it high overhead. She leaps toward O-bei, slinging the fireball toward O-bei's face.

O-bei brings the broad side of her sword up to deflect the blow, forcing it to explode over her blade.

I push up to my feet, gasping at the pain in the left side of my chest. With a groan, I press one hand against my side, grimacing at the strange looseness of one of my rib bones. Across the courtyard, we're already starting to lose ground—Ronin now has control of the kitsune, and they're battling to hold the courtyard against a growing number of ogres. I spot Shimada, Roji, Kiku, and Heihachi with them; Shiro, not at all. My heart aches. I don't know where Shiro has gone. Oni-chan doesn't appear to be anywhere in the courtyard, either. I can only hope and pray that they both still live.

On my right, a woman screams. O-bei stumbles back, clutching her right shoulder. Blood gushes through her fingers, and she struggles to hold on to her sword. She's facing me. Bright streaks of pain shoot across her face. I can't see how bad her injuries are, because the half-downed sun burns in my eyes.

Tamamo-no-Mae stands between us, her back to me.

"Do you want to continue with this nonsense?" Tamamo-no-Mae asks, advancing on O-bei. She grabs the shinigami by the front of her kimono. "You've already lost, *Lady* O-bei. Your foolish little rebellion ends now—"

I don't listen to anything more. Lunging forward, I take two steps and grab my sword out of the gutter. Tamamo-no-Mae rotates an ear toward me. I get a better grip on my sword. Tamamo-no-Mae shoves O-bei away and turns her head. There's no time to think about my next move; all I know is that I can't afford to lose O-bei. Not now, not with the sun setting.

I charge in, shrieking at Tamamo-no-Mae. She feints left, but this time, I'm quicker at tracking her movements. I pivot and swing my sword in her direction. I slice through the air, missing the kitsune by inches. With a snarl, she sidesteps my blade and slashes at my open flank. Her claws catch the fabric of the bag I wear around my chest. The silk rips, and the weight of the

Kusanagi's shards goes crashing into the roof tiles. The bag splits open, leaving the shards to glimmer in the sun.

Tamamo-no-Mae's eyes widen. A smile turns her lips. Before she can move, I dive toward her, thrusting my shoulder into her solar plexus. She loses her footing, and we go down, tumbling toward the edge of the roof. I barely manage to catch myself at the gutter, jamming one hand and my knee at the lip. My sword sails straight off the ledge and clatters onto the cobblestones below.

"Enough!" Tamamo-no-Mae shouts, heaving herself to her feet. Pushing off the gutter with one foot, I scramble toward the shards of the Kusanagi on my palms and knees. Furious, Tamamo-no-Mae rushes toward me, claws bared.

O-bei steps between us.

There's a meaty crunch, and O-bei's back goes rigid. Her head snaps backward, and her lips whisper something to the sky. She drops her sword, wavering on her feet. I see Tamamo-no-Mae's claws last, sticking out of O-bei's back. Blood drips off the ends of her fingers, spattering over the roof tiles.

Fury overtakes my good sense. I grab O-bei's sword, and its hilt hisses against my skin. Before Tamamo-no-Mae can pull her fingers from O-bei's body, I strike blind, bringing O-bei's sword down in a whistling arc. Someone screams—I don't know if it's the sword, Tamamo-no-Mae, or me.

Tamamo-no-Mae stumbles backward. Blood spurts.

We both stare in confusion at the severed stump of her arm.

THIRTY-TWO
Fujikawa Shrine

Kyoto, Japan

Tamamo-no-Mae shrieks in pain, stumbling out of reach. "This isn't over," she snarls, wrapping the length of her furisode sleeve around her injured arm. "Shuten-doji is rising, and now you have no cabal! Fools! May your ends be as pathetic as your useless lives!"

Tamamo-no-Mae blows two short blasts on her horn, and then disappears in a blinding streak of light.

With a gasp, O-bei wrenches Tamamo-no-Mae's severed hand from her chest. Spasms race from the wrist to the fingers, making the hand snap to and fro. It flicks O-bei's own blood over her face. Sneering, O-bei chucks it off the roof, grasps her chest, and falls to one knee. Thick black fluid pumps between her fingertips.

"O-bei!" I cry, dropping her sword. I hurry to her side, bracing her by the shoulder. She tries to jerk away, but manages only to crumple into a series of ragged coughs. I press my hand into her chest, trying to stanch the bleeding. *It can't end this way, not after everything we've done, not after everything we've suffered! Not like this!*

"How can I—I mean, w-what do you need me to do?" I ask her. "You're a death god, just tell me what to do! Can't you stop death?"

"No," O-bei rasps. Her shoulders slump. Something rattles in her chest, almost as if her heart has dried up and now clatters against dry rib bones. Shadows pool beneath her, circling like sharks. "The bitch hit her mark too well."

My eyes burn. A single, hot tear races down my cheek. I help O-bei lie back on the roof tiles, supporting her head on my knees. "You can't go," I say, fighting to keep the tears away. "You can't, we're so close, we have to keep fighting—"

"*You* have to keep fighting," O-bei says as one of my tears falls into her hair. I sniffle, wondering if I'm mourning her loss, the loss of our only way to defeat Shuten-doji, or both. "You failed to bring my seven shinigami, forcing me to settle for a filthy oni—"

I half chuckle at this, wiping my eyes.

O-bei draws a shaky breath. "But I need you to *win*, Kira. Promise me that my people will remain free. They have fought too long, and suffered too much, only to be pressed back into the service of a monster. If I didn't believe you capable, I wouldn't have saved your life."

"Okay," I say, nodding. My vision swims now, and I run the back of my hand under my nose.

"*Promise* me."

"I promise, Lady O-bei," I say, bobbing my head. "I promise we'll find a way to protect your people."

One by one, the others join us on the roof. Ronin finds us first, falling to his knees by O-bei's side. She turns her face toward him, then reaches up to trace his cheekbone with a finger. Her hand shakes, then falters. Ronin catches it, cradling it in his own.

Shimada and Roji arrive next. Shimada removes his hat, sinking to one knee beside Ronin. Heihachi crouches nearby, wiping his face with his palm. Yuza keeps a respectful distance, too, watching over the courtyard like a sentinel. Even Kiku seems to have found some manners. He sits on the edge of the roof, looking over and chewing on a bit of his beard.

As the sun sinks to three-quarters gone, Shiro limps toward us. My heart soars to see him alive, and then shatters when I see the look on his face. Oni-chan pads next to him, both creatures battered but breathing. Shiro kneels across from his brother. O-bei reaches for Shiro with her free hand, and he clasps it tight. Her blood runs down the roof in a black river, collecting in the gutter at the edge. In the courtyard beyond, countless corpses are scattered across the ground—mostly ogres, but I spot the kitsune among them, too. Death lies everywhere I look.

"Whatever . . . it takes . . . ," O-bei rasps to her children. "You . . . protect our people. . . . Understand?"

Ronin nods, his face devoid of emotion. Shiro sniffles and wipes at his eyes with the back of his sleeve. He meets my gaze for a moment, the despair he feels no doubt mirrored on my own face.

"Finish . . . my work . . . ," O-bei says, turning to Ronin.

"Yes, Mother," he says.

"And you . . . ," she says, turning toward Shiro. "Grow . . . a tail . . . it will make both of your mothers happy."

This makes Shiro half laugh, half sob, an unattractive combination that somehow feels like the only way to respond. I wish I could withdraw from this horribly private moment; it feels wrong to witness so much pain. And it feels worse to know that it's being suffered for my sake.

"Be good . . . to each other . . . ," O-bei says, and each word feels more painful than the last. "Remember . . . you only have your brother. . . ."

When the sunlight is no more than a glimmer on the tops of the mountains, O-bei slips away. Ronin reaches out and closes her eyes—a strangely human act. I cover my face with my hands, letting the tears pool in my palms. We have come so far, *too* far, to lose now. I don't know how to keep all the promises I've made to O-bei, or to Grandfather, or even to *myself* at this point. Our hopes for a cabal now lie dead in my lap, and the Kusanagi remains little more than a holy heap of trash.

"What happens to shinigami when they die?" I ask, hollow.

"They cease to be," Shimada replies. "It is the same fate Shuten-doji will suffer if we succeed."

In the east, the sky has begun to redden. *We don't have much time.* I see only one path to success left to me, one last desperate ploy to win.

As Ronin gathers O-bei's body into his arms, I lift my gaze to

Shimada. "Can you turn me into a shinigami, Shimada-sama? Is there time enough?"

"Kira!" Shiro says in a half gasp, half reprimand.

"We don't have any other choice," I say, rising to my feet. "I won't let O-bei give her life in vain."

Shiro leaps up. "We can find another way—"

"How, Shiro?" I say, taking the bag of broken shards and shaking it at him. "The Kusanagi no Tsurugi is broken beyond repair, and the blood moon is rising. We are *out* of options. We are *out* of time."

"That doesn't mean you have to give your life!" Shiro shouts, a big vein throbbing in his forehead.

"Enough," Shimada says, stepping between us. "I agree with your shrine guardian, Kira. Even if there was time enough for your transformation, defeating Shuten-doji is not worth your life. Not when we have other options."

"Then what do you suggest we do?" I say, not a little coldly.

"The same thing we did five hundred years ago," Roji says, crossing her arms over her chest. "We *run*."

"Where?" I say, not sure which admission shocks me more, the fact that Roji's willing to abandon our mission wholesale, or that she might have had something to do with the current state of the Kusanagi no Tsurugi. "It doesn't matter where we go— Shuten-doji *will* find us."

"Then we keep running," Shiro says, taking me by the hand. "I won't sit here and watch you end your life, Kira. My job is to protect this shrine, and *you* are its beating heart. If you die, not only do I fail my vows, but I fail the person I care most for in this world."

My words flee. I open and close my mouth like a koi, as if Shiro has managed to suck all the air from the space around us. I have no clever response or snappy comeback, because my anger deflates faster than the heat can build inside me.

"How can we protect the shrine if we abandon it?" I whisper to him.

He folds my hands in his. "Sword first, then the shrine."

I press my lips together, hating that he makes good sense. If we leave the shrine, it will most certainly be torn to bits by Shuten-doji's yokai; but if we don't protect the Kusanagi no Tsurugi, the loss of the shrine won't matter. Nothing will.

"I'm sorry to interrupt this nauseating moment," Roji says, crouching at the roof's edge, "but we should move now. Moon's rising."

The first sliver of a red moon appears on the eastern horizon. The shinigami turn their heads in unison, as if they can sense its energy.

"Roji's right, we need to leave," Shimada says. "Split up. Meet in Undertokyo at the Red Plum Inn—Roji and I will guard the priestess."

The other shinigami melt into the shadows. Even Kiku leaps from the rooftop in a huff, muttering something under his breath about Shuten-doji. Shiro kisses me on the forehead. "I'll see you soon."

"You're not coming with us?" I ask, looking back and forth

between him and Shimada.

"Someone's gotta keep an eye on Oni-chan," Shiro says with a grin.

"Better for each of us to travel alone," Shimada says. "But we cannot take that chance, not with the shards of the Kusanagi."

"Let's go, let's *go*, people!" Roji says, hustling me toward the edge of the roof. "We literally don't have all night."

As I drop to the ground, a flicker of light catches my attention. A golden ghost stands on a far veranda, dressed in an elegant red kimono. Her nine long tails fall behind her in an elegant, fluffy train. She radiates warmth, security, and kindness; almost like the shield that protected me in the Twilight Court, or the fire that sprang from my fingertips in the Iron Palace.

"Kuzunoha?" I whisper.

With a smile, she beckons to me. The air ripples around me. Time slows. Roji gets stuck leaping from the roof, as if someone hit the pause button on her in an action scene. Behind me, Oni-chan hovers mid-leap; and Shiro balances on one tiptoe, caught in the middle of his stride.

I turn back, and the kitsune spirit disappears around a corner.

"Wait!" I call, jogging after her, following the golden embers that float in her wake. They lead me to the gaping mouth of the motomiya, which now lies cast in shadow.

The embers trail down into the darkened cellar.

With a quick glance over my shoulder—and perhaps against my better judgment—I step inside.

THIRTY-THREE

Fujikawa Shrine

Kyoto, Japan

The cellar is empty.

The last of Kuzunoha's golden embers float in the air, sizzling out one by one. A whisper curls in one corner of the room. I turn to trace it, only to feel something scamper between my feet. My pulse flutters in my throat. I reach for my katana, remembering too late that I lost it fighting Tamamo-no-Mae.

"Who's there?" I say, stepping back as whispers take shape in my ears.

"Outcast."

"Failure."

"Dishonorable."

"Mutt."

Something moves on the razor's edge of my sight. It draws a raspy breath, then materializes in the cellar corner. In the dim light, I can barely make out the jagged outline of a pleated skirt and long, tangled locks of hair. The head spasms left as the body stutters forward, her joints popping in and out of their sockets with each step. Her head lolls back on her shoulders, exposing blackened pits where her eyes should be. A dark, oily substance drains from those sockets and dyes her cheeks black.

"You will never fit in . . . ," the ghost groans in Ayako's voice.

I step back. "I don't need to fit in, not with a monster like you."

A second voice adds: *"You can't fight . . . Kira . . ."* I whirl as a creature crawls from the well, this one pale with mud-splattered hair and fox ears. His eyeless gaze makes my whole soul recoil.

"That's not true," I tell him, balling my fists at my sides. "You know I've been training nonstop—"

"You're an embarrassment to the family." Spectral versions of my parents appear by the cellar door, side by side, their dark gazes empty of anything alive.

"I am the only one fighting to keep our family's legacy intact," I say, pivoting toward them. "And all I have ever done is try to be an honorable daughter."

"Honorable?" someone hisses. I spin, shocked to find O-bei behind me. She steps forward, her sightless gaze boring into me. With charred lips, she says, *"There was no honor in the way you let me die."*

A sixth voice slices through the darkness: *"Or the way you hid in the cellar while Ibaraki stole my life."* Grandfather steps from the shadows, oil oozing from his empty eyes. *"You left me to* die, *you coward. You do not deserve to bear my name!"*

Those words hit their mark, sinking between my ribs and piercing my heart. I close my eyes. My throat tightens. "I did what you asked me to do, Grandfather," but these words leave my lips on a whisper. My knees quake. The tremors echo through my bones and rattle in my skull. "I'm sorry. I'm so sorry."

"You're such a burden, Kira," Shiro says.

"An embarrassment to yourself and to our school," Ayako snaps.

"I wish you hadn't been born," Mother says.

They drag their bodies closer, their joints creaking and popping. I lift my gaze as the not-Mother reaches out and grabs me by the shoulder, driving her broken nails into my flesh.

"You're an outcast."

The specters circle me.

"You are a failure."

Their hands fall on my head, my shoulders, my arms.

"You aren't worthy of your name."

They speak in one voice now—the more I listen to it, the more I realize it sounds like my own. It tears the air from the room, making it difficult to breathe. Their nails break into my flesh, finding purchase to drag me down, down, *down.* Straight to my knees.

"You have already lost," they whisper to me. *"Give in, give up."*

"No," I say. The word is a small, hoarse thing. I swallow hard, focusing on one of Kuzunoha's glowing embers. I shake my head and say, "No," with more force. Gripping my sleeve, I yank the fabric away to expose my bracelet. The metal blazes, thrusting the shadows back. The specters shriek, covering their faces with their hands and bursting into clouds of black dust.

"My name is Kira Fujikawa," I say to the nameless thing I face. The dust rises from the ground and begins to coalesce into a new form. "I'm *not* a failure, not so long as the sun still rises—and *nothing* you can say will change that."

When the dust settles, I find myself staring into my own face. The creature has eyes like the backs of black beetles. She beckons me forward, asking me to join her at the empty altar. I step up, holding her strange, soulless gaze.

"I'm not ashamed of who I am," I tell her, taking the shards of the Kusanagi no Tsurugi from my back and resting them on the altar. "Not anymore."

The not-Kira closes her eyes and bows her head. She disintegrates mote by mote, the darkness spiraling away, leaving a brilliant, glowing being in its wake. I squint hard, holding up a hand to protect my eyes.

In the cellar's darkness, Kuzunoha glows like a golden star in the firmament. A floating crown of sunbeams spreads from the back of her head. She wears a multilayered Heian-era golden kimono, and her snow-white hair falls from her head in a long, unbroken sheet. My mouth drops open, so I bow deeply to keep myself from looking like a fool.

"You cannot wield the Kusanagi no Tsurugi with darkness in your soul," Kuzunoha says, her voice high and flutelike. She waves a hand over the altar, and my makeshift bag unrolls and opens, the silk lying flat at her command. The sword's shattered pieces rise into the air and puzzle themselves back together, but they do not fuse.

"Nor can I wield a shattered sword," I say, daring to lift my gaze to hers. "How do I make the Kusanagi no Tsurugi whole again?"

Kuzunoha smiles, filling my heart with the warmth of a summer's day. "My child, you have carried the answer with you for years."

"I don't understand."

"Do you not?"

"What have I carried for . . ." I trail off, lifting my left wrist. My sleeve falls back, exposing my bracelet. I know the charms by heart—leaping tigers, blooming chrysanthemums, a dragon in flight. But two of the charms are shaped like suns—one charm portrays her face rising from the mists. The other shows her rays glittering from a cave. Time has tarnished and blackened their faces, but gold glints along their ridges.

"These aren't charms," I say, sliding the bracelet off my wrist. "They're menuki for the hilt of the Kusanagi no Tsurugi, aren't they?"

Kuzunoha's smile widens. My hands tremble as I break the other charms away. Grandfather told me to protect this bracelet with my life; but he never told me the links weren't just holy, but *godly*. Did he even know? Or was the secret lost to time?

The Kusanagi no Tsurugi floats over the altar. Reverently, I fit the menuki into the hilt, under the diamond-shaped silk wrappings. I step back as a point of liquid light forms at the sword's tip. It melts along the blunt edge, filling cracks and veining the blade with gold. The rust flakes away, perhaps blown by a kami's breath. The hilt regains its luster, with twining birds, flowers, and blazing suns to decorate its hand guard.

A tiny shooting star races from tip to tang, leaving a razor-sharp blade in its wake.

Kuzunoha places her palms under the blade and hilt, lifts it, and offers it to me with a shallow bow. I accept it from her with both hands, bowing deeper.

When I rise, she has gone.

"Thank you," I whisper to the darkness. "I will not fail you, Kuzunoha."

Once my eyes readjust to the cellar's darkness, they find the faint outline of the cellar stairs. In the distance, I hear the shinigami calling my name. "Here!" I shout to them, taking the motomiya's stairs two at a time. I emerge into the night, finding the shrine cast in red moonlight. Overhead, the moon has risen into the sky, its face stained red with blood. "I'm here!" I shout.

The shinigami gather around the small shrine. Cast in the Kusanagi no Tsurugi's glittering light, I find myself surrounded by the shinigami and the souls in their protection. Hundreds of human spirits follow in their wakes—old and young, all dressed in white robes. Roji has only women in her care. Heihachi cradles a single child spirit, and I know it must be Sana. The sword even casts Kiku in a gentler light.

Shiro finds us last, and the spirits part for him as he approaches me. He looks different in the Kusanagi's light, his features a little more foxlike, with nine ghostly, black-tipped tails trailing in his wake. He wears his hoshi-no-tama around his neck.

"You did it," Shiro says, approaching me cautiously. I hold the blade up, displaying it to him. "How?"

"The menuki were missing," I say, and he grins. "I've had them on my bracelet all this time."

Shimada joins us. "No need to run now, eh?"

"No, there's not," I say.

A drumbeat rolls through the ground, quickening my blood. A great shock wave blasts through the shrine—*doom!*—making the buildings tremble. Cracks race like lightning along their walls. Tiles shatter and slide from the roofs.

A second *doom!* rolls through the shrine.

"They're battering down the gates," Shimada says. "To your positions, the enemy is upon us!"

We race to the main courtyard. Out front, the shrine gates heave inward, their big wooden bones bent and twisted. Massive splinters burst from new joints in the wood, looking like broken chopsticks. I'm not sure how much longer our gates will hold—we might have seconds before the demons break through.

Kiku charges forward, throwing his broad back against the shuddering gates. The remaining kitsune swarm around him, tutting mudras at the doors to bolster their defenses. Roji shouts something at me, but I can't hear her over the groan of splintering wood. Shiro takes my hand and shouts, "We stick together, okay?" I nod, but before I can respond, the demons break through our defenses.

The gates explode in. One door crumples like paper. The other one slams open like a pinball machine lever. It knocks into Kiku and tosses him like a rag doll, sending him sprawling across the cobblestones. With a roar, a massive oni charges into the court-yard, swinging his club in a wide arc. He must stand nearly ten feet tall, a towering, muscled *beast* in a tiger-skin kilt. Human skulls hang from a thick rope around his neck.

Shimada and Roji dodge his attack. Two crimson-skinned oni climb atop the gatehouse, surveying the shrine. One crouches down, rubbing his thick beard with one hand. He looks over his shoulder, then gestures to someone or something outside our walls. The third ogre leaps down, brandishing a club at Yuza. She dances out of his range.

I recognize the fourth and final oni who enters my shrine: this yokai stands taller than the first. His ropy red flesh looks like flayed muscle in the blood moon's light. A thick black mane of hair tumbles over his shoulders, one threaded with braids and bones. Four horns crown his forehead—two large, two small. He wears no armor, save for a kilt made of patterned silks and fur.

It leaves his chest bare, though his pectoral muscles look strong enough to repel steel.

This is Shuten-doji, Lord of Demons, King of Yomi. I recognize him from the stories I've read, and from the illustrations of him that have survived from ages past. But more than that, my soul recognizes the evil that emanates from him. A bright spark ignites in my heart. I grip the Kusanagi no Tsurugi and offer up a silent prayer to Amaterasu to help me strike true.

Shuten-doji stalks toward Kiku, slinging an oversize club off his shoulder. "You!" Shuten-doji snaps, his voice deep as a quake in the earth. "Traitor! Thief! You stole the Kusanagi no Tsurugi from my vaults, and betrayed your king and your people. You will die for your crimes, lowborn!"

Kiku scrambles to his feet, backing away from Shuten-doji until he stumbles into the front courtard pool. "You killed my family!" he shouts, spitting in the water. "And for what? For *nothing*! You are no king of mine, and the ogres would be better off without you!"

"Treason," Shuten-doji says, motioning to the ogres on the walls. "I will flay you alive, and then burn you for what you have done."

Shuten-doji moves so quickly he blurs, stepping in melee range of Kiku and stabbing a short sword into the other demon's chest. Kiku gurgles, his flesh ripping as Shuten-doji jams his sword up toward Kiku's sternum. The cries from my allies echo through the courtyard, but the only emotion I can comprehend in the moment is fury, and the only color I see is *red*.

The demon king yanks his knife from Kiku's body. As Kiku collapses into the pond, Shuten-doji turns to *me*. "As for *you*—give me that sword, girl. Or I will tear it from your broken hands!"

Those words shred whatever courage I held in my heart. Some-one screams my name as Shuten-doji charges toward me. I want to move, to dodge this attack, but my feet seem to have fused to the ground. Terror weighs my limbs down. Every muscle locks into place. Time slows. *"Move!"* I shriek at myself, but it's almost as if I'm held down by some dark magic, my body unable or unwilling to respond to my commands.

A gout of foxfire leaps from Shiro's hands, shaped like a nine-tailed fox. It slams into Shuten-doji's chest, scattering into a shower of cinders, and staggers him. Whatever spell Shuten-doji had on me breaks.

My rage pushes out my fear. I grip the Kusanagi no Tsurugi with both hands, recalling all the long hours of training I had with Roji. I'm no master; I'm not even good.

But I have to hope that I'm *enough*.

Shuten-doji regains his footing, shaking the last of Shiro's fire from his mane. Behind him, the shinigami battle his three lieu-tenants, three on three. Heihachi tugs a wounded Kiku from the water. The remaining kitsune hold the gate against a rising tide of yokai. We're desperately outnumbered, but the only demon who needs to die tonight—the one last death that will end all of this—is Shuten-doji.

"Do you not understand?" Shuten-doji shouts, lunging forward and swinging his club in an arc. Shiro dives out of the way, to my right; I leap backward. The weapon whistles past my nose. "Of all the priests in the world, I thought *you* would know what it means to be an outcast, Kira Fujikawa."

Shuten-doji draws his left foot up and brandishes his club high. He slams them into the ground in tandem, cracking the cobblestones. The ground bucks, forcing me to a knee. Shuten-doji swipes for me with his free hand, but I roll out of reach. Scrambling to my feet, I fight to catch my breath. It's already a ragged, shuddering thing.

"I sent your classmates to torment you, so that you might know oppression." He tracks me with his yellow-eyed gaze. "I wanted you to feel the same despair that my people have felt under Amaterasu's heel. I wanted you to *understand* us, but like all mortals, your gaze is pathetically short."

"Don't pretend you're some wise, compassionate leader," I snap, circling Shuten-doji, keeping the Kusanagi no Tsurugi between us like a barrier. "Not when you thrust a sword through Kiku's chest!"

"That fool deserved worse!" Shuten-doji rushes at me. Shiro leaps on his back, sinking his claws into the ogre's shoulder. Shuten-doji rips Shiro off with a roar, clutching him by the hair on the back of his head. Shiro snarls, clawing at Shuten-doji's face. In those precious, distracted seconds, I swoop in. Shuten-doji throws Shiro aside, but a second too late. I step close, slashing the

Kusanagi no Tsurugi across Shuten-doji's exposed chest. He pivots with a sharp howl, bringing his club down like a hammer—I dodge the blow, sidestepping his club, but not his fist.

It connects with my abdomen, punting me into the air. The pain inverts my world. I hurtle backward until I crash into the ground. I lose my grip on the Kusanagi and tumble for a few yards.

"Pathetic," Shuten-doji says as I struggle to push myself up, or even to *breathe*. My broken rib feels like it might be poking into one of my lungs. I blink the tears from my eyes, gaping like a fish left to die on land. "To think this is what Abe no Seimei's line has become! He would be ashamed of you, girl."

I push up to one knee with a half sob. The pain feels like a hot dagger between my third and fourth ribs. Clutching my chest with one hand, I take the Kusanagi no Tsurugi in the other. My palm is too slick to get a grip on the weapon. But if I remove my hand from my chest, I'm not sure I'll be able to keep upright. Bright fireworks of pain explode across my field of vision.

Fifteen yards to my left, Shiro gets to his feet, clutching his left forearm. It looks broken. Blood coats half his face, gushing from a cut hidden behind his hairline. Our eyes lock, and his pain amplifies my own. He can't fight with a broken arm, nor can he tut. I tremble, knowing that our survival now rests on my shoulders.

"If I'm so pathetic," I wheeze, turning back to Shuten-doji, "how did I land the first blow?"

Shuten-doji slings his club over one shoulder. I scored a line some ten inches across his flesh—it's no small wound, but it doesn't seem to concern him, either. "You cannot win. Even your shinigami are struggling to hold their ground against my lieutenants," he says, gesturing toward the shrine's main gate. I turn my head. Roji blocks an attack—barely—but her motions look sluggish. The left side of her breastplate has caved in, and dark blood oozes from her lip and coats her chin. Shimada dodges an attack, but he's limping. An inferno tears the shrine's gatehouse apart, and I see Yuza and Ronin darting among the flames, fighting off one of the lieutenants.

"Give me the Kusanagi no Tsurugi," Shuten-doji says, beckoning to me, "and let us end all this suffering."

"And what, you'll spare my life?" I ask with a short laugh.

Shuten-doji grins, throwing his club aside. "You're right, that does sound ridiculous. So be it, Kira of the Fujikawa Shrine. Bring me the sword, and then you die."

He twists his fingers into a tut so powerful, I feel it resonate in the air. Twin disks of fire appear to his left and right, spinning like sawblades. They rocket forward, carving twin lanes of molten rock on either side of me. The heat scorches my skin and dries the moisture from my eyes. *What is this fresh hell?!* I think, watching the red-bodied lava chew on the solid rock underfoot. The solid, cool stones I stand upon seem to be *sinking*, and I have no magical bracelet to protect me now.

The magma lanes corral me straight into Shuten-doji's arms. The molten rock is too wide to jump, trapping me between two fiery rivers of death. I lift my gaze. Shuten-doji watches me with a predatory focus, smile on his lips, his fingers slipping through another spell.

"Move, Kira!" Shiro shouts.

I lunge forward. The ground, two steps back, bursts into flame. Shuten-doji laughs. "A bird in a cage, indeed! Don't wait too long to come to me, little priestess—the stones are already melting away."

There might be fifty feet of free space between Shuten-doji and me. The lane isn't wide enough to allow me to attempt a frontal attack, not without burning off my foot or worse. At this rate, I would need wings to escape, or springs in my legs, or—

"Oni-chan," I whisper. The great cat stalks across the roof of the main shrine, licking his lips. It takes all my willpower not to call out to him, or even let myself look in his direction too long. Shuten-doji burns around a bit of ground beneath my feet.

"Oni-chan," I whisper again, calling him now, keeping my gaze on the demon king. The cat's ears perk.

"You'll have to speak up, little priestess," Shuten-doji says, taunting me. He licks his lips. "Unless you want me to make you cry."

I leap forward, rolling to avoid a double patch of magma. Biting back a sob of pain, I glare at Shuten-doji. "I said"—I rise to my feet, taking the deepest breath I can manage with a broken rib—"*Oni-chan!*"

Oni-chan roars as he leaps from the roof. Shuten-doji turns his head, but the giant nekomata covers the distance between us in two short bounds. He springs into Shuten-doji, staggering the ogre. The demon king takes a step back, his bare foot landing in molten rock. The blackened crust breaks open around his flesh, and red, bubbling lava swallows his leg to mid-calf.

Shuten-doji's scream breaks the sky. It hits my eardrums like a corkscrew and twists, spiking pain into my jaw, my temples, and my head. I'd clap my hands over my ears, but one hand holds the goddess's sword, and the other, my broken rib.

Still, I don't hesitate. Shiro leaps in, grabbing Shuten-doji by the mane, knocking the ogre off balance. Shiro is thrown clear as Shuten-doji tumbles back. Oni-chan's fangs are at his throat. For one heart-shattering, horrible moment, I think Oni-chan's going to land in a pool of lava, but Shuten-doji rips him off and throws him into a stone pillar. The cat slides to the ground with a whimper, then lies still.

I don't stop to look at the charred, burning stump of Shuten-doji's left leg, or even *think* about the smell of it—I charge to safety, passing his writhing, screaming form.

"Kira!" Shiro shouts at me, pain lacing his voice. "Strike now!"

I pivot, gritting my teeth and taking the Kusanagi in both hands. My heart in my throat, I drive the sword's tip toward Shuten-doji's broad back. It strikes home, but glances off his shoulder blade and slices though his trapezius instead.

I missed? How could I miss, he's right there—

Shuten-doji lunges for me, moving quick on his hands and feet. I dodge, kick a rock in his face, and run. He'll follow me, I *know* he'll follow me—I have the Kusanagi no Tsurugi, and neither of my friends poses him any threat. At least not anymore.

I run blind, half limping through the shrine. The blood moon now hangs low over the horizon, a festering tumor on the sky. The motomiya rises like a specter on my left. Skirting it, I step into the small hedge garden, hiding among the unkempt shrubs and Japanese maple. The cultured slopes of these bushes used to be Grandfather's great joy, but in the month since his death, they've gone wild. The loose pebbles crunch under my feet. I tuck myself behind a hedge and crouch down, breathing through the pain in my chest, scrambling to piece together a plan—*any* plan.

The wind carries a voice to me: *"Kagome, Kagome. Kago no naka no tori wa . . . circle you, circle you. The bird in the cage . . ."*

Something pokes me in my hip. Adjusting my leg, I reach into my pocket and pull out Shiro's fox omamori and the wedge of bloodstained wood I took from the motomiya. I tie them both to the Kusanagi's guard, hoping for a bit of fox luck and guidance from my ancestors.

"Little priestess . . . ," Shuten-doji sings, though the pain in his voice carries through his notes. "I have a gift for you. Come out, come out, and meet my pet. Or perhaps I will send it to find *you*."

The bushes rustle around me, releasing a low moan. Irregular footsteps crunch on the garden pebbles. I listen to them wander through the hedgerows, wondering what new torment stalks me now. Keeping my back to the hedge, I get to my feet, biting my tongue to keep from crying out in pain.

"Kir-aaaaa," something sobs.

I freeze, pinpointing the creature's location. It's one hedgerow over and starting to tear its way through. I'm in the middle of the garden, so there's nowhere left to hide.

"*Kir-aaa,*" it rasps again.

The bushes shudder, branches snapping like tiny limbs. A thin, gray-skinned hand shoots through the leaves. I lift the Kusanagi no Tsurugi one-handed, backing away from Shuten-doji's "gift." Another hand breaks through the barrier, making room for the creature's bulbous head and shoulders. It cries as it crawls through the hedge, tumbling out onto the ground with a *splat*. Its mouth isn't larger than a small plum, and its distended belly balloons from the creature's skeletal frame. It wears rags around its waist.

It's a gaki—a yokai that hungers eternally, wandering the earth in torment.

And it wears my grandfather's face.

"Grandfather?" I whisper, feeling like my heart's been impaled on my broken rib. The pathetic creature lifts its beady black gaze, whimpering. I limp to its side—a gaki poses no danger to me— and sink to my knees, tears welling in my eyes. "What have they done to you?"

The gaki opens its tiny mouth, muttering a mess of nonsensical syllables. Of all the things Shuten-doji has done to me, to my family, and to this shrine, turning Grandfather into a gaki might be among the worst.

The demon king has left me one choice.

I rise, swaying on my feet from the pain. Grandfather cranes his puny neck up to look at me. "I am sorry, Grandfather," I say, blinking away my tears. "I am so sorry."

Lifting the Kusanagi no Tsurugi, I place its tip between his brows.

Grandfather closes his eyes.

I push the sword through his skull.

The sword bursts into flame, consuming Grandfather's yokai body and burning it to ash. The fire sweeps over me, igniting a white-hot rage and scorching away my pain, grief, and fear. I stalk from the garden, soul on fire, and face my tormentor. On the periphery of my sight, I see the ghostly forms of my ancestors joining me. They light my path.

I find Shuten-doji waiting in the small courtyard. He leans on a makeshift crutch, his left leg half-gone, chest and back a mess of bloody wounds. "Did you like my gift, little priestess?"

I answer him with a bright blade in the shadows, one that opens him from shoulder to hip. When he doubles over in pain, I bring the Kusanagi no Tsurugi down on the back of his neck, slicing all the way through the sinew, muscle, and bone.

Shuten-doji is dead before he hits the ground.

Like Grandfather, he burns. I stand in the small courtyard outside the motomiya and watch the flames dance. One by one, the battered shinigami join me: Shimada. Roji. Yuza. Ronin. Heihachi.

We watch his body burn down to ash.

THIRTY-FOUR

Fujikawa Shrine

Kyoto, Japan

When dawn tiptoes over the shrine, I sit up, rubbing gritty crust out of my eyelashes. I spent most of the night resting beside Shiro in the assembly hall, listening to the crackle of funeral pyres outside. The scent of woodsmoke barely masks the earthier, meatier scents of burned hair, fur, and flesh. A low, thick haze hangs in the air outside, and ash coats my tongue.

Still, I want to see the sun rise.

Careful not to disturb Shiro, I slip from beneath the blanket we share. Every muscle in my back aches as I get to my feet. Shiro stirs but doesn't wake, his face a patchwork of bruises, blood, and dirt. Oni-chan snores, curled up in the crook of Shiro's knees. The cat now sports a new gash behind one ear, expertly sutured and already healing. He opens his yellow eye as I walk past, chuffs, and then pushes his face back into the blanket.

Kiku rests on a cot nearby, his torso wrapped in thick bandages. The shinigami promise me he'll survive—and I suppose their word is probably more trustworthy than any doctor's. Several kitsune have curled up together in a corner, using one another's tails for pillows. So few of them have survived—no, so few of *us*.

I can't pretend our realms are separate anymore; they belong in my world, and I'm a part of theirs. In the last month, I have seen more heroism and humanity from "monsters" than I have ever seen from men. I'm not afraid of the yokai. Not anymore.

I shuffle outside. Every breath sends a spike of pain through my chest, but the cold air feels good on my face. I brace myself against a wooden pillar. As the sky lightens, the last of the funeral pyres burn down to embers in the courtyard. Shimada, Roji, and Heihachi stand with their backs to me, watching the smoke and passing a flask around. Yuza and Ronin aren't anywhere in sight.

We won. Though the number of ash piles on the courtyard cobblestones might say otherwise. We won, but at a high cost. O-bei is dead, and Kiku teeters on the brink. Ronin has become a shinigami, and his relationship with Shiro may never recover. The Fujikawa Shrine is in desperate need of repairs—*again*—and its head priest was slain and turned into a demon. And now my parents are selling the shrine I fought so hard to save. They don't know what happened to Grandfather, and I don't have the heart to tell them.

We have won another sunrise. I tell myself that is victory enough.

"May I interrupt?"

I look up, surprised to see Shimada standing beside me. His red haori wears new bloodstains and tatters, and the stench of death clings to him. I hadn't seen him approach. "Of course," I say, though my voice isn't higher than a hoarse whisper. I cough and repeat myself, louder this time. "Of course."

He removes his sugegasa hat and palms it in one hand. Flipping it over, he reveals the rings of butterfly cocoons that line his hat. Most of them look like black, resinous scabs—I can see wings twitching in one or two of them, still slick inside their casings. Shimada points to one with felted, soft gray sides, as if it has been newly formed. "Your grandfather," he says gently.

I press a hand against my mouth and close my eyes, needing a moment of privacy. Gratitude and grief well inside me like waves, and when they slam into one another, my core shakes. Relief rolls out in their wake, too. I no longer fear for my grandfather's soul, now that it lies in the hands of the best shinigami in Yomi.

With no way other way to thank him, I drop into a deep bow. When I rise, I manage to compose myself long enough to say, "Thank you, Shimada."

"No need to thank me. I exist to serve the dead." He fits his hat atop his head, then hooks his thumbs into his belt. In the courtyard, Roji and Heihachi tend to a collapsing pyre, letting the logs burn down. "I am glad to find you awake—I wanted a chance to say goodbye."

"Goodbye?" I ask, knotting my brows together. "So soon?"

"Shuten-doji's death will upset the balance of power in Yomi," Shimada says. "Many will want to see the shinigami responsible for his demise pay the ultimate price for our defection, including the clans."

The ultimate price? "You mean the one O-bei paid?" I say.

He nods. "Roji and I will leave before sunrise. Yuza will likely join us in exile."

"And what about Heihachi and Ronin?" I ask. "Or Kiku?"

"Ronin left the shrine as O-bei's pyre burned low," Shimada says. "He gathered a handful of her ashes and disappeared. Neither Heihachi nor Kiku carries a shinigami's blade, so the clans' justice will not come for them. Or you, for that matter. Be cautious, however. Shuten-doji had many friends, and it is best that the Kusanagi no Tsurugi not fall into their control."

"I plan to return the blade to its rightful shrine in Nagoya," I say, reaching into my pocket and removing the menuki from within. The small suns glint in the predawn light. "*Without* the menuki, of course."

"A wise precaution."

"You seemed to recognize them on the day we met," I say, slipping the menuki back into my pocket. "Why didn't you tell me they were part of the sword?"

"I knew your bracelet had material from the Kusanagi no

Tsurugi," Shimada replies. "But I was not sure if you had an original piece of the blade, or if the links were forged from some alloy of its metals."

"You could have mentioned that fact," I say.

"Why?" he asks. "We had the pieces, but even I did not know how to put the blade together again. How did you do it?"

"I had help from an ancestor," I say, shooting him a grin. We listen to the wind for a moment before I get the courage to ask: "This wasn't the first time you defended the Fujikawa Shrine from Shuten-doji, was it?"

Shimada weighs me with a sideways look. "Perhaps not. One day, I may return here to summon your grandfather's spirit for you. When I do, I will tell you the story then."

My heart leaps. I bow to him as he steps off the veranda. "I would like that very much, Shimada-sama. Thank you."

The shinigami are gone before sunrise.

EIGHT WEEKS LATER
Fujikawa Shrine

Kyoto, Japan

Mother and Father finalize the sale of the Fujikawa Shrine on a festival day.

I stand on the veranda of the main hall at sunset, watching patrons enjoy the shrine grounds. Tonight, the first full moon of the new year will rise, and the Fujikawa Shrine is honoring the event by celebrating Koshōgatsu, or Little New Year. It's unorthodox to hold a moon-viewing party in the clutch of winter—but I couldn't think of a better way to celebrate the reopening of the shrine to the public. Even our new head priest, Yamamoto-san, deemed a moon-viewing party appropriate; I'm not sure what he knows about what happened here, but both Shiro and I are certain the old man can see through yokai glamours. After all, he came *highly* recommended by Goro.

I haven't met my parents' new business associates, nor was I invited to the closing. The shrine's new owners began reconstruction almost a month ago, and several buildings still wear their scaffolds like exoskeletons. Mother assured me I could continue working at the shrine, but after everything I've risked to protect this place, her promise seems hollow. She's placed our family's legacy in the hands of a faceless corporate entity, despite the blood and sweat I've spilled on these cobblestones, or the lives lost in defending this sacred ground.

For now, I am the last Fujikawa left to guard this place, and I will do so until the day I die.

"Kira?"

I turn, my red hakama swishing against the veranda. I smile when I see Shiro, who has escorted a prim-looking kitsune to see me. I'm surprised to find Shiro's companion in a business suit and tie—I'm not used to seeing kitsune in much of anything but shrine robes.

"This is Takeda-san," Shiro says. I exchange bows with our visitor. "He's here on behalf of the shrine's new owner."

I shoot Shiro a pointed look. *The representative of the shrine's new owner is a kitsune?* But out of respect to our guest, I don't ask this question.

"May I have a moment of your time, Fujikawa-san?" Takeda asks.

"Of course," I say, plastering a welcoming smile on my face.

The two men follow me into the shrine office, which has been scrubbed of the battles we planned and fought here. Gone are the maps, the black butterfly dust, any indication that this room has ever been inhabited by anything less ordinary than a kitsune shrine guardian.

"Would you like to take a seat, Takeda-san?" I ask.

"No, thank you," Takeda says, placing his briefcase on the desk with care. "I am here to deliver a document on behalf of my employer, and I won't take up too much of your time. It's a busy evening, is it not?"

"It is," I say with a smile, folding my hands in front of me. "In the best possible way."

Takeda pulls out a stack of papers from his briefcase. I swallow a knot of worry, determined to keep my heart in the right place. *At least they are allowing you to stay,* I tell myself. *At least you won't lose the shrine forever.*

Though I know that all of that could change on a whim. Unlike the generations of Fujikawa priests and priestesses who have come before me, my position here at the shrine is not asured. Not anymore.

Takeda separates the papers into three neat stacks on the desk. "These are transferral-of-ownership contracts," he explains to me carefully. "On your twenty-first birthday, my client will transfer the ownership of the Fujikawa Shrine to you—"

I can't help it: I gasp aloud. Tears spring to my eyes, and I can hardly blink fast enough to keep them back. I press a hand to my mouth, fighting to keep my composure. I desperately do not want to embarrass this man, this wonderful man who is handing me back the one and only thing I want in this world: my family's shrine.

"I am glad to see that I bring happy news," Takeda says gently.

"May I ask who your client is, Takeda-san?" I don't even care that my voice wobbles. Or at least I try not to care, because these emotions may be too big to contain.

"My client prefers not to be named, Miss Fujikawa," Takeda says with a bob of his head. "I hope you will respect his right to privacy."

"Of course," I reply, casting a questioning glance at Shiro. All Shiro does is reach into his pocket and produce my personal hanko—a personalized seal that bears my name, one I'll use throughout my life. He must have taken it from my desk in Grandfather's guest room. I give him a curious look and a half smile. "Did you know Takeda-san was coming today, Shiro?"

"I did," he says, offering me my hanko. "I've read the contracts, Kira. They're legitimate."

"Do you know this mystery client?" I ask, taking the seal.

"I do," Shiro replies. "But it's a secret that I'm going to keep."

I remove the cylindrical hanko from its case, wet it on the ink, and then stamp my name where Takeda indicates. He stacks two copies and slides them into his briefcase, then hands me the third copy.

"My client will continue to fund shrine renovations," Takeda says, removing his business card from a small case. He presents his card to me with both hands, and I accept it with mine. "In the meantime, if you need anything, please call me."

"Thank you," I say. We exchange bows, even though part of me wants to throw my arms around this man and sob. Someone has generously protected my family's legacy—something my parents didn't even want to do. In five years, the shrine will belong to me. *Forever.* My gratitude keeps trying to overwhelm me, but I'm careful to keep all that emotion at bay.

When Takeda is gone, I turn to Shiro. "What do you know?" I ask him, striding across the room. Shiro puts his hands up to ward me off, laughing.

"I promised not to tell," he says, especially as I grab him by the front of his kimono and bring my nose up straight to his. He bats me with his tails. "I *promised*, Kira. That has to mean something to you."

"You can tell me," I say as he puts his arms around me and walks us back two steps. "Who was it? Goro? Some unknown kitsune benefactor? Was it *you*?"

He throws his head back and laughs. "I'm *never* telling you, not as long as I live. But no, it wasn't me. And Goro's a priest, he doesn't have the money to buy an entire shrine!"

"You're rude," I say.

He nuzzles my nose. "You love me."

"Shut up."

"Who's the rude one now?" he asks, then kisses me. And every time our lips touch, I swear my heart burns like a miniature sun in my chest. He spreads warmth, light, and comfort through my system. But most of all, Shiro makes me feel like I'm *home*. He stood with me during one of the darkest nights of my life, not just for the sake of duty, but also for *me*. He didn't run when all seemed lost, and like me, he was ready to give his life to fight the monsters at our gates.

The bond between us goes so much deeper than mere romance or attraction—though I admit, the romance *is* fun.

"You love me," I whisper, twisting his words back on him. "Even when I'm rude."

"I do," he says with a grin. He takes my hand, tugging me toward the door. "C'mon, I think old man Yamamoto is going to need help with the ceremonies."

"That's Yamamoto-san to *you*," I say, remembering our conversation back in the office all those months ago. It may have been a lifetime now, or more. He laughs at me.

I am a girl surrounded by the monsters and spirits of an ancient world.

My world.

We have made our best efforts to research this novel to the fullest extent possible—including traveling through Japan and studying Shinto. We have prayed to kami in Kyoto, visited dive bars in Shibuya, and crisscrossed the country on shinkansen trains. We have listened to the rain on the steps of remote mountain temples, slept on futons in tatami rooms, and been nudged by hungry deer in Nara. While we acknowledge that our efforts aren't free of imperfections, we have tried to build an authentic, deep-rooted setting for Kira's adventures.

Any faults with the portrayal of Japanese culture in the story are our own, and we apologize humbly for any oversights made.

Stylistic choices were made to accommodate Western audiences—astute readers will notice that Japanese customs for given names and surnames have been largely replaced by Western ones. Most characters are on a first-name basis, even if they are merely acquaintances, which is unthinkable in Japan. We have also chosen to use honorifics in diaogue only, as the regular application of them felt disingenuous in Kira's internal voice.

Generally speaking, Kira is a more individualistic character than one might normally encounter in Japanese stories. We have tried, however, to balance out the individualistic tendencies of the

Western hero with collectivist conventions. Kira is a member of a *Super Sentai*–style group of heroes working toward a common cause, as opposed to the sole hero of the story. At times, her star is overshadowed by other characters'—particularly Shiro's—and it was important that her power progression remain moderate, as she could not possibly outperform better-trained warriors after a single month of training.

We have incorporated as many Japanese words as possible, especially in the case of words that have no English equivalent. We don't have ekiben in the United States, which is a pity. Ekiben are a delight to the senses! You will find a glossary at the conclusion of this section, should you need it.

Insofar as Shinto is concerned, we've taken pains to avoid showing sacred rituals on the page, outside of the temizu purification ritual. Referring to Shinto or any of its deities as "mythological" is inappropriate—Shinto is a living faith, and it deserves to be treated with equal reverence as Buddhism, Christianity, Islam, or any other world religion. For this reason, we have declined to name the kami housed in the Fujikawa Shrine; however, it's safe to consider it an Inari-aligned shrine, given its red torii gates.

Similarly, we took our cues from Japanese pop culture when considering which fantasy elements to include. The shinigami themselves are a blend of Tite Kubo's noble shinigami in *Bleach* and the monstrous ones found in Tsugumi Ohba and Takeshi Obata's *Death Note*. We also looked at magic systems steeped in onmyōdō and folklore, as well as the frequent appearances of the

Kusanagi no Tsurugi in manga, anime, and video games.

When the real Kusanagi no Tsurugi appears in public—as it did during the ascension of Emperor Naruhito in May 2019—it is placed in a beautifully wrapped box and shrouded from sight. It is one of three sacred artifacts in Japan's Imperial Regalia, all of which were inherited from Amaterasu-omikami. The blade is so holy, no photographs or illustrations of it exist. We have taken artistic liberties with its design for this novel.

As for our debt to Akira Kurosawa's immortal tale *Seven Samurai*—all the shinigami draw their names from the original seven samurai: Kambei Shimada, Gorōbei Katayama, Shichiroji, Kyūzō, Heihachi Hayashida, Katsushirō Okamoto, and Kikuchiyo. We split the character of Katsushiro into the two kitsune brothers, Shiro and Ronin. While the comparisons to Kurosawa's original tale end there, we wished to honor one of history's most remarkable storytellers by creating seven links back to his tale.

If you have enjoyed this novel and would like to explore further, we suggest you look to the creators, artists, and storytellers that inspired it:

Akira Kurosawa, *Seven Samurai* (film)
CLAMP, *xxxHolic* (manga)
CLAMP, *Magic Knight Rayearth* (manga)
Hayao Miyazaki, *Princess Mononoke* (film)
Hayao Miyazaki, *Spirited Away* (film)
Naoko Takeuchi, *Pretty Soldier Sailor Moon* (manga)

Rumiko Takahashi, *Inuyasha: A Feudal Fairy Tale* (manga)

Tite Kubo, *Bleach* (manga)

Tsugumi Ohba and Takeshi Obata, *Death Note* (manga)

And for a comprehensive illustrated English encyclopedia of yokai and other supernatural Japanese beings, please visit Matthew Meyer's Yokai.com.

Abe no Seimei: A historical figure who lived during the Heian period in Japan, Abe no Seimei was a legendary practitioner of onmyōdō who advised emperors and government officials.

Amaterasu: The chief deity of the Shinto faith, she is the goddess of the sun and of the universe.

Baka: An insult that means *idiot* or *fool*.

Bokuto: A wooden katana used for training in Japanese martial arts. More commonly known as a *bokken* in the United States.

Bonsai: The Japanese art of cultivating miniature trees that mimic the shapes of fully grown ones.

Chabudai: A short-legged table often used in traditional Japanese homes.

-chan: An honorific used for people the speaker finds endearing, particularly young women and girls. The male form of this honorific is *-kun*.

Ekiben: A boxed meal sold in train stations and aboard some long-distance trains in Japan.

Furisode: A woman's kimono characterized by elegant, draping sleeves. Furisode are formal kimono worn only by young, unmarried women for special occasions.

Futakuchi-onna: A female yokai that resembles a human woman, except she hides a second mouth at the back of her head.

Geta: A traditional sandal, generally worn with kimono and tabi socks.

Genkan: A lowered entryway for a house, apartment, or building located inside the front door. Shoes are removed in this space.

Hakama: Wide-legged, pleated Japanese trousers tied at the waist and worn with a kimono.

Haori: A jacket that hits at the mid-hip or thigh, worn open over a kimono-like garment called a *kosode*.

Hashira: The columns of a torii gate.

Hitodama: Magical balls of fire that float at night. Similar to will-o'-the-wisps, hitodama are thought to be the souls of the dead.

Hoshi-no-tama: A round or onion-shaped ball that contains either a kitsune's soul or the seat of its magical power.

Ibaraki: One of Shuten-doji's four oni lieutenants; generally considered to be the foulest and most dangerous one.

Itadakimasu: "Let's eat!" or "Thanks for the food!" Said before each meal, it is a way of thanking all the living things that contributed to the meal—including the hands that prepared it.

Jorōgumo: A half-woman, half-spider yokai, generally malevolent in nature.

Jorō spider: Enormous yellow-black spiders found throughout Japan. Jorō spiders weave golden-hued webs that can stretch up to a full meter in length.

Kami: A broad term describing the deities, venerated deceased mortals, natural phenomena, and ancestral spirits worshipped in Shinto. No one term in English expresses the full meaning of the word *kami*.

Kancho: A young child's prank that involves clasping the hands together so the index fingers point out, and then poking an unsuspecting victim in the rear end.

Katana: Traditional swords used by the samurai of ancient and feudal Japan.

Kendo: A martial art descended from kenjutsu.

Kenjutsu: The umbrella term for all schools of Japanese swordsmanship, particularly those used by samurai classes before the Meiji Restoration.

Kitsune: The Japanese word for *fox*. In English, the word *kitsune* refers to a fox yokai capable of shapeshifting into human form, usually to trick human beings. In Japan, foxes are seen as messengers of the gods, and they stand guard over Inari shrines.

Kitto katsu: "You're sure to win," a phrase used to wish someone good luck with a difficult endeavor. The phrase's phonetic similarities to the Kit Kat candy has made Kit Kats astronomically popular in Japan, where hundreds of varieties are available.

Kuzunoha: A legendary kitsune of Japanese folklore, known for being the mother of Abe no Semei.

Machiya: Wooden town houses typified by a first-floor storefront, with residential housing on the upper story. While machiya houses are common throughout Japan, they define the downtown architecture of Kyoto.

Miko: A Shinto shrine maiden. In modern times, the role of miko is generally seen as an after-school job for girls and women in high school or college.

Motomiya: A small shrine or "sub-shrine" located inside a larger shrine's boundaries.

Mudra: A ritual hand gesture in Buddhism, Hinduism, and Jainism. A mudra is a spiritual gesture employed in Indian classical dance, yoga, and many forms of martial arts in Japan.

Naginata: A weapon with a curved blade at the end of a long pole.

Nekomata: A mischievous cat yokai with two tails, with each tip burning with fire. The most dangerous types of these yokai can grow many times larger than a tiger or lion.

Nemaki: Kimono-style robes for sleeping or lounging.

Noren: A drape that hangs over the front of a door, window, or between rooms.

Oni: Supernatural ogres, demons, or trolls. Folklore typically portrays them as hulking beasts with horns, clad only on loincloths made from tiger pelts.

Onmyōdō: Japanese esoteric cosmology and astronomy, also involving practices of magic, divination, and exorcism.

Onmyōji: A practitioner of onmyōdō.

Otogi-zôshi: A group of roughly 350 short stories and folktales from feudal Japan.

Oeyama: Located in Kyoto Prefecture, Mount Oeyama is the traditional residence of Shuten-doji.

Rokurokubi: A type of yokai that appears as a beautiful woman with a long, snakelike neck.

Ryokan: A type of inn that generally features tatami-mat rooms, communal baths, etc.

-sama: An honorific for *lord*.

-san: An honorific that equates to Mr., Mrs., Ms., or Miss.

Sasumata: A feudal-era, two-pronged polearm used to trap intruders. Every school in Japan keeps sets of these "man catchers," which allow students and faculty to defend themselves from attackers.

-senpai: An honorific used to confer respect to one's seniors at school, work, etc.

Shikigami: A kami represented by a small ghost, able to be bound into folded-and-cut paper forms.

Shimenawa: Ropes of straw or hemp used to designate sacred spaces, natural features, or even special sumo wrestling rings.

Shinigami: Japanese "death gods" or psychopomps, traditionally responsible for taking human lives or guiding them into the afterlife.

Shinkansen (train): A bullet train capable of moving up to 200 miles per hour.

Shinto: The traditional religion of Japan, often used to describe kami worship and related theologies, rituals, and practices.

Shoji: A door, window, or room divider made of translucent paper over a frame of wood.

Shuten-doji: One of Japan's Three Great Evils, Shuten-doji is the mythical oni or demon leader of Japan.

Suzu bell: A round, hollow bell that contains pellets, somewhat like a jingle bell. Large ones are present in Shinto shrines and used to call to the shrine's kami.

Takamagahara: High heaven, where the gods dwell.

Tamamo-no-Mae: One of the Three Great Evils of Japan, Tamamo-no-Mae is a beautiful kitsune credited with deceiving an emperor and his court.

Temizu ritual: A purification ritual performed before entering a Shinto shrine, which cleanses the hands and mouth.

Tengu: A yokai that takes a variety of shapes, but usually is presented as a large, monstrous bird with anthropomorphized features.

Tennin: Spiritual beings in Japanese Buddhism that are similar to Western angels. They are generally unnaturally beautiful women dressed in ornate kimono—called *hagoromo*—that enable them to fly.

Tokonoma: A recessed area in traditional houses used to display artwork, flower arrangements, and other decor.

Torii: A traditional gate that marks the transition from the mundane world to the sacred one; most Shinto shrines have multiple torii gates along their main path, or *sandō*.

Tsukomogami: Tools that have grown old enough to obtain a kami or spirit.

Tut: Also known as *finger tutting*. A type of dance that involves intricate movements of the fingers, used in this novel as a verb to describe performing mudras.

Veranda: A roofed platform that runs along the outsides of buildings, known as a *hisashi* in Japan.

Yakitori: A chicken skewer grilled over a charcoal fire, often made as street food. Yakitori stands are often found outside large shrines.

Yokai: The supernatural monsters, ghosts, spirits, and demons found in Japanese folklore. Yokai can be benevolent, malevolent, mischievous, or anything in between.

Yomi: Literally "World of Darkness," or the land of the dead, which seems to have a geographical continuity with the living world. In some interpretations, it's synonymous with Western hell.

Yorimitsu: Also known as Minamoto no Raikō, a historical hero featured in many legends and tales—in Japanese folklore, he snuck into Shuten-doji's palace and beheaded the oni king.

Yuki-onna: Literally "snow woman," this yokai preys on travelers lost in snowstorms.

ACKNOWLEDGMENTS

Every book is a journey, but this one took me across the Pacific Ocean—first by plane, then by pen. I expected to battle demons on the page, but I wasn't prepared for the ones I faced in my own head. In the end, I'm grateful for the myriad things I've learned while working on this book.

To my agent, John M. Cusick, who was the first to advocate for this project and who later saved it—thank you. Without you, I don't think we would have made it to The End. May we see many more beginnings. Actually, we have too many beginnings this year—hold that thought until we have a few more endings in place!

To editor extraordinaire Alexandra Cooper—you are a paragon of patience, and my gratitude to you runs deep. You have shaped and guided this book with wisdom and grace, and I have learned so much about the writing craft from you. Thank you for never giving up on me, even when I was mired in the deep, murky pools of self-doubt. Your midnight emails gave me life!

To the talented crew at HarperCollins—you folks are a Super Sentai Squad for the ages. Thank you for all the hard work you've done on behalf of *Seven Deadly Shadows*.

To the friends who offered their insights, support, and edits throughout this process: Chersti Nieveen, Yamile Saied Méndez, Rebecca Sachiko Burton, Kate Coursey, and Tricia Levenseller. No matter where you left your imprints, they echo through this novel.

To my travel companion in Japan, Emily Coleman—what an incredible, life-changing trip we had! Thank you for helping me navigate the country by bus and train, for finding amazing places to eat, and for being so chill when I decided that biking three miles to Kyoto's Golden Pavilion "sounded like fun." How was I to know the journey was going to be almost entirely uphill?

And to our host in Kyoto, Atsuko Kusakabe—thank you for opening your beautiful home to us, for great late-night conversations, and for touring the Shimogamo Jinja with us. I have wandered far abroad, but Kyoto remains my favorite destination because of you.

To my family—both the one I was born to and the one I married into—thank you for respecting my writing time but still inviting me along, knowing my answer would be *I'm working!* I can't tell you how much it meant to me.

To dear friends: Dustin Hansen, Jolene Perry, Shawna Meske-Putnam, Michael Putnam, Zack Laine, and the gamers of Haven—thank you for keeping me company, keeping me sane, and keeping me laughing.

To all the Japanese storytellers, artists, and musicians who have influenced me from childhood—you shaped my inner world with your art, and I will carry your stories with me always. Thank you.

To the members of Twice—your music kept me dancing on

my darkest days, and I know Kira would love your work. Onces fighting!

Most important, much love and gratitude to my husband, Bo Jensen, who remained steadfast even when the night grew dark. You have been the most amazing partner in crime, sounding board, and bringer of hugs (and caffeine!) a writer could ever desire. Every day we spend together is the luckiest day.

—Courtney

They say when you hit rock bottom, only then will you know who your real friends and family are. The past couple of years have been extremely difficult, so I have an abundance of gratitude for those who stood by me through all the hard times:

Jacob, my home, love of a lifetime, best friend, and accomplice in all things adventurous.

The ones who give me gray hair but also put up with my whining about dishes, dirty laundry, or funky smells. You guys never cease to make my life a loud and happy one: Jessen, Keahi, Aiden, Kamaile, Elise, Lexi, Cale, Callista, and Lily.

My parents, Howard and Vicki, for keeping me alive and for their never-ending support.

Kristen and Mitch, for helping with the kids and all matters in life.

Stan and Ann Nagamatsu, for assisting with anything and everything.

Those who never fail to check on me and keep me going: Foxy, my sister from another mister; Fresh, Jcote, and Ahjack; Matt L. and Octavia O.; Robert Balenzuela, Michael Baker, Carson M., Victor Vilchiz, Ma, Del, and Alpha; and all my friends at OCD, BS2, and GT.

Brandon Sanderson, Dan Wells, Howard Tayler, Mary Robinette Kowal, and the entire Writing Excuses crew for allowing me to guest host for season thirteen.

My superhero agent, John Cusick, and everyone at Folio Literary Agency; editor, Alexandra Cooper, and the staff at HarperTeen; and coauthor, Courtney Alameda, for their undying patience.

All the doctors and specialists who brought me back from the almost-dead on many occasions.

Most of all, a huge hug to readers and bibliophiles everywhere.

—Valynne

9604